What Readers Are Saying... Before the Season...

"A really nice surprise! This is definitely an original Regency romance."

ANNE WOODLEY
Amazon.com Top 500 reviewer
patroness of the *Almack's List, Byron List,* Janeites, and the *Austen List*

"Beautifully written story, fast paced, and exciting from cover to cover. One of the best stories I have read!"

KELLI GLESIGE
book reviewer for www.ReaderViews.com

"In the vein of Jane Austen, Burkard weaves a delightful world, rich with detail. Her characters spring to life as they deal with their own struggles and prejudices.."

JANICE LAQUIERE
Logos Book Reviews

"Well-written, interesting, captivating, romantic, inspirational, and addictive, I highly recommend this book."

ARMCHAIRINTERVIEWS.COM

And from satisfied readers at Amazon.com...

"I laughed out loud and was also brought to tears while reading this beautifully written book."

ALICE TJIONG

"Beautifully written, touches your heart *and* keeps you entertained!"

DEBBIE HANNA

"A must-read story that will lift you up and stay in your thoughts long after you've finished the last chapter."

LISA G. SMITH

"A great, entertaining book! It had me caught from the first few pages and continued to reel me in page after page."

"Wonderful and beautiful book!"

"So good that I couldn't put it down! It made me laugh out loud and it made me cry…"

"Fun and inspirational. I enjoyed it from cover to cover and heartily recommend it to anyone who likes historical fiction!"

A peek at Linore's mail…

Christina writes…

"I received my copy of *Before the Season Ends* yesterday and have already finished it…I literally could not put it down…I can't wait for the sequel!"

Catherine writes…

"I got your book in the mail yesterday, started reading it, and could not put it down. It is delightful! It seems to me to be a bit like *Pride and Prejudice,* which is my very favorite novel of all time."

Viola writes…

"Just had to write a note and let you know that I have finished *Before the Season Ends.* It was great. Will there be another book about [Ariana] or her sisters?"

BEFORE THE SEASON ENDS

LINORE ROSE BURKARD

HARVEST HOUSE PUBLISHERS

EUGENE, OREGON

Cover by Dugan Design Group, Bloomington, Minnesota

This is a work of fiction. Names, characters, places, and incidents are products of the author's imagination or are used fictitiously. Any resemblance to actual persons, living or dead, or to events or locales, is entirely coincidental.

BEFORE THE SEASON ENDS
Copyright © 2008 by Linore Rose Burkard
Published by Harvest House Publishers
Eugene, Oregon 97402
www.harvesthousepublishers.com

Library of Congress Cataloging-in-Publication Data

Burkard, Linore Rose
Before the season ends / Linore Rose Burkard.
p. cm.
ISBN 978-0-7369-2551-8 (pbk.)
I. Title.
PS3602.U754B44 2008
813'.6—dc22

2008020667

Printed in the United States of America

08 09 10 11 12 13 14 15 / RDM-NI / 10 9 8 7 6 5 4 3 2 1

To the memory of my grandmother, Marie Rose,
for always believing; and my parents,
for their love of reading.

Special thanks to my editor, Nick Harrison,
who, (besides having a cool name) is great
to work with and who brought me to
Harvest House Publishers;
to Helen Hancox and Charlotte Hails,
my trusty British resource people, for their
friendship, suggestions, and corrections.
And to my wonderful husband, Michael,
the computer wiz, (where would I be without
my laptop?) who has never questioned my
obsession with writing;
and to my children,
for their patience and understanding.
You are all priceless!

One

Chesterton, Hertfordshire
England
1813

*O*mething would have to be done about Ariana.

All winter Miss Ariana Forsythe, aged nineteen, had been going about the house sighing.

"Mr. Hathaway is my lot in life!"

She spoke as though the prospect of that life was a great burden to bear, but one to which she had properly reconciled herself. When her declarations met with exasperation or reproach from her family—for no one else was convinced Mr. Hathaway, the rector, was her lot—she usually responded in a perplexed manner. Hadn't they understood that her calling was to wed a man of the cloth? Was there another man of God, other than their rector, available to her? No. It only stood to reason, therefore, that Mr. Hathaway was her lot in life. Their cold reception to the thought of the marriage was unfathomable.

When she was seventeen (a perfectly respectable marrying age), Ariana had romantic hopes about a young and brilliant assistant to the rector, one Mr. Stresham. It was shortly after meeting him, in fact, that she had formed the opinion the Almighty was calling her to marry a man of God. Mr. Stresham even had the approval of her parents. But the man soon took a situation in another parish without asking Ariana to accompany him as his wife. She was disappointed, but not one to give up easily, continued to speak of "the calling," waiting in hope for another Mr. Stresham of sorts. But no man came. And now she had reached the conclusion that Mr. Hathaway—Mr. Hathaway, the rector (approaching the age of sixty!), would have to do.

Her parents, Charles and Julia Forsythe, were sitting in their comfortably furnished morning room, Julia with a cup of tea before her, and Charles with his newspaper. A steady warmth was emanating from the hearth.

"What shall we do about Ariana?" Mrs. Forsythe, being an observant mother, had been growing in her conviction that the situation called for action.

"What do you suggest, my dear?" Her husband reluctantly folded his paper; he knew his wife wanted a discussion of the matter, and he would get precious little reading done until she had gotten it.

She held up a folded piece of foolscap, on which was written the annual letter from Agatha Bentley, Charles's sister, asking for Alberta, the eldest Forsythe daughter, for the season in London. It had arrived the day before.

Aunt Bentley was a childless wealthy widow and a hopeless socialite. For the past three years she had written annually to tell her brother and his wife why they ought to let her sponsor their eldest daughter for a London season. She owned a house in Mayfair (could anything be more respectable than that?) and knew a great number of the bigwigs in society. She had, in fact, that most important of commodities, which the Forsythes completely lacked: connexions. And as Charles's family were her only living relatives, she was prepared—even anxious—to serve as chaperon for her niece.

Much to the lady's frustration, Julia and Charles had annually extinguished her hopes, replying to her letters graciously but with the inevitable, "We cannot countenance a separation from our child at this time," and so on. Charles was unflinching on this point, never doubting his girls would reap a greater benefit by remaining beneath his own roof. They knew full well, moreover, that Aunt Bentley could not hope, with all her money and connexions, to find as suitable a husband for their offspring as was possible right in Chesterton.

And yet, due to the distressing state of affairs with Ariana, Julia wished to consider her latest offer. Waving the letter in her hand, she said, "I think we ought to oblige your sister this year. She must be lonely, poor thing, and besides removing Ariana from the parish, a visit to the city could prove beneficial for her education."

Ariana's father silently considered the matter. His eldest daughter, Alberta, was as good as wed, having recently accepted an offer of marriage—to no one's surprise—from John Norledge. Ariana, his second eldest, had been irksome in regard to the rector, but to pack her off to London? Surely the situation was not so dire as to warrant such a move.

"I think there is nothing else for it," Mrs. Forsythe said emphatically. "Ariana is determined about Mr. Hathaway and, even though we can forbid her to speak to the man, she will pine and sigh and like as not drive us to distraction!"

Taking a pipe out of his waistcoat pocket, though he no longer smoked, Mr. Forsythe absently rubbed the polished wood in his fingers.

"I recall other fanciful notions of our daughter's," he said finally, "and they slipped away in time. Recall, if you will, when she was above certain her destiny was to be a missionary to America. That desire faded. She fancies this, she fancies that; soon she will fancy another thing entirely, and we shan't hear another word about the 'wonderful rector' again."

Mrs. Forsythe's countenance, still attractive in her forties, became fretful.

"I grant that she has had strong…affections before. But this time, my dear, it is a complicated affection, for in this case it is the heart of the, ah, *affected* that we must consider. It has ideas of its own."

"Of its own?"

Mrs. Forsythe looked about the room to be certain no one else had entered. The servants were so practiced at coming and going quietly that their presence might not be marked. But no, it was only the two of them. She lowered her voice anyway.

"The rector! I do not think he intends to lose her! What could delight him more than a young, healthy wife who might fill his table with offspring?"

Mr. Forsythe shook his head. "Our rector is not the kind of man to think only of himself; he must agree with us on the obvious unsuitability of the match."

The rector in question was Thaddeus Admonicus Hathaway, of the Church in the Village Square. Mr. Hathaway was a good man. His sermons were grounded in sound religion, which meant they were based on orthodox Christian teaching. He was clever, and a popular dinner guest of the gentry, including the Forsythes. If these had not been true of him, Mr. Forsythe might have been as concerned as his wife. Knowing Mr. Hathaway, however, Charles Forsythe did not think a drastic action, such as sending his daughter to the bustling metropolis of London, was necessary.

Mrs. Forsythe chose not to argue with her spouse. She would simply commit the matter to prayer. If the Almighty decided that Ariana must be removed to Agatha's house, then He would make it clear to her husband. In her years of marriage she had discovered that God was the Great Communicator, and she had no right to try and usurp that power. Her part was to pray, sincerely and earnestly.

Mr. Forsythe gave his judgment: "I fear that rather than exerting a godly influence upon her aunt, Ariana might be drawn astray by the ungodliness of London society."

"Do you doubt her so much, Charles? This infatuation with Mr. Hathaway merely results from her youth, her admiration for his superior learning, and especially," she said, leaning forward and giving him a meaningful look, "for lack of a young man who has your approval! Have you not frowned upon every male who has approached her in the past? Why, Mr. Hathaway is the first whom you have failed to frighten off and only because he is our rector! 'Tis little wonder a young girl takes a fanciful notion into her head!"

When he made no answer, she added, while adjusting the frilly morning cap on her head, "Mr. Hathaway causes me concern!"

Mr. Forsythe's countenance was sober. " 'Tis my sister who warrants the concern. She will wish to make a match for our daughter—and she will not be content with just any *mister* I assure you. In addition to which, a girl as pretty as our daughter will undoubtedly attract attention of the wrong sort."

Julia was flustered for a moment, but countered, "Agatha is no threat to our child. We shall say we are sending Ariana to see the sights, take in the museums, and so forth. Surely there is no harm in that. A dinner party here or there should not be of concern. And Ariana is too intelligent to allow herself to be foisted upon an unsuitable man for a fortune or title."

Too intelligent? Charles thought of the aging minister who no one had had to "foist" her upon. Aloud he merely said, "I shall speak with her tonight. She shall be brought to reason, depend upon it. There will be no need to pack her off to London."

Two

*H*ad Ariana, once she set her mind upon something, ever been swayed by reason? This was the question on Mr. Forsythe's mind as he spoke with his daughter in his study that evening. He poked at the hearth with an iron instrument although the red coals were pouring out heat. It was, instead, the conversation that more rightly needed stirring, having gone cold; for Mr. Forsythe could not impress Ariana with the rector's unsuitability.

She had been preparing for bed when he summoned her and was therefore in a warm chemise nightdress and robe, her long, luminous blonde locks about her shoulders. Her feet were tucked up beneath the robe for warmth, and she absently twirled a strand of hair between her fingers. Her sparkling eyes—said to be the handsomest in the county—were fixed upon him in mild perplexity. Her bedside candle sat nearby, ready for the return trip upstairs.

"If God were to smile upon the union you desire," Mr. Forsythe told her gravely, turning from the fireplace to look at her, "then proof would be the blessing of your parents. But without the latter, you should not assume the former."

Ariana blinked, looking surprised at such a thought, and her father silently rejoiced that perhaps he had finally hit his mark. Then she smiled, and it was so placating and compliant a smile that he felt his first twinge of true alarm. And when she spoke, her tone was so maddeningly sweet that he might have lost his temper altogether.

"Mr. Hathaway says, even the most pious are apt to misread the will of the Almighty on occasion! And I can rest in the knowledge that marriage is a blessed estate to be much desired; and how could I, who am seeking to please God, err, if I marry into the church?"

Mr. Forsythe's face grew red. He set down the iron poker with his back to his daughter and made a grimace. Taking a breath to control the sudden rage he felt toward the minister, he put his hands upon his hips, and turned to face the girl. She was watching him cautiously.

"Has that man made an offer to you?" It came out in a bellow.

It was so uncharacteristic for Papa to lose his temper that Ariana felt the colour rise in her cheeks, and she clasped her hands together nervously.

"N-no!" It was true that she and the rector shared a tacit understanding, but there had as yet been no actual declaration. The damage had been done, however. Her father was clearly out of countenance. What would he do?

At the same moment, he was asking himself that very question. He was loathe to speak against God's servant, but he had to do something.

"Ariana—."

Her large eyes regarded him fearfully. They were light brown during calm moments, but colourful at the least excitement. Streaks of blue and green or even amethyst could sparkle in them, as well as health and youth, vigour and intelligence. Combined with her golden locks and delicate features, the young woman had a startlingly pleasing effect. He refused to allow her look of youthful innocence to sway him, however.

"I forbid you to speak with Mr. Hathaway from this day forward."

A flash of colour in her eyes revealed her alarm.

"But, Papa! What if Mr. Hathaway addresses me? I must answer him. I shan't be so disobliging as to not answer!"

Ariana and the older man had, of late, often held conversations after services, and it did seem likely he would not suffer her to pass by without a word. Therefore, after a moment's thought, Mr. Forsythe added, "You may nod. And I shall answer for you."

She was silent, regarding him with her restless eyes. In truth, she was trying to imagine merely nodding at Mr. Hathaway come the Sabbath. He was bound to think her impolite, she thought.

Mr. Forsythe had hoped to bring his daughter to reason, but that had not worked. She was vulnerable to persuasion by the minister, apparently, more so than to her father. He would have to take the case directly to the rector. Fortunately, he had until Sunday to think of an appropriate way to discuss the issue without injuring the friendship between the man and their family. He instructed Ariana to think no more of Mr. Hathaway, for a match between them could not be. And then he sent her off to bed.

∽◦∽

On the following Sunday things did not go quite as he planned.

For one thing, no sooner had Mr. Forsythe set foot out of doors after service than he was hailed by his friend Mr. Beckham (who happened to be the borough's M.P.) for Mr. Beckham had a matter he wished to be advised on.

Mr. Hathaway, as was his custom, stood at the door of the church shaking hands and speaking to the congregation as they exited. When Mrs. Forsythe came forth, he stopped her for conversation, knowing that her girls would be following her. Ariana, like her sisters, curtseyed politely, and waited for her mother. Mr. Hathaway soon moved his inquiries to her—as well as his admiring eyes, which had come alight— and the girl saw her mother's look of alarm with a sinking feeling in her breast. Why had her parents suddenly begun to oppose what she had been telling them all along? Mr. Hathaway was her lot in life!

∽◦∽

Indeed, Julia Forsythe saw that her instincts regarding the minister's feelings for her daughter had been correct. It was unfortunate that directly after this revelation she caught the avid faces of the Cranshaws fixed on her daughter and the rector. She saw, too, as they went off whispering and peering over their shoulders at the couple. Next, she was forced to accept looks of pitying disdain sent her by Mrs. Hennesy and Mrs. O'Doole, two of the Forsythes' neighbours, as they passed. She smiled at them through gritted teeth. It was the last straw, however, when the Misses Wenderson gave each other delighted gasps after spying Ariana in conversation with the older man. Julia realized then, to her horror, that her daughter and the minister had now become a matter of town gossip.

She sprang into action. It was not planned, considered, or prayed-over action, but every bone in her body declared that she knew—*yes!*—how to put an end to this business. She stalked over to her husband and insisted upon his immediate attention, apologizing as best she could to Mr. Beckham, whose conversation she had interrupted. Mr. Forsythe excused himself, concerned at the distress on his wife's face. Then, after some fierce whispering between the couple, he headed to where Ariana and Mr. Hathaway had their heads bent in conversation.

Ignoring a shocking urge to knock the two heads together, he merely cleared his throat loudly. It wasn't that he disliked Mr. Hathaway or even disagreed with his sermons; it was just that he wanted a son-in-law of whom he might feel fatherly, not brotherly. He would graciously extricate his child from the conversation and then simply ask the minister to refrain from singling out his daughter. Mr. Hathaway must learn that Ariana was henceforth not to be considered. This was his sole and utter intention. What happened instead was such a surprise—nay, a shock—that all he could do was comment later that God alone saw it coming.

∞∘∞

Ariana had noticed her father heavily approaching and felt a twinge of alarm. She nervously played with the handle of her parasol while trying to attend to Mr. Hathaway's conversation. He was saying how becoming she looked in her walking-out dress of white cambric, and she gave him a weak smile of gratitude; but here was Papa, and it was he who now commanded her attention. He had an uncommon look of purpose about him; a look which said that she, Ariana, was no doubt going to have to answer for speaking with the minister. Had he not forbidden her to do so? From beneath her bonnet, she gave him an apologetic smile as he reached them.

Then, she turned back to Mr. Hathaway, and simultaneously, in a single second, perfectly ruined Mr. Forsythe's planned speech. For in that one moment she had given the aged churchman a warm, brilliant smile; a smile that spoke volumes; a smile that Mr. Forsythe interpreted as saying, *Offer for me at any time, my dear Mr. Hathaway, and I shall not hesitate to accept you!* Or, *Why, here is my papa this very minute, and why should you not present your offer to him for me right now?* In any case, it was a smile that showed complete affability and approval for the man receiving it. To Mr. Forsythe, it was too provoking. He nodded curtly at the minister and said, in a clipped tone, "Ariana!"

"Yes, Papa?" Her voice sounded nervous.

"Go to the carriage, while I speak a word with the rector."

"Yes, Papa!" She shot him a knowing look before curtseying politely to Mr. Hathaway's fine bow, and went off in the direction of the family's equipage. After she had gone, Mr. Hathaway turned a veiled expression to Mr. Forsythe. Something in his eyes made the girl's father think he had been expecting a confrontation on the matter. He felt relief on that account, for it meant the man was aware that Miss Forsythe's family could hardly approve of such a match as he and Ariana would make.

With that realization, Mr. Forsythe did not have the heart, now that he was face to face with the man, to tell him the news outright: that Ariana was not to be considered by him. Instead he found himself speaking of the approaching season, his sister in London, and of "sending Ariana." The words spilled out with an accompanying sensation that it was the wisest course to take, despite his not having been convinced earlier. His wife desired this, he explained, but Mr. Hathaway's face went from red to white, and then slowly flushed red again, as he listened...

〜◦〜◦〜

Meanwhile, Ariana reached the carriage where the others were already ensconced inside. Beatrice and Lucy, the two youngest Forsythes at ages eleven and six, respectively, were now compensating for the enforced silence during the sermon with a barrage of chatter.

"Mama," Ariana said, after quickly seating herself between the younger girls. "Shall Papa be angry that I spoke to Mr. Hathaway? I had no choice!" Mrs. Forsythe held up a hand to silence her daughter.

"I do not think he will be; he is settling the matter at this moment, and I daresay he will be satisfied at having done so. Do not fret." She gave Ariana an encouraging smile, and she returned the gesture. (Did not Mama always smooth things over?) However, in a few minutes all smiles vanished. Mr. Forsythe appeared outside the coach, and he was panting with exertion.

"Charles? What has happened?" Mrs. Forsythe asked as the whole family stared at him in wonder. Even the two little ones had become instantly quiet at sight of their dignified Papa, all hot and red and wiping his brow.

He climbed inside the carriage and plopped down beside his wife, still too bewildered to speak, but gathering his thoughts. His clothing was askew and his hat had disappeared altogether. He took a few breaths, gave a backhanded bang on the wall behind him to alert the coachman to be off, and finally answered.

"I have just exchanged fisticuffs with the rector."

There was a moment of shocked silence and then a deluge of questions from the more mature occupants of the carriage—except Ariana. She was too busy trying not to blush in mortification. Though Alberta had eyed her accusingly at their father's announcement, no one else seemed ready to blame her.

From Mrs. Forsythe: "How could you fight a man who is older than you, not to mention, the rector!"

From Alberta: "I cannot imagine either of you raising your fists to one another!"

From Ariana, who could not maintain her silence a moment longer: "Indeed, Papa! How could you? How *could* you!"

"My dears!" he objected. "You mistake the matter! I assure you, I had no desire to fight the man, but he quite insisted upon it."

"How did it come to such a pass?" asked his wife, her expression pained at the thought of the ordeal, as indeed was Ariana's. With a look of dismay on his face, for he could not shake the feeling, Ariana's father described the event.

"He insisted I insulted him for his age, though I said absolutely nothing about it. When I merely agreed that I consider him beyond a proper age for my daughter—which is another thing entirely—he proposed fisticuffs to prove, he said, that he is just as fit a man as I. When I refused, he came at me, and I'm afraid I had no choice but to defend myself."

There was a moment's grave silence.

"I think he has abandoned reason," Mrs. Forsythe pronounced.

"The poor man would not stop coming at me and swiping his fists before my face, so I had no choice but to give him more than one good return."

"Did you hit him hard, Papa?" Ariana could not remove the dread in her tone.

"Yes." He turned back to his wife, adding, "But perhaps not hard enough. He said that unless I finish him off, he will not drop his suit with Ariana."

Mrs. Forsythe gasped. "He did not challenge you to a duel?"

"No. And I daresay, when he returns to reason, he won't."

She sighed with relief. "Yet he admits his aim is to court our daughter."

Mr. Forsythe nodded curtly. "Indeed he does."

Ariana, who was never good at keeping thoughts to herself, burst out, "I am utterly responsible for today's work! There is no answer for it except that you must part with me and allow me to wed the rector."

With a look of patience, Mr. Forsythe returned, "It seems, my dear, that we must, indeed, be parted from you." Ariana's face was one of pure surprise, thinking he meant to fulfill her request.

"It is to Hanover Square in London with you. Mr. Hathaway's

behaviour today confirms that you must be removed from his grasp." He and his wife looked at each other and nodded their agreement of this decision.

"London?" asked Alberta, startled.

"To Aunt Bentley," explained her mother. Ariana's mouth dropped in surprise, opened wider to complain—and then shut.

"Aunt Bentley!" exclaimed Alberta, with a tinge of jealousy. "Mama, you have said Aunt Bentley is practically a heathen! You cannot mean to send my sister there!"

"I am sure I overstated the case," said Mama, though she pulled a small fan from her reticule and began fanning herself. "I will not say your aunt is the model of a good Christian, my dears—indeed, I will not—but Ariana is going only for a visit, not to live with her."

The rest of the journey home was like a dream for Ariana. While her mother spoke about the fine entertainments and cultural offerings of the city, Ariana sat in a daze and listened. Like Alberta, she, too had been convinced she would never be the debutante her aunt desired to sponsor. While many a girl from the gentry was packed off to London at this time of year for the season, the Forsythes were too practical, spiritual, and financially encumbered for such frivolities. The family home, a modest manor, required servants, two carriages, horses, and with four young daughters and a wife, an astonishing amount of textile finery, not to mention the gentlemanly need for proper clothing for the man of the house. The girls had been instructed, moreover, on the largely frivolous pursuits of the season, so they had never felt they were missing anything of moment.

It turned out, however, that Mrs. Forsythe had experienced the thing called "the season" when she was younger, and it did have its worthwhile attractions: the opera, concerts, the ballet, theatre. And, far from feeling dejected that the rector, after all, was not her lot in life, Ariana felt an almost euphoric sense of freedom.

Three

*H*aving made the decision to remove Ariana from Mr. Hathaway's influence, Mr. Forsythe wanted it done speedily. He sent a letter to London the very day of his unfortunate confrontation with the rector via John Chilton, fastest messenger on horseback in the borough.

"Depend upon it," he told his wife, "he will be back to us by Thursday."

And so it was. Ariana and the rest of the family stood by early that evening while Mrs. Forsythe excitedly opened the burgundy seal on the rather thick letter from Hanover Square, and began to read:

My dearest Charles and Julia, I am exceedingly gratified that you will finally grant me the pleasure of introducing a niece to society. However, I consider it best to have Alberta. It is irregular for a younger sister to have a coming-out when the elder sister has not.

Mrs. Forsythe stopped reading and frowned. "Did you not mention our predicament concerning Ariana? Or that Alberta is betrothed?" The two girls exchanged bemused glances.

Mr. Forsythe removed his pipe, which was empty, from his mouth. "I did not think it pertinent to tell her…the bit about the rector, and so forth."

"Then, perhaps I shall go!" declared Alberta, to whom this had heretofore been a rather painful business. She agreed with her aunt that the eldest daughter must have the first coming-out.

"No, my dear, no," her mother said, in the voice of gentle maternal affection that all her girls adored. Like Ariana, Alberta was tall and slim, but she had darker hair (though it was still considered blonde), and her eyes were a pretty shade of Cornish blue.

Alberta's fashionably rounded shoulders sagged in disappointment, and she turned to head for the family's favourite room, the library. The rest of the family followed, with Mr. Forsythe closest on her heels.

"Now, now, if you went to your aunt, 'Berta, she would insist upon making a match for you. I daresay Mr. Norledge would little like it."

"She could make no match for me, Papa, for I am not willing to have it so."

"But it happens all the time, my dear!" put in Mrs. Forsythe. "Young ladies are commonly wed for the sake of a fortune or title, whether they be happy over it, or not."

"But you would never allow that," she returned, accurately.

"True." This time her father spoke. "But you will be among the upper class with your Aunt Bentley, and she will never stop trying. Your uncle worked under Pitt; he knew everyone, and your aunt maintained her social ties all these years."

"I will not seek a husband!" Alberta's eyes were threatening to spill tears.

"Who is to say a would-be husband shall not seek you? Is that not what the season is about? Meeting eligible partners? Being paraded about for the approval of young men? Many gels wait all their lives for this chance to induce an eligible young man to offer for them. And every mama with a son to marry off will be seeking the right young lady."

"Indeed," put in her mother. "The season is known as the marriage mart."

"And yet you will countenance *my* going?" Ariana asked in surprise.

"My dear, we are not against your getting married." Mrs. Forsythe smoothed out a wrinkle in her gown. "We only require a suitable mate. A man of faith, of course, but one nearer to your own age than Mr. Hathaway. You may meet that man in London, and if so, we shall rejoice with you. But we cannot endanger your sister's betrothal. The Norledge family would take it very ill indeed if we were to send Alberta to London, I daresay."

"When I return," Ariana replied soberly, "if the rector still sees fit to court me, will you allow him?"

"We can better answer that question," stated her papa in a firm voice, "when you return."

Mrs. Forsythe took up the letter again. She read: "*As time is of the essence, I must have your daughter as soon as possible. I am prepared, of course, to sponsor her at my own expense, which I hasten to assure you lest you have forgotten, shall be no hardship to me.*"

Mrs. Forsythe paused, her eyebrows raised, and Ariana took the moment to gasp, "How generous she is!"

"She has always offered to help," said Mrs. Forsythe. "But to take on the entire expense! Outfitting a young woman for a season. 'Tis remarkable, even for a rich old dame with nothing better to do with her fortune, I think." She ended on a chuckle, but Mr. Forsythe knew his sister better than his wife did, and had to comment.

"She is more concerned about her own reputation than in generosity. She won't be seen with a gel who is not as modish as she. If your aunt is nothing else, she is supremely 'in the mode.'"

"So, *in a fashion,* she is generous," stated his wife quickly in a droll tone. She and the older girls smiled again, while Beatrice asked, "What is funny?"

Mr. Forsythe frowned. "My sister ought not to incur the expenses which are properly the family's—Ariana's wardrobe, and whatnot—all those little fripperies which women think are vital to existence." Ariana and Alberta shared a look of amusement with their mama.

"But she *is* family, Papa."

"And the offer is freely made," added the girls' mother. There was silence for a moment and then the letter was raised once again and Mrs. Forsythe continued reading. "*There are shopping and fittings to consider, and just when the seamstresses are at their busiest. All this takes time, and it is urgent that you send her at once. (Please, Julia, do not try to copy the London fashions for your daughter from Chesterton. These things must be authentic!)"*

Ariana's head was beginning to spin with excitement. Her mother continued reading about traveling instructions and necessary stopovers at posting-houses, but Ariana kept repeating the phrase "shopping and fittings" to herself, and was quite unaware that she was smiling. She remained lost in thought while her mother told Dory to bring tea; and she was in a dreamy state, moreover, when her father relented and said if his sister truly wished to spend some of her own blunt on his child he would not object. (She could well afford it, he noted, having twice been widowed and both times left a fortune.)

Over tea and biscuits, after Mrs. Forsythe finished reading the many pages of the missive that included instructions regarding traveling arrangements, where to change horses, and so on, they decided that because Mrs. Bentley wished to hurry matters, they would send Ariana at once, in a matter of days. She would take with her a letter explaining fully why it was she, Ariana, who must go to London, and not Alberta, which they thought sufficient to settle the issue. While talk about London continued, Ariana was all ears. She heard her mother say, "The Regent's court can be wild, according to the papers—and it encourages the upper class towards wantonness."

"The Regent! Shall I meet him?" She met her sister's gaze with mock horror, and Alberta managed a wan smile. George, Prince of Wales, had been appointed regent two years prior due to a protracted illness of the king. He was recklessly extravagant, always in debt, and worse, rumoured to be something of a libertine.

"I hardly think so," answered her mama. "Your aunt is not the social dignitary she once was, and she's getting on in years. Remember she is Papa's elder sister."

"Of course our illustrious Regent prefers older women," Mr. Forsythe commented snidely. He was referring to a few well-known *liaisons* the prince was known to have had. "Even if Princess Caroline is peculiar, as they say," he inflected strongly, "I cannot respect a monarch who cheats!"

"Few of our monarchs have been known for their virtue, Papa." Ariana loved to read, and knew much regarding the history of the crown. But Papa always compared the Regent to his father, George III, who was a stellar example of fidelity, economy, and, until his illness, a most sound-thinking man.

Since his sentiments regarding the Regent were not new to anyone in the room, Mrs. Forsythe continued, "I am sure your aunt will properly care for you, my dear, or we should not give leave for you to go, no matter—" she stopped, not wishing to name the rector. "No matter what!" She nodded brightly to Ariana.

Alberta blew her nose lightly into an embroidered handkerchief, and Ariana turned troubled eyes to her. "'Berta, I am sorry you are not going. Pray, do not be out of countenance with me."

Her sister shook her head. "I shan't. Mama and Papa are right. Mr. Norledge would hate it dreadfully were I to go. It must be God's will for you." Alberta's mild tone and gentle look filled Ariana with gratitude for such a wonderful sister, and she gave her an impulsive hug that was returned with equal fervour.

Alberta was definitely the saintliest member of the family. She could overcome her disappointments so easily!

"But since you will be in my place," Alberta said, her eyes twinkling (and proving how thoroughly she had accepted the situation), "you must make an enormous success and marry a dashing nobleman!" Eyes alight, the sisters giggled, but Mr. Forsythe clucked his tongue at them.

"You will meet odd feathers of all colours in my sister's company, but we trust you to entertain no serious feelings for anyone of her ilk."

"Papa, Ariana knows I was only making fun."

"Still," he said, while a sleepy Lucy climbed up onto his lap and settled herself there, "many gels will set their caps at a man because of a fortune or how dashing he is. We expect wiser choices from you, Ariana. Never allow yourself to be drawn into the amusements of the season to the point that you neglect your spiritual offices." He paused, giving Ariana what he hoped was an expression of confident approval.

"Seek others of our faith—which I believe must be possible, for our Lord sent His angels even to Sodom for the sake of the upright living in its midst. Who knows but there may be upright ones among the upper class? Look at Wilberforce! There may be a *Lot* for you, my dear."

"Oh, *Papa!*" The idea of finding a Lot did not strike Ariana as pleasant in the least. There was a silence then, until Mrs. Forsythe stood, signaling to her daughter.

"Let us examine your wardrobe, Ariana. You have suitable gowns for both morning and evening, and I daresay your riding habit is not yet outmoded. I warrant even Agatha can only be happy if you bring some of what you will need."

This little speech sent new energy into Lucy, whose eyes shot open. The family lovingly called her the "little coquette," because she adored all manner of feminine attire, especially the fripperies which Mr. Forsythe had earlier referred to. She shot up off his lap and in a trice was following her sister and mother out of the room. Beatrice, too, scrambled after them.

"Mama," Ariana said thoughtfully, as they climbed the stairs, "I see no fault with any of my gowns save the gray kerseymere, which is fraying at the elbows; why should I not bring the rest? Perhaps Aunt will wish to update a few, but certainly that is more economical than bespeaking new things."

Mrs. Forsythe was thoughtful a moment. "I'm afraid Papa is right about your aunt—she is mindful of fashion to a fault." She stopped, surveying her daughter, her lips pursed in thought. Then she smiled. "But no one can be eager to put forth so much that to make do just a little cannot be deemed satisfactory. Yes! We shall pack the lot!"

Once inside Ariana's chamber she stood humming to herself while she went through the gowns in the armoire. Pulling out a plum-coloured, bombazine day dress, she held it out for inspection. "I do think," she said, "that it will please Agatha to shop for a young woman. Do not be surprised if she rejects more than half your wardrobe."

"May I have what she doesn't fancy for Ariana?" asked Beatrice, quickly.

"No." Her mother gave her a quelling look. "Alberta can certainly make better use of Ariana's cast-offs than you."

Lucy was watching, wide-eyed. "Did Aunt Bentley really have *two* husbands?"

"Not at the same time," chuckled Ariana. "But that does account for her fortune. Oh—I do fancy that gown!" Mrs. Forsythe had pulled forth a fetching afternoon dress in light gray figured silk with a small black leaf design, and trimmed with puffed gray crepe and jet beads. The skirt was flounced at the hem with black crepe and embroidered silk, and Ariana even had a matching pelisse of dark gray velvet lined with sarsnet. It was indeed a copy of a London fashion that their local seamstress had admirably copied from *Ackermann's,* and so valued by its wearer that it was only worn on the most important of occasions.

"May I wear it for the journey?"

"For the third day's journey when you shall be sure of arriving, yes."

"Third day!"

"It could be done in two, but your aunt is particular on this matter, and insists too much travel is fatiguing for a lady, even a young one like yourself. She is paying your shot at the coaching inns, so we should do as she says. Of course Dory will be with you," she added hurriedly, as Ariana's eyes revealed alarm at the thought of spending two nights in strange roadside inns.

Ariana was silent a moment. "Poor Aunt Bentley!" She was thinking of her widowhood. "How hard it must have been for her, to lose two husbands!"

"She was a good wife," said Mrs. Forsythe, "and indeed took it quite hard, both times." She looked brightly at Ariana and exclaimed, "Well, my dear, in every cloud a silver lining. The Lord is using her for your advantage. A young lady can hardly be comfortable in fashionable society if she feels inferior in appearance." She put down the clothing she had been holding and put her arms around her daughter. In a confidential tone she said, "I am very pleased for your sake that you will be going. There is nothing quite like a London season for a young lady. So many agreeable things to do and see! The balls! So much excitement! I believe our Lord is granting you this to some purpose, my love."

Then, as she led her daughter to sit on the bed, she added, "Do be on the lookout for that purpose. There is no doubt some good you can do there."

Ariana nodded, but her mother's gaze was far away. She was lost in the memories of her own debut in society, more than twenty years earlier.

"I remember my own come-out," she started to say, with great affection, but was interrupted by Lucy.

"Will Ariana find a husband in London, Mama?"

Smiling at Ariana, she answered, "Only the Lord knows, my love. But she may, you know. She may."

Four

One week later
Mayfair, London

Number 49 Hanover Square was posh and exclusive, which, being in Mayfair, was to be expected. Though Ariana had visited as a child with her family, she remembered nothing of the atmosphere of stolid wealth that pervaded the tree-lined street of Georgian brick homes, or the gleaming black iron railings which flanked doorways all the way down it, as far as one could see.

The railings of house number 49 fanned out toward the pavement in two graceful arcs. They were intricately designed and polished to a shine. Equally decorous black lamps sat elegantly above the railings on both sides of the door, and above the threshold, jutting out slightly over the steps, was an angelic sculptured awning.

Two cherubic faces smiled benignly down from the sculpture, and Ariana stopped and smiled herself. She, provincial Ariana Forsythe from the country, was about to embark on a London season of the sort that she had never imagined would come her way.

The journey to London by post chaise had indeed taken three days, including two stopovers at roadside inns. Mrs. Bentley had specified how to proceed right down to the littlest details, so that even Ariana's meals at these places were largely according to her suggestions. Dory had often dozed off in the carriage and encouraged Ariana to do the same, but she was too excited to sleep and chose to read whenever the light allowed.

Ariana had been forced to waken the maid upon their arrival, but true to form, Dory was instantly alert and bustled about seeing that Mrs. Bentley's servants missed no luggage, and that Ariana was expected and welcomed. A groom had appeared from the mews, and took charge of the carriage, leading the horses around the house. At the front door, Dory whispered a hurried goodbye, giving her charge a quick peck on the cheek before disappearing down the servants' entrance to the kitchens. Come morning, she would begin the journey back to Chesterton by herself. Ariana watched her go with a slight feeling of misgiving. Dory was her last connexion to home and family.

Ariana was ushered in by Haines, the butler, who, though he looked the part of the stern master of the staff, seemed to be a soft-hearted pretender.

"Your aunt will be pleased to learn you have safely arrived," he said, watching her with a staid expression, the result of training and long habit. For he was, in fact, pleased to find that the long-awaited niece of his mistress was a pretty young miss.

"Much obliged," Ariana said, while he helped relieve her of her bonnet, gloves, and pelisse. But when he reached to take her reticule, she nodded that she wished to keep it with her. It held the all-important letter explaining why she, Ariana, had come and not Alberta, as well as a small token of thanks for her aunt. The housekeeper arrived, and she curtseyed to Ariana.

"Mrs. Ruskin, at your service, ma'am. Welcome to London!"

Ariana thanked her and explained that from the time they had entered the outreaches of the city, she had been all eyes.

"Nothing like our busy city back in Chesterton, eh?" the housekeeper chuckled.

"Not at all," Ariana conceded. In fact, the strange sights and sounds—and smells—of busy London fascinated her. She had never seen such vendors, buildings, stalls, criers, carts of wares, or the manner of pedestrians and equipages as she had since they passed through Hampstead. Market day at home was crowded, of course, but nothing like this. Dory had been asleep when they entered the city, and Ariana was forced to keep her excitement to herself, even when the coach turned onto Fleet Street, a wide thoroughfare choked with traffic and well-dressed pedestrians.

An astonishing number of inviting shops lined both sides of the street as far down as the eye could see. Men and women of high fashion were coming and going about their daily affairs and Ariana marveled at them and their fine clothing. The coach made but little headway for a time, stopping every few minutes due to the traffic, and she had time to look and admire to her heart's content.

Then, while they sat waiting for room to manoeuvre, she noticed a pair of street waifs begging from door to door, only to be turned away again and again. A person here or there would give a coin, but her heart broke at sight of the poor little things.

One of them, a little girl with enormous brown eyes and raggedy hair, scrawny and unkempt, suddenly spied Ariana's compassionate gaze and started toward the vehicle as if on cue with a hand out-stretched. Ariana hurriedly felt for a coin in her reticule—she had a few pounds of her own as well as a small sum from Papa for pin money, and she eagerly desired to help this poor child. But a passing gentle-man saw the child's intent and stopped her with a cane, barring her path, and the little ragamuffin ran off. The gentleman tipped his hat and bowed, as though he had done Ariana a service. She looked away. She would not nod or acknowledge him; instead her heart felt heavy as the coach's wheels began to turn, moving them on.

After enduring more traffic, the carriage turned onto Oxford Street, a wider and less congested avenue, and they began to make headway. Finally they turned onto a smaller, quieter road. Ariana was admiring the rows of neat houses with their wrought-iron fences when the road widened into Hanover Square.

And now, here she was, inside her aunt's house. Mrs. Ruskin led her toward the staircase while Ariana's large eyes sparkled with pleasure, surveying the welcoming interior of the hall. Above her head was an elegant chandelier dripping with a score of candles, and to her right, a colourful tapestry on the wall. A gilt-edged, decoratively framed mirror hung elegantly above a little japanned table against the wall to her left.

"This way, my dear," said the housekeeper, after they climbed the stairs, and she escorted Ariana into a well-appointed parlour.

"Is there anything I can get you? Tea, perhaps?"

"I'd be obliged, thank you," she said, for in fact Ariana was hungry and thirsty. The housekeeper eyed her thoughtfully and added, "Perhaps a bite as well? A young lady must get an appetite from such a journey as you've had."

"That will be lovely, thank you." Ariana reflected with relief that kind servants usually meant the master—or mistress—was also kind.

She surveyed the light buff-yellow room, pleasantly illuminated with numerous wax candles, the good, expensive kind. Another rich chandelier was overhead, though unlit at present. There were two comfortable-looking sofas with embroidered flowers on them, a divan and two wing chairs, and a mound of hot coals in the hearth. An oval wooden table of a rich hue sat in the middle of the circle of furniture, and rested upon an oriental carpet. There were portraits on the wall of people dressed in old-fashioned, eighteenth-century styles, but still very pleasing to the eye.

The effect of it all was so warm and pretty and inviting that Ariana thought surely her Aunt Bentley must be warm and inviting herself. Perhaps not pretty, since she was Papa's elder sister, but warm and inviting would be very agreeable, indeed. She sat gingerly upon a sofa, placing her reticule lightly upon the table, careful not to disturb anything.

Moments later, she heard voices in the hall. The door opened and there was a swift change in the atmosphere as Mrs. Bentley, with a servant behind her, entered the room. Thoughts of her relation being warm and inviting flew away. Ariana came to her feet and beheld the woman who was her aunt.

Agatha Bentley was dressed richly in a heavy gown that reached the floor. It was adorned with sparkling gold-threaded embroidery at the wrists and hem. She had a shawl around her shoulders and tucked under her arms. She wore two very large jeweled rings on her hands, a multitude of heavy gold bracelets, and a jeweled headband. As if this wasn't enough to enlarge Ariana's expressive orbs, her relation's eyes were sharp and cold and her skin was very white. There was nothing in her face to remind one of Mr. Forsythe, Ariana's father; and unlike his sturdy features, hers were small and surprisingly delicate.

The house felt suddenly unwelcoming despite the fact that the servant carried a china tea service on a tray, with biscuits and small cakes on little plates. She placed the tray carefully upon the table near Ariana. The china was pretty, with fluted edges, delicate—and break-able, Ariana thought, for some reason.

Trying not to appear as if she were hungrily studying her niece, Mrs. Bentley smiled tremulously. It was not a warm smile, more like one the wearer hoped would be warm, but Ariana smiled in return and curtseyed. Her aunt felt infinite relief that the girl was attractive. All the finery she had in mind could not have hidden a pallid complexion or dumbness of expression. In fact, the girl had a calm, intelligent demeanour, rich blonde hair, and a rosy complexion. Her face was finely featured, with a lovely, chiseled nose, smooth cheekbones, and, most striking of all, light bluish-brown eyes that sparkled prettily, though they held a look of what? Mild alarm?

Perhaps she is peaked from traveling, thought Mrs. Bentley. She hoped it was not a permanent feature. She often found the best look-ing fruit invariably had the rottenest interiors and she supposed this applied to people as well. Would her handsome niece prove to be overly shy or inept at conversation? These faults were as fatal, in her social circle, as being ugly, or worse—poor! Aloud she said only, "So this is my niece! Welcome to my home," with an arm motion instructing Ariana to take her seat.

"You shouldn't have risen, you know," she added. "Ladies do not rise when company enters the room, unless it is royal company, of course."

Ariana nodded politely, and then said, "I am instructed to give you the best regards of my father and mother, and to say how very much obliged we are to you for sponsoring me." Having relieved herself of this speech restored her confidence somewhat, and she even remembered to give her aunt the small aromatic pomander fastened to a silk ribbon that she and her mother had fashioned as a present.

"For you," she said, handing it to Mrs. Bentley. "It's just a token, of course. Oh, and this letter, from Papa. Please read it now." She reached into her reticule and pulled out the sealed missive, handing it to her aunt with the pomander. Ariana could not feel quite at ease until Mrs. Bentley read the explanation of why she was there instead of Alberta.

The lady glanced fleetingly at the pomander with distaste, put it down on the table, and then ignored it. Likewise, she paid no attention to the letter in her hand but instead took a seat across from Ariana on a matching sofa. She gestured to the maid who was standing nearby, and the servant poured tea for them. Afterward, Mrs. Bentley dismissed her help and then sat sipping her tea, asking Ariana questions about the family, and trying not to openly study her niece while she answered.

Ariana eyed the letter uneasily, wondering if it would be rude to remind her aunt to read it. Meanwhile, her relation was congratulating herself for finally having got a niece to sponsor. During the season the need to secure advantageous matches for sons and daughters was hidden beneath a veneer of hospitality and party-going. Mrs. Bentley now had something to offer the mama looking to make a match for a son. This gave her the assurance of being included on more invitation lists than if she was alone.

Of course there was always the option of marrying Mr. Pellham, her dearest and most valued friend—who had proposed to her more than once—but he was merely a retired banker. And despite his wealth, retired bankers were not at all the sort of people admired by the *ton*. He, in turn, disdained any man who even faintly resembled a "fashionable," insisting they were all fops or dandies. This led him to treat nearly all of the *beau monde* with undisguised contempt. While Mrs. Bentley knew many of the elite were tolerant of eccentricities (most of them were eccentrics themselves) this tolerance did not extend to receiving condescension from a retired tradesman.

This was Mr. Pellham's only fault, but unfortunately it was a dire one for Mrs. Bentley, who had to choose between her dear, faithful friend, or involvement with the *ton*. During much of the year Mrs. Bentley was happy to forgo social climbing. Randolph Pellham was a frequent visitor, a deft opponent at cards, and kept her amused with accounts of exotic lands and destinations gleaned from a large collection of travel literature—his favourite reading material.

Meanwhile, Ariana was waiting to be offered a biscuit, wondering if she ought to volunteer to read the letter to her aunt. She was also quite desirous to see her bedchamber and to get a good night's sleep. Postinghouses were comfortable, but not the quietest of establishments, and, coupled with her excitement upon going to London, she hadn't slept a great deal since leaving Chesterton.

She was disappointed with her relation at this first meeting, but scolded herself for it. How blessed she was to be given this opportunity to experience a different lifestyle! She could not expect her aunt to be as comfortable as a dear old friend, or one's favourite gown. The two would need time to grow accustomed to one another. And surely she would have opportunity to make other acquaintances while in London. She was pulled from such thoughts by an unexpected voice at the door.

"You see, Mrs. B., all your worries were in vain. Your niece is well-mannered and much handsomer than you hoped, I warrant." The voice was male, and Ariana turned in surprise, unaware that someone had been beholding the meeting from the doorway. An elderly gentleman stood on the threshold with a friendly, "I told-you-so" sort of smile on his face, and he looked from Ariana to her aunt.

He was dressed gracefully in a rich black embroidered frock coat and buff trousers. He came toward them leaning on a golden-handled cane but walking with a great deal of dignity and with a smile on his moustached face. Ariana liked him at once; even before he said to Mrs. Bentley, "I daresay she is beautiful, in fact, and will make you proud to be her relation, and her chaperon."

The man then strode toward Ariana, who rose to her feet.

Aunt Bentley smiled at her visitor, but said to Ariana, "Did I not tell you a young lady remains seated when company enters the room? You do not rise for a gentleman, it is the other way round." The rebuke in her voice made Ariana blush and she quickly reclaimed her seat. The gentleman, who had come and stood before her, bowed politely and reached for her hand. He introduced himself as "Mr. Pellham, retired banker, reformed gambler, and the devoted gentleman-friend of this lovely lady, whom you call 'aunt.'" Ariana nodded (being unable to curtsey as she was sitting down), and said, "Miss Ariana Forsythe. How do you do?"

"Welcome to London, my dear," he said gravely, and then, noticing the pomander upon the table took it, sniffed, and said, "Lovely; I shall recommend your aunt hang it in her wardrobe."

Mrs. Bentley, however, had stopped with her teacup in midair, and was looking at Ariana strangely. "You are not Alberta? You are *not* my brother's eldest child?"

Ariana's face grew instantly rosy. "I am Ariana, the second eldest, Aunt." There was an awkward silence, except that her aunt took the sip of tea she had begun to take earlier, and then put down her cup.

"Why did you deceive me?" she asked, with one hand on her heart.

Ariana's expressive eyes grew larger. "Aunt Bentley, I gave you a letter from Papa, which I asked you to read directly. He explains everything in it; you would have understood the matter if you had read it at once."

"Would I indeed!" She looked at Mr. Pellham and remarked, "The young lady is quite outspoken, is she not?" Ariana's eyes dropped to her lap. Her aunt, if she chose, could send her right back to Chesterton.

"I beg your pardon, Aunt."

"Mm," was her reply, but her face lightened and she took up the letter and pried open the wax seal so that it did not crumble at all, and began to read. Mr. Pellham turned to Ariana.

"Allow me," he said, taking up a plate of biscuits and offering it to her. Ariana thanked him. She enjoyed what she ate, and when her aunt had read the letter she folded it and then looked at Ariana afresh.

"Well! At least I know who I have in my drawing room, now."

Ariana ate lightly and sipped tea, while listening to the two adults.

"I warrant I shall see less of you in the next few months than I have been accustomed to," said Mr. Pellham.

"Do you indeed think so?" She sounded highly gratified, understanding that he was referring to how busy she might be during the season.

"With Miss Ariana as your charge," he said, with a wink at Ariana, "I expect you shall be the toast of the town!" Another wink came Ariana's way, while her aunt gave a surprisingly feminine tinkle of laughter.

"You cannot think so!"

Ariana was amazed at the transformation in her relation. The hardness of her face melted and she looked exceedingly less formidable, even younger, than she had moments earlier. Mr. Pellham was the perfect antidote for Mrs. Bentley's sharp edges.

He looked at Ariana. "Is your niece aware of your grand plans for her?" Mrs. Bentley took a small sip of her tea but said nothing. "Under the aegis of your aunt," he said to Ariana, "you will attend the most fashionable dinner parties with the cream of society. You will meet more blue bloods I think, than you will wish to remember, and," he added, in a mischievous tone, "I would not want to be in your shoes for all the spices in India!" He paused and looked appraisingly at Ariana. "Do those plans agree with you?"

They both paused to hear her answer. "I suppose so," she stated, carefully. "Though I believe my parents wished me to see mostly the sights of London."

Mr. Pellham chuckled. "You will see sights among the *ton* like nowhere else on earth!"

"Randolph! The child is not referring to people, as you well know."

He gave her a patient look, but twirled his moustache and then whispered to Ariana, "I must behave myself." In a louder tone he said, "So you are referring, I take it, to museums and such?" He looked sideways at Mrs. Bentley to offer an expression of utter innocence, and Ariana bit her lip in order to hold back a giggle.

"Yes." She paused, thinking. "And St. Pauls, and the Royal Academy, and the British Gallery; a special exhibition of portrait artists is going on, you know!" Her eyes lit up as she spoke. "My papa had it from *The London Gazette!*"

"Capital!" he exclaimed. "Did you hear, Mrs. B.? A special exhibit of portraits!"

Mrs. Bentley nodded. "I did. If there is time," she added in an imperious tone, "Ariana may do such things. But social calls are given first consideration. The season is practically upon us, and we have precious few invitations. Fortunately," she added, smugly, "I already have an ace in hand! An invitation from Mrs. Royleforst for a picnic at Aspindon!" She paused, having expected to impress her audience, but her smile vanished as she realized the utter failure of the present company to appreciate the pleasure of receiving an invitation from the Paragon's only relation.

Both faces remained politely interested, however, so she went on. "The other few invitations are also impeccable, from the best families. The Hendersons, Lord and Lady Sherwood, Countess D'Amici." Her voice trailed off. "I think that's all I've had so far. We must procure more!" Looking earnestly at the others she added, "Without invitations, we are nothing." She smiled at Ariana with a self-satisfied expression. *How fortunate for my niece,* she was thinking, *that I am utterly capable of manoeuvring her successfully into society.*

"We can go to Hyde Park at the fashionable hour, and all of the popular haunts." With a finger waving expressively and an earnest expression, she continued, "Being seen, my gel, is as important as a dozen calls, if the timing is right! Being seen! But without invitations we are nothing."

Mr. Pellham was looking fondly at Ariana's aunt. "The three of us could make a fine company, and show your niece all she longs to see. We needn't care a fig for another invitation all season!" Ariana met his eyes and smiled her agreement, but Mrs. Bentley was shaking her head.

"My niece did not come to London for the company of two old crows! She is a debutante, Randolph. And I intend to see her debuted. Indeed, I am eager to do so." And she took a bite of a biscuit as if she had just settled the war with France.

"Will I go to court, then?" asked Ariana, surprised. She had heard that Queen Charlotte had stopped the practice of allowing young ladies to be presented, now that her son was Regent.

"If not, my gel, your first appearance at Almack's or any other place of social importance will be considered your debut. In fact, now I think on it, we must assure that you receive a proper notice; I will begin introductions as soon as your wardrobe is in hand."

"But there must be an agreeable time for cultural exhibits," Mr. Pellham inserted, hopefully. Mrs. Bentley made an uncomfortable sound in her throat.

"You know, Randolph, that I dread museums! So many *old* things. In addition to which Ariana may have no time for such. I have plans, things that she and I must do. Places we must go!" She stared at him a little wide-eyed, and he patted her hand soothingly.

"Of course, Mrs. B., of course. I shall escort your niece to cultural sights only when you have given your explicit leave. As for your balls and routs and assemblies, I am certain Miss Ariana will enjoy those with you. Neither of us is intent on depriving you of these pleasures."

"No, ma'am," added Ariana. "But I must say, my parents do expect me to avail myself of the sights while I am here."

"Oh, yes, I know!" her aunt sputtered, holding up the letter from her father. "I will not promise you—" she began, then stopped.

Mr. Pellham hurried to say, "You and I have enjoyed many days of touring town together, Mrs. B., and I recall that you much admired the interior of the Pantheon on Oxford Street, though we were not together when you saw it."

She registered the thought with a brief smile, but replied, "It burned down, which was a shame, and is now a theatre, I believe."

"You see, you do recall!" he persisted, pleased.

Mrs. Bentley sniffed. "I cannot say but there will be no time for such. But we shall see."

Ariana hoped there would be time. She longed to visit a museum or attend an art exhibit. Such things could stir her soul profoundly. Moreover, it would provide much to write home about and please her parents besides.

Mrs. Bentley stood up and reached for the bellpull. "I daresay you are tired, Ariana," she stated, in a way that Ariana knew she was being dismissed. She wasn't sorry. Mr. Pellham rose and gave her a fine bow.

"We will discuss an itinerary at a future time," he confided, in a loud whisper, and then Mrs. Ruskin was there to escort her to her chamber.

Mrs. Bentley watched her go with a gratifying sense of having done the right thing in sending for her. The gel was a pleasure to look on, sat up straight, held her teacup delicately, and made not a sound as she ate. In addition, beneath the flickering light of the candles, her niece's eyes shone golden. Unusual for eyes, but quite becoming, her chaperon decided.

It was more than she had hoped for.

Five

After breakfast the following morning, a seamstress and her girl arrived to measure Ariana for the all-important wardrobe. Mrs. Bentley wished to speedily outfit her niece, a thing she deemed doubly imperative after taking inventory of what Ariana had brought with her. Pretty fabrics, to be sure, but plainly cut and nothing out of the way. Mrs. Bentley dressed richly and with good taste; her niece must do so as well. Only the latest fashions and accoutrements of the first water, and all to be bespoken as speedily as possible. Why? Because Mrs. Royleforst's outdoor party was merely one week away, and it had taken on the significance—at least to Mrs. Bentley's mind—of ushering in the season.

The modiste brought fabric samples—more than existed in the entire linen draper's shop back in Chesterton, Ariana noticed—but exhorted Madame to visit her shop on Bond Street to see more. Heedless, her aunt turned pages of *Le Beau Monde,* a highbrow journal of fashion Ariana had never seen before, jumping from that to *La Belle Assemblee,* or, *Lady's Fashionable Companion,* stopping to order this morning dress, or that evening gown. Ariana tried to peek as often as possible, hearing such tantalizing names as "watered silk, beaded bombazine, printed muslin or calico or cotton, satin, net, chintz, sarsnet, or lace," but she was not once called upon for an opinion.

Mrs. Bentley gave long and detailed instructions on how she wished the gowns to be altered so they did not exactly mirror the ones on the pages. Her niece must appear as an Original. She specified changes in fabrics, trimmings and linings, buttons or sashes or lace; even which sort or colour of thread to be used.

Ariana shortly began to grow dumbstruck at the quantity of dresses her aunt was bespeaking. It was fascinating to hear her instructions, too, for she was no less than a genius at costume. She studied her aunt in astonishment for a clue as to why this woman, who seemed to be of sound mind, was spending a king's ransom on a niece she barely knew. Mrs. Ruskin stood nearby with pencil and paper in hand, listing every order and instruction and writing as fast as that poor woman could manage. As her hand moved down the paper, Ariana could do little more than watch, fascinated, and yet with a faint unease.

Had her parents realized that a London season could require so much? What if they knew of all this? She was certain her papa could never approve such an expenditure.

"Take note of this bonnet, Ariana," her aunt said suddenly, pulling her from her thoughts. Ariana obediently surveyed the page open before her aunt, and exclaimed, "How lovely!" It was a novel and elegant little piece of head wear, trimmed in Brussels lace and ribbon and sporting a dashing little ostrich feather. She instantly forgot her qualms and noted, boldly, "None of my bonnets has a real feather!"

"We shall look for one just like this," Mrs. Bentley said. "But we do not bespeak bonnets from the seamstress. We shall go to Pall Mall or Bond Street. Even Oxford Street or to a warehouse down on Piccadilly. Some very respectable shops are there, and I want a certain style of Grecian head wreath for you which I feel certain we shall find on Oxford Street."

When the modiste and her samples and catalogues had gone, Mrs. Bentley wrote a list of items that still needed to be purchased, saying each aloud as she thought of it. Ariana was again bewildered. Besides silk slippers and leather half-boots, fans and handkerchiefs, there were chemises and bonnets, gloves and stockings, ribbons, turbans, a shawl, a new pelisse, and perhaps a parasol or two. A proper corset might also be required, she said, staring thoughtfully (and to Ariana's acute discomfort) at her chest, which, she said, needed more of an uplift to fully benefit from the fashion.

"Aunt Bentley, please recall that I brought quite a few of these items with me from home. There is no need to—"

Mrs. Bentley looked up from her list with an absent expression, in thought, but then waved away what her niece had said. "You can use them if necessary, but I prefer you will use what I provide." She spoke quickly, in a tone that said to leave her to her thoughts and Ariana did not cavil again. But she sat there with the beginnings of a tiny, dark cloud above her head. Despite her delight at the beautiful house and her own agreeably comfortable bedchamber; and even at the prospect of wearing all the finery, she felt an unhappy discomfort.

Mrs. Bentley finished her list and summoned Haines to fetch the carriage. "We will shop directly," she informed her niece, who nodded from where she sat, in a lacy cambric morning dress and cap. "You need to change quickly. Put on that…er…pretty gray silk you had on yesterday."

"Wear it again?" she asked, surprised.

"Do you have a finer one?"

"No; that is my finest walking-out dress."

"Then wear it."

She called Harrietta, a servant just promoted to the position of lady's maid expressly for Ariana until she could hire a good French one (for they were best at fashioning the intricate hairstyles that were all the rage) to help her niece dress.

∞∞∞

Although Ariana was wary of the enormousness of her aunt's expenses on her account, she was nevertheless delighted when the carriage let them off in Pall Mall for shopping. The busy avenue bustled with carriages of all styles and sizes, and with crowds of pedestrians going in and out of fascinating highbrow shops. When they reached Harding, Howell & Co.'s Grand Fashionable Magazine, Mrs. Bentley turned decidedly and entered. It was a huge, high-ceilinged place with a great circular glassed dome in the centre of the ceiling which let in a good amount of light. On either side the walls were lined with large shelves holding all manner of haberdashery and millinery. Everywhere, they saw furs and fans, lustrous silks, muslins, lace, and gloves. Further inside another shop sported shelves of jewelery and ornamental articles, many in ormolu.

"A lady can procure most anything here, and in the first style of elegance and fashion," said Mrs. Bentley. Looking around at the numerous laden shelves and counters, Ariana did not doubt it.

They purchased six pairs of gloves, which Mrs. Bentley insisted was necessary; two three-quarter-length white satin for ball use, two of eggshell white for other entertainments, and two buff leather for walking out and informal occasions. The list was consulted: a few fans, a half-dozen embroidered floral starched white handkerchiefs, silk ribbons, artificial flowers (for use on bonnets and headdresses), stockings, and chemises—all purchased in a flurry of quick decisions which left Ariana astonished.

They were looking through a selection of very fine shawls when a woman's deep voice was heard, and Mrs. Bentley, without so much as looking up, hissed, "Good heavens! 'Tis Cecelia Worthington. She has not an original thought in her head!" Curious, Ariana turned to see a stout woman with dark hair coming their way. With her was a younger dark-haired woman, who managed to maintain an appearance of smiling smugness throughout their encounter. Both women wore large, cavernous bonnets.

"Mrs. Bentley! How delightful to see you!"

"And you, Mrs. Worthington." She added "Miss Worthington," with barely a nod to the young woman. The ladies curtseyed automatically, as did Ariana.

"I notice you are not alone," said the lady, looking curiously at Ariana. "Imagine my amazement when Sophia spotted you with this young woman. Ah, said I. Sophia darling, Mrs. Bentley has finally got herself a companion, the very thing I have told her to do numerous times. I am so pleased you have listened to reason, Mrs. Bentley."

"I do not have a companion, Mrs. Worthington." Mrs. Bentley's tone was cold, and she blinked condescendingly at the lady. "This," she said, motioning to Ariana, "is my niece. Allow me to present to you, my gel." And then, speaking to Ariana she said in introduction, "Mrs. Cecelia Worthington, and Miss Worthington." The Worthingtons curtseyed again, this time with indignation.

"My niece, Miss Forsythe," she concluded. Ariana curtseyed politely, though her cheeks were rosy due to the manner of the introduction. Mrs. Bentley had introduced the Worthingtons to her, instead of the other way around, as if she were the superior party, when in fact, as the newcomer and younger person, Ariana should have been presented to Mrs. Worthington. Not to mention that her aunt had named her as Miss Forsythe, signifying that she was the eldest daughter in her family, whereas she properly should be introduced as Miss Ariana Forsythe.

Mrs. Worthington was ruffled, but her curiosity was greater than her indignation and she asked, startled, "Your niece?" Her large eyes surveyed Ariana amazedly and her mouth nearly hung open. "I do not recall you having a niece, I clearly do not recall such a thing!"

"She is my only brother's child, I assure you, one of four, all of whom I may bring out at the proper time." Mrs. Bentley had not actually given any recent thought to whether she would bring out her other nieces, but it had struck her as advantageous to say so.

"Miss Forsythe," Mrs. Bentley continued, "is my first contribution to society and I must say I am greatly looking forward to having her received in all the finest drawing rooms in town."

Mrs. Worthington was still wide-eyed, but she picked up a little lorgnette she had hanging around her neck on a chain, and peered at Ariana through it. She took in the adorable face with a slight sinking feeling in her breast; the chit was going to outshine her own Sophia, that was sure. She next wondered if Ariana held a fortune, which would nail the matter entirely. A homely heiress was bad enough, but if this Miss Forsythe had both figure and fortune, why, there was nothing she could do to help her child at all. Not a thing.

"And I suppose...she brings with her a great dowry?" Her face wrinkled in fear of the reply, and sure enough, Mrs. Bentley supplied the information that, "Of course! She is my relation, is she not?"

Ariana forced herself not to contradict her aunt before strangers, but she would certainly have to speak with her on this subject. She knew for a fact that her dowry was middling, nothing to get in raptures over, and certainly not a sum to be called "great."

Mrs. Worthington let out an unconscious sigh. "Yes, I daresay, I daresay." It was a reluctant acceptance of Miss Forsythe's superior standing compared to her own daughter, who was merely somewhat pretty, though pale, and had a decent dowry, but nothing next to the amount she began to imagine Miss Forsythe must have.

Coming to her senses, she gushed, "My dear Miss Forsythe, you must know my Sophia! She is quite the little spy and will keep you abreast of all the latest happenings. Sophia quite prides herself upon being informed, do you not, my dear?"

Sophia nodded proudly and was about to say something when Mrs. Bentley interjected, taking Ariana's arm. "I am afraid, Cecelia, that we must finish shopping."

"We, too," Mrs. Worthington said at once. She proceeded to trail Ariana and her aunt, keeping up a stream of questions and conversation. Ariana made an attempt to speak with Miss Worthington, but the young lady was intently following what her mama and Mrs. Bentley were saying. A little spy, indeed, Ariana thought.

Mrs. Worthington never stopped talking, but managed nevertheless to stare sharply at every item or bauble purchased by Mrs. Bentley, and then had her daughter do the same. Ariana's chaperon, intent on her shopping, didn't seem to notice. At a counter displaying trinkets, Ariana's aunt picked out an unattractive brooch—quite out of character for her, and Ariana shrank at the thought of wearing it but said nothing out of respect for her relation. Holding it up, however, Mrs. Bentley praised it as just the thing to go with a certain gown she had in mind. The item was duly purchased by both parties.

Afterward, the younger lady suddenly asked, "Shall we meet

again next weekend, Miss Forsythe? You are of course invited to Aspindon?

Ariana finished paying for a pair of delicate tortoiseshell combs she had chosen for Alberta, and replied, "Aspindon?" It sounded familiar, but she wasn't certain.

Miss Worthington smiled. "Do not say that Mrs. Bentley has not had an invitation? What a pity; perhaps Mama can put in a word for her with Mrs. Royleforst. It's all her doing, you know."

"I think my aunt did mention an invitation from Mrs. Royleforst."

"Oh, my dear," the girl said, as if she were speaking to a much younger person, "if she had, you'd be certain of it! Mrs. Royleforst, you must know, is Mr. Mornay's aunt! Everyone knows," she said, lifting her eyes heavenward, "that Mr. Mornay would sooner die than host a large party himself. And there is great talk that he may not show—at his own estate! Can you imagine?"

She waited to see if Ariana could.

She then continued, "I hope he does show up, it's bound to be exciting, then. Of course I'd never speak to him myself, but I adore looking at him!" She smiled again.

"Oh, dear," Mrs. Worthington murmured, just then. "Come, Sophia darling, I see your papa! We must go!" Miss Worthington bobbed a curtsey while her mama rapidly expressed her hopes of seeing Ariana and her aunt again soon, and then they were off. Mrs. Worthington's loud tones could be heard fading as they went. Ariana's aunt made a few more purchases while Ariana bought hair ribbons to send home to her little sisters, which she placed in the paper that held Alberta's combs.

Before leaving, her aunt returned to the trinket counter and demanded to return the brooch she had just bought.

"I did think it a fright!" Ariana said in relief.

"I bought it so Mrs. Worthington would also. I daresay we may expect to see Sophia wearing it at some great affair. 'Twill serve her for copying me!" As they walked back to the carriage, followed by a footman carrying their boxes and packages, Ariana reflected on the mean-spirited act, greatly surprised by it. Suddenly remembering the conversation of Miss Worthington, she asked, "Do you know a Mr. Mornay?" Her aunt stopped in her tracks. Putting one hand upon her heart, she replied, "I do! Do *you* know him?" Her eyes, which were small, had become large in her face.

Surprised at the reaction, Ariana said, "No, indeed! I only ask in reference to something Miss Worthington mentioned."

"My word! You startled me!" cried her aunt, who now began walking again.

They stopped in a shop for half-boots and pattens. During the fitting Mrs. Bentley gave an opinion on how fashionable young ladies must have a great deal of footwear: shoes, boots, half-boots, pattens for rainy or snowy days, and, of course, slippers. Many pairs of slippers. Delicate satin was favoured for evening wear, and upon hearing that Ariana had brought only one pair (for her others were too worn), her aunt insisted she would need at least a half-dozen more.

They took the carriage to Oxford Street for the last stop of the day, a millinery shop, where Ariana tried on numerous bonnets. When they found one similar to the engraving in the catalogue, Ariana could not help feeling elated, despite it being so dear. A genuine peacock feather! Her head was swimming with all the new finery, but as they left, Ariana had one request of her aunt.

"May we stop at a bookshop, Aunt, before we return to the house?" Ariana was hoping to find a copy of one of Mrs. Burney's novels, having neglected to bring any with her. The Forsythes had never espoused the idea that novel reading was worthless, and Mrs. Burney's sympathetic female characters appealed to Ariana greatly.

Her aunt looked perplexed. "A bookshop? Whatever for? Not today, my dear. I'm fagged."

When they had returned to the carriage, Ariana had barely seated herself when her aunt turned her full attention to her niece.

"Now, tell me every word Sophia Worthington said regarding Mr. Mornay!" As the carriage rolled away from the curb, Ariana related the conversation to her aunt as best she remembered.

"Of course we shall be at Aspindon!" Aunt Bentley sputtered. "Impudent child!"

"What is Aspindon?"

During the rest of the ride home, her aunt filled her in on the mystery of Mr. Phillip Mornay, and Aspindon, his huge estate in Middlesex.

"Phillip Mornay," she said, after a few moments, "is the Paragon. Only Brummel, poor man, could hold a candle to him, but he of course is in the duns. Almost ruined, in fact. I should not be surprised," she admonished, "if he was to flee England tomorrow!" Even Ariana knew Beau Brummel was famous for his impeccable style, and for bringing the current men's fashion of dark pantaloons and sober costume into being.

"Mr. Mornay is also a leader in fashion," continued her aunt. "Though I grant he has no desire to be. The men copy him, however, from the way he ties his cravat to his style of shoe. What ninnies some men are!" She paused, looked at Ariana, and asserted, "The thing you must know about him, Ariana, is that he has no patience for young misses. It seems that every season there is a young female who is determined to ruin herself, and Mr. Mornay is obliging enough to provide her with the means."

"How terrible!"

"No, not in the way you think," she replied. "Mornay is a difficult, angry sort of man, and quite a favorite among the *ton*—but he never misuses a female bodily. I must grant him that. All he does, actually, is—well, *nothing!* He ignores the chit who is foolish enough to set her cap at him. And that is all he must do to assure her ruin. Her chances in society from then on are forever gone!"

"But why, Aunt Bentley? If there has been no impropriety?"

"Well, in some cases, the lady goes into a decline, though, mind you, I never believe in declines; I maintain they are a fiction for the purpose of arousing sympathy. But they rarely work." She paused. "In other cases, it is simply because society loves to love Mornay! If he pointedly snubs a woman—or a man, for that matter—other people quickly follow suit. He is a rogue of the first order, not because he particularly tries to be, but because he makes no effort not to be."

Her aunt drew out a handkerchief and wiped an imaginary drop of perspiration from her brow. "He is handsome, of great consequence, and unmarried. Were he married, I assure you, he would swiftly lose some of his power of influence." To Ariana's startled look, she added, "These are the ways, my gel, of society."

Six

*D*uring supper that evening, Aspindon was again on Mrs. Bentley's mind. "Mrs. Royleforst is playing hostess but it is unthinkable she would not require her nephew's presence—after all, it is his estate. So pray, remember to give that man a wide berth."

Ariana nodded.

"I daresay it will not be difficult for you; Mornay is ever discretionary and he manages to avoid more people than not. But keep in mind to stay away from him, because he can only mean trouble for a young lady."

Ariana decided earnestly to follow her aunt's advice in all points. She did not want trouble in any form, particularly on her first society outing.

Allowing a footman to put a serving of asparagus on her dish, she asked, "Will Mr. Pellham accompany us?"

Her aunt gave her a sideways glance. "Mr. Pellham does not..." she hesitated, choosing her words. "He does not endeavor to put himself forward."

"You mean backwards," a voice said, as Mr. Pellham himself entered the room. He was such a frequent visitor that his appearance was no longer announced by a servant, and both Ariana and Mrs. Bentley greeted him with smiles of pleasant surprise.

"It would be a great step backward for me to waste my time among a bunch of fops and lily-hoppers, who do nothing more than admire one another all day." With an easy air of familiarity he sat down adjacent to Mrs. Bentley and continued, "What's more, when they are not admiring each other, they are lambasting one another. I have no patience for such foolery."

Ariana stifled a grin.

A footman offered Mr. Pellham a plate that he declined with a wave of his hand, but a decanter of some liquid was brought and poured into his glass as if in the usual manner.

"Randolph would rather spend a quiet evening before a fire with one of his treasured volumes than a week at the finest country house," Aunt Bentley intoned dryly.

There was a silence, which Ariana broke by saying, "But fine country houses contain things that are worthy of admiration, even contemplation; paintings, old tapestries and styles of furniture, architecture. And old stories."

"Quite true, my dear," Mr. Pellham said, holding up his glass to Ariana. "I have no argument with *touring* the houses, it is having to talk with the owners which I find provoking." He took a sip from the glass and said, "Now, if more young ladies had the education and sense I find in your niece, Mrs. B., perhaps I might feel differently." Mrs. Bentley looked up from her food, which she had been absorbed in eating, but said nothing.

"Oh, dear," Ariana replied. "Do not compare me to those in the finest houses. I am sure they must be better educated than I!"

Mr. Pellham shook his head. "No, my dear, you mistake the matter. You are thinking that refinement and money go hand in hand. I assure you that, more often than one would think, such is not the case. This is precisely my contention with the aristocracy. With all their money and influence, they should be making the inventions. Exploring the planet! Bettering the condition of mankind." He gave a sidelong glance at Mrs. Bentley, who was paying him little heed. "Instead, they fuss over neckcloths and waistcoats and phaetons."

"Randolph, you simply do not understand that these things *are* evidences of refinement." Ariana's aunt had been listening, after all. "Taste! Only the well-bred man or woman has it."

"Bah!" He shook his head. "At any rate, Miss Ariana——"

"Randolph, you must address her as Miss Forsythe. I have quite decided upon her being Miss Forsythe."

"But Aunt," Ariana objected. "My sister is Miss Forsythe, Alberta, the eldest. I cannot use her address."

Mrs. Bentley held up one hand. "I am determined upon this point, Ariana. I want no talk of your sister's betrothal to a country squire; in fact, we must allow no talk of your elder sister at all, to be safe, which I assure you will occur if society knows you are not the eldest. And since your sister is not in London there is really no impropriety in using "Miss Forsythe" for your address. It is done, I assure you."

Ariana felt indignant. It wasn't done by her family, and she'd never heard of such a thing in Chesterton. She would write home and ask Mama's opinion. She also felt defensive and her words confirmed it. "My sister's betrothal is a proud fact, ma'am, and a triumph. Mr. Norledge is a Christian man above reproach, and from a fine old family."

"He is from an old family, you say?" She sounded doubtful. "Well, that is all very good, but I assure you I am only doing what is best on your account. Do not be affronted, my gel. No lady without a title, in my opinion, can sound quite dignified if her first name must be given at every introduction. And young ladies, especially, do not want to give the impression of being *missish* any more than they must on account of their youth."

"It does not seem honest, ma'am," she said, plainly.

"If your sister was in London, I should agree with you. But on account of her being in Chesterton, there is no harm in your using the designation. Enough of this! You will quickly grow accustomed to it, and I must insist upon this while you are in my charge." She studied her niece with a mildly dissatisfied expression. "In using this address for you I feel quite justified, for it is not misleading to allow anyone to think you are worthy of a high match, since you are indeed worthy on account of me. Talk of Squire Norledge could jeopardize our position. But there. Enough said."

Worthy of a high match? Was that indeed her aunt's goal for her? Papa had been right in guessing as much. She thrust the thought from her mind, reasoning that no husband could be forced upon her, aunt or no aunt; else her parents would not have let her come.

Mr. Pellham cleared his throat and said, "Let us return to our discussion of London sights. Miss Forsythe, you will tell me which places you most wish to see, and I will endeavour to assemble a schedule for us so that we might do as much as possible in an efficient manner."

"How good of you, Mr. Pellham!" Ariana's large, pretty eyes sparkled across the table at him. "I will make a list this very night!"

"Make your list if you must," Mrs. Bentley said, "but, Randolph, I insist Ariana will do nothing but be at my disposal this week for fittings and shopping, and who knows but that we may pay a few morning calls?" She strove to sound patient, but everyone in the room knew she was taxed at the least discussion of cultural exhibits.

"Please recall, Randolph, that my niece's purpose is to become a part of society, not to provide you with an excuse for roaming the town. I know you long to do so, but Ariana is accompanying me to Aspindon, and she must be prepared!"

Her tone clearly said, "End of discussion." Mr. Pellham winked at Ariana and stroked his moustache.

"Aspindon…is that not Mr. Mor*nou's* estate?"

"'Tis Mr. Mor*nay's* estate. How *can* you ruin a beautiful name like Mornay?" She swallowed a bite of food, and added, "Just think! A picnic on the grounds of Aspindon! The cream of the *ton* will be there. All the finest food, I am certain. 'Tis a rare treat, even for me."

Mrs. Bentley's face lit up with the thought of the coming day. "And who knows but that Mrs. Royleforst has arranged for us to see some small portion of the mansion?"

"One can always hope," Mr. Pellham said, in a droll voice. "Do be good enough to keep your niece far from that beast of a man."

Mrs. Bentley finished the last bite of food on her plate and said, "Mr. Mornay is not agreeable, I grant. But he is no beast, Randolph."

"Well," he replied, drying his moustache with a linen napkin from the table, "in any case, when your outdoor picnic is over, perhaps Miss Forsythe and I can have our outing."

Since her aunt did not object, Ariana remarked that she would be happy to do so, beginning, she thought, with the British Museum. "I have longed to see it," she added, "since learning it was formerly Montagu House; they say the painted staircase alone is worth the trip. Did you know, Aunt, that the first Duke of Montagu kept his second wife there, a poor mad creature, hidden from all her relations, and convinced that she was the Empress of China?"

To their interested expressions, she continued, "The duke had masqueraded himself as the Emperor of China to win her hand because it came with a great fortune, and she was mad, and wouldn't have anyone less. I have long wished to see the place."

"The Empress of China!" laughed Mrs. Bentley. "Upon my word, I fancy accompanying you when you visit."

"A capital idea, Mrs. B.!" Mr. Pellham was delighted. And so it was settled that the British Museum would be first on their agenda, and that Mrs. Bentley would join them, though artifacts and paintings, not Chinese Empresses, would be on the palate.

‹›‹›‹›

Early Friday morning, they were finally situated in Mrs. Bentley's best traveling coach, en route to Middlesex and the picnic at Aspindon. Ariana was all excitement. The modiste had been able to complete only one good promenade, or walking-out dress, in so short a time, but it was a sweet confection of white jaconet muslin with pink trim on the sleeves, the empire waist, and skirt edge. It had a high collar edged with lace, and a ribbon sash that formed a bow in back. Beneath the bow was a frilly pink trim that ran down the length of the gown in two columns, accentuating Ariana's tall, lithe figure. The sleeves were puffed and short, but there was a sturdy velvet spencer to wear over, which Ariana was especially thankful for, given the brisk weather.

She felt smart in her new clothing, and marveled at the luxurious attire upon her aunt, besides the comfort and elegance of the carriage. Mrs. Bentley wore a gown of figured silk, a matching turban with a fluffy ostrich feather, a good amount of jewels, and a gold-threaded shawl, which finished a look of comfortable opulence. She had a penchant for jewelery, but somehow it never looked overdone to the point of poor taste. Ariana realized her relation was satisfied only with the best—of just about everything. Not only wardrobe, but Ariana herself was expected to display superior accomplishments, and to behave with impeccable manners. Any flaw, no matter how trifling, was not beneath her aunt's notice.

Over the past week, Mrs. Bentley had put Ariana through the ordeal of demonstrating her abilities. She was asked to play the pianoforte, which Ariana knew she could do only tolerably. When she began playing a simple melody, the lady frowned and said, "She will need a tutor," to Mr. Pellham, who was listening and nodding.

For dancing, Mr. Pellham was her partner. Thank goodness for the kindly old gentleman! He spoke encouragingly to her, all the while managing to nod sympathetically at her aunt from time to time in response to her nonstop stream of commentary, which Ariana decided was the key to his huge popularity in Hanover Square.

Ariana's needlework (a sample of which came from home in order to be finished), was especially artful and promising, according to Mr. Pellham. Her drawing ability, superior. She did not sing overly well, but he remarked that no young lady could hope to master all the accomplishments, and that Ariana's grace of manner, coupled with her beauty, should satisfy anyone. In the end, he pronounced himself utterly satisfied with her.

Thankfully, Mrs. Bentley valued his opinion, but she continued to keep a sharp eye on her niece, particularly during meals, and was quick to point out anything that struck her as less than perfectly genteel in Ariana's person, bearing, or actions. It was wearisome, indeed.

"It was too bad of your sister to enter a betrothal just before the season." Mrs. Bentley's voice roused her from her thoughts. Ariana was startled, and could think of no proper response, so she said nothing.

" 'Tis irregular for the second sister to come out before the eldest." She looked deep in thought. "This is why 'tis imperative you are called Miss Forsythe rather than Miss Ariana. Pray, do not forget it!"

"My dear Aunt," Ariana gently suggested, "there is no irregularity in your bringing me out. At home, Alberta is much out. And no one could question my coming out in the least if they knew the reason why I am here and not my elder sister."

"That, my gel," she smiled back shrewdly, "is precisely what they must not understand! The country squire. *That* alone could ruin your prospects."

Ariana's face was a picture of mild alarm, as any reminder about the business of being "Miss Forsythe" awakened her concerns, and it showed in her large, expressive eyes. Her chaperon could not decide what gave them their allure: they were really an unpopular colour, being what one could only call light brown, but they held a sparkle that gave them the effect of gold, so unusual for eyes, that they held an undeniable beauty.

"I expect everyone shall be there," Aunt Bentley went on. "I daresay Mornay may have an announcement of some kind; imagine if he is to marry! That may be why Mrs. Royleforst has manoeuvred him into such a gathering. He is notorious for small parties of only his most intimate friends. What else could be afoot?"

Ariana's aunt looked at her as if she could supply an answer to the question, but Ariana looked blankly back at her. Such outright curiosity—nay, gossip—astonished her. And her aunt had not done: "I loathe long rides in the carriage." She shook her head. "One could overturn or encounter highwaymen! Such dangers are abroad these days!" She paused, settling herself more comfortably upon the cushions and added, "Of course it will be worth it to see Aspindon, but why could not Mrs. Royleforst have chosen Mr. Mornay's London house? Or someone else's? We have so many veritable palaces in town."

Ariana's eyes widened, but again her aunt barely paused. "Every unattached female of the *ton* will likely be there—setting their caps at Mornay, no doubt! An utter waste of time! That man is positively impervious to the female sex. The Paragon in appearance and style, he has all the airs, indeed, but does he ever show the least interest in doing his duty to his family name? No! We are all beginning to think he is the most determined bachelor in creation."

Ariana looked confused. "But did you not say an engagement might be announced? This very day?"

Aunt Bentley shrugged. "I was speculating. There must be some great cause for a *ton* party at Aspindon; and even Mr. Mornay must allow his need for an heir. But I didn't mean to suggest it is *likely*."

Looking sharply at Ariana, she admonished, "Never engage him in conversation. He is far beyond your depth, and heartlessly cutting in his remarks to young ladies."

"I would never—!"

"Oh—but I was talking about the ladies, and I wanted to say we must procure invitations." She wagged a finger at Ariana and said emphatically, "Without invitations we are nothing!"

Ariana nodded as if taking the point. She involuntarily cleared her throat, and resumed looking out the window of the coach. The crowded London streets were giving way to bits of landscape as they left the city proper, or "town," as her aunt called it. Ariana leaned her head back against the cushion and closed her eyes. She was looking forward to seeing the estate in Middlesex, for she had passed through the region on her trip to London and admired its beauty greatly. Nevertheless, sleepiness was coming upon her. How nice if she could sleep during the drive.

Seven

Aspindon, Middlesex

Ariana's aunt chattered in her gossipy fashion for much of the ride to Aspindon, so that when they turned into a long, winding drive about two and a quarter hours after their departure from Hanover Square, the younger girl had not been able to doze in the least. The scene before them now, however, began to revive her spirits. The drive was neatly framed on both sides by graceful lines of evergreen trees, which eventually came to an opening where Ariana caught her first sight of Aspindon.

Fully alert now, she beheld the large dwelling with awe. The house was breathtaking, both high and wide in the classical style and balanced beautifully on either side with four-storey pavilions made of cut, light-coloured stone. Three double-door entranceways were arched and overhung by balustrades, one in the centre and two at the pavilions. Far to one side, she saw the glass ceiling of a forcing-house behind a privet hedge, which also likely hid the servants' quarters.

Above the main entrance sat a huge Venetian window that reflected the sky gracefully as they drew nearer. Ariana felt a thrill of pleasure— she loved fine things—and could hardly take it all in: manicured grounds, liveried servants everywhere, other shiny black carriages ahead and behind. It all captured her interest.

After a footman helped her descend the carriage steps, she and her aunt joined a throng of guests on a wide lawn at one side of the house. Ariana looked at the people with a newcomer's eye, delighted by the beauty and finery they wore. She was thankful for her own expensive attire at that moment, seeing what a richly dressed crowd she was among.

She had on the bonnet with the peacock feather, another reason to rest easy. Looking around, she could not locate one bonnet or head-dressing lacking the same, or the fluffier ostrich feathers such as her aunt favoured.

On Ariana's feet were white kid slippers, and she saw many others wearing similar, or more delicate footwear, such as satin. Every young female was decked out in high-waisted chemise gowns like hers, reaching the ankle or the ground. There were a few in figured silk, like Mrs. Bentley, and one older lady in an exceedingly distasteful gauze creation, nearly transparent, with no underdress whatsoever. Ariana felt herself blushing and forced her eyes elsewhere. Her own gown, though light, was reassuringly modest. A revealing décolletage was fashionable but not necessary at every occasion, and Ariana's aunt had the sense to dress her niece with an eye for smart style that was more pleasing than exhibition.

The young woman, in fact, looked perfectly becoming in her ensemble, and stood out among the gathering as one of the more finely dressed. Though not aware of this, Ariana felt, smugly, that Aspindon was just the right place for her, the *elegant newcomer*. Crossing the lawn with her aunt, she breathed, "I cannot imagine a finer situation! The house and property are so proportionately fitting, so pleasant to behold."

"It is the Mornay estate; he is not called the Paragon for lack of taste."

"But surely he did not design the house," she said, being practical.

"Does it matter?" Her aunt was exasperated. She was searching the crowd with wide, sharp eyes, looking for her chief acquaintances. "Why, the whole world *is* here! Quite an illustrious beginning for you, Ariana. Do remember all I have taught you regarding…er…decorum and proper behaviour."

There were a multitude of canopied tables set about the grounds, all loaded with elegant-looking refreshments. Mrs. Bentley took Ariana by the arm and began earnestly seeking introductions. She was anxious to let it be known at the outset that she now had a niece staying with her. A pretty, genteel niece, of marriageable age. For her part, Ariana had never seen so many multi-coloured gowns, frilly parasols, sparkling sequins, and lavish embroidery, or such enormous, many-plumed bonnets. The quantity of weighty jewels, fobs, lorgnettes and quizzing glasses, shawls, headdresses, ruffled collars, intricate cravats, and colourful waistcoats was also an amazing sight to behold. She took it all in with the appreciation of the uninitiated, trying to commit to memory descriptions which she knew would amuse her family.

She smiled and curtseyed for each introduction, managing not to appear startled when she met a woman with two small patches on her face. Mama had spoken of this old style once; it had begun as a means of hiding imperfections but soon became a fashion in its own right. Most people had ceased to wear patches before the turn of the century, however, which was well above a decade earlier.

When she met a Mrs. Herley and her two daughters, Ariana's eyes met the older Miss Herley's and the two exchanged friendly smiles. The other sister, Miss Susan, was young enough for the schoolroom and clung close by her mama. While the older women chatted, Ariana looked to Miss Herley and offered, "I am staying with my aunt for the season."

"I wondered where you came from!" she immediately confided. "I never saw Mrs. Bentley with a young person in her company. But she is your aunt—now I see." She paused, and explained, "We live in London, and this is my second season."

"Indeed," Ariana nodded, impressed. Again they shared a smile.

"You are staying at Hanover Square, then?" Miss Herley asked. Ariana nodded.

"In Mayfair," Miss Herley pronounced, knowingly. "Town home for all the blue bloods and anyone who is anyone."

"Do you also live there?"

Miss Herley laughed and said, "No. We live on Burton Crescent, respectable to be sure, but too far from Mayfair to attract first sons, I assure you." Her amiable manner and infectious laugh communicated that it did not ruin her composure to allow that it was so.

"You, however, on Hanover Square, have much better prospects than I. Hanover Square is only a hop away from Grosvenor Square, and Grosvenor Square is just a skip away from Park Lane, whose inhabitants think they are royalty."

"I scarcely know my way around London," Ariana conceded.

"Park Lane is the most coveted address in the city—other than Carlton House, I suppose."

"I see," Ariana said, still smiling.

Miss Herley looked appraisingly at Ariana and then said, "You will not need a second season, as I have," in so serious a tone that Ariana had to laugh.

"I am not here to find a husband," she said, "as much as escape one." To her questioning look she explained about Mr. Hathaway the rector, and how her parents had not approved. They had sent her to London only to remove her from the situation.

Miss Herley murmured, "Well, that is the most unusual reason I have ever heard for coming to London." She paused. "But you will be glad you came, I am certain, and if you are not snatched up directly, I know nothing at all! Come, shall we walk?"

The chestnut-haired girl took Ariana's arm with easy warmth and Ariana silently thanked God for this newfound friend. Looking behind them, she saw her aunt immersed in conversation and decided it must be all right to explore. They passed two young men who looked interestedly at the girls, one giving a sudden impish wink in their direction. They pretended not to notice.

"Rascals!" chided Miss Herley. "And of no consequence at all; how they got here, I'll never know." She gave Ariana a glance. "Are you apprehensive? I was. I wondered endlessly how I should answer if one of the gentlemen approached me. Thankfully, I am much less anxious this season."

"I am intent only upon female conversation today," Ariana declared. "I must arm myself with friends before I even consider taking on the male population!"

Miss Herley giggled and looked at Ariana appreciatively. She then confided, "Most gentleman avoid debutantes like the plague. Do not be dispirited if it seems so to you—though it may not. I feel certain you will not reach the season's end without a betrothal."

"I am certain of no such thing," Ariana said with assurance. They stopped as they came abreast of a large group of guests, and just stood, watching and sharing thoughts, admiring a gown here, a pelisse or bonnet, there. A brooch and matching necklace as it was paraded by on a large, busty woman brought exclamations, as did the pastries they decided to try from a nearby table heaped with tantalizing confections.

They also admired finely dressed men, most sporting hats, dark jackets over colourful waistcoats, close-fitting pantaloons, and either shining black Hessians on their feet or dark slippers trimmed with buckles or other ornaments. Miss Herley giggled at the fops who were altogether too colourful, though Ariana more nearly pitied them, as she did the dandies who tried too hard at being fashionable. Some sported such stiffly starched high collars they had no freedom to turn their heads, but had to turn their entire body to speak or be spoken to.

Ariana remembered Mr. Pellham's remark about seeing "sights" among the *ton*, and had to concur that it was so. Astonishing, she thought, that to most of the people present, the extreme examples of fashion were perfectly ordinary.

At length Miss Herley suggested they see more of the property. Wide-eyed, Ariana agreed. As they started off, she noticed a particularly fine gentleman who stood out from the midst of a cluster of men.

She wondered if perhaps this was the famous Mr. Brummel, for his handsome demeanour, dark blue square-cut tailcoat with its high collar, immaculate white starched shirt, and beautiful cravat with a neat small knot fit everything she had ever read about him in the *Times*. As she considered this he suddenly looked up and their eyes met.

She read a look of faint surprise on his face, no doubt for her boldness. She meant to immediately drop her eyes, but somehow they lingered long enough to appreciate that his gaze was brooding, but intelligent. There was more than a hint of hauteur about the handsome face, and yet it seemed that if he would only smile, his would be an exceedingly agreeable smile.

She waited for it. Somehow she thought he was going to do it, smile at her, which made it difficult to pull her gaze away; until the look in his dark eyes became suddenly forbidding. She blushed and looked away then, feeling disappointed, and shaken by the sudden severity she had read on his countenance.

Miss Herley called, "Miss Forsythe!" at the same moment that Ariana suddenly collided into someone provoking a startled, "Oh-mmph!"

The lady she walked into gasped loudly, then stood, hands on her hips, glaring at Ariana. She was younger than Ariana's aunt, more near her mother's age, but dressed loudly in chartreuse and with an enormous bonnet upon her head. Some dark hair peeped out here and there in an untidy pattern, though her face was that of an aging beauty. The woman parted her lips indignantly and said, in loud, hollow tones, "I-beg-your-pardon!" She brushed off her gown as if contact with Ariana had tainted the fabric.

"Oh! I am sorry! I beg *your* pardon," Ariana cried.

"I daresay you should!" Still glaring at Ariana and with her hands on her hips she waited, apparently expecting her accoster to display deeper contrition. Not knowing what else to do, Ariana added, "I must be more careful; I do apologize." The woman showed no sign of softening, however.

"What is your name?" Her tone was imperious, and louder than Ariana liked.

"Miss Ar—Miss Forsythe, ma'am." She sensed that people were beginning to stare. Miss Herley stood by loyally, looking miserable. Propriety dictated that the older woman must dismiss her before she could leave, but horrified at the prospect of drawing such attention to herself, or of displeasing her aunt, Ariana took the moment to bob a quick curtsey, grab Miss Herley's hand, and make an escape.

"That was Lady Covington!" Miss Herley hissed, as soon as they were out of earshot. She turned and looked back in the direction of the mishap. "She wanted you to apologize more prettily, I think. She used to be a foremost hostess of the *ton* and is still one of the patronesses of Almack's! Without her approval, you may not get in!"

Ariana was only mildly daunted; Almack's was an establishment of spotless reputation with stringent standards of admission. Needless to say, if one was accepted there, one was accepted generally. But Ariana was determined to enjoy the day's outing and cared little about such a thing. After all, she had apologized. How elaborate must her apology be for a minor infraction?

"She wasn't hurt," Ariana replied, considering the matter. "She could have been more gracious."

"Of course she could have, Miss Forsythe, but that is one of the privileges of the nobility, is it not?" Smiling, Miss Herley continued, "To be as disagreeable as one wishes, without suffering the least consequence or loss of stature in society! If for nothing else, I wish I had a title simply to be as unreasonable as I chose, and with no one to gainsay me." Smiling, they walked on, and she added, "Well, let us hope Lady Covington forgets the incident. It cannot be good for you when you are new to society to begin with an enemy such as her."

"Enemy! Surely that is coming it strong!"

Miss Herley looked thoughtful. "Perhaps, but I daresay I would have tried to *seem* more sorry, to satisfy her, even though I was not." This was a gentle reproach, and Ariana laughed softly. "I shall apologize again when I see her next."

The other girl smiled. "Good. I should not want to see you absent from her routs, for Mama always makes us go."

They continued walking and chatting, and sooner than Ariana would have thought it possible to suggest, Miss Herley ventured, "Would you—would you like to call me—Lavinia?"

"Thank you, Lavinia," Ariana returned. "I should be glad to. And you must call me Ariana."

"Thank you," she said, with a pleased little smile. "What a fabulous name. It reminds me of Ariadne, the daughter of King Minos."

"Who fell in love with Theseus, ran off with him, and was abandoned by him later!" finished Ariana, in a droll voice. "I do hope we have no connexion other than like-sounding names!"

They then came upon a row of tight, tall, box hedges and Ariana wondered aloud what was behind them. "I have no doubt it must be a delightful garden," she mused.

"Perhaps statuary," suggested Lavinia, her eyes alight. "Shall we find the entrance?" Ariana nodded, and both girls giggled at the delightful mischief they were undertaking. The wall of greenery went on for quite some time with no break but after a sudden bend, Ariana pointed.

"Oh, there! It looks like a break in the hedge!" They picked up their stride. With a growing excitement, as if on cue, the two clasped hands and began running. In seconds it became a race. They dropped hands, lifted their skirts and, aching with laughter, ran wildly ahead. All thoughts of the finery they wore disappeared, and Ariana might have been in the little park surrounding her own home, so free she felt.

"I'm ahead!" Miss Herley was only a few steps behind.

"Not for long!" As Ariana careened around the corner of the hedge-row, for the second time that day she collided with another person. To her horror, it was the finely dressed gentleman she had seen earlier. His eyes did not hold the faint disapproval she had seen before; instead, they were ablaze with reproof.

Eight

Having come round the hedge as fast as she could, Ariana ran smack into the man. Why, oh, why did it have to be the same one she had seen earlier? Fortunately, he had lightning-quick reflexes, and broke the impact by instantly grasping Ariana's arms as she rushed against him. His grip was strong. His look severe. He was about to speak when Lavinia added to the insult he'd already endured by exploding pell-mell against them both, this time pushing Ariana right up against him.

"Do you *never* watch where you are going?" His voice was icier, if that was possible, than his eyes, which in themselves were ferocious. Oddly, however, she could only give heed to the fact that the gentleman, imposingly handsome from a distance, looked distressed at close range, as if the finery he wore belied the truth of a painful existence. The shock of seeing him this close had the uncanny effect of drowning out the regret she ought to have felt at her impropriety.

There was something fascinating about him, she had sensed that earlier. Time froze somehow while she took in a pair of brilliant gray-black eyes, deep with sparks, sparks of feelings, it seemed to her. They were intelligent eyes, and startlingly penetrating, and—*angry*. Suddenly she was back in the moment, and blushed deeply. She took an involuntary step back from the severe countenance. "We were searching...for an opening in the hedge. We didn't mean—I beg your pardon!"

"Yes!" squeaked Miss Herley. She was aghast, and hadn't spoken at all. The man smoothed his fine coat, his eyes still drawn in disapproval, and straightened his cravat.

"You were racing."

"Well—yes." Ariana's cheeks were burning hotly, both from the exertion of running and her embarrassment. She and Lavinia were still catching their breath.

"Racing," he repeated, disdainfully. "A child's game. Perhaps you had best race back to your mamas. They will undoubtedly be missing you."

Miss Herley immediately took Ariana's arm to obey, but Ariana stood her ground. She was shocked by his incivility, and as she had dealt so unsuccessfully with Lady Covington, something akin to determination rose in her breast now. She had to try more earnestly this time.

"Please; allow us to apologize!" She put a hand on Lavinia's arm as if to reassure her, for she could feel the other girl tugging at her to leave the scene. Wistfully, she added, "We meant no harm." The man did not soften his gaze, but raised one thick dark brow slightly, almost imperceptibly; but Ariana had seen it, and was encouraged enough to continue. "It was inappropriate for us to be running. I was at fault."

Miss Herley gasped, "Me, too!" Ariana glanced at her companion and conceded with a nod; she then turned back to the gentleman.

"We're terribly sorry."

"Yes, indeed!" Miss Herley's voice was higher than it had been earlier. Ariana could see that her friend, who had been so at ease when they'd met, was suffering a great deal of anxiety. Having no audience now (as there had been when she stumbled into Lady Covington) Ariana was not similarly afflicted. She was certain she was doing a superior job of smoothing things over with this gentleman. But he was scrutinizing her with fresh disgust.

Alarmed, she added, plainly, "Please say you'll forgive us!" and she tried to make light of it with a chuckle. "Surely you would not—"

"Enough! You have no business in this area of the estate. Go back to your mamas before I take you back!" At this outburst, Ariana lost her resolve to make peace—as well as her patience. He was no more civil than Lady Covington. Did these people think so highly of themselves that no one else's feelings mattered at all?

She crossed her arms and looked up at him with asperity. "*You* have no business speaking to us in such a manner! We meant no harm, and we have apologized!" Miss Herley stared at her friend in dumbstruck horror, while the gentleman, surprised, eyed her with a hint of a smile about his mouth.

"Your apology is not accepted; be *off* with you both!"

These words came out as something of a growl and Miss Herley turned immediately on her heel, not waiting for her companion this time. Ariana hesitated, searching his eyes for a moment—such rudeness seemed out of place in one so obviously refined. He raised an eyebrow at her and put his head back as if he, too, was taking stock of her. But Miss Herley had had enough, and if Ariana lacked the sense to move on before the situation grew worse, she did not, and she hurriedly went back and took Ariana's arm. With a sidelong timid glance at the man, she pulled Ariana on.

"Come!"

Ariana allowed herself to be moved along and fought the instant temptation to turn around and look back at the strange, beautiful man who was so thoroughly rude. When they had got out of earshot, Miss Herley said, "My word, but you frightened me! I thought I might swoon! A debutante standing up to Mr. Mornay!"

Ariana halted like one struck by lightning. "Mr. Mornay? Was that indeed *the* Mr. Mornay?" She was filled with a sudden dread.

"I thought you knew!…No wonder…" and she lapsed into silence.

"My aunt cautioned me to avoid him at all costs! And now—oh, I am certain to have ruined everything!"

"But he did go easy on us," Lavinia said softly. "He is a frightful fellow and capable of much worse. In fact," and her tone became philosophical, "having received a set-down from Mr. Mornay is rather like enduring a rite of passage, and other people will adore hearing about it!" Her face brightened. "Now we've had the 'rite,' I daresay it will give us a reason to draw some attention at our next social engagement. You'll see; women are all ears when it comes to the Paragon."

Ariana's large eyes were puzzled. "My aunt maintains that his disapproval is disastrous."

"But he disapproves of most everyone; He is disastrous only when he gives set-downs publicly."

"I see." Ariana had something to muse upon. To learn and understand if she was to make her way in this social world. She thought back on the encounter. "Dressed in perfect style, and yet without manners! Why is it always so?" Ariana spoke as though she had run into a hundred gentlemen and been subject to such treatment by them all.

"We did run *into* him," Lavinia reminded her, with a wry smile. "I am surprised he didn't take us by the arm and force us back to the company. That indeed would have been utterly humiliating!" They walked in silence for a ways. "He is a handsome man; do you not think so?"

Ariana smiled. "I suppose one must grant him that."

◦◦◦◦◦

"Goodness!" Lavinia started. "I promised Mama that I would help look after Susan! How could I forget?" The young women had decided to continue their exploration of the grounds rather than allow their afternoon to be ruined. They were far from the hedgerows, but still nowhere near the other guests.

"Then let us go to her," Ariana said.

"Oh, not you, Ariana. I'll only be a minute! I'm enjoying this walk today, I feel as though I've been shut up with Mama in the house for an age! I will get Susan and we will catch up with you."

Ariana, too, was enjoying the pretty grounds of Aspindon and the familiar feeling of being in the country rather than the city. But she looked around uncertainly. "Perhaps it's best if I go with you."

"But what if the incorrigible Mr. Mornay sees us and speaks to your

aunt, or my mama? I think it is safer for just me to go—he may have
an eye out for the two of us. While I'm gone, look about—perhaps
over there," she pointed toward a green field backed by a grove of
trees, "and find us a pleasant spot to sit and study the house. We can
try and commit it to memory, and see who can draw the best likeness
afterward, when we are home."

"Very well, "Ariana said. "But do tell Mrs. Bentley of my
whereabouts."

Lavinia nodded, already backing away. "I will. I won't be long!
Wait for me!"

"All right!"

Ariana walked along at a leisurely pace, taking in as much of the
landscape as she could. In one direction, after a gentle slope upwards,
she could see the sparkling surface of a pond. In another direction, the
little grove of trees, getting larger. Behind her, the house, elegant and
stately. She went steadily toward the grove only to find, when she got
right up to it, that it was not actually a grove at all. There was one single
monstrous tree, with many trunks branching out from one main low
foundation, like the arms of an idol from India she had once seen in
a book. She stood and stared at it, wishing she had her drawing book
and pencils with her. What a fascinating study it would be, and a great
addition to her modest collection of drawings.

But soon she had to change her mind; the innumerable branches
criss-crossed at so many points that only an artist more skilled than
she could properly get it on paper. Looking up at the branches, Ariana
was suddenly swept by a desire to sit among them. Why, there was a
little spot perfect for sitting, and from which she could easily survey
the scene around her. She could see if Lavinia—or anyone else—
approached. And it would afford her a luxurious view of the house
and grounds. Why not?

She studied the spot from a few angles: could it be reached? She
decided it could. She peeled off her gloves and felt the trunk. Rough,
but not so much that a lady could not climb it. She tucked her gloves
inside her reticule, removed her spencer, and placed her things upon

a stone behind the tree. After a look around to be certain no one was about, she lifted her gown, carefully raised one leg, and began to climb.

It was too bad her aunt had not allowed her to wear a pair of half-boots, but at least the kid slippers gave some traction whereas if she had worn her usual silk pair, she might not have attained her object at all (tree-climbing could be quite slippery). Nevertheless, it seemed like only seconds before she was sitting, quite happily, on a wide branch that was every bit as cozy as she had suspected it would be.

Wasn't this nice! Wearing a smile, she viewed the house and grounds, enjoying her secluded perch. Because of the many overhanging branches there was little likelihood that she could be seen where she sat, and a sigh of contentment escaped her. She put her head back, leisurely viewing the scene above and saw that at least three more wide branches spread out horizontally like hers. They looked equally superb for sitting.

Feeling like a child, Ariana stifled an involuntary giggle and climbed up to the next branch, which was lovely. In another minute she had to try the next; and finally, feeling she may as well go as high as was safely possible, she got up on the highest branch, which took a bit more effort. She had to stand and pull herself up, hoping as she did that brushing against the bark would not damage her gown. Perched atop the branch, peering out through the branches, Ariana had to congratulate herself. This was so far superior to the morning at home and the ride with her aunt in the coach, that it was well worth the effort. The sky was clear and clean, with nary a cloud. The house stood, dignified and solitary, in the middle of a large expanse of grass surrounded by hedgerows and evergreens, bushes and a terraced garden. Other than a slight chill in the air, she was enormously comfortable. There was no sign yet of Lavinia, but Ariana could wait.

She studied the house and tried to imagine what lay beyond its large, shining windows. What would it feel like to live in such a place? So many rooms! A vast property. It was more than she could imagine. And to think the owner was not even a happy person. Mr. Mornay was truly as unpleasant as her aunt had said, and it just proved that no amount of earthly possessions could make one happy.

It was with thoughts such as these that the minutes passed by. She kept a keen eye out for Miss Herley but the young woman never returned. After more time passed and still she did not appear, Ariana became alarmed. Had something happened? Was Mrs. Bentley fretting over her absence? Perhaps she had been gone overlong. Just as she decided to begin her descent, a group of loud guests came into view. She looked down at the ground. If she started now, could she make it without being seen?

The procession of elegantly clad ladies and gentlemen, ostrich and peacock feathers bobbing in the air, made its way jocularly across the grounds, in her direction. She drew off her bonnet, not wanting her own modest feather to be seen. She placed the hat gingerly in a nearby crevice, pulled her legs and dress up, and huddled, suddenly anxious, on her perch. She could hear the titters and snatches of conversation as they came wafting toward her. What had seemed so nice a circumstance only moments before had become a precarious one. If she was found in the tree, she would certainly be a laughingstock. And this, before having a chance to make a good impression on anyone! Her season would no doubt be ruined, and her aunt's also. How could she have made a mess of things so quickly?

The approaching crowd began to scatter apart. Were they playing a game? Some appeared to be searching for something. Voices were materializing on the breeze louder than before.

"Miss Forsythe! Miss Forsythe!" Ariana froze in alarm.

They were searching for her.

Nine

"**M**iss Forsythe!"

Ariana stiffened with fear. The whole party was searching for her! Had she been gone so long? But why else look for her? Her first thought was to scurry down, but it was too likely that someone might spot her. The humiliation would be unendurable. Her only choice was simply to huddle lower and try to remain unseen. To come forward now, to risk being spotted climbing down a tree, was too horrible a thought for words.

"Please, Miss Forsythe," she heard. "Let us rescue you! Let us be heroes!" Laughter.

Even if I am not discovered, she thought bitterly, *my name alone shall be sufficient to provoke derision.* The guests by now were making their way across the property in all directions, and Ariana watched helplessly. She held her breath whenever anyone approached the tree, but apparently it did not occur to them to actually search within it. No one had any reason to suppose she was hiding; they assumed if they only got within range of her, she would of course come forward. Only Ariana *was* hiding, and praying desperately that no one would find her.

After what felt like hours, though it must only have been minutes, the party began heading en masse toward the hedgerows. From where Ariana sat she could now see that behind the hedges were more of them: it was a maze. They were thinking she had become lost in it—what a relief! She waited for the last few stragglers to leave her area, but it was with increasing impatience. She was now longing to get down. There was still a party of four making its way leisurely across the lawn in her direction. How vexing! If it were not for them, she knew she could slip down easily and be none the worse for the incident.

As they got yet nearer, Ariana could hear the loud conversation that characterized people's voices when they were enjoying themselves socially.

"I say," a gentleman proclaimed, "Why do we not truly find this missing creature? Perhaps she is a ravishing beauty, and would reward her rescuer with a kiss!" There was the overcharged gasp of a female pretending to be offended.

"Upon my word, Hartley, but it would be the only way you could procure a kiss!"

Ariana recognized that voice—and the enormous bonnet. Lady Covington! Ariana's humiliation would be ten times worse if the countess discovered her. Mr. Hartley feigned offense. In an over-dry tone he objected, "I was speaking, my lady, to Mornay."

Mornay? Oh, goodness, not him again! But she stretched her neck to get a glimpse.

"I say this was planned!" spat out the Countess. "Mrs. Bentley has a great desire to put forth her niece, and she is nothing but a pretty child, I tell you. A mere child! I saw her earlier."

"Planned? I daresay, not; Mrs. Bentley seemed wild with worry." Mr. Hartley looked plaintively at the countess. But the second lady laughed.

"Worry? Mrs. Bentley most decidedly wanted her niece back, yes, but to say she was worried is going a good distance from the truth." After a meaningful pause, she added, "She was merely indignant that her niece, who is her key to invitations this year, was not forming acquaintances. In my opinion," she added importantly, "the young lady saw an opportunity to escape her aunt's expectations, and took it."

"My point exactly," stated Mr. Hartley. "It wasn't *planned*." The foursome were still approaching and now stopped a mere ten yards from Ariana's tree. The man named Hartley drew near Mr. Mornay.

"What do you say, Mornay? Is the wandering Miss Forsythe in dire need of help, or has she taken a flight of fancy and wished us all to the devil?" There was silence while the others awaited his response. It was just then that the hot-tempered man chanced to glance in Ariana's direction. The girl's heart beat so painfully and so loudly she thought it must surely give her away. And then it didn't matter. For Mr. Mornay, after looking at the others with an unreadable expression, glanced back toward the trees, and then right up to where she was perched, scrunched and uncomfortable, trying to make herself as small as possible.

Ariana felt roundly humiliated. Here was his moment for revenge. First, she had stared at him rudely. She hadn't meant to be rude, but she was sure it seemed so to him. Then, worse, she had trespassed on his property and collided into him at top speed. A dreadful shiver ran down her spine and drops of ungenteel sweat began to pop out on her forehead, despite a mild breeze.

Meanwhile, Mr. Mornay was squinting up at her. The others, though close behind him, were speaking among themselves and failed to notice the direction of his gaze. With a drooping heart, Ariana waited for his inevitable announcement. So much for thinking of herself as the *elegant newcomer*. Now she would be known as the absurd one! But the announcement did not come. Thinking it would, she had unknowingly raised her chin—she would face the worst with her head high.

Mr. Mornay turned suddenly to Hartley. "I doubt there is any need for...ahem...a hero." At this, the ladies laughed. "And if Miss— Forsythe, did you say?—has had the sense to leave the party, I can but congratulate her."

"Mornay, you beast!" chided Lady Covington, from within the reaches of her enormous, plumed bonnet. The gentleman was unmoved by the reproach and made no answer except his usual haughty expression. Mr. Hartley was smiling.

"In that case, let us escort these ladies back to the tables. I am in dire need of being rescued, myself. A touch of claret should do the trick!" They turned to go, smiling. Mr. Hartley politely held out his arm to the second lady, but to Ariana's amusement, Mr. Mornay did not offer his arm to Lady Covington. Her reaction was to pout and hurry to him, taking his arm brassily. He looked annoyed.

"Breathe easy, Mornay!" Her tone was loud and irked. "I have no delusions regarding your affections!" With that, they walked off.

Mr. Mornay had seen her, Ariana was certain. Why had he not revealed her? That was probably something she would never know. As they left, no one looked back at the tree, and she felt an enormous relief. Even while they were still in view, she could wait no longer and moved to edge herself down, and then, to her horror, discovered her gown was stuck!

She forced herself to relax, and then tried again. The resistance at the back of the gown persisted. Ariana reached as far as she could behind her, realized it was a ribbon from the back of her dress that was caught on the branch, but could not free the snagged piece. She took a deep breath and tried again, and was again without success. She felt tears coming to the surface of her eyes, but forced them away. It was all so provoking! When would this day end!

If she tore her gown she would never hear the end of it from Aunt Bentley. And bad as that was, it would be nothing next to the disdain that would arise when the whole party saw the result—for, with only the short spencer to wear over her dress, the torn fabric would be impossible to hide. Her legs were cramped and aching, and she was heartily sick of the tree. How foolish of her to climb it!

Ariana made one last attempt to get the ribbon free without having to force it. She could follow the snag with her fingers only so far. She had no choice and would have to let it tear. But wait—she hadn't thought to pray. She had breathed a prayer earlier about not being discovered, and so far God had been merciful. Mr. Mornay had seen her, but he hadn't shared his discovery.

Reflecting quickly on her behaviour, Ariana felt utterly unworthy of divine help. But she closed her eyes and prayed nevertheless. *Thank You, Father, that I do not need to earn Your favour. Thank You for freely giving it to me in Christ. Please help me get out of this tree without tear-ing my gown!*

She continued praying in a low voice, her eyes still closed, ending upon the words, "Oh, help me, *dear* Lord!" A polite cough came from below. She looked down in astonishment and saw that someone—Mr. Mornay!—was looking up at her with a dark countenance. Her heart jumped into her throat. How could it be? How could he have returned so quickly? And, even more puzzling, why?

Ten

M r. Mornay was leaning against the trunk of the tree with his arms folded as if he had been there for an age. He had thick dark hair and brows, and he was looking up at her with an inscrutable expression. He held a walking stick in his gloved right hand and Ariana felt herself blushing to the roots of her hair. He leaned the stick against the tree, removed his coat, and began making his way up toward her, saying a bit sourly, "I believe you are in need of assistance."

In only seconds he was beside her, and leaning past her shoulder to find the problem, lifted the piece of snagged fabric off the pointed branch that had caught it. He then let himself down to the branch beneath hers. Since Ariana's seat was a deal higher than where he stood, their eyes were nearly level. Again she was struck by the degree of movement in his dark eyes. And as before, she detected a sense of suppressed pain in his features. But he seemed about to give her a set-down, and she poised herself to receive it, clinging to her branch.

"Miss Forsythe, is it not?" He did not offer to introduce himself.

Ariana nodded, and uttered a faint, "I am much obliged to you, sir."

He looked at her severely. "You should be. It was exceedingly foolish to leave your friends and come off alone, putting yourself in a vulnerable position. Not only young and attractive, but alone and hidden from general view!" His voice was full of disgust, as if he had never met such a stupid creature in all his life. He paused for a moment.

"Are you not aware of dangers that may present themselves to careless young women like yourself?"

Ariana's face continued to burn. He must have noted it, but there was no softening on his features. She turned her head to avoid his eyes, now blazing with reproof, and suddenly seething indignation rose up within her. In most cases, her quick temper caused her problems. At this moment it came to her aid. She looked fully at him, meeting the raging sea of his black eyes and dared to defend herself.

"I did not plan, sir, for this to occur!"

"Does that signify?" His voice came out as a hiss, making it abundantly clear that to him, at least, it did not. "Has any young woman with the misfortune of being ill-used ever planned on having it so?"

She stubbornly returned his gaze, unconvinced there had been a risk of such danger. "This is a gathering of genteel people, gentlemen—"

"Gentlemen!" he sputtered, "are capable of the most heinous behaviour that any cove from London's darkest corners might be! In fact," he continued ruthlessly, "a gentleman may hazard more danger since he is least likely to suffer the penalty of law for his actions, no matter how abhorrent." His countenance was fierce, and Ariana felt as ashamed as when her own papa had occasion to scold her.

The logic of what he said made Ariana wonder if she had been at risk. Their eyes were in a deadlock while she weighed the idea. She could not help, again, but to be distracted by his swirling eyes, as different from the norm as hers were said to be. They were like tossing waves, changing before her, and yet not. She boldly met his blistering gaze, however, her own eyes reflective of the resentment she felt for being rudely awakened to dangers she had not imagined.

"I will assist you down." His voice was cold, but he was careful to hold the trunk with one hand, while receiving her firmly with his free arm as she lowered herself. The pleasant aroma of snuff greeted Ariana as he drew her closer in the rescue. Undoubtedly a fine brand. Many women, including her mama, were repulsed by its odour, but Ariana had never found it unpleasant. She and Mr. Mornay were in close proximity for only a few seconds, but it was enough for her to have the astonishing thought that not only did he look very nice, but he smelled quite nice, too.

Still holding her about the waist, he reached up and acquired the bonnet, handed it to her, and ordered, "Wait." He released her and let himself down to the next lower branch, again assisting her as she lowered herself. In that fashion, they made it to the ground. When Ariana was on the last branch he lifted her down with both hands.

She immediately busied herself by brushing off her gown, delaying having to say anything to him for as long as possible. He picked her spencer and reticule off the ground where she had left them, and held them out to her. Ariana took them and offered an obligatory "Thank you."

She took an apprehensive glance up at him, and found that *he* was studying her. He said nothing, but his countenance seemed less severe than it had earlier, and she decided it was a good time to make an exit.

"I am obliged to you, sir…and indeed, more so…if the danger you referred to was real."

He let out a soft gasp. "You can doubt it?"

Ariana's lips were pressed together stubbornly, and she pulled on her gloves with asperity. "If I did not, I could hardly enjoy the solitude I often cherish; I shan't be the sort of female who thinks there are dangers behind every tree or rock. I should never go out alone, then. Such a confining existence that would be!"

His countenance turned to a scowl. "Young women should not go out alone—or young men, for that matter." She was surprised by such a sentiment, but then decided it came from residing in London, a crowded city, so unlike her own small town.

"Perhaps I must behave differently here," she conceded, "though at home, I assure you, young ladies do go forth alone, and think nothing of it."

"Perhaps they think nothing of being a lady, then."

Ariana had no answer for this remark and just watched as he put his coat back on. Sophia Worthington's words, that she "adored watching"

Mr. Mornay suddenly flashed in her mind, and she looked away, embarrassed. He retrieved his cane, while she attempted to smooth her gown again. There were wrinkles in it, and with a sigh she gave up, and then realized he was looking on with obvious distaste.

"Is it that bad?" she asked.

"That depends upon your standard," was his evasive answer. "That's what comes of climbing trees in afternoon dress. May I ask what you were doing in the tree?"

She paused, giving him a curious look, but admitted, "I had no idea of climbing it until I saw what a strange, monstrous thing it was; somehow, it just seemed to…beckon to me."

One dark brow on the masculine face went up faintly, but he looked interested, not scornful, and she was encouraged. "And then I saw that those trunks, horizontal as they are, should make an agreeable vantage point from which to view the house."

"And so you climbed up," he finished for her.

"Yes."

"Right up to that high perch I found you in?"

"Not directly; I went higher for the advantage of a better view… indeed going higher than I intended at first." He was amused, and Ariana noticed with gratification a sparkle in the dark eyes.

"So you find this property agreeable?"

Ariana glanced around at the neat expanse of lawn and trees and sky and smiled. "I do." Thinking his silence was disagreement, she asked, "Do you not find it so?" He looked around them, but was silent. Ariana could not help shaking her head and pointed northward. "What a fine prospect! How serene and peaceful! How good for the soul it must be to view it often."

She glanced at him to find that he was looking at her, not the view, but he turned obediently and looked in the direction she pointed. He nodded, but said nothing. Turning back to her, the dark eyes seemed momentarily troubled, but he quickly regained control and the look was gone.

Ariana felt badly for him. There was something of grief in him.

As they started walking back toward the party, Ariana spoke first. "Will you allow *me* to apprise my aunt of my misadventure?" Her large eyes glittered up at him questioningly.

"You wish to inform her, then?" He was surprised.

"I shan't lie to her. And after having the entire company after me, I cannot think she will not ask questions." There was a silence then, and she moaned, "*Everyone* shall know of my folly!"

"What makes you suppose that?" His eyebrows rose.

"Mrs. Bentley is hard pressed to keep anything to herself." (Mr. Mornay, to his credit, did not so much as blink at this accurate appraisal.) "And now she will be scandalized and perhaps send me packing!" She met his eyes, her own full of resentment against the unjust persecution which she feared was forthcoming.

He studied her, not unkindly. "Packing to where?"

"Chesterton."

He nodded. "Not more than two days by coach."

"By carriage, yes, sir, it is. But in its few attractions…it may as well be across the ocean!"

"As bad as that?"

"Worse!" Ariana's emphatic utterance failed to take into account that she had never been discontented to live in Chesterton for her whole life.

"Not to mention fewer prospects of finding a husband," he interjected wickedly. But Ariana laughed.

"My prospects here are worse than at home, sir. Back home I am acquainted with a few men who consider the state of their souls before God; I do not think I shall meet so much as one in this company of whom I can say such a thing."

Now the black brows rose considerably. "You have been instructed, I think, regarding what to expect here."

Ariana nodded. "Yes." There was silence for a moment. "And now having been in London—where my papa brought us only once—I have been so close to seeing the British Museum which I have longed to see, art galleries, St. Paul's Cathedral, Hyde Park, and Vauxhall

Gardens; and so many attractions—only now to be thrust back home without so much as a glimpse! I shall be forever cast down!"

Ariana was amazed to find herself conversing comfortably with the man she had considered rude and arrogant only moments before. His tone and attitude had changed considerably; he now seemed an agreeable gentleman. Indeed, one with understanding and compassion. She did not know what to make of it.

He could not resist making his point yet again. "Perhaps it will serve as a lesson to you, so that in future you are more careful of your surroundings." This time she did not cavil, choosing to remain silent, until he added, "Be thankful that only your season is ruined, and not something much worse."

This was provoking. "Your misapprehensions are without warrant," she said, trying unsuccessfully to hide her annoyance. "I fail to see danger. These grounds were safe when I arrived, and so they are, now." They stopped walking, and Mr. Mornay crossed his arms while receiving the brunt of her indignation. Her tone calmed. "You are too strong in your case, sir."

He said nothing for a moment, but then, in a smooth, low voice stated chillingly, "You are assuming, of course, that I myself could pose no danger to you." Ariana blinked and felt a little grip of fear on her heart. She said nothing. He leaned in closer upon her and asked, in that same sinewy voice, "Do you know for a fact that I pose no danger to you?" His voice was silken and smooth and—scary. Her eyes widened, but he suddenly retreated. "As a matter of fact, I do not."

"I never thought as much." There was relief in her voice.

He turned forbidding eyes on her. "But for all you knew, I could have! You obviously afford yourself the luxury of trusting strangers. No young woman, no matter how well off she is, can afford that!"

"I—I beg your pardon." She had nearly stammered, and flushed pink. He looked at her steadily for a moment, and then held out his arm.

"Come. I shall return you to your aunt."

Shyly, she accepted his arm. She had seldom been escorted by anyone other than her father, and it was pleasant to be led by Mr. Mornay. In addition, she recalled how he had not offered his arm to Lady Covington, earlier, and she was flattered that he had done so for her.

She kept her eyes averted as they walked.

"I should hope that when you again come out, if indeed you do, your behaviour shall be improved." Instead of answering with a rejoinder, which was her immediate impulse, she decided to show him that she could, when she tried, control her temper.

"I shall endeavour to make it so."

He gave her a surprised glance. "What, is all the fight gone from you? Pity. I was enjoying it."

Ariana was speechless.

Eleven

When Ariana and Mr. Mornay rounded a bend which brought them into view of the guests—as many as had made their way out of the maze—an excited buzz began to circulate. Mr. Mornay with a young lady on his arm was not a common sight.

"How will your family in Chesterton receive you, when you have been cast back upon them in so untimely a fashion, with no suitor, no prospects?" he asked.

She met his gaze with a faint smile. "I had no hopes of finding a suitor, sir, and if I must return home, then my family and I will accept that it is God's will." A little unconscious sigh escaped her.

"Now, now, do you blame the Almighty for your own misbehaviour?" he asked in mock reprimand.

Ariana looked up at him in surprise. "By no means. But I do know that what the Lord allows has a purpose. It may be that my misbehaviour, as you put it, was ordained to spare me from a greater ill that might have befallen me had I stayed with my aunt longer."

He expressed interest in her answer, but there was no time for further conversation. As their presence was noticed more widely, people began to sweep in their direction.

"And if you are *not* sent packing, Miss Forsythe, I trust you may be able to bear that as well," Mr. Mornay said. There was no time for Ariana to ask what he meant. The missing debutante had reappeared and the attention of the guests was on them. A small throng soon surrounded them, with many shouting out questions and jests, but Mr. Mornay, now leading Ariana by the elbow, ignored them, moving determinedly to an astonished Mrs. Bentley, who was standing with a glass in one hand and the other upon her heart when he presented her with her niece.

"Is all well?" she asked, her demeanour anything but positive.

"Certainly." Mr. Mornay's voice was commanding. Ariana had not yet opened her mouth when he swiftly continued, "Your niece was surveying the grounds when I chanced to spot her." His eyes met hers for the briefest second; enough for her to understand that he was not going to divulge the details. A silent thank you went forth from her own expressive eyes.

"What, *alone?*" It didn't look well for a young lady to go about unescorted, and Mrs. Bentley's voice conveyed her dread at this idea.

He ignored the question. "She was impatient to rejoin you as soon as she understood that you were the least bit flummoxed by her absence."

Mrs. Bentley sighed in open relief, suddenly comprehending that her niece was not in disgrace with her host. She nodded, exclaiming, "My dear Mr. Mornay! You are too good! Too good, indeed. How can I thank you for bringing her back safely to us?"

"Not at all," he said with a brief nod of his head. He then turned to leave, stopping only to bow slightly to Ariana. Mrs. Bentley's eyes glittered in her head. Ariana was grateful for his simple explanation, and curtseyed nicely to him. She had not precisely wished to join her aunt as soon as possible, as he had said, but otherwise his words were true and had spared her from ridicule and the vexation of being sent packing.

It so completely lacked sensationalism, in fact, that soon the guests were back to playing lawn games such as bowling on greens, eating the delicacies prepared by the kitchens at Aspindon, and engaging in the usual conversation, teasing, and gossip that accompanied any *ton* gathering.

✎⌘✎

Mrs. Henrietta Royleforst knew her nephew, was suspicious of his explanation regarding Mrs. Bentley's missing niece, and, in short, did not believe a word of it. At the soonest moment, therefore, she motioned for Ariana to come to her.

Henrietta Royleforst was a large woman, and sat upon a wing chair that had been brought from the house for her comfort. When Ariana approached her, she took her gold-rimmed lorgnette and held it before her eyes. Ariana curtseyed politely, and had not finished the motion before the lady came straight to the point:

"How did you happen upon the favour of my nephew?"

"Your nephew, ma'am?"

"Mr. Mornay! You didn't know?"

"Oh, yes, I—"

"Humph! What is your name?"

"Miss Forsythe."

"Of course you are Miss Forsythe! The whole party knows you are Miss Forsythe! What is your *Christian* name?"

Ariana bristled at the tone, thinking that Mrs. Royleforst and her nephew were not unlike in temperament. Her chin rose. "Ariana, ma'am."

"Oh! I suppose you think it a pretty name, eh?" She did not wait for an answer. "And how did you happen, Miss Ariana Forsythe, to impress my nephew favourably?"

Recalling the ire he had displayed at their meeting, Ariana had to say, "I hardly think that is the case, ma'am."

"I shall be the judge of that," she replied dryly. "Did he behave abominably to you? Has he told you in no uncertain terms that you are *quite* beneath his notice?"

Surprising questions! But she kept her countenance. "No-o-o."

Mrs. Royleforst nodded blandly but her curious eyes grew suddenly thoughtful. Ariana shifted on her feet. Perhaps she could distract the lady. "May I fetch you a refreshment, Mrs. Royleforst?"

"Ah!" She crinkled up her eyes happily. "So you do know who I am! But you try to change the subject. Tell me what you think of Phillip."

"Phillip?"

"My nephew, of course. I daresay he must have introduced himself?"

Ariana again shifted on her feet. "No, he did not." She coloured, though she was not certain why this admission should be at all humiliating to her.

"Oh?" Clearly Mrs. Royleforst was after something, but with each answer Ariana provided the woman seemed to grow more confused. "And how did you chance to meet?" Her small eyes were intent as they awaited a reply.

"It was as your nephew said, ma'am. I was, er, *exploring* when he happened upon me."

Her eyes narrowed. "And you maintain he simply proceeded to return you to your aunt, without a single scathing remark? 'Tisn't his style!"

Ariana gave a wry smile. "I did not say there had been no scathing remarks, ma'am."

"Ah." She nodded knowingly. "Where were you when he found you?" Again she listened keenly for the response.

"On...on the property." Her reply was hopeless, but she dared not say more.

Mrs. Royleforst gave another loud "Humph! What fustian!" She put down the lorgnette she had been peering through, one eye closed, using first one eye and then the other, and gave Ariana a surprised, wide-eyed look. Her eyes were small and red in her large, ponderous face, giving the impression that she most assuredly needed the lorgnette. She wore an old-fashioned mobcap upon her head of untidy locks, but otherwise attempted to fit the mould of fashion despite her large size. Her ample crimson gown was of a rich velvety fabric, and she wore the popular satin slippers, in a matching hue, on her wide feet.

In a shrewd undertone she said, "I understand my nephew quite well. He obviously favoured you! If you wish to have my assistance you must give me no more Banbury tales! I need an account I can trust, and then I shall know how to direct you."

Ariana looked at her helplessly. "Upon my honour, ma'am, I cannot say with the least integrity that your nephew favoured me!"

"Ah! You simply do not know him!" She sat back in her cushions, unhappily. "This is tiresome, Miss Forsythe, and I cannot abide it! You have told me nothing in all this time!"

"Is that so?" It was Mr. Mornay. Ariana and Mrs. Royleforst looked up at the tall figure with surprise.

"It *is* that bad, I assure you!" the old woman complained. "What a vexatious creature! She gives me no information whatsoever!"

Mr. Mornay looked appreciatively at his aunt, but said, "You exert yourself too much, and without cause."

She gave him a narrowed look. "You are my nephew! Tell me who this gel is to you, and do not, pray, offer me any fustian, for I've just had a bellyful of that."

With the hint of a smile he said, "I wish I'd heard it."

The lady then stabbed at his foot with her walking stick. "You are disrespectful, sir!"

"My dear ma'am," he exclaimed innocently. "If I were to be disrespectful then I should tell you outright—" he leaned down and spoke softly—"that you should mind your own business."

Mrs. Royleforst harrumphed loudly enough to make others turn and look. "You are not like your father, sir! Or your mother, for that matter! If you are not my business!" She pulled out a handkerchief. "I am sure I do not know what is. My brother's only living child! My last relation!"

"There, there, ma'am." A painfully thin, middle-aged woman with tightly drawn-back hair had just returned from a refreshment table. She was carrying a plate of delicacies for her mistress, for she was Mrs. Royleforst's paid companion. She had remained at a polite distance for as long as she could stand to, and now rushed over to console her employer who was evidently severely displeased.

"Doctor says not to get yourself all astir, ma'am." The companion had a high, nervous voice. Her shyness was great, but loyalty and affection for her mistress won out momentarily. She placed the tray on a little table near her mistress and then looked accusingly at Mr. Mornay—but soon tore her eyes from that formidable face, having temporarily forgotten how much he frightened her.

A handful of men across the way hailed Mornay, then, and he gave a bow to his aunt and then disappeared into their midst. Ariana took the chance to curtsey and walk away herself. When she looked back, the lady was sitting happily helping herself to the confections on the tray in front of her. She no longer looked the least out of countenance. And then Ariana saw Miss Herley waving to her and coming toward her hurriedly, so she turned and started closing the gap between them.

"I am dreadfully sorry, my dear Ariana! May I still call you by your name? I was utterly horrified by what the consequences might be, but when your aunt inquired I was forced to tell her we had been exploring the grounds. She insisted upon alarming herself with the notion of you going forth on your own, and forbade me to get you, but would have the whole party do so!" Her sincere brown eyes looked hopefully at Ariana. "I dreaded to see them all go forth, as if it were a huge joke. I am miserably sorry, Ariana. Your aunt kept her eyes strictly upon me or I would have returned to you!"

Ariana was nodding understandingly throughout this hurried speech. "It seems to have turned out well," she said. "And in any case, it was certainly no fault of yours that I allowed myself to stay unaccompanied."

"You are too kind; We both know I encouraged you to it!"

"But I enjoyed it."

"You did?"

"Until I saw everyone looking for me. That changed matters rather swiftly, I assure you!" She was touched by Lavinia's heartfelt apology. "Think no more of it," she told her friend. "I am not vexed. Mr. Mornay did an astonishing job of smoothing things over for me."

"Astonishing, indeed! I nearly froze from surprise when I saw you on his arm! He was not vexed? However did you manage that? You must tell me every detail!"

The girls spoke at length, spending the rest of the afternoon mostly in one another's presence. They exchanged promises to keep in touch. Mrs. Bentley, meanwhile, had time to mingle, extending and receiving invitations, and had high hopes of filling her parlour with fashionables for many days to come. High hopes, indeed, and thanks to her niece whose appearance upon the arm of the Paragon made her instantly an object of great curiosity. Mrs. Bentley determined that not even during the whole long ride home would she mention the matter of Ariana's long absence from her side that day, so pleased was she with the result.

Twelve

Mayfair, London

The days following Aspindon saw a steady stream of callers at the house in Hanover Square. Far from being the laughing-stock she had feared, Ariana was all the rage. Mrs. Bentley's parlour was rarely empty and the hallway tray overflowed with cards from callers. The older lady couldn't have been more satisfied—except for one catch.

During their day away, Mr. Pellham had taken a nasty fall, badly injuring his right ankle. His surgeon had wrapped the leg up prettily over a mash of grated comfrey roots, administered laudanum, and gave strict orders for bed rest. Mrs. Bentley was loath to leave her own parlour lest she miss important calls from high-standing members of the *ton;* but it rankled her nerves to know that Mr. P. needed her and she was not there. She saw nothing for it.

Ariana began to wonder why the pair did not marry, but dared not ask. As for the sudden popularity of their drawing room, it aston-ished her that it was on account of the taciturn Mr. Mornay. He had unwittingly made it instantly fashionable to know Ariana, and simply because he was the Paragon: dashing in figure, all the mode in dress, and, perhaps most importantly, fantastically rich. (Any of these qualities by themselves could capture the imagination of unwed females; but to possess all three in one man! It made Ariana laugh to herself when she heard one woman say, "He lacks a title, but only the fussiest females can hold that against him. As for myself, I certainly would not!")

The circumstance of owing her success to him was outrageous to Ariana, but she nevertheless quickly grew to appreciate that it was a blessing. She'd been given the opportunity to make the acquaintance of many people, including other lovely young women, while her aunt chatted with their mamas. She did not enjoy the love of gossip held by many. And, it was disconcerting that, although Mr. Mornay was a preferred topic of conversation, all that she learned of him was largely negative. He possessed an acid tongue (something Ariana could easily attest to); he ignored people who bored him; he more often than not refused invitations and when he did accept them, could not be depended upon to show. He was exasperating and decidedly cutting in his remarks, yet he remained an object of admiration and even affection.

This, Ariana felt, was due to the fact that he could, when he chose, display a winsome charm and thoughtfulness that made his quick temper forgivable. She had experienced a measure of that charm and it was distinctly pleasant.

Finally, as if all that wasn't enough, Mr. Mornay was said to be immune to female charms. Any seasoned lady worth her salt, therefore, was compelled to tip her cap at Mr. Mornay though it brought out the worst in his nature. Even the notorious married flirts of high society had failed to lure him into their grasp. Indeed, it was an annual point of wagering, speculation, and conversation to see which ladies would develop the *tendre* for Mr. Mornay, and wind up with ruined hopes.

Hearing such reports hardly raised him in Ariana's estimation, and by the end of the week, she wished heartily not to fall again into his path. Or almost did. It was one thing to hear tales about him, but no matter how much she was swayed by the general consensus regarding his character, she could not forget the moments of kindness in his voice; or that he had actually done nothing unforgivable toward her.

Still, she was sensible enough to realize that his placid behaviour to her on one occasion might not be repeated, so she determined to be wary of him.

∞○∞

There was one thing that was lacking in Ariana's social success. Two of the patronesses of Almack's—Lady Covington and Lady Hollingsford—had not called upon Ariana and her aunt. Only ladies with so-called "vouchers" could be admitted to Almack's, and only the patronesses of Almack's could issue them. Therefore it was paramount these ladies be singularly satisfied the debutante in question was worthy of admittance. Two of the four patronesses had called, however. The vouchers were promised, and their ladyships' absence was not to be dwelt upon.

The cultural expeditions, as Mr. Pellham called the intended jaunts he and Ariana had hoped to take together, were postponed indefinitely. Mrs. Bentley kept her niece busy returning calls in any case, and they were welcomed into the most elite drawing rooms in Mayfair, where the art of keeping up a lively banter, Ariana found, was both fun and challenging. She could not always hold her own, but it seemed that Mr. Mornay's favour had preceded her, and if she momentarily faltered for a smart reply, she was kindly helped along by various hosts or hostesses. Ariana discovered, too, that silence, accompanied by a knowing look, could be response enough to satisfy a company. And her natural habit of speaking her mind was often mistaken for wit, to her advantage.

One night she and her aunt attended a card party at the exclusive residence of Lord and Lady Sherwood. Ariana dreaded the evening, for it promised to be an exceedingly proper affair. Her aunt warned her that the Sherwoods took their cards seriously and wagers were likely to run prodigiously high; Ariana was not, under any circumstances, to accept an invitation to play. This presented no dilemma, since gambling was no temptation for her.

The Sherwoods' home was more luxurious than her aunt's. Ariana could have been happily entertained giving an inspection to the abundance of splendid paintings and numerous trinkets in the large rooms, but she was ushered off to one side of the main drawing room with other young ladies who were not playing cards. She already recognized a good number of the other girls, and they treated her with deference, introducing any strangers until she had met everyone; she was not neglected for a moment.

Far into the evening, two latecomers arrived. One gentleman was unknown to Ariana, the other, the much-maligned Mr. Mornay. Ariana felt a surprising reaction within herself. A slight flutter, a mild rush of colour to her cheeks. She had heard so much about him by this time that her reaction to his presence could not be neutral. This, surely, was the reason she became suddenly self-conscious. This, too, the reason she vowed instantly not to say a word to the man, but hoped every second he would see and greet her.

Seated beside her was a lovely young Spanish girl named Miss Isabella, who offered the information that the other man was Lord Horatio, a second son who could expect two thousand a year. Ariana nodded sagely, having grown quickly accustomed to this unusual manner of learning about others in society. The gentlemen were greeted warmly, though Mr. Mornay more effusively, Ariana thought. They were quickly ushered to the main card table. Later, during a break in play, Mr. Hartley came and bowed politely to the circle of young ladies, exchanging small talk with a few, including Ariana. Lord Horatio looked brightly in their direction, but Mr. Mornay behaved as if the party consisted solely of those nearest him.

Miss Isabella shuddered. "May Mr. Mornay continue to keep his *deestance,* for I understand he can have nothing civil to speak to a *señorita.* My mama say to avoid him at all costs!"

Ariana said nothing but stole a glance his way. It happened that Mr. Mornay looked up from the table then also. Their eyes met and Ariana found herself in the precise predicament she had been in once before: his gaze immediately arrested hers, and she found herself hoping he might be on the verge of a smile.

He wasn't, of course. In fact, he showed no sign of recognition other than a faint change in his demeanour. Ariana noted with gratification that at least he did not scowl; that was something. Lord Horatio claimed his friend's attention and Mr. Mornay looked away, but Miss Isabella had witnessed the silent eye match and hissed, "He is bound to insult you, now you have claimed *hees* attention!"

Ariana spoke her thoughts aloud. "I wager that he must labour under some hidden anguish which causes so unnatural a response in him."

"No, no! It is not *heeden*," Isabella answered. "He is out of countenance because everyone wants to *teep* their cap at him because he is *reech* and handsome."

∽∾○∾∾

A few hours later, the group of intent card-players stood up, and congratulations for Lady Sherwood could be heard. As they began to disperse around the room, Lady Sherwood, looking very pleased with herself (for she must have won a great deal of money) announced that the refreshment room was open. As people headed in that direction, Ariana did likewise but had to stop as if by a great tug on her heart when she came abreast of a beautiful Reynolds portrait.

Lord Horatio, meanwhile, had stopped Mr. Mornay while the crowd was thinning into the other room. "I say, Mornay, you threw that game, letting her ladyship win! What the deuce for? With such stakes!"

"You give me too much credit, Horatio," was the reply, with a short laugh.

"No, upon my word! You could have had that round and you know it!" Mr. Mornay did not reply, but helped himself to the smallest pinch of snuff.

Lord Horatio continued. "You've heard the same rumours I have, that the Sherwoods are in narrow straits these days! Upon my soul, but if you aren't a sentimental fellow beneath all that crust, after all."

Mornay stiffened. "That is the most imbecilic notion I have ever known you to entertain. Now go plague somebody else with your devilish ideas!"

Lord Horatio chuckled. "Oh, very well, deny it if you like. But I know what I know—" He stopped short as they both noticed Ariana at that moment. She had unwittingly abandoned the painting and had turned her head in astonishment upon hearing such a remarkable dialogue. She was still in front of the large, ornately framed canvas, but looking at the two men, delighted with the notion that her Mr. Mornay was actually a secret do-gooder, for she instantly gave credit to Lord Horatio's suspicion.

She looked very pretty in full evening dress with the long, empire-waisted white gown and matching white gloves that reached her elbows. Her hair was done high upon her head and she was standing, with a small smile upon her mouth, looking at Mr. Mornay as if he were an angel. Now it made perfect sense, his helping her that day at his estate.

She realized her position with a short gasp. "I beg your pardon!" She would have turned on her heel immediately but Mr. Mornay held out a hand for her to stop.

"Horatio, I must speak to this young woman a moment."

The young lord instantly had a nervous alarm in his eyes. He looked cautiously at his friend. "Do not do it, Mornay." His tone was low, and wistful. He wanted to think of a reason to bring away this fetching young lady so that Mornay could not be unspeakably rude to her, as he was certain his friend was about to be. Having nothing come to mind in way of a rescue, however, he bowed helplessly to Ariana, and strode reluctantly away, saying, "Do follow shortly; Lady Sherwood will be waiting to fall at your feet, I should think."

This was meant as a joke, but Mr. Mornay did not smile. He was looking severely at Ariana, who was realizing what an enormous blunder she had made. Again! She had done the very thing she had repeatedly been warned against, allowing Mr. Mornay to see her admiring him. She turned veiled eyes to his swirling dark countenance.

"Do you make it a habit to listen to private conversations?" His tone was soft—and venomous.

"Of course not!"

"Nevertheless, you have deliberately overheard one of mine. Do not think, Miss...er..." He had forgotten her name!

"Ariana. Forsythe!" She had given her first name out of habit and she blushed.

"Miss Forsythe." He ignored the mistake. "Do not imagine Lord Horatio was near the mark in what he supposed."

She said nothing, but only continued to face him, feeling her heart beating painfully. Why was she afraid of him? She must have heard too many reports of how awful he could be.

"For your information," he continued, sourly, "if I did throw a hand, it would not be a misguided effort of good will."

"You owe me no explanation, sir!" Her voice lacked strength. She put one hand to her throat, a nervous mannerism she was unaware of.

"Indeed, not! But as your meddling results in a misleading assessment of my character due to Horatio's delusion, I prefer to keep the record straight."

There was a brief silence, but Ariana's weakness of speaking her mind surfaced. Her voice was not as even or unruffled as his, but she managed to say: "I have heard a great deal about your character of late. And nothing would have convinced me of any redeeming qualities within it. I am too persuaded already of your *overwhelming* depravity, so an explanation is hardly necessary!"

He eyed her with surprise. Her outburst seemed to have restored his good humour. She had met his stinging rebuke with her own poisoned dart. Though Ariana's face was blazing from embarrassment and self-reproof, his had become unarmed. She was surprised by this startling change in demeanour, and suddenly self-conscious. It began to be borne in upon her that she had indeed listened to a private conversation and she owed him an apology.

She could not meet his eyes. "I am sorry for having listened to your conversation; it was—rude of me…and…wrong. I do not know why I did! Good evening!" With that, she whirled around and hurried toward the refreshment room, hoping no one would notice her late entrance.

Lord Horatio looked anxiously at Ariana as she entered the dining room. She was flushed, to be sure, but not hysterical, and he decided that Mornay had either gone easy on her or she had nerves of steel.

As people helped themselves to drinks, fruit ices, pastries, nuts, and fresh fruit, Ariana discreetly took her place near her aunt, who whispered, "Where have you been!" A few minutes later, Lord Horatio politely requested an introduction. She discovered his lordship was witty and pleasant, and she greatly enjoyed the minutes she and her aunt had of his company. He had an admiring attitude toward Ariana that made the blush on her cheeks remain; and when he had gone, suddenly Mr. Mornay was there, bowing politely.

"I notice your niece did not play this evening," he said lightly to Mrs. Bentley.

She looked at him wide-eyed. "Well! With you and the Sherwoods playing, I should think not! I positively forbade her from doing so."

He nodded. "Perhaps another time, then. I should like to see how she gets on."

He looked at Ariana who instantly professed, "I do not play for wagers, sir, on any occasion."

"And what is your reason? I feel you must have a particular reason, by your manner of stating it."

"Yes; It is against my principles. Card-playing is innocent enough, but, when combined with gaming, it is ruinous. You know that fortunes are lost at cards."

"There are those," he returned with the briefest look in Lady Sherwood's direction, "who would say that fortunes are won."

She answered slowly, trying not to be distracted by his dark good looks. "Yes. At the expense of those who lose."

He studied her with the hint of a smile. "Certainly I agree that one shouldn't play unless one can afford to lose."

"And therein lies the problem." Her eyes flashed, a quick spark of bluish-green was in them, and then was gone. "Those given to gaming always think they can afford to play; and if not, no longer care. I submit that gaming at cards is ruinous, and should never be encouraged."

He bowed politely and turned away.

Thirteen

Mrs. Bentley was silent for most of the twenty-minute drive home from the Sherwoods' house. "I believe," she said at long last, "Mr. Mornay means to discover your situation."

Ariana looked wide-eyed at her aunt. "What on earth for? He can have no interest in me."

"No, indeed, not," her aunt quickly agreed. "Someone else must have inquired, perhaps Lord Horatio." She thought for another moment and said, "I shall write to your father, to see what's what, though I daresay there will be little coming from that corner, eh?"

Ariana nodded. "Five hundred pounds, at most, I believe. And perhaps some plate. Very little by London standards." She hoped this would dissuade her aunt from any thought of seeking a match for her.

"Lord Horatio is only a second son, of course, but of excellent pedigree. If he is interested in you," said her chaperon, rubbing her chin thoughtfully, "then I shall transfer to you a sum I have put aside."

"I could not accept it, Aunt Bentley!"

Her aunt raised her chin. "Don't be absurd. Of course you can accept it. What are childless relations for?"

Ariana eyed her uncertainly. Was she actually making a joke? "But—"

"The money belongs to me, and if it will help you marry into a noble family then I consider it better spent on your account than elsewhere.

In addition to which, if you marry Lord Horatio, you can help your sisters find equally advantageous matches. They may not have your style, I grant, but that is secondary. You will be Lady Horatio—"

"Aunt Bentley! Lord Horatio has hardly spoken to me. You are too hasty in your thoughts, I am persuaded."

"No, but he looked at you, my gel, quite noticeably. I own he was taken with you."

They arrived at the house and the conversation ended. With a heavy heart, Ariana went up to her room. As Harrietta helped her undress, she ruminated on her aunt's plans for her. It wasn't enough that Ariana was gowned and coifed in the first order of fashion. Now Aunt Bentley wished to endow her in the hope she would make a famous match, which meant marrying one of the rich society gentlemen of title or exceptional heritage, regardless of their faith—or their lack of it.

Lord Horatio was an agreeable man; perhaps he held with her beliefs? But he seemed to be in tight with Mr. Mornay, in which case she had to doubt the possibility of his taking religion seriously.

At home, Papa often questioned the girls about their readings in the prayer book or the Bible, and wonderful conversations and ideas ensued. They discussed the election of the saints, the parables of the Lord, the providence of God and His hand on the affairs of men—oh, so many things. Matters that few in her aunt's circles she knew of could, or would wish to, hold their own on. Mrs. Bentley (just as Papa had warned) was practically a heathen. She was a church-going, generous heathen, to be sure, but her generosity was not without obligation: Ariana was supposed to find a husband among this circle of London's wealthy elite.

Thinking of her parents, she suddenly recalled that she had not got a single answer to her letters, thus far. It was decidedly unusual for them not to respond. She would write and tell them of Aunt Bentley's latest idea regarding Lord Horatio and of enhancing her dowry. Papa would certainly have something to say about that!

Before getting into bed, Ariana fell to her knees and began to earnestly pray. *Heavenly Father, keep me for Your purpose; I pray that, despite my aunt's desires, only You would choose a husband for me. And let it be a man who cares for the things of God. Let me not keep the attention of anyone who is not pleasing in Your sight. Lead my steps and guard my path, Lord!*

After praying for everyone who came to mind, Ariana went to bed. Her aunt's words came back to trouble her, and she slept only with difficulty. *"Mr. Mornay means to discover your situation...You shall be Lady Horatio..."*

~~~

In the next few days a great quiet descended at Hanover Square. Morning calls ceased. Completely. Abruptly. Just like that. Worse yet, when Ariana and Mrs. Bentley took the carriage out to make calls of their own, not one lady received them. At each home, after taking Mrs. Bentley's card inside, a servant had returned to give the dubious information that his mistress was not at home. Mrs. Bentley was far too shrewd to think it could be coincidental, but she refused to believe they were being snubbed. *How could it be so?*

On the bright side, they had time to spend with Mr. Pellham. He had insisted upon being moved from his chamber to a comfortable spot in his drawing room, and received them there. Mrs. Bentley filled him in on the latest *on-dits* to which he would invariably reply, "So 'tis with high society, Mrs. B.," or, "Not a farthing of sense among all that brass!"

He had begun endeavouring to walk with the help of crutches. This was very encouraging to both Ariana's aunt and the gentleman himself. It was nonetheless a surprise to find Mr. Pellham in the parlour at Hanover Square late Friday afternoon. Two burly footmen were supporting him in lieu of the crutches, but his spirits seemed higher than they had for many a day. Mrs. Bentley was beside herself for a few moments, shouting shrilly to the servants. Indeed, her affection for the old gentleman was nowhere more evident than when she was giving orders on his behalf.

"Come, come, get some blankets and pillows down here directly!"

"Charlie and John, move this settee nearer the window, and get a card table here at once."

"Haines, tell cook we have a dinner guest, and bring him his drink—you know what he likes."

"Goodness, Molly, you know Mr. Pellham must have the *Times!* You've been employed here for days, already! Whatever is that silly broadsheet? Bring it here."

Molly's face was ashen. "They's givin' these out on the street, mum," she explained, after handing it over.

Molly was the newest chambermaid in Mrs. Bentley's household, and always averted her eyes when Ariana entered a room, or passed her in a hall. Somehow it was different from the way other servants displayed that they expected to be ignored. Ariana sensed fear in the girl, and supposed it was due to timidity, or perhaps from having served in a cruel household; so she tried to spare the girl's feelings by ignoring her in turn.

Mrs. Bentley glanced quickly at the broadsheet and then threw it upon the table. "I've no time for gossip, now," she scolded.

When Ariana felt it was safe enough to enter the room, Mr. Pellham greeted her warmly. "My dear, I warrant I shall be up and about before you know it. Our little outings will begin, I assure you."

"I am happy to see you looking so well," Ariana offered. "When you do recover, I will of course be honoured by your company on those outings, I promise you."

A knock on the front door below was heard, but Ariana paid no attention, knowing it was probably a cart monger or some such person. Haines was well-trained in handling them. But it was not a vendor of wares. The butler judiciously led the visitors to the second parlour and announced, when he came to the door of the best one, "Mr. Mornay and Lord Horatio, ma'am, in the second parlour. Shall I bring them here?"

Both ladies were dismayed by the illustrious guests. Mrs. Bentley smiled to herself, however, interpreting the call as confirmation of his lordship's interest in her niece. Ariana felt a strong sense of caution, but she was also curious. She would not give the slightest hint of encouragement to his lordship, lest indeed he was interested in furthering their acquaintance as her aunt suspected. She would merely be polite.

"Come, Ariana," her aunt said. "Randolph, we shall return presently, when the gentlemen have gone."

"Bring them here!" he admonished.

"But Randolph, you dislike my friends!"

"Have they come to see you or your niece?"

She put a hand over her heart. "I cannot say!"

"Bring them on." His tone had the sound of a man ready to face the enemy. "I wish to see how these gadflies are treating Ariana!"

Mrs. Bentley folded her arms across her chest. "Are you determined to be civil? I cannot subject Mr. Mornay to—"

"Oh, bring them forth, Mrs. B.! I daresay your Mr. Mor*nou* can handle an old codger like me!" He was enjoying himself. Ariana got up smilingly from the escritoire in the corner of the room, and went to sit by him on the sofa. Her aunt surveyed her.

"Your gown! Quickly! To your chamber and out of it! Out of it!"

Ariana was wearing an afternoon dress she had brought from home. It was not unbecoming, but too plain to satisfy her fastidious aunt, who had agreed to let her niece wear it only on account of there being no visitors to entertain, and to save her finer garments for needful occasions.

"To be seen in that, in front of Mornay! I won't have it." Mrs. Bentley was practically impelling Ariana across the floor in her rush. Ariana scooted past the second parlour, thankful the door was shut, and hurried to her chamber. Her aunt was fast on her heels, and she strode directly to the bellpull and yanked it energetically more than once. A few servants rushed in the room to be told, "Get Harrietta!" in the lady's well-known impatient tone.

Poor Harrietta came rushing in breathless, holding onto her cap. "Yes, ma'am! "

"Help!" Ariana's chaperon motioned toward a dress she had selected, while she removed the long muslin over her niece's head. "We must change Miss Forsythe speedily! We have important guests."

She had chosen an afternoon dress of deep aubergine, sprinkled liberally with tiny flowers of white and yellow. A light-coloured spencer with puffed, banded sleeves went with it, and there was a small cherusse at the neck which framed her face quite becomingly.

"Even Mornay will have to approve," Mrs. Bentley said, watching as Harrietta set upon her niece with vigour. "I will explain Mr. Pellham's unfortunate accident to our guests, and bring them to the first parlour. Make haste!" And Mrs. Bentley quickly exited to do just that.

Ariana thought she could have spared the words. "You have more determined energy than my old nurse!"

"I daresay your old nurse did not have Mrs. Bentley to answer to," was the quick reply. When the gown and spencer were on and adjusted and fastened, Harrietta scrutinized her young miss and exclaimed, "Now for the hair!"

"I put it up myself!"

"Indeed, miss, an' it shows! You must let me fuss it up a little."

Ariana sat down reluctantly. She felt that queer little flutter in her stomach, which Mr. Mornay's presence always brought about. She hardly liked the man, but his presence was a bit exciting given his wide renown, not to mention her earlier encounters with him. That must be the reason, she thought, while Harrietta finished styling her hair, gingerly placing two tortoiseshell combs in advantageous positions, that her heart was beating so fast.

⟆⟨०⟩⟅

When she entered the parlour, the gentlemen (except for Mr. Pellham) stood politely and bowed. Ariana meant only to give a cool nod in way of greeting, but when she saw Lord Horatio's eyes alight at her entrance, her natural good humour took over and she permitted herself to smile. Her countenance faltered when she met the dark eyes of Mr.

Mornay, but she sat down calmly and let her aunt pour her a cup of tea from the tray upon the table.

"Glad you could join us, my gel," said her aunt, as if Ariana's presence was a surprise. Lord Horatio added, "Yes! Very glad." Ariana gave a little smile and tried not to look again at the other gentleman, but ended up shooting a quick glance in his direction. He had said nothing, and his countenance was unreadable as usual, though his eyes were fastened upon her.

He was dressed comfortably in another fine outfit. She had barely noticed gentlemen's clothing in the past, but when in his presence, why was it she had to take note? There was nothing loud or colourful in his dress, and yet he managed to somehow exude a presence that was downright daunting. Even Lord Horatio, whose clothing was undoubtedly costly, looked slightly askew beside his dignified friend.

Mrs. Bentley turned to her niece. "My gel, we have been discussing a matter that seems to have us all perplexed, and perhaps you may be able to shed light on the subject."

"I?" Ariana asked, surprised.

"Miss Forsythe, without alarming you unnecessarily," said his lordship, "we came to inform you and your aunt that Lady Covington (one of the patronesses of Almack's, you know) has made it her mission to not only bar you from that Assembly, but to spread doubts throughout the *ton* about your character. Your aunt says there has been a decline in visitors, which makes it plain that Lady Covington's scheme is working."

"*She* is behind that?" Ariana gasped.

"Preposterous!" Everyone looked in surprise at Mr. Pellham. He had spoken out of loyalty, forgetting for the moment his wish to remain aloof from the company. Mrs. Bentley had warned her guests that he was a dear old friend, but a noted eccentric, and not to expect any conversation from him. Mr. Pellham seemed quite as surprised by his sudden contribution as the rest of the occupants of the room, and he cleared his throat uncomfortably.

"Indeed," said his lordship, after a moment of uncertainty as to whether to respond or not. "To be plain about it, Miss Forsythe, the countess has used Mr. Mornay's name to cast a dreadful slur upon yours."

"Upon my word!" Mrs. Bentley's hand flew to her heart.

Ariana was looking in perplexity at the men. "What sort of a slur, my lord?"

Mr. Mornay chose that moment to enter the conversation.

"She claims that you have...favoured me with certain of your charms, which, let us say, would cause the sturdiest reputation to topple. In addition, she maintains that you cherish the illusion the impropriety will force an *event*." He eyed her keenly.

Mr. Pellham cleared his throat loudly, barely managing to contain his displeasure. He searched for his cane and would have banged it upon the floor, only it was at home, since he had used footmen for his support, not the walking stick. Ariana nodded at the sympathy and outrage she saw in his eyes, correctly interpreting his expression. Mr. Mornay refused to even look in his direction though Lord Horatio gave him an uncomfortable glance before returning his gaze to Ariana, who had gone pale.

"An *event!*" She knew what an "event" referred to: marriage. "Between us?"

When he nodded, her paleness gave way to a ridiculous embarrassment that sent a crimson streak across her cheeks. Then, as it all sank in on her, it became hurtful. That anyone should foster such lies about her! In moments, she was blinking back tears, feeling a terrible sense of injustice. Nothing she had done deserved so nasty an attack by a fellow human being. Ariana looked in agitation to her aunt, her own hand rushing to her breast as if to calm herself. Her aunt was regarding her with an equally agonized expression.

"My gel; I am beyond words! I cannot account for this animosity!"

Ariana forced herself to think clearly; she must remain calm. A glance at Mr. Mornay sent a fresh wave of humiliation over her, and her cheeks burned brighter than ever.

"So this is what everyone now believes of me?" She kept her eyes averted, too mortified to do else. Lord Horatio frowned and shifted in his seat. Ariana hated to think of what Mr. Mornay must have thought when he first heard the falsehood. Oh, it was too unbearable!

"Not everyone," he said just then, to her utter relief. "But the mere scent of a scandal around a young woman's name in society is rather like having the plague; they won't come near you until they know of a certainty that you are safe."

Mrs. Bentley was now holding a handkerchief to her mouth as if she might moan audibly. Everything had been going so perfectly... until this!

Mr. Mornay was studying Ariana's reaction. Suddenly he said, "As to the charges, which are nearly as much against me as you, I was convinced they were not your claims, Miss Forsythe, or I would not have come to your drawing room, believe me. Since the countess has abused my name in her scheme, however, I find it is beyond my powers of self-restraint to stay aloof from the situation. For this reason, you will have me as your ally in the matter."

"Humph!" murmured Mr. Pellham, in what was actually a sound of approval. He had forgotten, once again, that he would be heard by everyone else and looked around apologetically.

"You are a godsend, Mr. Mornay!" Mrs. Bentley felt remarkably revived. Having the Paragon on their side changed everything.

Ariana's defeated expression lifted enough so that her eyes glittered gratefully across the room at him. As could happen at times, they were suddenly sparkling gold, like jewels in her face, he thought; lively, intelligent jewels that were focused on him in evident gratitude.

"I am much obliged to you," she said simply.

He nodded.

"Is there any reason you know of, Miss Forsythe, why the countess would single you out like this?" Lord Horatio looked intently at her.

"*Think,* Ariana! I have never been in love with Lady Covington, but I maintain we have never quarreled, either. I am severely provoked by this, most severely!" Mrs. Bentley gave her niece an exasperated stare. "It is exceedingly good of these gentlemen to come to our aid. We must give them some explanation, and you alone, I daresay, must know it. No one else does."

There was silence while Ariana decided how to reply. She folded her hands upon her lap and said, "I think I am able to supply a reason." She looked about apologetically. "It is really quite simple; astonishingly so!" All eyes in the room were fastened upon her and not a sound was heard. She looked up, facing the circle of inquisitors and confessed. "At Mr. Mornay's estate I walked into the countess, awkwardly, but not intentionally. I apologized immediately but she was not mollified in the least, I am afraid."

Lord Horatio had been leaning forward in his seat but at her words he sat back with a plop. "Is that all? That's preposterous!"

Ariana's eyes stayed far from the face of Mr. Mornay, for she had also collided into him on the very same day and had no doubt but that he was thinking of it.

"How on earth, Ariana! However could you do such a thing? What were you about?"

Ariana shut her eyes for a moment, knowing exactly what she had been about, and she flushed pink afresh at the memory. She had been staring, transfixed, at the peculiarly arresting gaze of the man across the room, as they both very well knew. She said nothing, therefore, but her gaze came up to peek at his face, and something in those inscrutable dark eyes made her think that he absolutely remembered: he had witnessed the whole thing.

"Ariana? Well?"

She answered falteringly. "I was—I think—that is, I failed to see her coming. I believe it was entirely my fault."

"Obviously." Mrs. Bentley's eyebrows had risen exceedingly, and her tone was dry. "But what were you occupied with?" How annoying of her aunt to ask her again! Ariana glanced once more at the man watching her and thought that his silent expression now held a lively interest in the proceedings which did little to help her state of mind. Odious man! What could she say?

"Does it signify, Aunt? The thing is I offended Lady Covington and I did not cower at her feet afterward as she would have liked."

"Ariana!" Mrs. Bentley glanced nervously at the gentlemen. But his lordship let out a delighted laugh and even Mr. Mornay's stern features cracked into a smile. Mr. Pellham could not allow the moment to pass him by in silence, so he again cleared his throat loudly in support of Ariana.

"Ma,am, I do think Miss Forsythe has the right of it, indeed." Lord Horatio came to her defense. On his account only, Mrs. Bentley refrained from firing a riposte at her ungenteel niece.

"There is only one thing to do, and that is to gain an audience with her ladyship so Ariana may apologize prettily; publicly, so that her ladyship's sensibilities will be satisfied." Mrs. Bentley looked to the two men for approval of her scheme, but they looked doubtful.

"I daresay going public would be a great risk," ventured Lord Horatio. "Lady Covington could hardly pass up the opportunity to finish what she has begun, which is to ruin a young lady's reputation."

"Is she so cruel?" Ariana's eyes were large in her face.

His lordship's head bobbed vigorously. "The countess is a lady she-devil, if you will pardon the expression."

"But she must respect me!" interjected Mrs. Bentley. "The other patronesses have promised us vouchers. Will she not show some kindness to my niece for my sake?"

Mr. Mornay gave the answer. "She delights in...shall we say, vendettas. And it would indeed give her great pleasure if you go crawling to her for help, particularly in public." A moment's tense silence passed, and he added, "But I hasten to add it would have no effect upon the rumour regarding Miss Forsythe and myself. Were the countess to forgive you wholeheartedly, it would make little difference, for the seed of doubt she planted has been growing in the minds of people."

"Perhaps if we see her privately?" Mrs. Bentley's tone revealed she had little confidence in the suggestion.

"I would not recommend it." He spoke lightly but with such utter weight to his words that Ariana's aunt knew she was defeated and threw up her hands.

"Then what shall we do, Mr. Mornay? I beg you to find some answer for us!"

Another silence descended, and all eyes turned to the Paragon. His reputation forbade him to do anything for anybody except himself, but he had helped Ariana down from the tree and protected her from humiliation. She still suspected that he had indeed allowed Lady Sherwood to win at cards in order to do them some good. She watched him now, certain that if anyone could refute the falsehoods, it would have to be he.

Mr. Mornay met Ariana's gaze, and then looked to her aunt. "It would not do for me to simply deny Lady Covington's accusations. Society would humour me, perhaps, but not believe me, and Miss Forsythe would remain in social disgrace. Likewise, if Miss Forsythe simply denies them, no one will believe her."

A sense of frustration settled over Ariana. It seemed there was nothing she could do to help her situation. He cleared his throat.

"I am forming the opinion as we speak that only a drastic action will answer." The company waited breathlessly to hear what the "drastic action" would be. Mr. Mornay did not keep them waiting long.

"Lady Covington is depending upon me to behave in my usual cavalier manner, and to keep my distance from your niece. Indeed, under normal circumstances that is precisely how things should have turned out, for it is simply my style. Naturally that would not be taken as a reflection of her character, but only of mine. In light of the countess's accusations, my attitude toward your niece will decide all. It goes without saying I would publicly avoid her at all costs if the charges were true. Therefore, my usual manner of conduct would be taken, regarding Miss Forsythe, as a confirmation of the allegations."

Every word the Paragon spoke increased Ariana's feeling of helplessness. The thought came to her, however, to ask for Divine help. She could pray, at least. Silently she began to pray from her heart: *Father*

God, even Mr. Mornay cannot decide my fate—only You can! Send me the help I need. Clear my name!

She had not prayed eloquently or gratefully, but out of desperation. And yet, the next moment she heard Mr. Mornay saying words she knew came in response to that prayer.

"The only answer which will serve is to convince society that I have determined to court Miss Forsythe. If they believe she has been foolish enough to set her cap at me then they must be made to believe I return the sentiment. If I am seen to behave in a proper manner toward her, no one shall entertain the notion of an impropriety. No man of my position would court a woman he has already abused."

While the others digested this startling conclusion, Mr. Mornay, contemplating the matter added, "They must be convinced that I am, shall we say, smitten?"

Fourteen

To the astonished faces around him, Mr. Mornay smiled neatly and then crossed his legs comfortably.

"Bravo, Mornay! That will turn the tables on Lady Covington, I daresay! She will be happy to forget Miss Forsythe's existence—if she can!" His lordship looked around for agreement. Mrs. Bentley dabbed at one eye, which did not seem to be wet after all.

"Ingenious, Mr. Mornay!" She waved her little white handkerchief in the air. "Ingenious! And so generous and good of you. I am quite overcome with gratitude."

"And you, Miss Forsythe?" Ariana had been quiet since his announcement, and Mr. Mornay looked at her now. "My intention is to outmanoeuvre the countess, which will serve to rescue your reputation. I cannot abide to see her succeed in her vicious scheme. But I care very little about what is said regarding me; you must be eager to do this, or I am content to let the matter lie where it will."

Ariana looked across the little circle of furniture at him.

"It appears I am at your mercy, Mr. Mornay. I should be greatly obliged to you for your invaluable help in the matter. Instruct me on what I must do, and I will, I promise you, do whatever you say."

"Very good, my gel!" Mrs. Bentley was relieved that her niece had spoken with meekness and humility, as befitted her station.

In her heart, Ariana almost wished to be ousted from the exacting but hypocritical society she found herself in. But not due to shame; not

to lies. No, she would have to stay and fight. She thanked God that
the volatile Mr. Mornay had come to her aid—again. There was an
awkward silence in the room for a few moments while the two beheld
each other, and then the men rose to their feet. Ariana and her aunt
rose also, but the chaperon had an alarming thought.

"Mr. Mornay!" Her hand was over her heart. "What will we say
when there is no event?" This was a circumstance that no one had
thought of. His eyebrow rose in the way it tended to, and a faint smile
appeared on the handsome face.

"I suppose we will have to account for that," the Paragon
conceded.

"That should pose no dilemma, ma'am," piped in his lordship.
"When Miss Forsythe accepts another proposal, it will simply be given
out that she and Mornay decided they did not suit."

He smiled, looking around for approbation, but Mrs. Bentley asked,
dryly, "Another proposal? Whom do you suppose will dare to approach
her if Mr. Mornay is believed to have taken a serious interest in her?"

Lord Horatio said, "I could, I suppose, myself…that is…"

Ariana's cheeks grew instantly warm. Mr. Mornay was not similarly
affected and stated in a firm tone, "When the scandal has been sufficiently quenched, Miss Forsythe will be free to take a disgust of me."
The others smiled, and he turned to Ariana. "Which should present
little difficulty for one who is already *fully convinced of my overwhelming depravity.*"

Ariana looked away hurriedly. Although she had thought him terrible, he was fast acting in a fashion to change that impression.

"Ariana! I should hope Mr. Mornay is mistaken," Aunt Bentley
scolded. "Certainly you cannot hold him in such a thought as that."

"No, ma'am, I am sure I do not." She answered quietly, forcing
herself to meet his eyes. His expression was faintly bemused, but not
injured. He offered a short bow. He often had that near-smile on his
face, she was beginning to realize. Perhaps he was not as irascible as he
pretended. Perhaps most people were too frightened of him to notice
that he barked, but did not bite.

"When may we begin?" Mrs. Bentley was eager to see the tide of societal approval turn in their favour.

"The sooner the better." Lord Horatio was ever helpful.

"Perhaps Miss Forsythe and I could take a drive right now," Mornay offered. "'Tis past five-thirty and the park will be teeming. Our triumph over the evil countess," he grinned, "can begin."

"Yes, of course!" Ariana felt suddenly breathless. It had not dawned upon her until that moment that she would of necessity be spending time with Mr. Mornay. Perhaps alone. The fluttering in her stomach had subsided, but now returned in full force.

"I'll take you home, Horatio," Mornay said, "and then take a leisurely pass through Hyde Park with Miss Forsythe."

Mrs. Bentley's face lit up. "I have it! Let my carriage convey his lordship so that the two of you may be seen together at once."

And so it happened.

Since Mr. Mornay had not brought a servant, one of Mrs. Bentley's footmen jumped on the back of his open curricle, to act as chaperon. Despite it being an open equipage, a chaperon was deemed necessary in light of the rumour regarding the pair.

Wishing to avoid the traffic on Oxford Street, Mr. Mornay took the carriage west, passing Hanover Square and Brook Street, part way around Grosvenor Square (the other side of which housed his own residence) and onto upper Brook Street, and then a turn onto Park Lane. They followed the lane for a few impressive streets, while Ariana enjoyed viewing the succession of mansions. She glanced at her companion who was intent on manoeuvring the curricle, and thought what a shame that Phillip Mornay could be so good-looking and intelligent and gentlemanly—at times—and yet averse to marriage. (Not that *she* wanted to marry him! No, indeed!)

After all, was he not nearing thirty, and yet had never been associated with a single engagement? As she watched the way he smoothly handled the team, a pair of elegant matched chestnuts, she mused that someone so nice in appearance ought to possess less aloofness of character.

They made a sharp left turn onto Tyburn Turnpike and then a

right, passing easily through the wide Cumberland Gate entrance to Hyde Park, Ariana rippling with excitement at her first visit to the famous spot.

"Here we are," Mornay said. "Just in time to find the place teeming."

Teeming, indeed. The number of equipages on the open lanes of the park surprised her. Here was a popular pastime the likes of which she'd had no idea of. People were literally everywhere. On horse, on foot, and in carriages, of all styles and sizes. Mr. Mornay stopped their vehicle by Hyde Park Lodge, from where he made innumerable careful introductions, always allowing that Miss Forsythe was honouring him with her company. Ariana met many a peer and like luminaries, most of whom shortly halted upon spying the pair, to come and give their greetings. To those too afraid to approach the Paragon, he occasionally nodded or motioned them forward, and they came, like subjects to a king. Ariana felt she could imagine being a queen.

Raised brows and astonished faces were swiftly followed by impressed looks—and invitations. Ariana could not help but to enjoy the bewildered respect she received. Without exception, she was treated like royalty.

"Why, Mr. Mornay! Miss Forsythe! What a pleasure! And such a *surprise!*" Mamas with their daughters did not know if they were more surprised to see Mr. Mornay accost them in a friendly manner, or that Mr. Mornay with Miss Forsythe had done so. Was this not the outcast Miss Forsythe? The same Miss Forsythe Lady Covington severely disapproved of? *What was a mother to think?*

All the women promised sincerely to call at Hanover Square at the soonest convenience. Ariana was much heartened to see relief on many faces; a fact that meant she was genuinely liked. People had been frightened away by Lady Covington's lies, but they were happy to find her in society with the Paragon; this meant they could safely enjoy her company again. In addition, instead of appearing as a grasping female hoping to win a prize, she was now seen as the object of affection by the singular renowned bachelor.

He seemed well satisfied when they exited the park a good hour later. He drove Ariana back to her aunt's home. As he pulled to a stop, he turned his dark eyes thoughtfully upon her. He paused, thinking before saying, "I shall call for you on Saturday evening, say, at half-past nine?"

"Tomorrow evening? Yes, if—if you wish."

He gave her a bemused look. He had expected a warmer reception to his invitation.

"I do wish." He wore that half-smile; was he poking fun at her? Since she wasn't sure whether he was, or whether she ought to laugh or not, she decided to just smile demurely and then turned to leave.

"Wait," he ordered, jumping down on his side and going around to help her down. With his hands about her waist he set her lightly upon her feet. They surveyed one another. Mr. Mornay still wore that bemused expression, as if he found her amusing. Rather like an appealing little puppy, she thought, later. Appealing, but infinitely inferior.... But she smiled politely.

"I am much obliged for the drive and... for all of your help."

He nodded. "Until tomorrow evening, then. And wear one of your finer evening dresses."

"One of my finer?"

"Yes." He paused, studying her. "Do you have a satin and gauze?" He was referring to a sophisticated style in which the underdress of satin was worn beneath a coverlet or overdress of net or gauze. The satin underneath showed through and, depending on how the bodice was cut, the gown could either be a sweet or tempting confection.

"I believe I do."

"Let us hope so."

Her large eyes sparkled with curiosity regarding what he had in mind for the evening, but she felt suddenly too timid to ask.

"Anything more?" She gave him a smile, and was pleased when he surprised her with one of his own, making her acutely aware that she had never seen him smile fully before.

"That should do it. I have seen enough of you to know that you either have a knack for fashion or your mama does."

"It is my aunt who has the knack."

"Of course." He nodded, knowingly. With that, Ariana curtseyed and then walked self-consciously toward the steps of the house. She felt the strange, beautiful eyes of Mr. Mornay on her and did not take a good, deep breath until Haines had closed the front door and was helping her off with her spencer.

❧

Mrs. Bentley shook her head in amazement. "Mr. Mornay has rescued you! Mornay himself! He has gone against the countess on your behalf! I promise you, there shall be one unhappy lady the night you walk into Almack's."

Ariana sat in a comfortable wing chair across from the older woman and poured herself a cup of tea from the service that Haines had put out while they were speaking.

"Why do you suppose he has helped me?" She settled herself more comfortably in her chair.

"I must think 'tis for his lordship's sake. Certainly you are not the first female said to have tipped her cap at him, nor would you have been the first to suffer a ruined season on his account, although you may well be the youngest. Generally, it is the more experienced femme fatales of society—like Lady Covington herself—who attempt to win over the Paragon. Of course many others swoon for him but they have the sense not to display it." She picked up her delicate china cup and took a sip. "That is the only explanation I can think of. He has indeed performed a service for us, no matter what moved him to it, and we are obliged to him."

"He told me to expect him on Saturday evening." Ariana knew this would be received rapturously and was not surprised when Mrs. Bentley's mouth dropped and her hand went to her heart.

"He means to do more for you, then! Where is he taking you?"

"He didn't say. But he told me to be sure and wear one of my finer evening gowns. He asked if I had one of satin and gauze. I do, don't I?"

"Yes, of course." She sat back on the sofa, stunned. "A finer gown! Satin and gauze. We have no invitations for tomorrow evening, and I have not heard of any entertainments. What could he be thinking?"

"Could it be he intends to take me to Almack's?"

Her aunt looked at her silently for a moment, preoccupied with her own ideas. "No. 'Tisn't open. Only on Wednesday nights, my gel. And, at any rate, I cannot believe he would be caught alive at Almack's! The men of his set find it a dead bore. They only go on occasion to show they *can*."

A minute passed. "It must be something popular on account of her ladyship." Her aunt laughed. "To think that of all the men in society, she chose to involve you with Mr. Mornay! It is a great stroke of luck for you, my gel."

Ariana did not wish to point out that it could not be called "luck" to be embroiled in a scandal; or that she did not credit "luck" with the events of her life. Despite the humiliation of the situation, she accepted that somehow it was part of God's plan for her.

"When this is over," continued the older lady, "you will be the toast of the town, for even without an event you are the first lady in London who can claim to have had Mornay's affections! Lucky for us he wishes to punish the countess."

Ariana's heart sank at these words. "But I do not wish to be in the middle of their quarrel. I think I must refuse to go any further with this."

Mrs. Bentley's response was immediate and grave. " 'Tis your quarrel, also, Ariana. Lady Covington has sunk her claws into you, for no good reason. Happy or not, you must help the matter. In the end, every single family in the Society Book will want to know you!" Ariana's face was downcast, but she nodded. Mrs. Bentley laughed, saying, "This entire outcome must be the veriest thing sent from heaven!"

Ariana looked up at that, struck by the thought. She excused herself and went directly to her chamber eager to read the afternoon's collect, and especially, to pray. Sent from heaven? Indeed it had to be, all of her circumstances, though she did not see how any of it could work in her favour in a spiritual sense. In a worldly sense, yes, she was gaining social favour and success by her relationship with Mr. Mornay. But she knew that true success would be finding others of her faith, or helping in some small way to further God's kingdom.

Ariana fell to her knees, resolved to be thankful for every good thing in her life—including even worldly social success. Only God knew how He might use this for good.

She prayed over the matter, asking for blessings on what was to come, and for Mr. Mornay for his goodness in helping her. She prayed for strength to forgive the countess, and for that lady to come to repentance and salvation. She asked, if possible, to be used by God to help others seek His face. When she prayed for her family, she remembered that it was time to write again, even though she had still not had a reply. After committing that puzzling matter to the Lord as well, she spent an hour writing a long missive detailing the startling turn of events the day had brought. She began by describing her new impressions of Mr. Mornay, who was, she wrote, "not nearly as mean-hearted as I earlier took him for."

Fifteen

*A*riana was considering doing without breakfast except for a cup of strong tea. She'd been aware from the moment she arose that she would be seeing Mr. Mornay later, for the familiar knot in her stomach was present. She no longer felt frightened of him, but it was useless to pretend she was wholly indifferent.

Mrs. Bentley, who always took toast with butter and drank her only cup of chocolate for the day in the morning, was chipper and talkative about the coming night.

"'Tis no doubt a private dinner party at an exclusive address."

"Oh, dear; I fear the amount of conversation necessary in such a situation."

Her aunt waved her hand. "Never mind that; they shall be concerned with pleasing you! A lady friend of Mr. Mornay's." She tittered gleefully. "And to think—it is all a hoax! I could give Lady Covington a kiss of gratitude! If she only knew the good she has done us, I warrant she would turn green."

A hoax? Ariana put down her teacup. She had not thought of it as such, and now took a fresh dislike of the situation. But what else could be done? Certainly she had the right to prove the countess's accusations false, since they were false.

"Well, we shall see later what is up. Be assured I will not allow you to leave this house with a gentleman, even Mornay, without knowing precisely what his plans are. I will ask him when he arrives." She studied Ariana as if for the first time, her mind obviously working at some idea, and Ariana waited to hear it. She was coming to recognize this look on her aunt's face. It meant there was something significant on her mind, and it was only a matter of minutes or seconds before she would voice the thought.

"Could it be he truly has a *tendre* for you, my gel?"

"Dear me, no!" Ariana said vehemently. "I am astounded he is helping me, for he has given me numerous set-downs, I assure you! Nothing could be clearer, Aunt, but that he is not overly fond of me."

Mrs. Bentley was not really surprised at this response, for after all, *who could win Mornay?*

"Well, it is certain he does not overly dislike you, either. If he had a disgust of you I am prodigiously sure it would have prevented him from coming to your aid. Mornay is not the man to hide his dislikes, and when it comes to young females I avow he has had more than his share. Now I think on it, when you are with him tonight, be careful not to do anything to make him feel you are developing an attraction. Nothing is more certain to bring about his disapproval!"

Ariana stared at her relation, trying to digest the strange advice. She was not artful enough to hide her true feelings, even when she tried, but fortunately there was nothing to hide in this case. Mr. Mornay was handsome, but not at all the type of man she could ever consider as a marriage prospect. He was, in fact, the furthest thing from her idea of a future mate.

Mrs. Bentley took a sip of her chocolate and let it linger on her tongue before swallowing with a satisfactory little gulp.

"Look, my gel, the newest issue of *La Belle Assemblee!* It arrived just today."

Ariana could not share her aunt's pleasure, as she was fretting. "What if I do something foolish before his friends? I am much younger than he... He'll despise me!"

Her aunt raised calm eyes to Ariana's troubled ones. "I have seen you interacting with enough people to know you are no fool, Ariana; you are more sensible than I could have hoped. I daresay you will know how to behave." She took a bite of her toast. "He despises most people, in any case, so it will be no great thing if you are added to the number, though I do not think it likely. He behaved gallantly to you, yesterday. But do not set your heart on pleasing him, for such is not possible. And he is, after all, far out of your league…though I hate to admit it. Enjoy his attentions while they last, and the social success they will bring. That is my advice to you, my dear."

My dear. The words rang pleasantly in Ariana's ears for she did not recall her aunt ever referring to her in any way but as, "my gel."

"Thank you, Aunt. I shall keep in mind what you have said."

❦

After breakfast Mrs. Bentley announced they would visit Mr. Pellham, and Ariana was glad for the diversion. She would be glad of anything that took her thoughts off the coming evening.

Mr. Pellham's residence was on Lower Brook Street, just past the Square. They found him nestled cosily upon a sofa in the drawing room with his leg well positioned off the floor. A small table was pulled up, and a chair, so that he and Mrs. Bentley could play their favorite game of cards, two-player whist. Ariana sat comfortably across from them upon a plush wing chair and read *The Italian* for the second time. Mid-afternoon they had tea with scones and fresh berries. Berries were hard to procure unless one's servant was quick, for they sold out prodigiously fast on the street. Ariana found herself able to eat, and enjoyed it more than she had expected.

By the time Mrs. Bentley announced their departure Ariana felt quite relaxed. The dear patient was assured of another visit shortly though he remonstrated that "an old invalid" was not worth the trouble.

"Nonsense!" Mrs. Bentley declared and Ariana echoed the thought, then added, "And what would you like to read, next?" For sometimes she read aloud to him to ease his boredom.

"You choose the book, my dear," he replied with a characteristic wink. Meanwhile, Ariana's aunt gave orders to his servants, double-checked that the doctor had stopped in, and made sure a good supper was ordered before they left.

Once back at Hanover Square, the knot in Ariana's stomach slowly returned. To distract herself, she worked on her sewing canvas, brought from home, but could not enjoy it. She wrote another letter, staring absently at Molly who was cleaning the grate, while she thought of what to include. The day at Hyde Park with the Paragon was news her family would enjoy, but the thought of Mr. Mornay only sent her into fresh tremors. Instead, she wrote a light and humorous letter to her younger sisters, who would feel important receiving their own missive. When she'd sealed it, Molly, who had never approached her once before, suddenly came alive.

She came and curtseyed, and swallowing nervously, asked, "Kin I take it to Mr. Haines for ye, mum?" It was no trouble for Ariana to leave it on the hall tray downstairs herself, but she smiled in pleasure that the little chambermaid had found some courage.

"Certainly. Thank you," she said kindly, handing over her correspondence. Molly flew from the room.

Afterward, she picked up the new fashion catalogue, but nothing, it seemed, could dispel the uneasy feeling in her being.

She finally thought to pray, scolding herself for not having done so in the first place. Why was it often true that the more reason she had to pray, the less she seemed inclined to do it? She began by confessing this weakness, then thanking the Lord for all the good things He had brought into her life. Unexpectedly, it became a special time of communing with God. As could happen at times, she felt a very reassuring presence of the Holy Spirit; she was not alone.

She prayed at length about her unusual relationship with Mr. Mornay. It was tempting, truly tempting, to think something had gone awry; that if she had been more in prayer, perhaps, none of the trouble with Lady Covington would have started to begin with. It was hard to trust that the Lord would have engineered her spending time with such a man as Mr. Mornay.

She remembered, however, that even a sparrow did not fall to the ground apart from God's will, and that the hairs on her head were numbered. In light of this, how could she fail to believe He was indeed directing her path? Had she not long been praying He would guide her during her stay in London? That he would spare her from evil? Surely she had to trust that whatever came her way came from His hand, no matter how it looked.

As she prayed, she grew aware that the thought of the time spent with Mr. Mornay in his open curricle was decidedly pleasant. She was enjoying his attention. No matter the reason he was giving it had almost nothing to do with her, personally. She was nothing more than a means of refuting Lady Covington's lies; of beating her at her own game. And suddenly she felt that somehow she was going to willingly be the means. All at once, her heart was more in it. They were not intent on hurting Lady Covington. On the contrary, their actions in representing themselves as a pair were only defensive ones. The countess had thrown the fiery brand. They were merely snuffing it out.

It was daunting to realize that despite his temper, his coolness, or his disdain, it was nevertheless agreeable to be with the Paragon. On the occasions when she had met his temper with her own, he had actually enjoyed it. And there was no escaping his pleasing elegance and comportment, his confident manners. When he chose to, he could be a vastly pleasant companion. Those piercing dark eyes and his bemused expressions—she was growing to like all of it. Goodness, what was she thinking? Not only a confirmed bachelor, but a good deal older than she and "out of her league." She prayed for strength to resist the earthly charms of Mr. Mornay, committing herself and the coming evening into God's hands.

Just as she finished praying, her aunt came to her chamber with Harrietta. It was time to prepare for the evening at hand. She found it outlandish when Mrs. Bentley insisted she soak in a hot tub only to follow it with a quick plunge into tepid water that set her teeth shivering. Her aunt called this "polishing the skin." Harrietta then took over, trimming her nails both on her feet and hands, and supplying her with an enormous array of vials and lotions, perfumes and powders, and other mysterious liquids. Some were for her face and neck, others for her hands, elbows, and even her feet.

Afterward Ariana was allowed a small meal.

"Now we shall earnestly prepare for the evening," her aunt informed her. Ariana had to wonder what they had been doing all along, if not earnestly preparing for the evening. Before she had finished the small rations on her plate, she was stopped.

"You don't want to eat overmuch, Ariana, as I intend to have you corseted beneath that gown."

Aunt Bentley and Harrietta fussed over her hair, chemise, stays, stockings, and finally the gown. Over a silk-satin underdress of light pink, she wore a net coverlet which was embroidered in a leaf motif with gray and silver thread. A band of the silk-satin ran across the empire waist and more bands were intertwined in the short, puffed sleeves. By the time the two women had finished, Ariana felt more than ready to face the Paragon. Her hair was coifed elegantly atop her head, except for two coils of curls on the sides of her face, which was fashionable. Ariana wished she had jet black hair, but Mama always said her lighter tresses matched the light in her eyes, and indeed, this night her words rang true. She was a picture of sparkling, beauteous youth.

Still, Mrs. Bentley insisted upon embellishing her appearance with the loan of a matching set of jewels consisting of a necklace, earrings, brooch, and bracelet. And, as a last dignifying element, a tiara: the delicate headpiece was placed gingerly over her head and fastened into place with pins. When at last she stood quietly resplendent in her gown, long white gloves, and pink silk-satin slippers, even Mrs. Bentley had to smile.

"You do me credit, my gel," she said, almost affectionately. "Even Mornay will be smitten, I daresay, eh, Harrietta?"

"Oh, yes, ma'am!" breathed the servant. She was fully as pleased as her mistress. "So tall and strikin' as miss is, just like a princess!"

"I thought at first you might be too tall," her aunt admitted, "but it turns out that 'tall' can be statuesque."

Ariana had been waiting for fifteen minutes in the parlour when Mr. Mornay appeared, precisely on time at half-past nine. She nodded a greeting from her seat in return of a very fine bow. He was dressed in exquisite evening wear. He wore a dark, tailored frock coat and black cloth pantaloons. An immaculate white starched shirt could be seen beneath a gold-embroidered satin waistcoat. His cravat was starched and tied neatly beneath his firm chin. There was a single fob hanging from his belt, a handkerchief just visible in the waistcoat pocket, and buff gloves on his hands. Instead of an ostentatious bicorne, which was popular, he wore a top hat and polished black shoes. As usual, he wore the perfectly tailored attire looking as natural as though he were at home before the fire, in a favorite robe.

He stopped past the doorway and surveyed Ariana, who, despite herself, came to her feet. She had too much nervous energy to refrain. Mrs. Bentley, feeling proud of her niece's appearance, said nothing— and waited. Breathlessly.

Ariana tried not to squirm beneath his gaze. When he started toward her he said to her aunt, "My compliments, ma'am; she looks just right. Not too sophisticated for her age, and yet not too missish for Carlton House."

Mrs. Bentley had been about to take a breath of relief when she gasped instead, putting her hand on her heart as was her manner.

"Carlton House! Is that where you're taking her?"

He looked amused. "Didn't you know?"

"Indeed, we did not!" When his gaze met Ariana's she just shook her head, signifying she had not known, and he smiled gently. "I suppose I forgot to mention that, eh?"

She smiled in return. "I'm afraid you did."

When he reached her his hand went up toward her neck, and she took a little step backward. He had reached for her necklace and now he was looking at it, turning it over in his hands. Eventually he let it down gently but then studied the brooch that was pinned to her bodice.

"Pretty," he murmured, "but not necessary." He proceeded to remove it while Ariana shot a look of uncertainty at her aunt, who stood by helplessly. Mrs. Bentley started mumbling in the background about the quality of the jewels but he ignored her, and taking Ariana's two hands he held them up, examining the bracelet about her right, gloved wrist. He put her arms back down and took a step back, surveying her from head to toe. Then he took the bangled hand and gently pulled off the gleaming bit of jewelery. He surveyed her again.

"There. Now she's perfect."

Ariana felt momentarily affronted by his audacity at taking off the jewels, but then gave in to amusement. Who better than the Paragon to say what she looked best in? And he had pronounced her appearance to be perfect! Who could argue with that? She gave him an amused look while he returned the jewelery to her aunt. When he turned again and saw her expression, he smiled.

"Are you quite certain you now approve of me?" Her tone was teasing.

"As a matter of fact, Miss Forsythe, I am." Turning to her aunt he added, "Remarkable, is it not?"

"Indeed, it 'tis!" She was not certain if he had meant that Ariana was remarkable or that his approval of her was remarkable. Either way, she was satisfied, more, floating on air. And yet there was still a matter to be discussed...

"Mr. Mornay," Mrs. Bentley began.

He looked expectantly in her direction.

"My niece has not been presented to the prince; does this not pose a difficulty?"

"I am certain, ma'am, that the prince will demand the introduction as soon as he is given to understand I have brought her," Mornay replied. He was as polite as anyone had ever heard him but Mrs. Bentley's face settled into a frown.

"But is that not precarious? I fear the Regent may as likely demand she be removed from the royal presence!"

"Never!" He looked amused. "If it helps to settle your mind, Lord Horatio is already informing the prince of my intentions. He shall be eager to meet her."

Mrs. Bentley's face softened. She was decidedly not the most affectionate of relations, but she was, after all, Ariana's chaperon and responsible for the girl. She cleared her throat. "Is it not irregular for a gel so young to attend one of the Regent's parties?"

Haines appeared in the doorway with Ariana's pelisse held carefully in his arms. Mr. Mornay had walked round about Ariana, still examining her appearance minutely, but he looked over at Ariana's aunt.

"If I thought so, Mrs. Bentley, I would not be taking her." He took the garment from Haines and helped Ariana into it. It was a luxurious pelisse, an expenditure that was shockingly high even for Mrs. Bentley, but it was ermine-lined and edged, worth every shilling, and it looked exactly right on Ariana in her finery. If Mrs. Bentley had ever entertained doubts about that purchase, she was happy now to have done it.

"But you must allow she is young for the Carlton House set. Is it quite—the thing—for her?" Mr. Mornay was by now escorting Ariana from the room, but he hesitated. "I assure you, Miss Forsythe will find the evening agreeable. She will be my responsibility."

"I am aware of the Regent's habit of all-night entertainments." Mrs. Bentley's dry tone made him stop again. "Pray remember that Ariana is only just out. She is not used to such things and you may have to cut your evening short."

"You have my word." He was striving to be patient.

"In that case, I am much obliged to you! Much obliged!" She followed behind the pair as they went downstairs and toward the door. "Enjoy yourself, Ariana!" Her wish was heartfelt, surprising even herself. She had not expected to grow fond of the girl.

Sixteen

Carlton House

*W*hen they were comfortably seated in Mr. Mornay's luxurious black coach, sitting across from each other as was proper, Ariana removed the hood of her pelisse. The flicker of the single lamp made the velvet-lined interior cosy, and accented glimmers of her sunlight-coloured hair. Mr. Mornay surveyed her silently for a moment, then asked, "I trust our destination agrees with you?"

"Of course! I never dreamt of being a guest at Carlton House!"

"Shall you enjoy it, then?"

"Indeed, I must!" She gave a glowing smile. "If the Regent is anything near as extravagant regarding his town residence as he is said to be, I am sure it will be most diverting."

"Carlton House is one of his favourite indulgences. You will not be disappointed."

"I understand he has a great interest in art, and collects paintings." The idea thrilled her. She hoped to have a chance to view some.

"Indeed; as well as plate, jewelery, horses, military uniforms, drawers, women, and debts." It was a shameful list, but Ariana had to laugh out loud. *Drawers!*

A comfortable brief silence passed. "Do you expect Lady Covington will be there?"

"Let us hope she will be." This was a blow to Ariana, and yet hardly a surprise. She had wondered all along that her ladyship might be the reason Mr. Mornay had taken up her cause to begin with. Perhaps she was a love interest of his! Perhaps he was merely hoping to pique her jealousy with Ariana.

Her face must have betrayed these tumultuous thoughts.

"Does that distress you? You're not frightened of her, are you?"

Ariana's chin went up. "No."

"Good." But could he tell she was disturbed at the thought of seeing her nemesis? She tried not to dwell on it, but fears did assail her. What if the countess accused her in public? Right there, in Carlton House? What if she made a scene? Ariana had no idea what to expect.

She reminded herself that much prayer had gone into the evening; and that it was truly an enormous stroke of luck—no, a *blessing*—to be seeing the Regent's establishment. And meeting the Regent! And, on the arm of Mr. Mornay! Goodness, could this really be happening?

"Is it a special occasion tonight?" she asked.

He slowly smiled. "To whom? Do *you* think it is special?"

She blushed. "I meant, for the Regent."

He gazed at her for a moment. "No. Prinny often throws parties. He'd do it every night if he could get away with it, which is to say, afford it."

Prinny! It did not sound dignified enough for a prince to her mind, whether his reputation as a libertine and hedonist was true or not. But Mr. Mornay was smiling, and what a smile he had! She had to return the gesture.

❧

When they reached Pall Mall they joined a crush of carriages. It took minutes of crawling through traffic to draw up beneath the portico but at least Ariana had been able to take a leisurely view of her first glimpse of Carlton House. The multitude of carriage lamps and the bright flambeaux of the palace lit up the night. She could easily see the imposing structure she had only seen in drawings before. There was the distinct centre and two wings which were visible from the street. Along the front, the portico was lined with tall Corinthian columns. It certainly did fit the Regent as a man of great dignity despite his many reported failings in character.

After Mr. Mornay had handed her down from the coach, she was suddenly struck by a fit of nerves. She confided, holding tightly to his arm, "I am suddenly distressed, Mr. Mornay!"

His face took on a bland look, as if he thought, *This is what comes of escorting a debutante to Carlton House!*

"Oh? In what manner?"

She instinctively moved closer to him, not wanting to be overheard by anyone else. The gray-black eyes were intently upon her.

"I cannot tell. I fear I am going to be—"

He thought she was going to say, "ill."

"Shy."

He shook his head. "Did you say, shy?"

"Yes."

He put his head back and surveyed her with that little smile playing about his mouth.

"Don't worry. I will protect you from the countess, and from the prince!"

"But I may be shy with everyone!"

"I should think you would, this being your first encounter with a member of the royal family. Do not even think of it—Prinny has pretensions only for himself, I assure you." They passed through the row of columns lining the entrance. "Try to enjoy your surroundings, one or two of the guests—if possible, which is doubtful."

Did she see his eyes sparkle when he spoke? She had; he really was laughing at people most of the time!

"And do sample the refreshments, which will be excellent."

Ariana was not reassured and clung to his arm. "Will you be nearby? All night?"

Something in the tone of her voice made him stop and look down at her, startled. He was used to women wanting him nearby. They wanted to be seen with him, they wanted prestige, they hoped to win his affection, or, failing that, at least his fortune. But here was Ariana Forsythe, young and beautiful, earnest and appealing, wanting him nearby for safety. For security. It was an entirely unfamiliar feeling.

Awkwardly, he patted the hand clinging to his arm. He was not accustomed to showing affection. "I shall endeavour to stay near you. There may be inevitable separations, but I will see they are not prolonged."

∽∾◊∾∽

The Regent enjoyed entertainments of a large scale. In addition to carefully chosen regulars at his table, therefore, recent acquaintances, members of Parliament or his government, a few military men, royalty-seekers and more, could often be found gracing his presence as well. This evening was no exception, and by the time Ariana and her escort had arrived, the interior hall of Carlton House was teeming with the social elite.

Inside the magnificent high-ceilinged hall, Mr. Mornay ignored those hailing him and led Ariana to a velvet-cushioned bench and apologized for the necessity of leaving her only to contrive the introduction. With a polite bow he turned to go, but suddenly a jovial crowd came swarming from all directions as if on cue. They were surrounded by scads of well-dressed upper-class personages in moments. When Lord Horatio stood forth and then another man stepped from behind others and came forward—a man she immediately recognized as the prince—she was too confused by the suddenness of it all to even think of being nervous.

Ariana recognized him not only because of the numerous likenesses of him she had seen in the past, but because he was clad loudly in a shimmering green silken jacket and trousers, with a voluminous matching cape in shot silk. He sported a showy cravat and jeweled rings on his hands, all of which spoke volumes about his status in society. He made a large figure, helped not in the least by the cape, which enrobed him. But none of the reports Ariana had heard regarding the luxury and elegance of the palace or the prince had been exaggerated. He was not the most handsome presence in the place, but he certainly commanded a very proper awe in his carriage and bearing.

"Ho, 'tis true!" He had a loud voice, and came rapidly up to them. "Now this *is* a singular event! Mornay, you devil, you astonish me!" He turned to Lord Horatio. "Horatio, my sincerest apology; our friend has indeed brought a lady to my house!" He sounded delighted. He shook Mr. Mornay's hand smilingly. "Congratulations, old man! This is divine. Introduce her to me!"

Mr. Mornay spoke something into the prince's ear, and the Regent reacted in a startled manner. "Oh?" He turned and hissed at the nearest footman. "Get this beastly cape off of me!"

To Mr. Mornay he said curtly, "Obliged." He turned to Ariana. "Now then." He was tall and heavily fleshed on his face, but he had intelligent gray eyes, and curly light brown hair, which was just beginning to gray.

When her name was given she managed a graceful curtsey, and, to her relief, a calm smile when the prince exclaimed, "I am delighted, Miss Forsythe. I daresay Mornay will be a different man, now. You must lead us in discovering his softer side!"

The whole company paused, awaiting her reply. The manner of her response would be crucial to acceptance in these circles. Her stomach was churning with nerves, but she forced a smile.

"I should be honoured to lead Mr. Mornay himself in discovering it." She paused and gave her companion a wry look. "Assuming, of course, that it exists." Her remark, as usual, was artless and honest; Ariana had simply stated what she felt was true. But the company loved it and burst into laughter. She had unwittingly conveyed that she was not intimidated by the usually fearsome Mr. Mornay, and could meet his sharp tongue with apropos remarks of her own.

At the crowd's response, Ariana smiled in earnest and laughed. The Regent then offered his assessment. "She is all sunlight, Mornay! The very thing you lack!" Then, without so much as a by-your-leave, he took Ariana's hand and placed it upon his arm. She shot a look of alarm at Mr. Mornay, but he was listening to someone and missed it.

Meanwhile, the Regent walked her down the sumptuously decorated hall through a richly ornamented octagonal room. A grand staircase on one side, a gigantic skylight (which His Royal Highness pointed out, with the information that to appreciate it one had to view it in daylight) above. Everything Ariana saw blended into impressions…There was no time to take in the richness of details, and every nook and cranny had them. Ornaments, embellishments, tapestries, immense golden-framed paintings, polished and ornate furniture, exotic or graceful wallpapers, sculptures, rich fabrics, drapery…could a prince with such taste be condemned for great expenditures?

Her head was swimming at the richness and yet she could scarcely give heed to it all for she was overwhelmed at being upon the arm of the Prince Regent himself!

They entered a grand, magnificently lit room where people were milling about in conversation, though it ceased the instant the prince's presence was noticed. He retained his hold on Ariana's hand, which rested on his silken sleeve, and began circling the room.

"This is Miss Forsythe. Mornay's lady!" He said it over and over to the curtseying ladies and the bowing gentlemen whom they passed. Ariana tried to smile at the faces who looked at her in stark amazement or curiosity, but she was also searching frantically for Mr. Mornay. There! She saw him, but he was smiling and chatting with another gentleman, ignoring the Regent's antics. She hoped he would remember his promise to look after her.

Now His Royal Highness began pointing out people for her and naming them, including some slight *on-dit* about each and proving that, as was reputed of him, he was a witty and gracious host.

"There is Mrs. Siddons, the actress; have you seen her on stage? She is my particular friend." Ariana had not, but she knew of her from reading the papers, including that she had just retired from the theatre. He pointed in another direction.

"There is Lady Jersey, a very dear and particular friend." Her lady-ship was watching and beckoned to him, and so, keeping Ariana's hand upon his arm, he led her over.

Lady Jersey was an attractive woman who looked, Ariana thought, about her mother's age. She was elegantly clad and wore a necklace of large jewels, and all Ariana could remember else about her afterward was that she had oddly cold eyes, even when she smiled. Ariana was blithely unaware that her ladyship was considered the prince's mistress, which was fortunate, or her blushing countenance might have revealed her disapproval of such a relationship.

Aside from that encounter the Regent made her feel at ease, so that when he expressed his amazement and admiration that she had melted the legendary stone heart of Mornay, she was able to instantly profess she had no knowledge of doing so. He took this as a modest denial. Once the room had been circled he stopped and threw up a heavy arm in a flourish.

"Let us have dancing!" There was an immediate cry of approval from the boisterous guests, and the musicians, the prince's own band, began to play at once. His Royal Highness made a polite bow as the first strains of a country dance began, and Ariana's heart leapt as she realized he meant to dance with her. She automatically curtseyed, placed her hand once again on his arm which he was holding out with a smile; and she prayed that her trembling limbs were not evident.

The eyes of everyone in the room were on them and Ariana was thankful for the countless occasions she and Alberta had practiced this dance—a minuet—at home to pass the time. Others scrambled onto the floor to join in the figures and as she waited there with the Regent, Ariana had to keep telling herself that it was all very real; she was stand-ing up with the prince, King George's son! Wait 'til her mother and father heard of it! Even Aunt Bentley would surely be astonished!

Though the prince had grown large over the years, he was fond of dancing and still capable of short-term gracefulness. Ariana found herself enjoying the dance, and the prince made amiable remarks whenever they came abreast of each other or waited for others to complete their figures. It was startling to enjoy the company of this Royal—a man her family had never approved of.

After she had been returned to her escort (who had after all been watching her on the dance floor, with that near-smile) one person after another came requesting an introduction to her. One man asked for a dance, and Ariana blushed lightly in confusion. Could one refuse graciously without giving offense? She looked uncertainly at Mr. Mornay. Perhaps he could help her. But he mistook her questioning look as a request for permission to accept the gentleman, and nodded imperceptibly for her to do so. Now she felt compelled to accept. She would have preferred to stay at Mr. Mornay's side and watch the others dance. She wanted to take in every inch of her surroundings as well as the glamorous occupants of the room. But the prince had set a precedent among a crowd who loved to follow precedents, and so Ariana stood up for every dance. Some of her partners were men that Mr. Pellham would have unhesitatingly declared "veritable tulips," or "pinks of the *ton,*" and she studied them for the sole purpose of giving their descriptions later on.

Between dances Mr. Mornay murmured, "Miss Forsythe, I do believe you are the rage this evening."

"*You* are ever the rage, and their interest in me is only on your account," Ariana returned.

He eyed her for a moment. "Can you be so certain?"

More dancing. Some gentlemen made a show of eliciting permission from her distinguished escort, one man adding that it was the first time he had the honour of "borrowing something belonging to Mornay." Ariana blushed, but Mr. Mornay did not demur. It was a relief when Lord Horatio asked her to stand up with him. A man she knew, hurrah.

"Ah, but I think I should have the honour, Horatio," Mornay said. "She is, after all, by the prince's account, my lady, is she not?"

"A stroke of luck, Mornay, that he should have announced it so!" Lord Horatio looked around. "And the house is packed!" But he had not released Ariana's gloved hand, and he placed it upon his arm now. "You never stand up to dance, and since you have allowed your charming partner to dance with most every gentleman here, I insist you grant me the opportunity."

"Another time," Mornay pressed. "I hear the strains of a waltz, and I fancy myself in the right mood for one."

"A rare mood, indeed!" Lord Horatio declared with no small surprise on his face.

Ariana was equally surprised, but not unhappy. Lord Horatio reluctantly released her arm, requesting that she promise him a future dance, which she did, gladly.

Mr. Mornay held out his arm. "May I have the honour, Miss Forsythe?"

"You may, indeed!"

"Beware, Mornay." Lord Horatio spoke as they started off for the dance. "You may chase her until she catches you." He gave them an affable flourish with his arm, motioning them onto the floor, and there was no time for a response to the cryptic warning.

Seventeen

As they took to the floor, Ariana was conscious of deference being given them. Everyone scrambled to make room for the couple. Some men shouted out amiable jests to Mornay, which he completely ignored.

Instead, he again congratulated Ariana on her "success."

"It is evident that with the gentlemen I seem to be."

"Indeed. We have only to see if Lady Hollingsford will approach you."

To Ariana's questioning look, he added, "She is the most powerful of the hostesses of Almack's. If she gives you her blessing tonight, then our *counterattack* is a success." He actually sounded playful.

From then on, they spoke little. Ariana was happy to give her full attention to the dance, enjoying every moment of proximity to the man she was beginning to admire. She would not have guessed that a gentleman who danced so little in society could yet dance so well. He swept her along smoothly, making the steps seem more simple than she had found them before, in practice. She suddenly realized this was her first public waltz (at Carlton House, no less!) and yet she had nothing to worry about, thanks to Mr. Mornay's strong lead.

In addition, she was flattered because she had attended many a ball with her aunt during which he failed to stand up even once. Their eyes met and Ariana smiled. Was it her imagination? Or was he looking at her differently? His swirling dark eyes were intently upon her but for once Ariana felt no incrimination coming from them. It was a surprisingly pleasant experience. *Too* pleasant. She must guard her heart!

Mr. Mornay was exactly the sort of man her father had warned about. A man of fashion, fortune, and figure but without an interest in the things of God; without an active religion. She must not lose her heart to him.

Meanwhile, the company was bubbling with the thought that Mr. Mornay had fallen for a debutante.

The floor was slowly clearing of other couples as everyone was curious to enjoy the sight of the Paragon doing a waltz. Even the prince, seated now, looked on with great pleasure, nodding his head in time.

"This is too far outside Mornay's style," one man spoke into the prince's ear, "for it not to be a genuine *tendre!*" Another was heard to say, "Did she truly come upon his arm? I thought Prinny was joking!" After this night, no one would doubt he had declared his affections. He had broken precedents with Miss Forsythe. If it had not already been completely quelled, the question of possible improprieties was now laid soundly to rest.

From the edge of the room, Lady Covington eyed the couple narrowly, alone in her doubts regarding the relationship. She felt prodigiously indignant that the two people she had purposely entangled in spurious lies were now a bona fide, completely respectable, couple. Mr. Mornay appeared to be solicitous of his companion, the very opposite of the brute she had claimed him to be. And to top all, he stood up for a waltz. They were ruining her scheme, and it was utterly provoking!

‿◦‿◦‿◦

It was near midnight when Mr. Mornay took Ariana for refreshments, which was simply a matter of going through a great opened double-door to an adjoining chamber. The floor was carpeted, footmen abounded, and, though the menu was service *a' la française,* there were servants to carve one's meat or fill one's glass.

As for the room itself, Ariana delighted in the rich wallpaper, the elegant trimmings, beautiful china, and golden utensils. The damasked table glittered with sparkling crystal and delectable dishes. She was a princess in another world tonight, a dream world where all of life was beautiful. What a stark contrast to the filth of many London streets where she saw far more destitution and poverty from her carriage window than she had dreamed existed. She made a determination, while basking in the splendour around her, that if God saw fit to some-day make her a woman of means like her aunt, she would espouse the cause of the poor. There had to be something she could do for them.

Mr. Mornay stood back politely while Ariana chose refreshments. She accepted slices of beef and turkey *au jus* from a footman, then helped herself to cold ham with French mustard, apricot tart, and Maids of Honour; herbed asparagus and green beans; a poached pear and raspberry cream. There were many more dishes beckoning her attention but Ariana was in a state of high excitement and not certain she could even consume the contents on her plate.

The guests came and went for refreshments at will, the men standing politely back while the ladies helped themselves. Once Ariana had finished eating, Mr. Mornay escorted her back to the ballroom, leaving then to have a bite himself. She soon found herself surrounded by a group of boisterous guests who were telling stories. She was fascinated by tales of those who had encountered highwaymen or footpads, even in Mayfair! A footpad, she was assured, would slit a man's throat for mere shillings.

And then, just as Mr. Mornay hoped, Lady Hollingsford came up to Ariana.

"Miss Forsythe, upon my honour, however did you manage to claim Mr. Mornay's affections?"

Ariana smiled while her ladyship surveyed her with curious eyes. She gave the only answer she could. "I can take no credit where none is due, my lady. I am afraid Mr. Mornay's affections remain at large, as always."

"No, but he escorted you here, did he not?" She waited, mouth slightly ajar so that a few small white teeth were revealed.

"Indeed, ma'am, but—"

Lady Hollingsford nodded thoughtfully, and patted Ariana's arm.

"Do not fret on account of Lady Covington! She shall be brought 'round, I warrant you. Almack's is open to you at any time! I shall send vouchers to your aunt directly."

"I am much obliged, ma'am."

Lady Hollingsford smiled, nodded her head regally, and then strode elegantly off.

Mr. Mornay returned to Ariana's side almost instantly.

"That went well?"

"Yes, she promised me Almack's."

"Very good." He straightened up and looked around. "Then I may take you home."

"So soon?"

Her escort smiled. "I promised your aunt I'd return you at a decent hour and it is past two, now." Time had flown by.

"Oh, but I have not—oh it doesn't signify; yes, let us go."

But one brow on the handsome face was raised. "Is there someone in particular you haven't danced with that you are longing to? I can arrange it if you like." He sounded irked, but Ariana giggled, and then covered her mouth for a small yawn.

"No! If I stand up with one more gentleman I will stamp on his feet to be excused!" She looked up at him. "I only hoped to see more of the house. We passed so many marvelous paintings. Had I not been on the arm of His Royal Highness I would have stopped to view them."

The ire left his tone.

"I see. But I must get you home. You can view the paintings another time."

"Another time?" Her eyes lit with amusement. "I do not expect there shall be another time, sir."

"One never knows, does one?" His response was enigmatic.

He led them to the prince, to take their leave. Again the Regent made much of Ariana, and thanked her for coming to his house. He was exceedingly gracious. Later, after a servant allowed Ariana to pick her pelisse from a coat room, Mr. Mornay escorted her out of the lavish establishment and onto the street. A servant had already been dispatched to alert his coachman to bring round the carriage.

The air was surprisingly chilly, and Ariana was thankful for the warmth of her coat as she pulled it closer around her. While they waited she could not help looking about cautiously for the presence of any footpads. The conversation indoors had given her imagination frights, despite the reassuring company beside her. Mr. Mornay was in good health, and strong—she remembered that from their encounter on his estate. But it was still a relief when they were finally seated in the coach.

As the wheels began turning and the carriage moved away from the mansion on Pall Mall, Ariana craned her neck to get a last look at the building. How extraordinary, that she had been there, danced in its ballroom, with the Regent and Mr. Mornay! When she turned back and saw that familiar half-smile on her companion's face, she grinned sheepishly.

And then she was aware, suddenly, of being tired. Meeting all those people, lords and ladies of all ranks, and Lady Hollingsford offering her Almack's—it had been a momentous night, and now the effects were settling in. Her head found its way to rest against the cushion, but her feet, shod only in the fashionable but flimsy silk slippers, were aching. She reached down and rubbed one, hoping to be discreet, but his eyes, sharp as always, noticed immediately.

"Your feet are sore! Perhaps I should have warned you not to take to the floor so often."

"I would that you had; how does one begin to say 'no,' when she has already said 'yes,' to others, without giving offence?"

"Did you indeed wish to?"

"Yes; aside from the prince—" She looked away. "And you." She dared not meet his eyes. "I had no interest in dancing." She paused. "I do not enjoy proximity with strangers."

"Nor do I."

Again she rested her head on the cushions.

"I am afraid I kept you out too late."

"No." But her tone was weak. "It was wonderful. I enjoyed nearly every minute!"

"Nearly?" There was laughter in his voice.

She raised her head to explain. "Standing up with the Regent is not something one does every day, and I daresay I might have swooned!"

He smiled at her exaggeration.

"And the countess did nothing but send me the most astonishing dark looks! I realize she is not my friend but I cannot account for such animosity."

After a moment of ensuing silence he offered, "You were a deal more than she had anticipated being up against."

Ariana was flattered, but embarrassed. "Thank you."

He nodded, and they lapsed into silence for the remainder of the drive. When they pulled up in front of her aunt's house she heard a servant come round and lower the steps. Mr. Mornay exited the carriage first and then assisted her by holding one of her gloved hands as she carefully descended. They did not speak as they walked to the door, and Ariana was incredibly aware that he had not released her hand. When Haines appeared, she turned to Mr. Mornay with a curtsey.

"I am greatly obliged to you. I had a wonderful evening that I shall never forget."

"I am glad of it," he said, lightly. Then, when she would have reclaimed her hand to leave, he instead raised and kissed it, and then bowed. In another moment she was inside the house, and the door had shut behind her. Haines helped her out of the expensive pelisse but she barely noticed. She was too busy going over that parting light kiss to her hand.

It may have been nothing more than a polite gesture, or the usual gracious manner he might have exhibited to anyone in her place; but Ariana hoped her face had not betrayed the pleasure she felt. Mr. Mornay's expression was somewhat sombre, and when he nodded, she'd turned and entered the house. Nothing more than that, it had all taken only seconds, and yet, why did she feel as if somehow her life was changing?

⋐∽∘∾⋑

Ariana found herself obliged to tell precisely what had taken place at Carlton House in exhausting detail. Mrs. Bentley wanted to know everything, from who was present to what they wore, what they said to her, and more. She wanted descriptions of the delicacies offered, and the names of every gentleman she stood up with. She was exasperated when Ariana could only remember a few, all of them married men. Her idea was to keep up an acquaintance with the eligible men who had shown an interest in Ariana, knowing such a thing could easily bud into a romance.

Even the servants were compelled to be curious and asked the young miss questions (if they "could be so bold") when they came upon her alone. It amused Ariana the way Molly, especially, would scramble to listen if she came within earshot. She refused to meet Ariana's eyes, still, but nevertheless displayed a noticeable curiosity about her. In all, the servants' treatment of Ariana, which had always been respectful, became even more so.

Her aunt also had to know, of course, how things went with Mr. Mornay. When she revealed that he had kissed her hand, even Mrs. Bentley was uncertain whether or not it signified. She had begun to raise her hopes—only faintly—after the way he had approved of Ariana. In the past she had heard him acknowledge, if pressed, that a female was within the mode, or "all the rage," but she had never seen him personally gratified by it as he apparently had been with Ariana. She supposed that since he was her escort, it gave him a bit more of a possessive feeling, but it seemed to her that what she was sensing in him went beyond that. Nevertheless, she would quickly concede defeat, for after all, *who could win Mornay?*

She could not be disappointed with her niece if she failed to do what countless other females had failed at. And now, with guaranteed access to Almack's, and Lady Covington's slanders proven groundless, everything was going superbly.

~~~∽~o~∾~~~

Ariana found herself thinking strongly of Mr. Mornay during her quiet moments or when she prayed. She included him faithfully in her orisons, praying that his private pain, whatever it was, would find healing in heaven's balm. She did not dare ask to win his heart, but prayed fervently that God would. She was praying for him, she told herself, because he had been providential in helping her. At times, however, it crept across her conscience that she had enjoyed his company overmuch and would like nothing better than to see him again.

Mr. Pellham, meanwhile, was still in need of visitors. Ariana and her aunt often spent afternoons in his drawing room, keeping his spirits up with simple diversions. His leg had started to heal but the doctor's opinion was that Mr. Pellham's convalescence had just begun. At Mr. Pellham's age, bones did not heal quickly and one could not be too careful. This was the very thing most liable to vex Mr. Pellham's free-spirited mind, and thus he was out of sorts for days.

Ariana tried to amuse him out of his gloominess by reading light-hearted fare aloud, such as Pope's *The Rape of the Lock*, or, Shakespeare's *Much Ado About Nothing*. She and Mrs. Bentley played more card games than either of them cared to, for his sake. But there was nothing they could do to help his leg.

"I am a miserable specimen of a man," he lamented one day. "One small misstep, and look at me, abed for weeks! Why do you bother calling upon me any longer? I shall never be the companion you used to know. And I have escorted Ariana nowhere at all!"

Mrs. Bentley could hardly tell him to stop spouting nonsense when he was so uneasy in mind and unwell in body, as she would have done at another time. And Ariana did not wish to say she was greatly enjoying her stay in London without their intended jaunts.

And so they played another game of cards.

Eighteen

Mr. Mornay had a box at Drury Lane, so when he sent word that Ariana would be accompanying him to the theatre in the evening, she was rippling with excitement.

It became, in fact, the start of an amazing two weeks during which she appeared on his arm not only at the theatre, but at the ballet, opera, and many private entertainments as well. She was forming the opinion that a life without these pursuits was dull, indeed. During an aria she would close her eyes in bliss and just—*listen*. During the ballet, she fixed her gaze on the dancers until her eyes ached and watered. It was all so beautiful! And Mr. Mornay enjoyed watching her taking it all in, and hearing her express her impressions, afterward.

Mrs. Bentley accompanied them as often as the Paragon would allow, although he was more aloof when she was present. Ariana's aunt, however, was in her glory. She delighted in being spotted in Mornay's box, and her little white handkerchief had seen more usage of late, as she waved it around at every acquaintance, than in all its history.

Ariana was able to wear all the finery in her newly acquired wardrobe and people who barely knew her treated her with the utmost respect. Famous now as "Lady Mornay," as they called her, things could not have been any better. Then, surprisingly, word went around that the countess had been cornered at a dinner party and made to confess the truth: her allegations had been a hoax. When Ariana heard this she was stunned with relief. She thanked God for allowing truth to triumph. The only glitch in her happiness was a nagging concern for her family, for they still had not written a single response to her many letters. It was so unlike her parents and Alberta not to write; something had to be wrong, and it worried her.

She wanted so much for them to share in the triumph of her reputation being completely restored. She wanted most of all to hear their opinion of Mr. Mornay, and to know their thoughts on all he had done for her since that day at Aspindon. It failed to dawn upon her that now the scandal was utterly without credit, she and Mr. Mornay no longer had need to appear involved with one another. She had not let herself forget that his attentions were temporary, but neither did she dwell upon the fact that they must, in due time, cease.

She was unprepared, therefore, when the day came for her charmed life to end. It happened when Mr. Mornay brought her home from an afternoon concert, and indicated he wished to come into the house. Sitting across from her in the drawing room, he appeared less than comfortable, which was decidedly unusual for him.

Ariana was pleased he had asked to come in, and, after ordering tea, sat across from him expectantly. Her large eyes were shining as they tended to do, but his were dark.

He leaned forward in his seat, and Ariana saw he wanted to speak to her.

"I am leaving town for about a fortnight. I have business to attend to, my estate, you know, and other holdings." He produced an elegant blue Sevres snuffbox from an inside pocket of his waistcoat. "I suggest you give it out while I am away that we have had a disagreement." He took the smallest pinch of snuff, snapped the box shut with one hand, and replaced it to the pocket. Ariana's face had lost its expectant glow, but she was listening intently, betraying nary a hint of disappointment. He instructed how she should answer the inevitable inquiries, gallantly offering to take all the blame for the failure of the relationship.

"If you say I have been beastly and unforgivable, no one will doubt you." He gave a wry smile, but Ariana would not have it.

"I could never say such a thing," she insisted.

"Why not?" He seemed surprised.

"It isn't true." Her wide eyes regarded him prettily and he shifted in his seat.

"Do not force me to behave in such a manner; that mustn't be the only way to do this."

To do this. The words echoed in her mind with an empty ring. She wanted to ask, *to do what?* She wanted to make him spell it out for her. If he wanted to stop seeing her, though she knew it had been coming, she was not yet inclined to help him do it.

As Haines brought in the tea tray (after a peremptory sound at the door) he sensed tension in the room, coming chiefly from the gentleman's direction. After he had gone, Mr. Mornay resumed his unsavoury task.

"Miss Forsythe." He watched her gracefully pour him a cup of steaming liquid. "I will put it to you plainly. The countess has assuredly lost her appetite for reproaching you, and I believe there is not a whit of doubt in society regarding your good name."

At these words she spilled a little tea while filling her own cup, but ignored it.

"Yes, I agree." She put down the teapot and faced him. His usual manner of being completely in control of every situation seemed to have deserted him. He was regarding her earnestly, yet almost nervously—and suddenly Ariana felt ashamed of herself. He had done nothing except help her, and it was now her turn to be gracious. She took a breath to muster her courage and eyed him steadily.

"Do not fret on my account, Mr. Mornay. I assure you I have long been prepared for this moment."

He practically jumped to his feet.

"Very well." He looked at her helplessly. "And you are free, now, of course, to do as you wish. We did what was necessary, and now, I think, before your season is over, you must be given space to make further acquaintances. I mustn't continue to prevent other prospects from approaching you."

"Yes, of course."

He looked at her searchingly for a few seconds. "When I return, if you need to contact me I encourage you to do so."

"Thank you."

There was an awkward silence. He acted as though he had expected a much worse time of it, for indeed he had. Wouldn't it have been usual for the lady to reach hysterics, or at the least declare she would suffer a decline directly? Ariana, however, was even now smiling at him reassuringly. While he watched, she took a delicate sip of tea.

In truth, she was waiting for him to leave; maintaining control of her emotions for his sake, but at great effort. Of course it was necessary for him to do as he was doing. It was not his fault she had been thoroughly enjoying her time with him or that she would miss the excitement of his company. He had done a superb job of rescuing her from social ruin, but that job was accomplished. Thanks to him, Ariana was considered good *ton*.

She forced another smile. "I apologize for not being very grateful just now; I suppose you took me by surprise."

He did the eyebrow gesture. Here he was unceremoniously abandoning her, and *she* was apologizing to him? She even came to her feet.

"I am more obliged to you than I can say. There is no one who could have helped me as you have, and I am sure no one with whom I could have enjoyed myself, more." She clasped and unclasped her hands. "I only wish there was something I could do for you in return." There was no mistaking her sincerity.

He seemed surprised and for once, caught without a response. He answered slowly.

"You have done something for me, just now, and I thank you." He bowed politely, and replaced his hat. "You will excuse me, now."

"Of course." He turned to leave so quickly that Ariana curtseyed to his retreating figure. At the door, however, he stopped and looked back at her.

"Goodbye, Miss Forsythe."

She bobbed another curtsey. "Goodbye. God bless you!"

She watched him leave, his black boots gleaming in the light from the window. She went and stood discreetly by the drapes, so she could see when he left the house below. She wiped away tears which were allowed to come out now, watching as he disappeared into his expensive black carriage. Turning back she thought, *What if I should never see him again?*

The thought disturbed her. She sat back down, heavily, and wept until her handkerchief was soaked.

She knew she ought not to be so upset over a man who was not suitable as a husband; she knew he was truly the farthest thing from the mate she had imagined. But she felt alone, now he was gone. As alone as when she had first left home. Only this time, it felt much, much worse.

Nineteen

*T*he days following Mr. Mornay's departure were dreary indeed. Ariana was distraught at the uncertainty of ever seeing him again socially. She missed his little witticisms and swirling eyes. She missed the gallant way he treated her, the laughter in his voice when she amused him, and the firm air of assurance about him. Though Mrs. Bentley had her own box at Drury Lane, it was unthinkable to make use of it. Ariana would be accosted with an onslaught of curiosity were she to appear anywhere but in Mr. Mornay's box. She did not feel ready to face such an inquisition.

Another disturbing factor was the lack of news from home. The longer her time away, the more it vexed her. She might return home, she thought, simply to get an explanation. She was restless and bored without Mr. Mornay's company at any rate. The only thing preventing her from acting on the plan was the small worry that her papa might not allow her to return to Hanover Square. If that were to happen she would surely never set eyes on Mr. Mornay again. And so the question of why her family had not replied to her letters remained a nagging concern.

She moped about the house for a full week before the pall of his absence began to lift, and she came to her senses. She had forgotten the simple truth that all her steps were in God's hands. His plans for her were the only important ones. She began to spend more time in prayer, giving all her hopes and dreams to the Lord. Indeed, she gave

Mr. Mornay to Him, praying only for his salvation. And she gave her family and her worries to Him. Whatever was behind their lack of correspondence, she felt sure it could be easily explained—somehow.

It helped that Lord Horatio called. Ariana had already received a visitor who mentioned seeing Mr. Mornay the previous evening. She stayed outwardly calm at hearing this, but inside her heart was churning with the thought that he had returned.

"My dear Miss Forsythe," his lordship said, with a sincere smile, and neat bow. "'Tis delightful to see you."

Ariana had received him wearing a morning gown that draped her tall frame gracefully. Her hair was in ringlets about her head, decorated with a wide band of taffeta. Mrs. Bentley joined them in the parlour, happy to see Ariana receiving guests again.

When he was seated and small talk was out of the way, his lordship looked directly at Ariana. "Are you well, Miss Forsythe? No one sees you about of late; are you hiding yourself at home?"

"I am home a great deal, but not in hiding, my lord!" she replied.

"She is far too much at home, your lordship, but cannot be pulled from her books and the fireside," Aunt Bentley offered. "Why do not you insist upon her going out? She will listen to you." Lord Horatio looked in consternation at Ariana, who was directing a patient look at her relation. He said, in a low tone, "'Tis said you are suffering a decline; on account of Mornay, you know." Ariana's mouth gaped in indignation for a second.

"Upon my word!" she said at last. "People have far too little to do if they must continually invent calamities!"

Lord Horatio smiled. "Indeed; nevertheless I insist, as your aunt suggested, that you leave your house more often and be seen wearing smiles. The talk has begun, and your parlour is bound to be full in the next few days with the curious—unless you act now and nip it in the bud."

"The talk has begun," she repeated. "By whom?"

Her richly dressed friend shrugged. "Does one ever know? The point is, once in circulation it only gets worse."

Ariana eyed him gratefully. "Thank you for calling and letting me know. I will be sure to resume my morning ride in the park tomorrow."

"Come for a drive with me now. The sun is out, and though the air has a chill, it is a fine, clear day." His tone was soft, but not so much that Mrs. Bentley hadn't heard.

"How kind of you! Do go, my gel!"

But her niece needed no persuasion. She thanked his lordship and went to get her bonnet and pelisse while he checked that his curricle was still at the curb. Sometimes the groom would walk the horses if they became impatient—but there it was, a neat equipage on two wheels that was just the thing for a drive about town.

Soon he and Ariana were seated in the vehicle and he snapped the reins to set off. They began moving smartly down the Square, turning onto Brook Street. Mayfair was usually busy with delivery carts and wagons, strollers, posh carriages, and passers-by. They waved gaily at anyone they knew and Ariana made it a point to give especially brilliant smiles. A carriage stopped by theirs near Berkeley Square, causing Lord Horatio to pull up the horses abruptly, all so that one lady could tell Miss Forsythe she was much relieved to see her out and about. His lordship then had an idea.

"Would a turn through the park be agreeable, Miss Forsythe?"

It was earlier than the fashionable "hour" for being seen, which meant the lanes would be less crowded and they could actually enjoy the scenery. On a whim he added, "Why do we not pass by Grosvenor Square on the way and see if Mornay is about?" Ariana stiffened at mention of his name, but did not demur.

Grosvenor Square was not on the way. It would have been more direct had they gone straight down Mount Street to Park Lane, but Ariana was not aware of this. The suggestion to pass by the Paragon's establishment was made in such a breezy tone, however, that she looked at her companion suspiciously. Was he testing her for a reaction?

As they approached the square, her pulse quickened. Lord Horatio diverted her by naming many of the grand houses they were passing, and telling brief facts about the owners. When they drew near Mornay's house, his lordship cried, "Good luck! 'Tis the man himself!" He slowed the equipage and Mr. Mornay, who was affectionately stroking the mane of one of his horses and speaking softly in its ear, looked up as they came aside him.

"Are you coming or going?" Her companion's voice was jolly.

Mr. Mornay issued instructions to his groom who led off the team, and stepped over to where they had stopped in the street. He bowed to Ariana, looking at her with keen interest.

"I've just returned home. What are you about?"

"Headed for the park. Just taking a drive."

Mornay turned his attention to Ariana. "How do you do, Miss Forsythe?"

"Well, I thank you." she said, trying to decide whether to disguise or admit her pleasure. "And you? Are you well?"

He gave only a short nod for answer. "Are you certain you're well? I have heard otherwise." His look was mildly reproving.

"I have been home a great deal, but aside from that there is no foundation for what you heard," she assured him.

He nodded again, noting that the sparkle in her eyes had not diminished, nor the colour in her cheeks. Without thinking, he said, "Thank you, Horatio." He stepped back and gave another short bow to Ariana.

"What did he thank you for?" She felt as though she had missed something of the interaction.

Lord Horatio came to attention and looked thoughtful for a moment, but then shrugged.

"I suppose for stopping by." He turned and gave her a guarded look. He did not mention Mornay's concern about the rumour of a decline, or that he had expressed his wish to see Miss Forsythe, but dared not call upon her himself. The scheme of going by his house had been Lord Horatio's impulse and it had paid off; Mornay got to see his little protégée.

The following day Ariana took that early ride in the park

accompanied by her aunt's groom on another mount. She went down the Ladies' Mile and stopped to chat with more than a few acquaintances. She returned home and had only changed into a morning gown when callers began to arrive. By late afternoon Ariana felt certain all question of her having fallen into a decline must have surely been put to rest. Lavinia and her mama were the last callers, for they, too, had heard the rumour.

"Tomorrow I have determined to accompany you to the museum you have longed to see," Lavinia announced, "if you have no previous engagements."

"I haven't!"

"Excellent! Mama says our coachman may take us. I'll come for you at eleven o'clock!"

∽∾०∾∽

Ariana had seen Lavinia often at balls and card parties, but this was the first time they would spend all day in each other's company. She dressed excitedly, urging Harrietta to hurry with her hair so she would be ready on time. There was already a pencil and paper in her reticule so she could take notes for Mr. Pellham's sake. He would enjoy hearing her account read aloud.

When the Herleys' coach rumbled to a stop at the curb Ariana called out to notify her aunt, and then hurried through the front door to the carriage. To her surprise, there were two gentlemen with Lavinia. She was introduced to one Lord Antoine Holliwell, and Mr. O'Brien was introduced to her, with the information that she and he had similar interests in religion. She shot Lavinia a knowing look, catching on immediately that the meeting was no coincidence.

As they rode through London streets, she discovered that Mr. O'Brien hoped to enter the church. There was a living in his parish that was soon to be vacated and he had high expectations it would be given him. His sincere love for the church and God gave his speech an animation that was endearing. He even mentioned things from his private devotions that reassured Ariana that his was a genuine faith.

Her parents had raised her almost as a Methodist (which would have been shocking to many of her acquaintance, had she told them) though they never renounced the Anglican faith. Her papa had strong sympathies with the Methodists and the Dissenters. So this upbringing included discernment to see the difference between a minister who took his vocation as a sacred calling versus the one who viewed it as merely an occupation that paid the bills. It was the difference between what the Methodists would call soul-saving faith versus mere religion. It was immensely heartening for Ariana to finally make the acquaintance of a person who understood the same distinction.

Mr. O'Brien had light, sandy-coloured hair. He was tall and slim and good-natured. His appearance was neat and clean, and his voice gentle and earnest. Ariana liked him at once. He, in turn, was fascinated with Miss Forsythe. She was, indeed, too good to be true! A lady of faith that echoed his own and with such beauty as made his heart quake.

When the coach rolled to a stop Ariana looked eagerly out the window but was disappointed to see a row of circular townhouses, recognizing Burton Crescent, where the Herleys lived.

"Lavinia? What of the museum?"

"Museum?" Mr. O'Brien looked blank. He evidently knew nothing of it.

"Oh, dear me, how could I have forgot to tell you?" Lavinia giggled. "I am dreadfully sorry; I promised Lord Antoine a grand meal at our table. Pray, do not be cross and hold it against me. I will make it up to you, my dear Ariana, I give you my word as your friend!" When she saw that Ariana was out of countenance she turned to Lord Antoine.

"You see? She *is* disappointed!" Then, to Ariana, she added, "I insist you forgive me, for it was Lord Antoine, you must know, who would not be agreeable to visiting the museum."

"Guilty as charged," said the young man, holding his hands up in a gesture of admission. He did not bother to apologize, however, and Ariana did indeed feel cross. Lavinia giggled again at something his lordship said as they exited the coach. Mr. O'Brien alone seemed cognizant of the degree of Ariana's disappointment, though he had no hand in causing it. He looked at her gravely and apologized for her dissatisfaction.

"There was no mention of a museum outing to me." He helped her from the carriage by lightly holding one hand.

"No? But Miss Herley agreed only yesterday that we should go today. I am astonished she has changed the plan without informing me."

He nodded, but then smiled shyly. "I was told I was to endeavour to offset your loneliness." When she only looked up at him in surprise, he added, "With Mr. (here he stopped and swallowed) Mornay away."

Ariana blushed. "I assure you there is no need. Mr. Mornay and I are…" He watched her hopefully. "Only acquaintances."

"That's splendid!" He came up short and said, "I beg your pardon. I only meant—" His eyes were a torment of confusion, making her laugh.

"I know what you meant, Mr. O'Brien."

❧

The day at the Herleys' passed pleasantly. When Lavinia had a moment she confided to Ariana she had been loath to change their plans but it had been necessary since it gave her the opportunity to entertain his lordship.

"You have your Mr. Mornay, and you have made all the most splendid connexions, but I made none. Can you understand, Ariana, why I had to do as his lordship wanted? I daresay Mama would have disowned me if I muddled this chance. She has ever had her heart set on my making a match with a nobleman!"

"Miss Herley?" They both heard his lordship's voice, but it was further back in the house and not an immediate threat. They spoke hurriedly.

"I understand. But please do not refer to the man as 'my' Mr. Mornay. That is not the case."

"Perhaps not any longer," she said, taking a quick glance around to be certain no one had found them out. "But you are by all accounts a success, while I am still, in this my second season, alone."

Suddenly Lavinia had tears in her eyes and she almost shocked Ariana with a hug.

"My dear! I believe he really finds me agreeable! I'm so…frightened!" She whispered heavily into Ariana's ear.

"Why are you frightened?" Ariana asked. "If he finds you agreeable, surely that is a good thing."

Lavinia wiped her eyes hastily, using her skirt. She didn't meet Ariana's eyes, but said, "You are a such comfort to me, my dear."

Ariana was puzzled, but there was no time for further discussion. Lord Antoine appeared in the doorway, a look of satisfaction on his face for locating Miss Herley. Mr. O'Brien was playing with the younger members of the family in the parlour, and Ariana regarded the scene with a little smile.

Later, when the carriage was summoned to take Ariana home, it was well into the evening. Both gentlemen were to accompany her in the carriage before being delivered to their own residences. Ariana was grateful the drive went quickly; she did not enjoy Lord Antoine in the least, and Mr. O'Brien's constant attempts to converse became tiresome. She felt weary.

She did, however, give Mr. O'Brien leave to call upon her. He asked her permission shyly, which was unnecessary because she was quite happy to have made his acquaintance: a man of respectability, a good countenance, and sincere religion!

He called two days later. Ariana was riding in Hyde Park with a friend and missed his visit, but her aunt had not.

"Ariana, a third son!" Ariana was still in her riding habit, but Mrs. Bentley would not be put off. She followed her niece right into her chamber to complain.

"He will get nothing. *Nothing!*"

Ariana patiently explained why his friendship was of value to her, besides the fact that she found him utterly agreeable.

Her aunt stared at her wide-eyed. "He will get *nothing!* Are you comprehending me?"

"My dear Aunt," and she gave her relative her most patient look. "You must know that my first concern is not with the size of a man's fortune or inheritance."

"Then let it be your second concern," came the reply, spoken dryly. "Goodness knows it will concern you the rest of your life." Ariana raised her eyes heavenward. She could no more deny Mr. O'Brien the chance to strengthen their acquaintance than she could wish away her attraction to Mr. Mornay. Life, she was beginning to realize, came at you with its hands full, but what it held in its hands did not always obey the rules of your mind or heart—or even your better judgment.

She knew that Mrs. Bentley had written a list with the names of wealthy gentlemen, and was planning on inviting them, one at a time, to dinner to better acquaint them with her and emphasize her availability. Mr. Mornay had cleared the way for Ariana to be accepted in the most aristocratic gatherings in town. Her aunt had seized that happenstance to issue invitations to the most aristocratic unmarried men available. And yet Ariana sighed with relief whenever regrets came by mail or messenger. Most people's calendars it seemed, had little room for new invitations at mid-season.

✿◦✿◦✿

Mr. O'Brien called three times in which he failed to find Miss Forsythe at home. On the fourth occasion, he was informed she was home, but busy entertaining other callers. He left a card each time, which was getting irksome, for he had no wish to order new ones. He tried, since obtaining the little cards with his name on them, to make them last.

Finally the day came when the young man managed to find Ariana at home. Mrs. Bentley sat stiffly in the parlour determined to give them no time alone. No matter. Ariana enjoyed their conversation very much, even when it was evident they held different views regarding the providence of God in the affairs of men. They held lively discourse over the topic while Mrs. Bentley sat by yawning. The older woman was relieved when she could announce that the proper time for a polite call had passed.

Taking Ariana to see Mr. Pellham more often was an excuse to remove her from the parlour. Besides, Mrs. Bentley was growing alarmed at Mr. Pellham's slow rate of recovery. She sometimes wearied of her hours at his side playing cards, or letting him read aloud from a travel book, though, so Ariana played at cards with him, or sometimes chess. There was not much else the man could still enjoy without his usual freedom.

Twenty

*S*hortly after the day at Lavinia's house, Ariana was sitting quietly in the library reading when a footman found her there.

"Your presence, mum, is needed in the parlour."

"Is there a caller?"

"Ay, mum, and the mistress is still out."

Ariana straightened her gown and ran her hand over her hair which was done up in the usual way. She was glad that, if Mr. O'Brien was calling, her aunt was not yet returned. But when she opened the door to the parlour, the man who quickly spun around from the window to offer a polite bow was Phillip Mornay.

Ariana greeted him with a brief curtsey. "How nice of you to call." She made an effort to keep her greeting polite and calm, rather than effusive. "Have you been offered refreshments?" Haines knew to do that, but it seemed a safe thing to say.

"I have, thank you."

She motioned for him to take a seat.

He seemed to be studying Ariana as at their last meeting. When several awkwardly silent moments had passed, Mr. Mornay asked, "Do you expect your aunt soon?"

"I cannot say; she went making calls to her dowager friends," Ariana replied. Mr. Mornay nodded. Then after a few more seconds of awkward silence, he said, "I hoped to ask her leave to take you from the house, today. There is a couple in my coach at this moment—friends of mine—and we thought you might find it agreeable to join us on a visit to Vauxhall. 'Twas an impulsively made decision, and I apologize for the lack of notice."

But Ariana's face lit up. "I would like that very much, I thank you."

"Are you certain your aunt would give you leave?"

Ariana gave a wry grin, and said, "Mrs. Bentley would no sooner deny you, sir, than the king or queen!"

He nodded again and another small silence ensued.

"I am pleased to see you're looking well," he offered.

"As are you," Ariana returned the compliment and then excused herself to make ready for the outing. She hurried pell-mell to her chamber (after quietly closing the door on her guest) to change from slippers into a pair of leather half-boots, her heart soaring. She certainly hadn't expected Mr. Mornay to call on her again! She prayed for him each and every night, and had shed a few tears, but she had been making steady progress in removing him from her thoughts. Until now.

After getting her bonnet and reticule, and notifying Haines of their destination for her aunt, they left the house. Mr. Mornay shooed away the footman and handed Ariana into the coach.

The lady seated inside was a pleasant-looking young woman by the name of Miss Dorsett, and her companion, Mr. Hartley, equally amiable in his greeting. Ariana felt sure it was going to be a very agreeable outing.

Miss Dorsett's brown hair curled about a modestly fashionable bonnet and her hazel eyes smiled a great deal. Mr. Hartley had reddish-brown hair with a stylish lick, but nothing so loud in his attire that one could mistake him for a pink.

During the drive Ariana exchanged pleasantries with the couple, not surprised that Mr. Mornay's comments were few. His eyes were milder than she remembered them, and he looked at her often. Now and then he even gave her a hint of a smile. It made her feel they were back at their easy method of being together, as when they had gone to the opera or theatre as a couple. Miss Dorsett and Mr. Hartley kept up a cheerful banter that made the atmosphere lighter for everyone. Talk turned to London.

"Are you enjoying your stay in town?" Mr. Hartley asked Ariana. "I am very much indeed."

This caught Mr. Mornay's interest. "Have you seen some of the places you wished to, then?"

Ariana tried to ignore the familiar pangs in her stomach as she met his gaze. "I have, with you to thank." She turned to the others and explained. "Mr. Mornay escorted me on many a delightful evening to the opera and theatre and ballet. I feel certain today's excursion will be another delight which I will be in his debt for."

"What other sights are you hoping to see, Miss Forsythe? Do name them for us." Miss Dorsett's eyes regarded her earnestly.

Ariana paused to think. "The Royal Academy, the Tower, the British Museum, The Egyptian Hall; and, oh, I must not forget St. Paul's Cathedral and Westminster." She spoke a little about the architectural styles of the noted cathedrals. "And I would like to tour a missionary society I know of, and a charity school, if I may."

Mr. Hartley expressed surprise at this last comment, and Ariana added, "I have long desired to educate myself on how the less fortunate of society are helped—"

"Bravo, Miss Forsythe!" Mr. Hartley said. "I say, I haven't stepped into a church since before my first season. Why do we not all take a tour together sometime, eh, Mornay?"

Before he could answer, Ariana did. "Perhaps, Mr. Hartley, you should try going first upon a *Sunday*." She had not been able to resist offering the advice to one who admitted outright to neglecting Sunday services, though Mr. Hartley had not addressed his remark to her. Miss Dorsett's lips were suddenly compressed as she endeavoured not to laugh. Mr. Hartley laughed rather too much, belatedly realizing her earnestness; and Mr. Mornay's eyes came alight though he said nothing.

Ariana then turned to Miss Dorsett. "And you, Miss Dorsett? Do you know of any house of worship we should all endeavour to see?"

Miss Dorsett considered the question a moment, then said, "I think perhaps St. Paul's for its architecture after the way you have described it. You make it sound fascinating." As an afterthought she added, "And, I assure you, Miss Forsythe, I attend church every week." Ariana offered a companionable smile.

The bridge toward Vauxhall was a toll road, and it slowed their progress, but soon they had reached the gardens and were out of the carriage. Mr. Hartley, the self-appointed tour guide, turned to Ariana with enthusiasm.

"This is a famous site, Miss Forsythe, that you will surely appreciate. The gardens are lovely and there are many little amusements within the park to keep one diverted."

Ariana was indeed struck by the natural beauty. It was early for flowers but there were primroses and crocuses, and the trees, while not yet in bud, were still a welcome sight after the drab London streets. Ariana was still unused to the sooty air and unpleasant aromas, and, worst of all, the presence of so many starkly poor people. It made her feel helpless, for she failed to devise any scheme for helping so many needy souls. This was another reason she wished to visit the charity schools and foundations begun by Christian Societies in London—of which there were many. She needed to know that much was being done and especially if there was a role for her in aiding such work. But she tried to shake off such thoughts and enjoy her surroundings.

The foursome naturally separated into couples. The others led the way, and Mr. Mornay and Ariana followed a little distance behind. Ariana exclaimed about the prettiness of the primroses and stopped to lean down and take a whiff.

Mr. Mornay took the opportunity of their being alone to say, "Miss Forsythe, I called upon you to see how you are getting on."

"Thank you for your thoughtfulness," she replied. He seemed doubly tall and imposing from where she was, near the flowers, at the moment. She came to her full height and added, "Unless Mr. Pellham refuses to recover, I may still look forward to his taking me about."

"He is still abed?" He looked surprised. "Perhaps he lacks the right medical man. I will send my doctor to see him."

Ariana started to speak her approval, but before she began, he was speaking again.

"More to the point, Ariana, I've been stricken with guilt on account of my hasty departure from you. If I had not abruptly abandoned you there would have been no rumour about a decline." He paused, searching her face. "Be plain with me. Have you been distressed?"

Ariana was taken aback by his sudden question, and by the fact he had used her Christian name. And yet it seemed quite natural for him to do so and she liked it a great deal, but it made her flush.

"I was indeed sorry." She hesitated, wondering whether to hazard the whole truth. Well, why not? Honesty had always been her policy.

"I thought I should never see you again and I was distressed on that account." She took a quick peek at his eyes. "I was not overly distressed; I do not think one could call it a decline. But I did miss your company." She couldn't help blushing furiously.

"Thank you."

"I have prayed for you often."

"*Prayed* for me?" He looked astounded.

"Yes, for your salvation. All of mankind needs salvation."

He thought, *She thinks I am the devil himself!* There was a silence then, which he broke by saying, "Then I *have* distressed you; I am sorry for it."

"My dear Mr. Mornay, you needn't be sorry." She looked up at him. "I am indebted to your kindness, and happy to pray for you. I promise you there is no one I pray for more often than you."

His brows furrowed. But any words he might have said had to wait. A voice was approaching, exclaiming, "Miss Forsythe! What a happy meeting!"

It was Mr. O'Brien coming their way in the company of a young woman and an older one.

"Did I not tell you about Miss Forsythe?" The threesome stopped near them and nodded, smilingly, at Ariana. Ahead of them, Mr.

Hartley and Miss Dorsett turned, saw the meeting, and waited, staying a polite distance away.

"Allow me to present Miss Forsythe to you, Mama!" The older lady was smiling amiably at Ariana, but Mr. Mornay broke in. In a lazy voice that belied the substance of what he spoke, he said to Mr. O'Brien: "I daresay your mama should be introduced to Miss Forsythe." His voice was lazy and light but hit its mark. There was an awkward silence during which Mr. O'Brien recognized Mr. Mornay and paled; the women lost their smiles, and Ariana felt an uncomfortable alarm. With a glowering look at her companion, Ariana said, "Do, I pray you, Mr. O'Brien, introduce me to your mama! I should be honoured to know her!"

Mr. O'Brien glanced at Mr. Mornay. "Perhaps another day, Miss Forsythe. It was an ill-timed meeting, I see. Good day." He took each lady by an arm and hurried them off.

Anticipating Ariana's reaction Mornay said, "He was thoroughly improper. You are by far the social superior and should be treated as such."

Ariana could not remain silent. "I am beyond ashamed, Mr. Mornay! How will I face Mr. O'Brien again? How can I meet his family? They are bound to think I am the most pretentious...odious—!"

"You mistake the matter," Mornay interrupted. "It was a simple enough blunder on your young friend's part, but I fail to understand why you should be the least flummoxed by it. It was their mistake, not yours."

"No! It was *your* mistake!"

The raised brows were his only response. They had reached the others, and Mr. Hartley asked if they would be agreeable to a gondola ride.

Mr. Mornay searched the sky a moment. "The wind is picking up."

Ariana looked around at the sky and there were indeed gray clouds scudding in, bringing a chilling breeze. She was happy for her warm spencer.

Mr. Hartley scoffed. "What's a little wind? Miss Dorsett has never been on a gondola and I am determined to give her the opportunity! Come, Mornay, be sporting!"

He looked at Ariana who instantly offered, "I have never been on one, either!"

"Then you ought not to miss this chance. There are costumed boatmen in Venetian-style barks," Hartley explained, to which both ladies expressed delighted anticipation. Even Mr. Mornay could not be impervious to this and he reluctantly agreed.

"If we go directly," Mr. Hartley said, "I think the weather will hold for a quick outing."

At the river they were told in stilted English that only two people per boat was the preference.

"He is a thief," warned Mr. Mornay. "I have been on one with four people, in the past."

Mr. Hartley, ever pleasant, said, "We shall have to enjoy ourselves separately. Miss Dorsett and I will go in one and you two in the next. We'll meet back on shore afterward."

⚬⚬◦⚬⚬

After Ariana had settled on a wooden seat inside the narrow vessel, holding on to the sides for support, Mr. Mornay took his seat in front of her so they faced each other. Ariana waved gaily at Miss Dorsett and Mr. Hartley in the other boat, and they waved back with equal fervor.

Soon the boats began to separate and eventually Ariana found herself virtually alone with Mr. Mornay. There were other crafts afloat, but not in their vicinity. The water became lighter and darker in appearance as the sun went alternately in and out of the heavy clouds overhead, and a breeze tugged playfully at Ariana's bonnet.

"You must endeavour to see Vauxhall at night," Mornay said. "In the summer there are fireworks most every evening."

"Yes, so I have heard," she said.

"Mr. Pellham will no doubt insist upon taking you."

"I hope he shall," Ariana said quietly.

Mornay looked at her silently for a moment, and then offered, "Have no admirers—for I'm sure there are many—offered to take you to the museums or other sights?"

Blushing, Ariana thought of the numerous young bucks that often sought her hand for the dance floor, and her cheeks grew even warmer. She had been under the suspicion for some time that her "admirers" thought, mistakenly, that she was of a rich family. For this reason, she had refused any offers for outings or sightseeings, allowing herself only a harmless dance with most gentlemen. Mr. O'Brien was an exception, as was Mr. Mornay.

As for Mr. Mornay, since he was quite rich (and therefore not seeking a fortune) and was not going to offer for her, she felt perfectly comfortable accepting his invitations for an outing, such as today's. But many of the beau monde were eagerly seeking wealthy brides, and Ariana was entitled to only a modest share of a modest estate, despite the wealthy appearance she presented. It was a difficult and precarious position to be in, and one she was not enjoying.

"There have been invitations…but I have not felt comfortable in accepting them."

"Why is that?" His voice was inquisitive and almost caring, and she wanted to tell him everything about her circumstances. She had never considered hiding them from anyone intentionally, but suddenly she felt a new, insidious fear. What if Mr. Mornay would no longer associate with her if he knew her true state of affairs?

On the other hand, if he did refuse to know her afterward, then she could only be well rid of him. A real friend would not be swayed by one's lack of wealth—wasn't that true? She peeked up at him, wondering.

"Does no one interest you?" His dark eyes were upon hers, veiled and indecipherable as always. For once, she wished she knew what lay behind that veil. But once again, she had to be honest.

"I have discovered only one gentleman with whom I can speak of spiritual things—Mr. O'Brien—who may very well never speak to me again! In addition he alone can have no false hopes regarding me, for he understands my background completely."

Mr. Mornay sat forward, studying her face. "What kind of spiritual things? And what do you mean by 'false hopes?' Answer that question first."

Ariana was silent a moment. She looked around at the water and the darkening sky, felt a breeze, and shivered. "I hardly know how to begin. You see, I am not what I appear to be."

The raised brow. The little bemused expression.

"Do go on, Ariana; I am living to hear this explanation."

"You mock me, but you will see I am in earnest!" Her face looked adorably so.

"I have no doubt whatsoever you are in earnest. Pray, continue."

She took another deep breath. "Why did you treat Mr. O'Brien so poorly?"

"Do not change the subject. I will answer that question at a later time if you insist, but you were going to explain how you are not what you appear to be."

"But this *is* to the point," she insisted. "I know why you treated him badly, but I would like you to say why, in your own words."

"You sound like my old tutor."

"Well?" Her expression was expectant. "Are you going to answer my question?"

Now Mr. Mornay sighed. "It isn't unusual for me to be unpleasant, Ariana, you surely realize that by now."

"But you can be prodigiously pleasant! Indeed, you are capable of the finest manners. There is a reason you do not like him, and it is because he is—below you. He is not wealthy, or popular, or so fashionable as you."

"To a small extent I suppose you have hit the mark." He was irritated. "What difference does it make? Are you fond of him? Did I insult the man you favour?"

"'Tisn't *that!*"

"Wait! I have it." He paused. "He is timid, devilishly boring, and shabby genteel. I daresay you won't like my saying so, but those are my reasons."

"Just as I thought!"

He smiled at the way her face puckered up in thought.

"Why do you smile?"

And then she lowered her head and covered her face with her hands to repress tears that momentarily threatened. When she was certain of having quenched them, she looked up and added, more calmly, "I find Mr. O'Brien to be courteous and gracious and above all things, interesting in his conversation! As for being 'shabby genteel,' I do not lay the blame at a man's door for what he was born into."

Mr. Mornay sat forward in concern, realizing the degree of distress she felt. Of course it was ridiculous what she was saying. People were judged by their birth, fair or not. He would have spoken, but she hadn't finished.

"You yourself would have nothing, nothing at all, if God did not see fit to give it to you! How can you be so arrogant and proud of something you merely received?"

Perhaps Mr. Mornay had not thought of his circumstances in that light for a long time. But he astonished her with his next remark, spoken lightly.

"Well, said, indeed. I am an arrogant beast and I know it. But this is nothing new. Why does it vex you so?"

"*Because*—" She was holding back tears once more, and annoyed at herself for it. "There is no reason why you should see fit to know me!"

The dark eyes beholding her sent a little spark up to their tumultuous surface.

"I have never found you to be to be overly timid," he said. "Proper, perhaps, but with a scandalous wont to speak plainly that I find wholly rejuvenating."

"But what of being shabby genteel, Mr. Mornay? Has it never occurred to you that I may be a part of that dreaded class?"

He gave her a surprised look. "Are you telling me that you are? But no, for by all appearances you must be free from that danger."

Ariana stood up in agitation.

"I told you I am not what I appear to be! Did I not say that, precisely?"

He was concerned to see her swaying in the moving boat.

"Sit down!"

"No!" She objected immediately to his tone.

"You are swaying; I will not sit by and watch you take an unwelcome swim. Now, take your seat!" This severe tone never failed to raise her own temper, and she surveyed him stubbornly. It was true she was swaying, but she had complete control of herself. The bench her legs leaned up against, though it reached only halfway above her ankles, anchored her.

"I am exceedingly sorry you have called upon me when you no longer have need to! Now that Lady Covington has withdrawn her claws from me, you are perfectly free to ignore me!"

His frown deepened further. "Ariana!" That firm, daunting voice. "*Take your seat!*" But she ignored him, focusing only on the throes of her predicament.

"Oh! My aunt has meant well, but she has ensured my ruin!" This sounded very dramatic and even Mr. Mornay had to respond.

"Whatever are you talking about!" When she did not answer but only continued to survey him with blazing eyes, he surprised her by reverting to a seldom-heard, kinder tone.

"I have upset you. You must know that my ill manners are not personal, to either you or your friend. I am afraid you are unaware of what a habitually unpleasant being I can be."

The admission did seem to help, for her expression softened.

"You know of course, that I hold you in high regard," he went on in an extra measure of appeasement that was not lost on her. At first her eyes flashed prettily but then her face sobered.

"No amount of your regard can help. 'Tis based upon an assumption about me that is not true."

His eyes darkened, and she shot forward with this: "I am not a wealthy woman, and my family is probably what you would call shabby genteel. Yes, by your standards I feel sure this is the case!"

He was silent a moment, while his thoughts sped behind his eyes. "How did your family manage your wardrobe?"

In a subdued tone, she explained. "They did not manage it. My aunt for her own sake, insisted upon embellishing my things. She has bespoken almost my entire wardrobe! She was far too extravagant but would brook no reasoning in the matter!" Shame-faced, she admitted, "I have hardly accepted any invitations from gentlemen for fear my appearance has given false hopes—I only received your attentions on account of Lady Covington, and because I knew you would not be putting your hopes on me."

There. She had told him the truth, but it had cost her no little effort, and she found, to her dismay, that she would like nothing better than to throw herself at the feet of God just now. She badly wanted to cry.

Mr. Mornay stood up and gently led her to sit, then shifted uneasily in his own seat.

"Ariana," he intoned softly, saying her name like it was silk on his tongue. "I would never have made such ill-chosen remarks had I known—"

"'Tis better you did. Now you realize who I am." Her voice sounded pitiful, and her heart beat strongly. She was shocked at the sudden anger and hopelessness she felt regarding Mr. Mornay. Why was she reacting like this? Why should she care if he never wished to see her again? Had she not already decided he was wholly unsuitable for her? He was arrogant, and his superior attitude was not to be borne! Why then was she distressed?

With such tumultuous thoughts, and finding it difficult to meet his gaze, she could not remain seated and came again to her feet. A cold breeze had picked up and it felt good across her hot face. Ariana made a pretty figure standing there inside the boat, and she raised one gloved hand to shield her eyes from a sudden streak of the near-setting sun, which had broken through the clouds. She could not make out the other boat. Her reticule hung from her wrist.

"I cannot find their boat. Perhaps they have returned to shore. May we?"

"By all means."

A surprisingly cold wind blew and Ariana shuddered. Mr. Mornay told the boatman to return them to shore, at the same time leaning forward to bring his companion back to a sitting position. Unfortunately, as the boat turned into the wind, and just as he went to reach for her, she fell sideways. With barely a gasp she went headlong into the middle of the river, just like that, making a single splash no louder than a jumping fish might have done.

Twenty-One

"*A*riana!"

Mr. Mornay leapt to prevent her from going overboard, but too late. He watched as her feet sank beneath the dark, cold water and she disappeared from sight. The sky was growing darker by the second, which in turn made the water darker.

"Stop the boat! Stop!" he ordered the boatman. After a few terrible seconds of seeing nothing, Ariana's head, covered by a dripping bonnet, struggled to the surface. She was unable to stay afloat, however, having never learned to swim, and began to flounder.

The boatman was trying desperately to turn around, but they floated farther and farther from the struggling girl. Mr. Mornay meanwhile, grumbling under his breath, undid his neckcloth and removed it. This was followed quickly by his double-breasted jacket, after which he jumped, boots and all, in a beautiful dive, into the murky water.

A strong swimmer, he swam masterfully toward Ariana, got his arm around her, and pulled her head out of the water. With an arm around her, he dragged her back toward the boat and with the help of the boatman managed to hoist her, dripping wet, aboard; then he pulled himself over the side.

Ariana was collapsed silently across a wooden bench, not able to cough or breathe. Mr. Mornay turned her over with both arms, a look of intense concern on his face. She began coughing and he lifted her up in his arms. In a minute, during which she coughed and expelled some water, she became alert.

"Are you all right?" His voice was gentle.

She nodded, but she felt ill and was feeling the shame of having caused such a disaster. Tears filled her eyes. She shivered and Mornay pulled her up to huddle against him. Spying his jacket, he managed to lean forward and clutch it and then wrap it around her shoulders. Despite a chemise beneath the thin muslin dress, Ariana's gown clung like a second skin. The bonnet was dripping large rivulets down her face and neck, and her reticule hung, dripping, from her wrist.

"Take off the bonnet," Mornay said.

She obeyed.

The weather, meanwhile, was rapidly growing worse. The mildly chilly air had completely given way to a cold front, and the threatening sky was growing darker by the second. Both of the drenched people in the boat were quickly feeling the effects of the sharp drop in temperature.

The boatman was apologizing profusely, but Ariana's companion was not in a forgiving mood. No matter it had not been the man's fault.

"Enough!" he spat out. "It will suffice if you can manage to take us ashore without another disaster!" Ariana shivered uncontrollably. The combination of cold air and frigid water, along with the frightening struggle to stay afloat, left her weak and shaking. She snuggled against Mr. Mornay, forgetting any concern other than warmth, and he allowed it, closing strong arms around her.

She felt sick and weak and full of self-reproach for her behaviour. Mr. Mornay looked helplessly at the dripping young woman in his arms, not daring to guess how he himself must look. His starched shirt was sodden and his hat (which he had forgotten to remove) was nowhere to be seen.

At the shore, there was no sign of Mr. Hartley and Miss Dorsett. Mr. Mornay managed to jump out of the boat, but this proved too much for Ariana, still weak from her brush with drowning. Her companion lifted her out. He waited to receive their remaining items, which were strewn about the craft, from the boatman. Then he started off, carrying Ariana.

"I can walk," she said uncertainly. Her rescuer ignored her.

"I am sh-sh-shaking!" She was alarmed at the violence of the tremors racking her limbs, and that she could not make them stop. Even her voice shook when she spoke. She was not sure if the trembling was on account of the cold or from fright. Perhaps both.

"Hush!" He was taking long strides, going as fast as possible, for Mr. Mornay was not impervious to the cold any more than Ariana. His garments were wet and tight and he did not have the benefit of his jacket, as she did. In addition, the water trapped in his boots was like a little extra measure of cold, and the accompanying slosh with each step was one he did not relish.

"Your c-c-coat sh-sh-should be on y-y-you."

"No." The biting air was beginning to sting. She felt awful on his account and was glad to see they were approaching the gated entrance to the gardens. Ariana's rescuer hurried forward and passed through the gate. It took only moments before they spotted his carriage. The coachman was walking the horses, but a single shout from Mr. Mornay brought them hurrying the team forward.

"Wh-wh-what of Mr. Ha-Hartley and Miss D-D-D-Dorsett?"

His reply was brusque. "Mr. Hartley and Miss Dorsett are dry; they will engage a hack. We must see to ourselves."

When the coach drew up a groom jumped from behind. "Sir! Are you well?"

'No! Open the door quickly, man!" The words sounded almost like a growl.

Once inside the carriage, he put Ariana gently upon the cushion, but she exclaimed involuntarily when she felt her cold, wet garments.

"Remove the wet spencer and then put my jacket on properly," Mornay insisted.

She stood and began to do as told while he punched the ceiling to signal his coachman to start off. She fell backward no sooner than the wheels began to turn, but he caught and steadied her. Afterward, she took her seat more carefully, hating the feel of the wet cloth against her skin. Mr. Mornay had pulled a small blanket from beneath a seat and motioned her to move beside him. For the sake of warmth they would share the same cushion.

He spread out the blanket, endeavouring to cover them both as much as possible, Ariana especially. She huddled against him as close as she dared. Then she sat up to pull her sopping half-boots off, looked at him apologetically for the delay, but proceeded to turn away and removed her soaked stockings as well. Then, satisfied there was nothing else she could do to improve her situation, she settled down against him, tucking her cold feet up, and he arranged the blanket over them again.

Funny, Ariana thought, settled there with his arm about her; what they had argued about seemed so insignificant, now. Safety and comfort had temporarily overcome all other concerns. And Mr. Mornay had been concerned about her; he had jumped in after her, despite the fact that had she listened to him earlier, she never would have fallen in. In addition, he might have ordered the boatman to rescue her. After all, he was notoriously fussy about his apparel, but he had done it himself without hesitation.

Another shiver ran through her body.

"Is it very bad?"

"No; I'm better actually. See, my voice has stopped trembling." Then, soberly. "How will you ever forgive me for this?"

He let out a small laugh. Ariana looked up sharply in surprise. He wasn't even angry!

"Somehow, I never need to forgive you for anything," he said. "Unlike nearly everyone else I know!"

There was a little smile on his mouth. But Ariana looked quickly away. They were much closer than usual and it was disconcerting, to say the least.

"But it was my fault."

"I upset you. It was my fault."

"You are determined to think so, I see, and I, for once, will not argue with you."

They both smiled knowingly at that.

The coachman was doing his best but the roads were crowded and their progress was slow. Ariana was uncomfortable and still could not feel fully warm, though of course it was immeasurably nicer huddling against the warmth and strength of her companion in the carriage, than it had been outside. As she squirmed about trying to find a warmer position, Mr. Mornay made a clucking sound with his tongue and lifted her off the seat, onto his lap. He then adjusted the blanket so that she was entirely covered.

"Forgive me," he said, as he lifted her. "But I think this is necessary. Perhaps in future you shall see the wisdom in heeding my instructions." There was a playful inflection in his tone and she wanted to glance at him to smile, but she dared not. Their faces might touch if she did. (Just the thought made her blush.) But she had to sigh with contentment at feeling the first real comfort since her mishap.

The carriage finally drew up outside her aunt's house. Mornay lifted her off his lap and began to rise from his seat.

"Do not trouble yourself to come in! I can walk now, I am feeling much improved," she insisted.

"Without your boots on?" he murmured, going past her to exit the carriage ahead of her. When she came forth, grimacing at the blast of cold air which hit her, he took her right up in his arms as before. Ariana had her bonnet, spencer, half boots, and stockings in her arms, as well as the sopping reticule, but she let them fall on her lap so she could entwine one arm around his neck. She felt more secure that way.

When they reached the front door it opened ahead of them, since Haines had a man watching for Miss Forsythe's return to report to his mistress.

Ariana looked up at the stern, handsome face and apologized. "I am sorry now that I took my boots off, making you do this again."

"I should have done so in any case," he said.

That silenced her for the time being. A much astonished Haines received them, trying not to gawk openly at the sight of the Paragon looking all undone, carrying a sodden Miss Forsythe into the house as if it were not the least unusual. Moreover, she was wearing a man's jacket and was barefooted!

Mr. Mornay marched right into the house and up the staircase. Passing the best parlour he strode determinedly on, toward the bedchambers, Ariana still ensconced snugly in his arms.

"Which is your chamber?" he asked mildly, as if he was likely to carry her into her bedchamber on any number of occasions.

"Second door on the right," she uttered, feeling dazed. Molly, large-eyed, froze at sight of them, just watching, until sight of Mr. Mornay's expression sent her scurrying to open the door ahead of them. He moved past her to lay his charge gently down upon the chintz-covered bed.

"Raise the fire!" His bark caught Molly, who was still looking on in wonderment, by surprise, that she jumped, but then dropped a split-second curtsey and scrambled to the hearth. There was already a small flame in the grate, so her task was not difficult. Mr. Mornay was used to giving orders and continued, "Call the maid to help Miss Forsythe with her clothing."

He turned to Ariana. "You need to change out of your wet things immediately."

"Yes, but you must stay and warm yourself," she said.

"Only for a moment."

The servants began scurrying about, the word having spread that some accident had befallen the pair, and that they were thoroughly soaked. Mrs. Bentley's voice could be heard shouting orders shrilly. She soon appeared looking bewildered and concerned.

She saw Mr. Mornay and put her hand to her heart.

"Mornay, for pity's sake! What has happened?" She went to Ariana and felt her skin. "Dreadfully cold!"

Mr. Mornay gave her a short account, laying out it had been an accident caused by the boatman's hasty turning of the vessel.

"You both fell in?" she asked, doubtfully.

"No, ma'am, I fell in," Ariana said. "Mr. Mornay rescued me."

Mrs. Bentley, still wearing a look of great consternation, ushered Ariana off her bed and behind a screen where she and Harrietta hurriedly stripped her of the wet items and put a warm, dry nightdress on her. Another housemaid, meanwhile, changed the damp blanket on the bed to a good, dry one. Ariana resumed her place, this time beneath the sheets, and sat up looking charming beneath a large white cap with laced edging to keep her head warm.

Mrs. Bentley continued to shout orders. "Harrietta—a hot bath up here as soon as possible!" "Hot tea for Miss Forsythe." "Tell cook to make a compress!" "No, Betty, get the woolen blankets! And do not dawdle!" She turned to Mr. Mornay. "I will have you taken care of in the next room."

"I thank you, no, I must be off."

She studied his face a moment, as if she couldn't believe what she'd heard. "But, you are wet and cold! And with this frightful turn in the weather. Of all the bad timing! So unseasonable and chilling. I cannot allow it, not even for you, Mornay!"

He walked over to the fire and stood close by it for some moments, stretching out his hands, and felt some relief. But the thought of his own fire and house, so near by, beckoned to him as the place he'd be most comfortable.

"I am obliged, but no." He went to Ariana's bedside and reached for her hand.

"Do let my aunt provide you with some warm attire!" she insisted. She was horrified he meant to continue home without help. "I am sure she possesses some fine clothing of my uncle's."

The fact that Mr. Bentley had been dead for nearly a decade and that his clothing would be dreadfully outdated did not matter a whit to Ariana. But of course it mattered very much to Mr. Mornay, even in this dire circumstance, for he declined hastily with an odd look on his face.

"I regret our outing met with such disaster." He smiled ruefully, still holding her hand.

"It was all my wicked doing! I am dreadfully sorry!"

"See that you eat something, and keep to your bed for awhile. I have no doubt I shall do the same."

"I pray you do." She had a thought. "What of your friends? I am distressed we had to abandon them."

"I'll send a carriage." With that, he dropped a soft kiss on her hand and a polite bow, then turned to leave. He stopped to tell Ariana's chaperon to send him word when she was certain Ariana was recovered. And then he was gone. Mrs. Bentley was standing in the background, all eyes, and her little mind was spinning wheels. First she saw to it that a few good, warm blankets were sent off with Mr. Mornay. Then she came back to Ariana, all in a flutter.

A servant followed with a tea tray, and Mrs. Bentley poured a cup of the steaming liquid for her niece.

"Here, drink this quickly. It will warm you on the inside." While she sipped, her aunt hovered nearby, pacing and thinking and then asked for Ariana's recounting of what had happened upon the water. After hearing the full account, far from being angry at Ariana's petulance and stubbornness, Aunt Bentley seemed excited.

"Mr. Mornay has called upon you when he no longer needs to; Lady Covington's accusations are wholly forgotten. I think it signifies! And the way he parted from you just now. I maintain I have never, in all my days, seen that man speak so kindly to anyone. And he kissed your hand so gently."

"But I was rather ill when he first took me from the water," Ariana said. "I don't know if I was breathing. I think it must have affected him. He is not heartless, you know."

Mrs. Bentley continued her thought. "Indeed, Ariana, under normal circumstances I should think an incident like today's would have sent the Paragon into a fury such as would make a body quake to be near him. But no, he was hardly concerned about his own condition or discomfort—not even his clothing! He looked only to you." The more she thought on it, the more she was convinced that Mr. Phillip Mornay had a serious *tendre* for her niece. She was cautiously ecstatic;

it would be delicate going from here on. Mr. Mornay was not someone to be easily managed.

"My dear Aunt," Ariana said, seeing that familiar scheming look on the lady's face. "I daresay you are presuming too much. Mr. Mornay has no intentions toward me."

"He is not the sort of man to take up a flirtation. If he continues his interest with you then I shall be convinced." A knock at the door revealed four footmen who shuffled into the room carrying a large tub of steaming water. After they had gone, and Ariana was luxuriating in the glorious warmth, her aunt came and stood nearby. Momentarily, she asked, "If Mornay is interested in you, will you encourage him?" It had suddenly occurred to her that perhaps her niece was hindering the matter, not helping it as she ought.

Ariana decided she must end her aunt's speculations quite firmly. "Just today, Aunt, he made it abundantly clear that he despises members of my class!" Her voice was earnest or her aunt would have doubted her hearing.

"Fustian! Your class is the same as mine, and while I grant that he seems generally to despise the majority of people, he does not despise you, no matter what your class. I tell you, upon my word, if Mr. Mornay decides to hold you in favour, he shall do so, devil may care what your circumstances!" After a moment's thought she added, "He does not need a fortune, goodness knows, and he should likely be quite content to have a bride who can wear all the mode to his fastidious satisfaction." She looked at her niece. "Some women look absurd with the least little feather on their bonnets, but not you, my dear. You will do him credit, I assure you."

Ariana sighed deeply. "Do not place your hopes on the match, Aunt. I myself have no such expectation, and I am certain Mr. Mornay's thoughts are equally wide of that mark." She looked plaintively up at the dowager. "May I get out, now? I think I'm hungry."

Twenty-Two

*L*ater that week Mrs. Bentley sent word to inquire after Mr. Mornay, and dared to include an invitation for tea, if he was well. Unfortunately, he was not. He had suffered the cold longer than Ariana, taken a stiff drink when he reached home, and was now laid up with an ague that, according to his doctor, threatened to turn into pleurisy if he was not careful.

He sent round a polite apology, mentioning how pleased he was to learn that Ariana was completely recovered; a fact which Mrs. Bentley attributed to his hasty intervention on her behalf.

Ariana was conscience-stricken, knowing her stubbornness was to blame for the entire incident. She hesitated over whether to send an apology, a letter of thanks, or both. In the meantime, Mr. O'Brien called. It was an awkward meeting, but Ariana was sincerely relieved to see him.

"I am so obliged you have come." She offered him a seat with an outstretched arm.

"Thank you, Miss Forsythe. I felt it necessary to apologize for what happened."

"Oh, I beg you, do not even think of it." Her face grew rosy. "Mr. Mornay was in the wrong, I assure you."

"Apologize?" Mrs. Bentley had come to attention. "For what?"

"There is no need," Ariana insisted.

"It is generous of you to say so." Mr. O'Brien was all admiration.

"No need for what? Apologize for what?" A chaperon had to know! "No, not generous, only fair. I assure you it was all a mistake."

"You are too good, Miss Forsythe." The young man was relieved and pleased. "And perhaps I may bring my sister with me on my next call? She is still intent on meeting you, as well as my mama."

"Your *mama?*" The indignant tone of the older lady suddenly captured their attention, and they turned to face Mrs. Bentley. She had a newspaper before her and was sitting on a wing chair, adjacent to the pair.

"Oh, yes, ma'am. I have told her of Miss Forsythe's superior qualities—"

"Young man." Aunt Bentley's voice was severe. "You hardly know my niece! I think it is too soon to bring your family to meet her." This set-down was sufficiently humiliating that Mr. O'Brien only mumbled, "I beg your pardon."

Ariana was astonished at her relation and hurried to change the topic.

"And what have you been reading for devotions of late, Mr. O'Brien? I love to hear what others are learning of our faith."

✦✦✦✦✦

Mr. O'Brien called again the next morning. And the two days following that. Over the course of these visits he and Ariana had discussed his family, her family, the royal family, and today, the future family he hoped to have. Mrs. Bentley did not like the subject, feeling correctly that he was alluding to his wish to include Ariana in his plans. The younger girl sensed the same thing. She tried to envision the family he spoke of, children around the table, with her as the mother. But something did not feel right, and her smiles faltered during the discussion.

She felt the Lord had sent Mr. O'Brien to steady her confused soul, to be the beacon of light she needed during these trying times of tumultuous happenings with Mr. Mornay. So why was there hesitation regarding him in her soul? It was different from the way she hesitated over Mr. Mornay. With that man, her heart was in danger, but her head knew he was not suitable. With Mr. O'Brien, the opposite was true. In her heart, she couldn't quite fully embrace him, though her head assured her he was perfect husband-material.

Her aunt's assertions that Mr. Mornay might be entertaining a *tendre* for her had sent her into a frightful discomposure for just these reasons. She liked Mr. Mornay overmuch, though he was not at all the sort of man she ought to like. Mr. O'Brien, on the other hand, was the kind of gentleman who should have set her heart dreaming, but, no sooner than he left her, she would find herself wondering when she would next see the other man.

Her prayer times were now full of self-reproaches, and she earnestly sought the Lord's help. *If it is Your will, take away this foolish, foolish attraction to Mr. Mornay, and show me, please, if Mr. O'Brien is the man You have chosen for me. I am a senseless, emotional creature! You must change my heart, and my feelings, to comply with Your plan!*

To her mind, it was impossible that God could be actually leading her and Mr. Mornay together (though she would have liked to think it so), for that gentleman, though not without good qualities, was not a man of faith. Disqualified, therefore. No exceptions. She had been raised to marry a man who lived by his religion, and the Paragon did not.

Mr. O'Brien, on the other hand, had grown up in the faith, and was intent on becoming a clergyman for all the best reasons. To preach the gospel. To better society. To extend charity.

Now, if he made her an offer, what could be easier to decipher as God's will?

⋙ઝ⋘

Nearly two weeks had passed, with no further word from Mr. Mornay. Ariana was worried about him. Was he dangerously ill? She might have inadvertently ruined his existence!

She had all along continued to pray for his health and well-being, but when no news came she ventured to suggest she and her aunt call upon him. It was not done for ladies to call upon a gentleman, and she expected a fight with her aunt, but there was none. This should have warned her that Mrs. Bentley had some scheme in mind, but Ariana, not the scheming sort herself, was blithely unaware, and pleased that her aunt had agreed.

Mrs. Bentley in fact was delighted at the idea, and did not divulge that she knew for a certainty Mr. Mornay had been steadily recovering, and would likely have soon called upon them. Instead, she instructed Haines to summon the carriage.

Ariana began to regret her suggestion after it was so joyously received, but there was no shirking it now. And perhaps the encounter would put to rest these absurd notions of her aunt's regarding Mr. Mornay's interest in her.

∽∽◌∾∾

The butler at Grosvenor Square received the ladies doubtfully, taking Mrs. Bentley's card, but leaving them in the hall until he consulted his master. When he returned, it was clear he was cognizant of having erred in their regard, and his manner became apologetically gracious. They were ushered cordially upstairs into the first floor drawing room, and served excellent tea. Mr. Mornay, they were told, would be in attendance momentarily.

When he entered the room a few minutes later, Ariana felt a strange mix of emotions. Her stomach gave a small lurch at sight of him. She was heartily glad to see him, remorseful for the trouble she had caused him, and suddenly felt shy when thinking of their last encounter. *Had she really sat upon his lap?*

He looked to be in good spirits, was dressed in his usual faultless style, but his face bore the evidence of having been ill. His eyes were shadowed, it seemed to her, and his manner almost entirely without the playful tension he seemed to thrive upon. He bowed politely and took a seat across from them in the well-appointed French-style parlour.

The room was fittingly masculine and yet no less elegant than Mrs. Bentley's parlour. Dark woodwork framed the doorways and walls, and wainscoting filled the lower half while the upper was Sevres blue. The mantel was crowned with greenery, two matching Chinoiserie vases, and a small Romanesque statue. The windows were draped with heavy gold and blue fabric with golden tassels at the edges.

When he had thanked them for troubling to visit, Mr. Mornay rested his eyes upon Ariana, and remarked that she was looking in as fine health as he had ever seen her. Something about his manner made it evident to Ariana he was not the least bit changed toward her despite the revelation of her circumstances. Suddenly she was very glad she had thought to visit.

"Much improved," he replied when questioned about his own health. He didn't offer details of the near two weeks of misery he had suffered. Somehow, however, Ariana knew. She could see it on his face.

"I can hardly tell you how dreadfully sorry I have been, Mr. Mornay," she offered. "If I only were not so foolishly stubborn!"

"If you were not so foolishly stubborn," he returned smartly, "I daresay your company would not be as entertaining as it is." They smiled at each other. Mrs. Bentley's eyes lit up at this announcement; her mind turned cartwheels. But she was in a flummox about how to confront the man. She wanted to come straight to the point and demand to know if he had intentions toward her niece, but one did not make demands on Mr. Mornay. His temper was famous and she had no desire to find herself at the brunt of it. Ariana, of course, would be mortified at the least mention of the topic, but that did not signify. There were things a chaperon had to know!

Suddenly she hit upon an idea: She would propose a social function and ask him point blank to guarantee making an appearance. He was known to be fussy about these things, and passed up twice as many invitations as he received. So she could be fairly confident of the matter by his response. But what sort of function? What could it be?

The answer, of course, was obvious. A ball was the thing. She could just envision the little printed invitation:

Mrs. Agatha Bentley requests the pleasure of Mr. Phillip Mornay's company at an Evening Party, on Friday, 4ᵗʰ June. An answer will oblige. Dancing.

While she was thinking thus, she found the eyes of their host upon her. Those piercing eyes, looking through to her soul! Or so it seemed, and without further contemplation, she found herself issuing the invitation. "My dear Mr. Mornay, I intend to hold a ball in Ariana's honour, and may I hope to be sure of your coming?"

Ariana's mouth nearly dropped open, for she had been given no information regarding such a thing. Further, was it polite to ask him outright as she had done? Her face took on a rosy hue.

But Mrs. Bentley was determined to have some insight into the matter of where his feelings lay. She smiled nervously and waited, ready to celebrate a victory, but Mr. Mornay's countenance was not promising.

He glanced at Ariana. "I should rather speak to you privately but since Ariana is no stranger to what I am about to say, I will speak in her presence." He paused and sighed.

"Mrs. Bentley, I commend you for wanting the best for your niece. If, after we have spoken, you still wish to go forward with this scheme, I will give you my word to attend your affair—assuming I am able to. However—" His look became severe. "You are making things exceedingly difficult for Ariana. How is she to find the match she desires, and can hope to win, while you shamelessly embellish her appearance so? You are putting her forward in society in a way that is not honest. If it is discovered she is not from the sort of family she appears to be from, there will be no less than a scandal."

Mrs. Bentley's face became alarmingly red.

Mercilessly, Mr. Mornay continued. "I doubt even I could rescue her from a second scandal!"

Taking a moment to recover from the shock of such a direct challenge, Mrs. Bentley made her reply. "Ariana is my niece and her family is of spotless reputation! I can see no difficulty there, sir!" Her voice was fraught with indignation. Ariana saw that Mrs. Bentley's fingers gripped her reticule so tightly her knuckles were white. The younger girl sat by, tense and unhappy, not knowing what to say.

Mr. Mornay, cool as always, wasn't the least put out. "She is not, however, a great fortune. How is she to know a true friend from a grasping one? I am convinced, as you must be yourself, that that handful of idiotic admirers who run after her at every social function think she is an heiress."

Now Mrs. Bentley's face froze in horrified disbelief. But she rallied her strength with sudden conviction, and it was such a strong conviction that even Mr. Mornay's severe countenance could not prevent her from voicing it. She cried, in response to his undeserved accusation, "Most of the young bucks these days, sir, give Ariana a wide berth, and for only one reason: because they think she is yours!" With a great deep breath, and in a rare, triumphant tone, she continued. "Mr. Mornay! If anyone is responsible for putting her forward in society, it is *you* more than I!" Mrs. Bentley's eyes were wide with the power of righteous indignation. "You have taken her to Carlton House, danced with her, taken her to the opera and ballet! The theatre! These are no small things!" She gave a magnificent pause to let him digest what she had said, and added, in a less agonized tone, "It gives one the impression, does it not, that if the venerable Mr. Mornay knows and approves of this gel, then she must be of excellent standing. And for that matter, though she is not to inherit a fortune, she does have claim to a respectable sum!"

He sat transfixed, a small smile coming upon his features.

"Upon my word," he breathed, rubbing his chin thoughtfully. "I suppose I *am* guilty in the matter."

Ariana's face was stiff with restraint for she was endeavouring not to protest. She was feeling terribly hurt, despite the fact that everything which had been said about her was true.

Mr. Mornay, his eyes alight with mirth, looked at Ariana and then back to Mrs. Bentley.

"They're keeping away from her still, you say? And on my account? Cowards! I would have thought my absence from town—and from her side—was enough for anyone who wished to approach her to do so. And for Ariana to encourage someone. But that brings us right back to the problem, does it not? Whom can she encourage?"

Mrs. Bentley did not hesitate to press her advantage, for this was precisely the question she hoped herself to settle once and for all.

"Obviously," she intoned, "it would be a man who has not whittled away his fortune at cards or debauchery as have so many men these days. It would have to be a man who does not need a wealthy bride; it would have to be a man like—*you!*"

Ariana breathed in sharply from shock. The words hung in the air, while that queer little smile played about Mr. Mornay's mouth, though his brows were raised. Mrs. Bentley sat still, her eyes large in her face and her heart beat almost painfully in her chest. What would he say to *that?*

But the answer never came. Before he could reply, Ariana shot up out of her chair. She could tolerate the situation no longer.

"This cannot be borne! Mr. Mornay!" She turned to him in glorious indignation. "I *forbid* you to say another word!"

His eyes were not without compassion, but he couldn't erase the smile upon his face. This was exactly the kind of behaviour in Ariana he most enjoyed. Mrs. Bentley's countenance, meanwhile, had fallen mightily. This was exactly the kind of behaviour in Ariana she most dreaded.

Ariana, heedless of her aunt's reproving demeanour, continued. "Aunt Bentley, I pray you would not…force the matter! I am not ruined by your generosity or by Mr. Mornay's past attentions! I expect any day to receive an offer that I intend to accept, and therefore all of this is entirely unnecessary!"

And then, striding for the formal double doors of the room, she announced, "Please. We must go."

Mr. Mornay's eyes followed her.

"An offer from whom?" His tone conveyed that he had every right to know.

Ariana glanced at him, startled, but ignored the question, her hand upon the doorknob.

"Come, please, Aunt, we have presumed upon Mr. Mornay's hospitality long enough."

"Ariana! An offer from whom? You said you expected any day to receive an offer. What is the name of the gentleman, if you please?"

Ariana hesitated. She did not want to admit that she did not know of a certainty that Mr. O'Brien was about to offer for her, as she had rashly stated. It had seemed that way, to be sure, but what if she was wrong? She could not say his name. Her aunt, to her surprise, came to her rescue.

"I imagine 'tis that young sprig, O'Brien!" Her distaste for him was evident.

Mr. Mornay's swirling eyes turned darkly upon Ariana.

"O'Brien!"

Ariana refused to meet his eyes and clutched the doorknob tighter. From behind her, he added, "Surely we can do better than that."

What did he mean, *we?*

"Mr. O'Brien is perfectly respectable!" She had turned to face both of the others with this exclamation.

Mrs. Bentley let out a moan. "Respectable, indeed!"

"I will not discuss this!" Ariana gave Mr. Mornay a hurried curtsey, and babbled, "I am greatly relieved to see you are recovered…and… and much obliged for the tea!" Again she took hold of the doorknob, this time starting to turn it. Mr. Mornay jumped to his feet and strode quickly to her and took her hand.

She endeavoured to pull it away, but he held it fast; and addressed her aunt.

"Mrs. Bentley, are you indeed allowing O'Brien enough time to press his suit with your niece? In view of your, eh, largess toward her, did you not expect to net a higher yield?"

"Mr. Mornay, I resent that!" Ariana's eyes blazed at him.

"Oh, but she did!" He had to laugh as he spoke. "She expected *me!*"

"I daresay I did *not* expect an offer from you." Mrs. Bentley was also offended, although what he had said was quite true.

Ariana managed to loosen her hand from his and snatched it away. Without a word she turned on her heel and opened the door and hurried from the room.

Mrs. Bentley turned to the Paragon. "There, you have offended her."

"And so have you," he said, unpleasantly.

The chaperon did not know what else to say. She stood up to leave, but had a thought.

"I shall send an invitation for the ball, which I mean to hold."

"Do that." His dark eyes were indecipherable.

As Mrs. Bentley descended the stairway, she decided she could not be angry with Ariana. None of this confusion was truly her fault. It concerned her, but she had not done anything amiss. In addition—and this was the strongest factor which influenced her just now—it seemed to her that despite all he had said, Mr. Mornay cared about her niece after all. He did not wish to admit the fact, but the conviction that he did, of a surety, feel more for Ariana than he had expressed, was from that day on a constant thought with her. What to do about it was the question. Mr. Mornay might take himself off once the season ended. Most of the upper class families abandoned town as soon as Parliament shut its doors. That signified the end of the season. What if Mr. Mornay did the same? There had to be something a chaperon could do!

She thought of the upcoming ball in her home and a little light went on in her head. *The ball's the thing, in which to catch the conscience of the king!* If a king's conscience could be caught, she reasoned, nodding her head silently, then surely Mr. Mornay must be vulnerable—to the right plan. And it must be soon. Before the season ends. Hadn't Mornay as much as promised to attend their ball? This meant she could count on his coming—and plan for it.

Twenty-Three

*M*rs. Bentley was not sorry she had suggested giving a ball. True, she had not thought of doing so in the past, for it was a great trouble and a great expense, particularly since she had put forth so much for Ariana already. In addition, one was never certain it would be a success. But with Ariana so popular, and Mr. Mornay promising to attend, a success was virtually guaranteed.

Mornay had been perfectly on the mark in suggesting that she, Mrs. Bentley, was hoping for a greater catch than O'Brien. And if the Paragon never did come round, then all the more reason to encourage Ariana to realize there were many, many other fish in the sea.

Some of the possibilities, in fact, were of the peerage. Although her niece did not possess a fortune, she had beauty, grace, and charm, and even, occasionally, the odd touch of wit. (Not to mention a rich aunt with good taste and connexions!) These endowments had caused many an uneven match in the past, and were sure to do so in Ariana's case. The thing was certain to happen; it was only a matter of time...

∽∾⊙∾∾

Ariana realized her aunt was placing exceptional hopes upon the upcoming ball, for she insisted on taking her shopping for a new gown for the occasion. And that was only the beginning of a spree of amazing expenditures that made Ariana quake in her shoes. She tried to dissuade her aunt on the grounds there was no guarantee of her ever being reimbursed. Mrs. Bentley had got the idea in her head, however, that Mr. Mornay was eventually going to offer for her niece, and, in view of that, could any expense be considered too great?

She had firm ideas of what sort of gown she wanted for Ariana, but the first modiste they visited, a Frenchwoman, insisted that Ariana's gown could not be too sophisticated. Was not mademoiselle a debutante? It did not become women so young to wear gowns more fitting for seasoned ladies. Ariana agreed heartily and urged her aunt to listen. But Mrs. Bentley was offended and ended up taking them elsewhere. They returned to the busy street.

"To get the match we are seeking, we need a little more incentive."

"But I do not seek a high match! You are bringing this requirement upon me if you insist upon spending so much!" Ariana had to hiss beneath her breath so that passersby did not hear this exchange, for it would no doubt have caused much mirth. Her words were in vain, however, as her aunt ignored her. Still, she implored, "My family will never be able to repay you—and then you will not take my sisters when they come of age."

Her aunt gave her a doubtful look. "Do not fret about repaying me. I never required it. But getting the right husband for you will be satisfying, indeed."

Ariana's heart sank. But she determined never to agree to a match that failed to honour her family or her own convictions. As they stepped up into the next seamstress's shop, she ventured to remind her aunt of the lovely pink and gray net gown she'd worn to Carlton House. It was at the house, waiting for another use.

"Allow me to be the judge of what is suitable," Aunt Bentley said. "You take too much upon yourself. If you must know, I feel Mr. Mornay has more of a *tendre* for you than he allows. You must appear in as sophisticated apparel as we can manage."

"Is that why? For Mr. Mornay?"

When her aunt did not bother to answer, she added, hoping to sound ominous, "This is my first season, and he of all men will be sensible of my being dressed unsuitably!"

"You have the style and the presence to wear the gown I have in mind for you." While they waited to be helped, she added, "His bachelorhood is famous, and no doubt difficult to give up. He needs a little more incentive." She looked steadily at Ariana for a few moments. "I feel very strongly, Ariana, that you *will* be his wife."

"But the man denied outright that he has intentions toward me, Aunt! What could be clearer?" Bitterly, she added, "He actually laughed at the idea, do you not recall?" A tear popped into her eyes, but she hastily shook it away. Why on earth should she cry about that?

Mrs. Bentley looked at her almost fondly. "I am satisfied upon this point, Ariana, and I mean only to help him grow aware of it."

～♡～

There was a ball at the Seton's a few days after the shopping. During the interval the Paragon had called upon Ariana and taken her out in his open gig. Before they even left the curb he inquired mildly whether Ariana had yet received an offer from Mr. O'Brien, to which she coloured, since she had not. But she was relieved to own that Mr. O'Brien had been away visiting family.

When she next saw him at the Seton's ball, the evening was well past its peak. Ariana had been anxious for the night to be over, but her spirits perked up when she noticed his tall head above the crowd coming toward her. Her stomach gave its customary lurch, and she was thankful to be seated upon a cushioned wall bench taking a rest as he drew up to her. He was gallant as usual, and sat beside her after making his signature polite bow.

Ariana waited for him to begin the conversation.

"How do you find the ball?"

"I have stood up for nearly every dance," was her evasive reply.

"Excellent." At that moment, a Mr. Chesley returned to Ariana with two cups of lemonade in his hands. He was a second son who could look forward to one thousand a year, but when he saw Mr. Mornay sitting beside the delightful Miss Forsythe, his face sank.

"I say, Mornay," he said grudgingly, as he handed one cup to Ariana. "This seat was taken. Miss Forsythe is no doubt too polite to inform you that I only left to get us some refreshment."

"Very good of you," was the maddening response. He relieved Mr. Chesley of the other cup, ignored the glaring eyes and compressed lips and added, "I wish to speak with Miss Forsythe. We'll let you know when your attentions are required."

Ariana had not objected to Mr. Chesley's attentions. He was a vicar's son, first of all, which raised him inestimably in her sight, and he had asked to stand up with her two times. She was far from inclined to object to Mr. Mornay, however, so she said nothing, but smiled weakly at Mr. Chesley, who, inspired by that little kindness, dared to face the giant.

"This is just your style, Mornay! Shouldn't you be at White's or Boodles?"

Mr. Mornay was not a stranger to either of the gentlemen's clubs, but he merely eyed the younger man with disdain.

"Tsk, tsk, Mr. Chesley, have a temper, do we? Do not provoke me, my boy, for I guarantee you shall regret it." Mr. Chesley's face glowered angrily and he stood there for a moment deciding whether to respond; but then Mr. Mornay added, in a light, venomous voice, "Be off with you!"

Young Chesley bowed stiffly to Ariana, glared again at Mr. Mornay, and turned on his heel, stomping away across the room. Ariana turned gently accusing eyes upon her companion.

"Was that necessary?"

"I only, ever, do what is necessary."

She took a breath, and hazarded a second question. "Do you disapprove of Mr. Chesley?"

Mr. Mornay met her gaze and then answered lazily. "Oh, not in any important way. Just your run-o'-the mill devil's cub, you know. Beginning to kick at the bit, too. If he keeps it up, I may even manage to like him."

"Why do you call him a devil's cub? He is the son of a vicar!"

"'Tis just an expression." Then, "Are you particularly fond of him?" He looked into her eyes as he asked.

She looked out at the ballroom, uncomfortable beneath the gaze that always made her feel as if he could see right through her.

"I hardly know him. But I should endeavour to defend anyone from being called a 'devil's cub,' unless it were patently true."

If he did not feel remorse, he at least apologized prettily, begging her pardon and vowing never to call any other young sprig a "devil's cub" in her presence. Ariana smiled, her light tan eyes flecked with gold beneath the lights of dozens and dozens of candles overhead in chandeliers. They sat chatting after that for nearly fifteen minutes. Mr. Mornay's conversation afforded her no small pleasure, for he was one of the few people who did not harp upon Mr. S____'s fortune, or Lady P____'s jewels, and so on. She had acquired a disgust of such gossip in an amazingly short time.

Just then, the Master of Ceremonies announced the next dance would be the last for the night. Mr. Mornay looked at her.

"I hope you are not engaged, for I've a notion to dance with you. If," he added politely, "you would grant me the honour?"

For a moment, her heart soared, but then Ariana frowned. If only he had asked this of her at any previous ball.

"I should be very glad to, I assure you, but my aunt has forbidden me to accept any invitation to dance."

He looked at her silently a moment. "Did you not say you had been dancing this evening?"

She met his gaze with difficulty. "Yes. I am afraid this applies only to...you." She shrank from saying it, and looked at him apologetically.

"Only to me? Where is your aunt?" His voice did not sound angry or even venomous as she well knew it could, but the set of his jaw was not promising.

"She only means to—"

"She means to plague me!" But there was a droll expression about his mouth as if he recognized the situation was not without humour. He came to his feet, and Mr. Chesley, who was watching them with eagle eyes from across the large room, came to attention. Perhaps Mornay was leaving, he thought. But no. He watched while the man he detested held out his arm to the charming Miss Forsythe, who stood up uncertainly.

He took her by the elbow and led her forth.

"You cannot mean to make me disobey my aunt?"

"No. But was this your wish, as well?"

"Not in the least, I assure you."

He was silent a moment. "Is it true the young men are avoiding you on my account?"

"Only when you are present. And I must say 'tis a welcome relief!"

"Am I frightening away a man you admire now?" He looked briefly about the room.

"No, I promise you, you are not."

"Then the only reason she denies me your company on the dance floor is to vex me." He had to smile. "Your aunt means to make it a battle, does she?"

"No, surely not." She felt an alarm at the idea. Mr. Mornay always won his battles, and she did not want him under the impression that her chaperon wished to take him on. He was silent another moment, still leading her past all the dancers with one hand propelling her by the arm, keeping close behind her. When they reached a quieter space he stopped and faced her.

"I hope you would say so, Ariana, if you preferred that I keep my distance from you. Do not be so missish that you fail to let me know." When he paused, waiting for her to speak, her feelings were so much the opposite that all she could safely do was to shrug her shoulders.

"What, me, turn away the Paragon?" she said in a teasing tone.

"Do not call me that. I am acutely conscious of how little I fit that description."

"I beg your pardon," she said, touched by his admission.

He now continued leading them slowly from the ballroom.

"Is Mr. O'Brien aware you are disposed to accept his offer?" This seemed an abrupt change of subject, but she went with it.

"I think not." A second later she added, "I am uncertain, actually, regarding the matter. I made that rash statement at your house because my aunt mortified me!"

He stopped. "Do you mean, he is not preparing to offer for you?"

"Oh, I think he is. But whether I shall accept him is not certain. I am determined to be open-minded; I enjoy his company, and he is intent on entering the church."

A raised brow and a little smile. "Is that all it takes to gain your approval?" He had a further thought but did not speak it: That anyone with the right connexions and the money could enter the church.

Ariana's face was flushed, however, for it occurred to her that had Mr. O'Brien been intent on any other occupation, he would immediately have appeared less eligible to her. Mr. Mornay was exactly right! It was that easy to gain her approval! It was a terrible realization.

"Is something wrong?"

She looked up at him, but had no words to say what she felt.

"What is it? You are not well."

"No. I am not." She was oddly at a loss and just looked at him helplessly.

"I will see you home."

She always enjoyed his self-assurance, and he displayed it now, putting her hand firmly upon his arm and taking her toward the hall and door.

"I am not ill, precisely." She did want to leave, though. She had been bored for much of the evening, finding a commonplace ball was no longer something to excite her sensibilities. Mr. Mornay was virtually the only man she would have delighted to dance with, and her aunt had denied her that pleasure. And now, having suddenly realized the shallowness of her attraction to Mr. O'Brien, it threw into sharp relief all of the stronger, truer feelings she had been fighting to suppress for Mr. Mornay.

"I must find Aunt Bentley," she said. "To let her know." He changed direction, going toward the room set aside for cards. Her aunt often abandoned the ballroom in favor of the card table, though she played strictly for small wagers only. She was far too sensible to hazard great sums. In addition, she had seen Ariana happily dancing enough nights away to know the girl would be fine left to herself. She did not need her aunt hovering about at every occasion, after all.

Thus, they found her engaged in a game of whist. It was the start of the third rubber but she would not be ready to leave until it had finished.

Mrs. Bentley saw Mr. Mornay and felt a twinge of satisfaction. He had come to complain about being banned, had he? But then she noticed Ariana looking strained; so when he informed her he would be escorting the girl home, she could only eye him doubtfully. She would have liked to deny him—and somehow she felt he knew it—but she was losing the present game and wanted to regain her few pounds. In addition, the ladies around the table were impressed that the Paragon was prepared to see her niece home. Under the circumstances, how could she say no?

Mr. Mornay was not one to miss an advantage when it came his way. In minutes, therefore, he was handing Ariana into his plush black coach. He might have been denied a dance, but his male pride was now fully restored. He enjoyed having charge of Ariana.

When comfortably seated across from her in the carriage, he struck the wall to signal them off. He lit the interior lamp, and it was evident her face was still crestfallen. Try as he might, he could not remember what had passed between them that might have caused it.

"Are you ill?" His voice was gentle.

She shook her head.

There was silence then, until he asked, "Is it something I said? 'Twould not be the first time I plagued your sensibilities."

He was rewarded with a brief smile, but nothing more.

"Ariana, this is unlike you!" He sat forward in his seat and looked at her questioningly. "I would much prefer to be subjected to one of your outbursts than to have you silent. Pray, if there is anything I have done, tell me!"

"But there isn't!" She looked at him fully then, and, without knowing herself what was about to happen, burst into tears and covered her face with her hands.

Mr. Mornay was dismayed. He felt helpless. It was not something he was accustomed to.

"Ariana!" he said, softly, handing her his handkerchief. When she continued to cry silently he moved from the cushion across from her and sat beside her, in what he hoped was a supportive gesture. He tried to lift her face so he could see her, but she refused to turn her head. This left him sitting there continuing to feel that awful helplessness, without a clue as to what he should do. Her blonde hair shone golden beneath the glow of the lamp and he gently cleared the side of her face of any stray tendrils.

He sat beside her until her shoulders ceased to rock, and he could tell she was calming down. He had a strong urge to put her upon his lap but realized the romantic implications, and could not bring himself to do it. He wished for a moment that he was her father or brother; it would allow him to be more affectionate without raising any false hopes. For he had long ago realized his utter unsuitability for marriage; no, not even with Ariana, despite the feelings of protectiveness she aroused in him.

Suddenly, Ariana raised her head, and slowly turned to face him. Her eyes were puffy and adorable. Her cheeks and the tip of her nose were quite pink and this too was not unbecoming. He stifled a smile.

"Forgive me!" she declared. "I am more fatigued than I thought."

"But are you well, now?" He spoke mildly. "What was troubling you?"

When she looked at him, endeavouring to choose her words, she glanced at the neat mouth and clean-shaven jaw, the tidy cravat. He was still sitting close to her and his proximity was startling. She turned away again, without having answered, and suddenly Mr. Mornay knew.

He was not alarmed or annoyed, as was his usual response to any woman who intimated she found him attractive. Indeed, he felt a rush of concern for Ariana—he did not want to hurt her. This was a decidedly unusual predicament, and for a few moments he was at a loss again, not knowing what to do. He reached over and took her hand, and held it firmly in his own.

"Ariana, I would like to help you, only I find myself uncertain how to do that. If you think of something I can do for you, please let me know."

She nodded, and let out a small, "thank you." But she continued to keep her face turned away from his. This charmed him, for it was completely void of manipulation. Ariana never did anything intentionally aimed at attracting him to her—aside from just being herself—and that, in itself, he found attractive. Her lack of artifice, of deliberate attempts to gain his attention, was refreshingly welcome. There was no question, moreover, of her being after his money or anything of his. Ariana genuinely liked him. He knew it, but all he could think to do was to grasp her hand in his own.

Somehow, he would have to help Ariana Forsythe. He had unwittingly been a part of causing her problems, as her aunt had pointed out, and he needed to make it right. But he could not bring himself to change the relationship from the platonic one they had settled into. Why? He did not know.

When the coach pulled up to 49 Hanover Square, the two in the carriage were still as they had been. Mr. Mornay gave Ariana's hand a squeeze, and spoke softly into her ear.

"I'll see you the night of the ball. If you need me for anything before then, do not hesitate to inform me." Looking at the side of her face, he felt a great affection for her, but that same sense of helplessness overcame him, so that he rose and left the coach to help her down. He walked her to the door and kissed her hand.

She tried to smile before he left. "Good night. Pray forget my behaviour tonight. I am sorry for having cried."

"Do not be," he said, holding up one hand. "I am not the least put out by it. My only concern is for you."

Ariana looked up at him and blinked in surprise. For a moment she looked ready to burst into a fresh torrent of tears.

"Good night, Mr. Mornay!"

She swept into the house. With a grave nod of the head, Haines closed the door after her.

Twenty-Four

There hadn't been a ball at Hanover Square for more than a decade—not since the master was alive. The servants, for this reason, were in a tizzy. They were falling over each other during the special cleanings and preparations which must go beforehand, since even Mrs. Ruskin seemed confused about who should be doing what.

Ariana was compelled to give her opinions, which, to her surprise, were immediately implemented. The servants, unbeknownst to her, had placed her in their highest esteem because she was often found reading either her Bible or the prayer book. Many of the servants were devout, and took heart to see a copy of *The Book of Common Prayer* in use at Hanover Square.

Gilded invitations had been sent. The house was washed, waxed, polished, and aired. Then it was polished once more until the woodwork shone and the floors sparkled. Every nook and cranny, every utensil, was given painstaking attention. Extra servants were hired, including an undercook to help with the enormous food preparations. Cook remained in the kitchen for an entire day before the event, thinking that if all went well she would die happy. Certain specialties were ordered out, such as an exquisite cake from *Gunter's*, with little beautifully formed marzipan figures on top. When Ariana saw the cake, she burst into tears and retreated to her room.

It was too much to bear. She had resigned herself to the realization that what she felt for Mr. Mornay was a deepening love, and that in itself was a great reason to despair. She had an acute awareness that, despite her feelings for him, he could never return them. He maintained a semblance of caring for her—thus his displeasure at being denied the dance—but it was not love. Rather, it was more like a brotherly affection.

Worse, she knew it was wrong to love him. How could she love a man who had no interest in the things of God? Had she seen him, even once, at St. George's on a Sunday? No!

And why did she not love Mr. O'Brien who was a sincere, devout man? Was there ever more reason to despair? And yet Aunt Bentley was determined to treat her as if she deserved the best of matches. Ariana worried that her aunt might become a laughingstock on her account. If she did not marry money, her relation would be maligned for having made her a spectacle. Society would regard the lady with a mixture of pity and distaste. Ariana felt an enormous pressure with each expenditure, which was why the beautiful cake from *Gunter's* had sent her to her chamber in tears. The utter hopelessness of it all had driven her there.

She had sent a wild letter to her parents, imploring them to answer her correspondence; begging for their advice and counsel. Their silence was incomprehensible and felt as a sort of punishment; but, to what purpose? Surely if they wished to reprove her, they would do so in writing, or send for her outright.

If only Mr. Mornay were a devout man! But he was not. Ariana fell to her knees many times to pray over the matter, but felt so agitated she could barely concentrate. The still, small voice of God which she desperately wanted to hear, was lost amidst the noise of her own unhappy thoughts. She wanted to be still before the Lord, to open her heart and mind to His counsel while reading Scripture—but found it exceedingly difficult to do so.

∽⚬∽

The morning of the event found the house bedecked with numerous floral garlands bearing sugarcoated fruit and berries. They hung from the mantels and adorned the curtained windows. They were spread across clean, white tablecloths. They were even outside, on the iron railings of the house. A small fountain was brought in and set up at one end of the dining room. It had an adorable little cherub seated on its outer rim, which normally Ariana would have delighted to see, but now her heart sank.

Again she retreated to her chamber. Harrietta had earlier set her hair with papers and left them to be taken out later. She had time, therefore, to be alone, though the household hummed with the extra commotion of preparations. Mrs. Bentley, moreover, wanted her niece to get plenty of rest. Little did she realize she was causing Ariana to lose sleep instead.

Ariana opened her Bible numerous times only to find she was too distraught to take comfort there. But she prayed. If her mind wandered, she brought it back and prayed more. Eventually she got to that place of feeling herself in God's very presence, and she confessed all that was heavy upon her heart. She detailed every last bit, keeping back nothing. Her love for Mr. Mornay was put out and despaired upon, yet she did not sense a whit of condemnation for it from the Lord.

Eventually, upon opening her Bible yet again, her eyes fell upon these words from the epistle of 1 Peter: "*Casting all your care upon him; for he careth for you.*" Prayer again followed but more easily, now. It had been laborious to take her deepest feelings before the Lord, but how rewarding a labour! She felt a renewed sense of God's love for her. It was just what she needed, and she was filled with gratitude. She had ever been in His hands, and was still so now. What He allowed, He allowed for a purpose. It was not for her to control her aunt, not even her spending; it was not for her to control her life. That was the Lord's prerogative. Finally, she felt amply reassured. God cared about her. He would take care of her.

She fell into an exhausted sleep. The tensions of the past week had taken their toll. She wasn't awakened until her aunt sought her out two hours before the guests were expected, to begin her personal preparations.

❧

The response to Mrs. Bentley's invitations was so great she was concerned there would be a crush. Every hostess infinitely preferred a crowd to its opposite, but a crush was another matter: important members of the *ton* must not suffer. Mrs. Bentley did her best, therefore, to encourage guests to roam a suite of rooms in addition to the newly polished ballroom and supper room. Wooden tables draped with linen, holding large bowls of negus or lemonade, staffed by a servant, were placed throughout the rooms in hopes of offsetting too great a crowd in any one of them. Of course a card room was set up, with plenty of seats around the walls for the dowagers, who would delight in watching and gossiping.

Ariana's mind, when her aunt bade her get dressed, was not on accommodating the guests. As she washed in a warm bath she reaffirmed her resolve to trust the evening's events to God. She endured the quick plunge into cold water with a prayer on her lips, and found, by the time she was being dressed and fussed over, that she was actually beginning to look forward to the night. All of her acquaintance would be there, and she would have friends about her. Really, there was nothing to dread.

It helped soothe her spirits when she was attired. A girl could hardly remain gloomy when sporting a beautiful new evening dress. The second modiste had outdone herself with a splendid confection of a gown. It was exquisite white satin, trimmed at the bust, the quarter-length puffed sleeves, and at the hem. The gown had a lower décolletage than her other gowns, a high but slim train gathering in the back, and was embroidered with white and gold thread.

She wore three-quarter length white satin gloves with gold-threaded satin buttons on the sides, and matching silk-satin slippers on her feet. Her hair was curled into dozens of tight ringlets, as opposed to the simple chignon she often favoured; and in front, her head displayed a diamond-studded tiara, wider than the modest specimen she had worn to past events. The stunning ornament was said by Aunt Bentley to be a relic from her heyday, which the lady had happily resurrected for the occasion, as well as an eye-catching gold filigree collar necklace with a large twinkling diamond in its centre.

Mrs. Bentley helped with the dressing as usual, fussing and complaining, and feeling that a great deal of pokes, prods, and pulls on the fabric were necessary. Ariana was used to this, and withstood it admirably. When it was finished, the older lady stood back to survey her niece. She made no comment at first, but bade Ariana turn round, slowly. When the aunt looked again at her charge, she came forth with a rare full smile.

"A triumph, my dear. Indeed, a triumph." She paused and made a little frown. "Breathe not to a soul the name of the modiste, for I intend to make her my own, and I do not want half the *ton* hankering there and making her prices go up provokingly. And there is one more thing necessary," she added, "and I know just what to use!"

Mrs. Bentley disappeared toward her own chamber. In a minute she was back carrying a shawl made of fine gauze silk, gold-threaded in an intricate design around the edges in a wide margin. She draped this artfully across Ariana's arm and around behind her, to the other arm.

"Now you have the elegant look. I daresay you will have offers made to you tonight!"

Ariana resisted the temptation of letting this remark disturb her. Instead she repeated to herself, *He cares for me. He will take care of me. He cares for me. He will take care of me!*

۞

At exactly half past nine the guests began to arrive. Ariana stood beside her aunt receiving them, and no one could have guessed she had ever dreaded the evening. More than one young lady and gentleman whispered urgently to one another that she was looking "shockingly well!"

"She is like an altogether different angel," declared one besotted young man, who was certain Ariana was an heiress. "In the past, a cherub, and now, a seraph! An exquisite seraph!"

Many others felt similarly. Mr. Mornay had been precisely on the mark when he suggested they all thought she was an heiress. Those who had looked into her family and found only the evidence of modest gentry living, were stumped.

Ariana dressed in the first order of fashion, and with exquisite taste. That, plus the fact that the Paragon chose to keep company with her often, and the quality of this ball, the furnishings, the house, the food—it all shouted *wealth*.

People had long understood that her aunt was rich, but no one suspected that anyone, not even a rich relation with no children of her own, would finance a young lady to the degree that Ariana had been.

While greeting guests, Ariana was startled when Miss Worthington, for once ignoring her mama's conversation, instead settled an unnerving little smile and knowing look upon Ariana. It was uncannily familiar to Mr. Mornay's expression of understanding, and for a moment she just stared at the girl stupidly in return. What could it mean?

She decided to ignore the chit—she had no time to do otherwise, in any case, with a roomful of guests to mingle among. A few admirers flocked around, but Ariana found herself searching for that tall, dark head. Where was Mr. Mornay? The dancing would soon begin, and she would be hard-pressed for time once it did.

She took a seat to rest and was soon in the midst of friends and hopeful admirers. While she listened to the light banter around her, there came a sudden change in the atmosphere. The young bucks began to scatter; others moved off in pairs. Looking about, she was pleased to find that the source of the disruption was Mr. Mornay.

He had approached Ariana, and when he saw her his countenance changed swiftly and to an unexpected end. All in his path quickly strove to be out of it. Ariana herself gulped involuntarily as her admirers vanished in every direction, for she, too, caught a glimpse of that formidable face.

Mr. Mornay bowed stiffly, and just looked at her with distaste. In fact, he seemed to be growing angrier while she watched. Miss Herley had dared to stay by her friend's side to this point, but he looked at her now scathingly, and without a word, managed to send her away as well. Ariana was clinging to her arm, hardly knowing it until Miss Herley firmly but gently removed her arm from Ariana's grip.

"I am sorry, my dear," she said in earnest, "but I must give Mr. Mornay leave to speak with you."

"Lavinia!"

"Really, dearest; but I shan't be far."

Ariana realized it was inevitable. "Very well."

Now it was just the two of them. In such a crowd, and yet Ariana felt suddenly alone with a frightful man she could hardly reconcile with the man who had been so kind of late.

"Come to your feet, so I can see you better." So this was his greeting! She rose.

"You see what your presence does; all the young men have quite abandoned me!" She smiled bravely, but he did not return it. There was none of the friendliness about him she had come to know, nor a jot of the warmth he had displayed toward her at their last meeting. Ariana was rediscovering what had seemed so frightful in him when they first met. Even silent as he was now, he could be vastly intimidating.

At length he began. "I am astonished by your appearance; it is unlike you to wear the fashion to such an extreme." He motioned at her tiara, at the beautiful shawl draped about her, at the collar necklace.

"These aren't *mine!*" She wanted to explain that her costume had been chosen for her, that her aunt had decided upon it all, and that it wasn't her fault.

"And does that signify? You are shamefully overdone, or should I say (with a pointed look at her décolletage) underdone?" His eyes blazed with reproof. "Particularly, for one who has no desire to mislead anyone regarding her situation. Or am I mistaken in that? For I see your aunt has invited every unwed blue blood in England!"

Ariana gasped at his hurtful remarks. She had not assembled the guest list aside from a few names. Nor had she bespoken the gown, or wished to. But his words stung so that she found herself defending it.

"I grant it is not my usual style, but no one else is shocked by it, and I daresay it is not...immodest! I have received, on the contrary, countless compliments!"

"People in these circles would compliment a cock if it wore an ostrich feather!" he declared.

Ariana stood speechless for a moment. She waved her fan rapidly over her face.

"You are utterly disheartening, sir! I will not subject myself to this." She would have turned on her heels, but with a lightning-quick grasp he took her arm and walked beside her.

"Society is no longer certain if you are mine or not; we can put that question to rest tonight. Since you wish to flirt with titled gentlemen, in fact, I can speak a word for you with any of them, beginning, if you like, with the richest." He was hissing in her ear, and Ariana blinked back tears. She felt as if he had struck her, and she halted, stung, though he was endeavouring to move her toward an old, ornately dressed peer.

Suppressing tears, she turned on him.

"I should have thought you knew me better than to say such a thing!" She paused, again fanning herself rapidly. "You have made your obligatory appearance; why do you not *leave?*" She freed her arm from his and whirled off, hardly knowing in which direction.

"Pay no attention, whatever he said." Ariana turned in surprise to see Lady Covington looking at her knowingly. She had been invited at the last minute, at Ariana's insistence, for she saw this as a way of obeying the biblical exhortation to "seek peace and ensue it." Evidently the countess was relieved to end the animosity as she had accepted the invitation.

Ariana tried to hide her distress with a smile. The countess was the last person in the world she wished to speak to at the moment, especially if her ladyship had witnessed the exchange with Mr. Mornay.

Should she ask for the countess's opinion of her gown and jewelery? But no, for this was the woman who regularly wore outrageous bonnets and indeed, was sporting a headdress full of feathers at the moment.

She thanked her politely, adding that she was pleased her ladyship had come to their ball. Lavinia was then at her side. She had been staying within sight of her friend since the Paragon's arrival.

"What happened, dearest? Mr. Mornay looks out of countenance and so do you."

Ariana glanced at him. He was still watching her with a deep scowl.

"He insists my clothing is overdone! And I've too much jewelery. Do you think so, Lavinia? Please give me your true opinion!"

Lavinia was surprised at what seemed to her a trifling matter. But she obediently gave her friend the once-over, and shook her head.

"I think you look wonderful!"

"Top-o'-the trees," added the countess, still shamelessly eavesdropping. "You are certainly bedecked, my dear, but becomingly so."

Mr. Mornay started in their direction, and Ariana, determined not to speak another word to him, excused herself rapidly and walked away. Mr. O'Brien had been nearby, waiting to have her to himself, and he instantly befriended her now, tucking her arm into his.

Mr. Mornay kept to his purpose, seeking Ariana's aunt. He was intent on registering a very pointed complaint. Mrs. Bentley saw him approaching, made her excuses to the lady she was chatting with, and came forward to meet him, feeling triumph was at hand. His first words, however, astonished her.

"What can you have been thinking when you gave your approval to such an outlandish outfit for Ariana?" He had not even bothered to bow.

Mrs. Bentley's hand went to her heart. "But everyone is unanimous in thinking Ariana's gown is beyond the latest mode!"

"Yes, *quite* beyond. My point exactly."

It was so difficult to make any response to the glaring black eyes studying her disapprovingly that Mrs. Bentley stood there helplessly. Many people, when up against Mornay, did not respond other than standing the brunt of disapproval as well as possible, and then making for solitude where they could collapse in private. Mrs. Bentley feared she was soon to join their ranks.

Ariana, meanwhile, was doing her best to mind Mr. O'Brien's light banter, but her heart, still smarting from the earlier encounter, was not with him. She had hoped to find Mr. Mornay sympathetic to her predicament, thinking he, of all people, understood it. They might have laughed together at her aunt's latest scheme to garnish approval— and offers—for her niece. Instead, he reacted as if she had personally offended him.

The chamber group began a country dance tune. Ariana had long since promised away many dances, the first of which she was required by custom to give to the highest ranking man present. It happened to be a duke whose name she could not recall. Fortunately she had merely to say, "Your Grace," to most anything he said, with a little nod of her head, so the memory lapse didn't signify.

Her next dance partner was Mr. O'Brien, who made repeated attempts to speak when they came abreast of each other or face-to-face. Something about having an urgent matter to discuss with her.

No, she thought. It could not be tonight. She had enough on her mind. However, Mr. O'Brien's apparent approval of her was comforting, as was that of Lord Horatio during the next dance. When he made conversation, his genuine admiring tones restored her feelings sufficiently so she no longer felt the need to cry. She refused to peek, but she was curious whether or not Mr. Mornay had left. It was grossly unfair that she cared about his opinion of her, but useless to deny it. Despite her anger and hurt, she dreaded discovering that he'd gone.

After the dance Lord Horatio released her reluctantly as the Reverend and Mrs. Chesley, the parents of Harold Chesley, one of her admirers, hailed her. Lord Horatio had been determined to find out this night once and for all if Mornay had intentions. He had suspected such and forced himself to keep his distance from Miss Forsythe. But here the season was past midway and his friend had made no declaration. Fair was fair, and if Mornay wasn't smart enough to snatch up the lady, he certainly was!

Ariana had noticed that Mr. Chesley was sporting a cravat nearly as high and stiff as those the fops wore, but she determined to be polite to his parents in any case. Mr. O'Brien then appeared again at her side, and seemed impatient; nor did he release Ariana's arm from his own during her conversation with the couple.

Mr. O'Brien had decided to offer Ariana marriage some time ago; but Mrs. Bentley's eagle eye had always been upon him, affording him no time alone with Ariana. He saw tonight as the chance to speak to her, if only for a few minutes, to settle the matter. The sudden appearance of Mr. Mornay was another reason he was fretting. Why on earth did that man insist upon hanging about Ariana? Everyone knew he would no sooner marry than be bitten by a snake! But his continual presence around her was definitely making him nervous.

And then as he stood by Ariana waiting for the Chesleys' interminable conversation to end, he saw Mrs. Bentley motioning frantically from across the room. Did she want him? No, it was Ariana. Glad for a legitimate reason to interrupt, he proclaimed, "Excuse me, but your aunt is beckoning for you, my dear." He gave the Chesleys a short, relieved smile.

Ariana looked across the room, saw her aunt waving her handkerchief vigorously at her, and agreed. She smiled, excused herself from the Chesleys—and Mr. O'Brien, whose features dropped in disappointment—and hurried to cross the ballroom to her relation. With a start, she saw that Mr. Mornay, whose figure had been hidden by a romanesque bust on a pedestal, was beside her aunt. She took a breath and continued.

When she approached them she saw that her aunt had been crying. Mrs. Bentley, *crying!* Her eyes were red and a little puffy, and she was holding her handkerchief to one eye even now.

"I have called you, my dear, to insist you give Mr. Mornay your next dance," Aunt Bentley stammered.

Ariana looked at Mornay in surprise. Did he truly want a dance with her? Was he no longer angry? Or was he seeking an opportunity to give her a further set-down? While her thoughts raced thus, she noticed he was looking at her differently now without a trace of anger. In addition, he had a drawn, resigned look about his face. He appeared nearly as distraught as her aunt.

"But I am promised to another gentleman for the next dance," Ariana said.

"That is of no account; if Mr. Mornay wants to dance with you, he must be allowed." Her aunt dabbed at her eyes again.

"You have been too hard on my aunt, Mr. Mornay!" Ariana said in rebuke. "Is it not enough for you to provoke me? Must you upset her also?"

"No, no, no! Forget that, my dear!" Mrs. Bentley looked distressed.

Ariana looked from one to the other and saw unmistakable signs of tension.

"What has happened? You both look as fearsome as ghosts." She attempted a laugh, but no one joined her.

Mrs. Bentley gave a little sigh, glanced at Mr. Mornay, and then drew Ariana in close to her.

"We will make the announcement after he speaks to you," she hissed, "but Mr. Mornay has offered for you. You are to marry him!"

Ariana's expressive eyes widened, and colour rushed into her cheeks. Mr. Mornay's scolding voice interrupted her shock.

"You should not have told her like that!" More calmly, he said, "I wanted to speak to her myself, first." He looked at Ariana. "I apologize for the suddenness of this—I see it has surprised you. Come, take a turn with me about the room."

Twenty-Five

*A*riana accepted Mr. Mornay's arm, astounded at what she had just heard. But there was lightness about her heart, and suddenly she was blinking back tears of an entirely different sort from those she had struggled against earlier. Mr. Mornay had offered for her! He must love her!

He led her forward, but they could not speak. The late comers had all arrived, and the ball had now reached the level of a genuine crush. He dropped her arm and took her hand firmly and began making his way across the room. Some people stopped him, intent on conversing with the Paragon, but he was brusque to the point of rudeness.

"Not *now!*" The forbidding hiss was sufficient so that people turned away in mortification. Ariana was also hailed, but she was pulled on by Mr. Mornay's grasp, and could only blurt, "Good evening!" Her smile was so great, however, that it drew curiosity, and soon the guests noticed that the Paragon was leading her. A ripple of excitement swept through the crowd.

Conflicting feelings were sweeping through Ariana. Amazement, happiness, yes; but also an unwelcome sense of caution. A nagging voice that even now was insisting she could not accept a man who was practically a heathen. How irritating to be reminded of it!

Suddenly Mr. Pellham was before her, and Ariana stopped in delight. She pulled strongly against her companion's firm grip so resolutely that Mr. Mornay came to a halt.

"Mr. Pellham!" Ariana said in delight. "You have no crutches! And you have come to our ball!"

The man smiled and bowed, first to Ariana, and then, unbelievably, to Mr. Mornay, who was also surprised.

"I believe I have this man to thank. He sent his personal physician to me, who prescribed a new physic for the pain in my leg, and what do you know? After the pain was gone, I found I was regaining use of my leg! It is stronger every day, my dear!"

Ariana impulsively gave Mr. Pellham a hug. "I daresay it is Mr. Mornay who deserves your gratitude—and mine."

He looked directly at the Paragon. "Thank you, sir. You have done me a great service." He reached forth his hand, a thing which was unimaginable not long ago, and shook the hand of Ariana's companion, who was uncharacteristically smiling back at him.

But the crowd was pressing in, and after Ariana had directed Mr. Pellham to her aunt, they continued on. After leaving the ballroom the couple went through a succession of occupied rooms: sitting room, card room, supper room. Now and then her suitor would look over at Ariana, and she marvelled at what she saw in his eyes: unmistakable affection and admiration. She felt elated, as though her feet hardly touched the floor. But they were nearing the front door and he was still moving determinedly on.

"Where are you taking us?"

"To a place where we can speak without shouting."

Haines, seeing the young mistress, was going to suggest she needed a coat, but one look at Mr. Mornay's face reminded him that silence could indeed be golden.

When they hesitated momentarily at the door, Ariana took the moment to gasp, "Not outside! What will people say?" This was a useless argument to present to him for he cared very little what people said. In fact, that appeared to settle the matter for him. He motioned for the butler to open the door.

"I shan't go! There must be a room in the house where we can talk." Her eyes were suddenly alight. "I know! The servants' quarters. Or the kitchen."

He frowned. The thought of declaring his love in such a place struck him as absurd.

"No, we'll go outside."

"Very well." Her tone was reluctant. "But I need something warmer than gauze," motioning at her shawl. He eyed the butler who immediately moved off to fetch an appropriate garment. When he returned with a pelisse, he would have helped his young mistress into it except the sagacious-eyed gentleman insisted upon that honour.

Outside on the pavement, Ariana looked up at him, studying his face. She had never looked at him with the thought that he cared so much for her; enough to marry her! It was an amazing, wonderful feeling.

"Did you *really* offer for me?" She felt unable to grasp it.

He looked down at her warmly. "I did. Are you astonished?"

She nodded.

"So am I." He continued to look at her as they walked, arm in arm, and asked lazily, "Any other reactions?"

She realized the lazy tone was due to his vulnerability. A cover.

"I *love* you, Phillip Mornay; how could I feel, except wonderful?"

He stopped walking, impulsively wanting to pull her up against him, but could not. The only people about were the coachmen, grooms, and a few footmen waiting around their equipages for the return of their employers, but it was not proper to display affection publicly and he would not do it.

Instead, he began moving them hurriedly out to the street.

"Where to, now?"

He made no answer, but was looking for his own equipage.

"I cannot ride in your carriage. That would be improper!"

He whistled loudly, getting the attention of every servant on the block, but his own man heard it and from down the street Ariana could see a team being led to turn around to their direction. He turned patient eyes to hers.

"Did I not escort you home in my carriage only a week or so ago? And that was before we were betrothed; I assure you there is nothing scandalous about taking a short spin with me, now."

"But a betrothal cannot be announced, yet. You must know there are—concerns—to discuss, first."

He looked at her searchingly. "If you mean finances—"

"No!" She blushed pink.

"Then what?"

The carriage pulled up in front of them and he led her toward the door. A liveried footman jumped from the back, quickly let down the steps, and stood aside.

Ariana stopped and stood firm, refusing to move. Mr. Mornay looked at his servant and said, "Go to the back, Charles." The man obediently went to the rear of the vehicle and climbed onto his perch. Ariana's suitor did not relish having his remarks overheard by servants. He gave her another of his patient looks.

"I am a man who has just discovered he is in love," he said. "*With you*. Now come with me into my carriage and let us talk about it."

Ariana still hesitated. "There are people," she motioned toward the house, "who are watching. They will see if I get in your carriage. You said yourself I could not survive a second scandal!"

"There will be no scandal, unless you force me to pick you up and carry you! Now, be a good girl, and do as I say." He motioned toward the open door.

She took a deep breath, thinking. "Oh, very well!" She moved forward and he handed her up, giving an uncustomary look toward heaven.

He mouthed the words, "Thank you."

〜◦◇◦〜

There were crowds at the windows of Mrs. Bentley's house, and when the couple disappeared into the coach, somebody shouted the news. There followed a great deal of excitement as the *on-dit* went buzzing through the rooms.

"Is the carriage moving?" Someone had asked loudly, and the room quieted while the answer was awaited.

"Yes! The coach is moving. Leaving the street, now!" More whispering and exclaiming and shaking of heads accompanied this news and again made its way through the house. Mr. O'Brien's head went back in stunned defeat. He stood, almost reeling with the disappointment. Lord Horatio heard and nodded to himself. He wasn't nearly as surprised as Mr. O'Brien, though the news was disappointing. He began to look around at other ladies in the room with new eyes. He wanted a wife.

When Mrs. Bentley heard, her hand flew up to her heart, but Mr. Pellham patted her other hand.

"All will be well. They are to marry, after all."

"Yes." She nodded. Then, coming to herself she exclaimed, "Everyone must know! That will answer any question of impropriety!" She looked at her longtime friend. "Notify the orchestra to do a flourish. We must have everyone's attention!"

He did not move, however, but stood looking at Mrs. Bentley with an expression she did not recognize.

"Why, Randolph! Whatever is the matter? Why are you standing there staring at me?"

"I will not make the announcement," and he shook his head firmly. "Unless you consent to make another one. That you will marry me."

"Oh, my dear man," she crooned. "'Tis a sweet thought, but you cannot expect me to make that decision *now*. Not when I have so much happening already! Please, Randolph."

He realized his timing was unfortunate for her, but he stood his ground. Once more he shook his gray-white head. "No, my dear Mrs. B., we have gone on like this for too long; I realized when I was indisposed that you are invaluable to me. In fact, I cannot live without you! Not any longer!"

Mrs. Bentley shook her head, tears appearing in her watery blue eyes.

"Oh, Randolph! But think of the disagreements we shall have whenever I wish to entertain my friends—you despise them!"

"No. I shan't behave that way any more. Not when I realize how terribly wrong I was about Mr. Mornay. If that man, with his reputation, can turn out to be like an angel sent to help me—only think how wrong I must be about others!"

He was still shaking his head, reproachfully. "I shall never again behave so disrespectfully to anyone of your acquaintance!"

Mrs. Bentley's eyes grew large with wonder and joy. All she could do was breathe, "Oh, Randolph!" while staring at her beloved with large eyes. His expression mirrored her own. They nodded at each other and grasped hands for a few seconds. Then he went to the corner of musicians to make his announcements.

∽◦∾

"I should not have agreed to this! May we just sit at the curb?"

Mr. Mornay had not bothered to sit across from Ariana, and they were facing each other on the cushion, her hands snugly enfolded in his.

"No, we best not," he said. "They will come pouring out of the house, and I do not relish having the mob peeking in my window." The coach continued moving, and left the street to circle the area.

He squeezed her hands.

"First of all, I apologize for my monstrous behaviour to you earlier." He raised and kissed her hands, one at a time. "I can be an insufferable beast and I know it."

"And for what you've done since?"

There was an immediate sparkle in his eye. "Do you mean the manner in which I dragged you from your home, from warmth, and safety and society?"

"That is precisely what I mean!"

"Well, perhaps it escapes your notice, but your aunt, I believe, did mention I intend to marry you. Does that help matters?"

She shook her head. "Directly after I convinced myself you should never care for me in that way!"

"No, my sweet; I convinced you. Forgive me!" He pulled her toward him and Ariana gladly threw her arms around his neck. She rested her head against him and then their faces were touching. She loved the feel of her cheek against his face, but then he drew back his head and kissed her.

He broke apart from her when he felt the wetness of a tear against his skin.

"What is it? Have I offended you?" There was silence. "Ariana?"

"I—don't—know—wh-what—to—do!"

He moved apart enough to see her.

"What do you mean?" His voice was caring and gentle, and Ariana again pressed her head against him. She couldn't help then, but to put her arms once more about his neck. It felt wonderful to be able to—it was like a dream.

"Oh, Ariana!" he cried, softly, strengthening his embrace. He was surprised and once again moved apart enough to raise her face, though he could not see her eyes clearly in the dark. Passing street lamps gave some illumination, but not enough for him to read her emotions from her face and eyes.

"Is it that I forced you to come with me?"

"No." He waited for her to continue. "I have been praying about you for as long as I have known you; for your salvation, you see. And I have always prayed that God would lead me to the right man; the one He has chosen for me. But I had—I have—no indication…that you could be him!"

"No indication?" He was surprised. "That I was falling in love with you? I thought I was the only one who failed to notice that." He was silent a moment, thinking. "Surely you marked my attentions to you."

"No, you misunderstand me. I mean that I have—no—indication that *God* has chosen you for me!"

"But you have every indication."

She was giving him the death knell of their betrothal, and he sounded amazingly calm.

"How is that?"

"I am the one who has offered for you, and received your aunt's approval; I have cared for you; I am able to take further care of you and solve your social quandary. You will not have to fret on account of your aunt misrepresenting you, or for not having a fortune. I am the one who saved you from the countess's lies; and I saved your life when you might have drowned. In fact, now I think on it, I've saved you a good many times."

He was speaking in a soothing, serious tone. He was taking her concerns to heart, and answering them as best he could, as best he knew how. When he had finished his list, including their encounter at his estate in the tree when he had not revealed her, he gently pulled her forward and gave her a kiss.

"And now it must be official," he said in a droll tone, "that Mr. Mornay is God's choice for Ariana Forsythe. I certainly believe it was God who brought you to me!"

"I wish I could believe that!"

"Why shouldn't you?"

She hesitated, wondering how much it might upset him to hear the truth.

"There is a verse from Scripture regarding marriage. It says: *Be ye not unequally yoked together with unbelievers.* It is a direct command not to marry anyone outside the faith."

"But I am the same faith as you. Church of England, born and raised."

"That is a religion. You were born into a religion. Faith is a different matter."

He sat back, exasperated. "I don't understand your point, Ariana."

She began again. "Faith causes a man to seek his Creator, to want communion with Him. To desire to please Him." There was silence a moment.

"You think I am the veriest pagan, but I assure you that is not the case."

Another silence.

"I know to you there is no dilemma, but it is very real for me.

I assure you. I must tell you, the outcome—our being wed—is more precarious than you think. In fact, the question of our betrothal—"

"Question? There is no question, Ariana. It is evident to me we must wed, and, as soon as the proper arrangements can be made. I have already charged your aunt with that business. Except for your wedding gown, which I intend to oversee—"

"Mr. Mornay! This cannot go forward until you have my parents' blessing!"

"I have received permission from your aunt—your guardian at the moment. And I can assure you in any case there isn't a single mama in London who would dream of withholding permission from her daughter to marry me."

"My family is bound to be an exception," Ariana countered. "I feel certain the outcome is more precarious than you assume."

He was growing angry. They moved apart, though they were still seated beside one another.

"You said earlier, you had been praying about me since we met," he recounted. "Why is that not enough? Or, pray on, if you like. Pray all you want! But some things have to be, and—" his tone changed. "May I remind you, you are sitting beside me, inside my closed carriage at night, alone? That not many minutes ago you were practically upon my lap? I hate to think you will find this disagreeable, but every rule of society dictates we must be betrothed or your reputation is shattered."

"But I said I shouldn't come!"

They both sat fuming silently for a minute.

"I do not mean to be difficult," she continued. "I am merely trying to do what's right. I hope you can understand that."

His answer was immediate. "The right thing is to avoid the appearance of evil, is it not?"

She was surprised that he apparently did know some scripture. "Yes."

"Then you must accept the necessity of our marriage. If you defer now, the whole of London society will be scandalized. There is nothing else for it."

"I must think on this." She was feeling confused, and hated to be disagreeable to him. "I am convinced that to marry you—though I am heartily sorry to say it—would be wrong. It dishonours my beliefs."

"Is your family Methodist?"

"No. But my papa has given me a great deal of their teachings."

"So this is why you favoured Mr. O'Brien?" His tone was bitter.

"I never favoured him over you in my heart. Only in my head."

"Tell me again. The verse you mentioned."

"*Be ye not unequally yoked together with unbelievers.* Second epistle to the Corinthians, chapter six, verse fourteen." He had listened intently and now he leaned toward her with a sudden thought.

"I realize I am not the model of virtue you hoped for, but I am not an unbeliever. I do believe in God! Your objection is groundless."

Ariana eyed him uncertainly. Even in the dark of the carriage, his exceptional eyes glowed out at her, deep, intent, and—and—earnest. But she had to give voice to her thought.

"The devil believes in God, too, and trembles, Scripture says." She felt as if his eyes would bore holes into hers.

"Are you comparing me to *him?*"

"No!" She shifted in her seat. "I am showing you that general belief is not the same as faith. Faith is believing, yes, but 'tis more than that. Christ died on the cross for your soul! Until you understand the value of that—there can be no hope for us."

There was a deep silence this time until she asked, "Have you put your soul in His hands, Phillip?" His name rolled off her tongue before she realized it, and she blushed.

He hesitated before answering. "I see that you make a great distinction, but nevertheless it says not to be bound to an unbeliever, and I stand upon my claim that I am not one."

She looked at him despairingly.

"Ariana, it is useless; all of London will soon learn of our betrothal. Your aunt has informed her guests by now. The fact is we are bound to one another. I do dare to entertain the hope, however, that you will soon find this agreeable."

There was a deafening silence until Ariana asked, in a petulant tone, why he hadn't approached her first, instead of her aunt.

"Yes, I see it was a mistake," he murmured. "But I hardly knew myself I was going to offer for you. When I realized it, I could only think I had to do it before O'Brien had a chance to."

"Would you please return me home?" Ariana said.

"At once. But—is this your way of telling me that you do not care for me? Is that the real cause of your hesitation?"

"No! I have been miserably aware of late that I care for you all too much!" Even as she spoke, they were suddenly back in a warm embrace. Why did it feel so wonderful to be in his arms? He strengthened his hold on her and moved her upon his lap for a kiss. To herself she thought, *If I did not love you, Phillip Mornay, I would have no dilemma!*

The carriage returned to Hanover Square.

Twenty-Six

When Mr. Mornay's carriage pulled up to the curb, it was far up the street from house number 49. He turned to Ariana.

"Everything we have discussed can be resolved once we are wed. There will be plenty of time for you to instruct me, and I promise," here he lifted her hand to his lips, "to allow you to do so." He then leaned forward and kissed her cheek, and moved to kiss her mouth but she turned her face away.

"I cannot sufficiently instruct you."

"Hush!" He tried to kiss her again but was equally without success. He took and held her, however, and spoke softly into her ear.

"I love you, Ariana. I cannot say how or why I began to love you the moment I found you in that confounded tree, but I did! And then your large eyes, and your wonderful innocence—coupled with as brave a temper as mine is fierce—undid my three decades of bachelorhood. And, the absurd thing is, I'm afraid it took me until tonight to realize it."

Ariana, her head resting lightly against him, felt enormously pleased. But she lifted her head up to object.

"You did not love me so soon! When I saw you at the Sherwood's card party, you forgot my name. I distinctly recall!"

He smiled wryly. "No, I pretended to forget your name."

This fascinated her. "Why?"

He leaned his head back.

"To put you in your place, I suppose. I have found it an effective discouragement for hopeful females."

They were both smiling and she laughed. "Did you think I was setting my cap at you?"

"Until you told me how convinced you were of my 'utter depravity.' I gather you are no less convinced today than you were then, eh?"

"Oh, no." She spoke softly. "Without Christ, you are utterly depraved before God, as are we all; but I think you're wonderful!"

He tried to kiss her again, and this time succeeded.

A few minutes later they were strolling toward the house, her arm snugly in his.

"Ariana, we are betrothed, and it must be so."

She looked at him helplessly.

"There is still time—as much as you need—to settle your doubts. But I will not lose you." He stopped walking, looking at her earnestly. "Before tonight, I should have thought you would be happy to find your future entwined with mine. I felt certain you...wanted me." The words left his mouth with difficulty, and Ariana's defences, what little she had, crumbled.

"You were right, indeed."

He took both her hands. "Then why are you putting this wall between us?"

They searched each other's eyes.

"I do not mean to put anything between us." She was speaking slowly, choosing her words. "I am telling you what is between us, so you may remove the obstacle."

They resumed walking in silence until they reached the house.

"Do you mind if I say goodnight here?" she asked. "I should like to read and pray."

"Then read and pray. By all means." He took and kissed her hand warmly, and watched with a sigh while she disappeared into the house.

∽〇∾

Harrietta was scandalized to find Ariana in her chamber so early, for it was scarcely twelve-thirty. The ball was likely to go on for hours yet, she pointed out. Ariana deferred, knowing that if she returned, there would be no end of questions and congratulations and attention. She was in no mood for it. She herself still had questions. How could she marry Mr. Mornay? How could she not? And why had this longtime bachelor fallen for her charms, when she had taken no pains to win his affection? *What was she to do?*

This was the question she presented to the Lord in prayer that evening. She fell to her knees beside the bed, and Harrietta, knowing when Ariana fell to her knees she tended to remain that way for a long time, realized nothing was going to persuade the young miss to return to the ballroom. She went to find Haines, her superior, to let him inform the mistress.

∽∘∾

The betrothal was a divine bit of gossip, and people left the house intent on spreading it. There were always other places one could go in town, no matter the hour, and soon the fabulous *on-dit* had been passed along so the Regent himself heard it.

It was never disclosed exactly how the thing had come about. Mrs. Bentley made it a point to keep to herself the remarkable account of what had happened when she spoke with Mr. Mornay at the ball.

He had approached her with a bitter pill to swallow: all her troubles with Ariana's wardrobe had worked quite the opposite as she had hoped. He even accused her of behaving scandalously in the matter— a crime she denied with indignation.

"Scandalous? I am convinced no one else thinks so!" The color had already faded from her cheeks.

"Perhaps no one else thinks, madam." His tone was venomous. "I tell you, you have ruined the child!"

"Child?" Mrs. Bentley was beginning to feel weak. "I daresay my niece is young, but she is no child. Look at her. You can see for your-self—" It chanced that Ariana came into full view just then, and it was obvious that Mrs. Bentley's words were true. Ariana was a beautiful young woman—especially this evening, in her new gown.

Mr. Mornay was not to be appeased.

"You see, ma'am, what you have done."

All of the dear lady's hopes began to fade away like a procession of candles being snuffed out, one by one. She thought she knew what would please Mr. Mornay, but now was confused. The truly vexatious thing was she had expressly bespoken the gown with him in mind!

"I thought you should approve of such a gown!"

"Not on Ariana!"

Suddenly Mrs. Bentley was dabbing at tears. She thought—no, she knew—he cared for her niece, but for him to take a disgust of Ariana now, when she had taken such pains to prepare the girl for him—it was too, too provoking! She had never been the sort of female to depend upon salts, but she felt in need of them now.

"I warrant she is still the same—child," she ventured weakly. "I have only dressed up what was there all along." He was staring out at the dancers watching for every glimpse of her, and made no reply.

Mrs. Bentley was irked. "This is too unbearable, Mornay! When I expressly ordered that gown for you!"

He looked at her with a raised brow. Whatever was she talking about? For him? The noise of the room must have affected his hear-ing. He continued to give his attention to Ariana on the dance floor. She was moving to the music, stepping forward, then back, doing a graceful circle and smiling up into her dance partner's face, looking so lovely…

Mrs. Bentley shed a few tears from sheer frustration. But suddenly she had a rare insight. She, too, was watching Ariana and she could see nothing amiss in her appearance. The girl was beautiful. But then, wait, that was it! She was looking *too* beautiful. Too beautiful for a man who was denying he was in love, at any rate.

She looked up at the man beside her, wiping the last tear from her eye, and pronounced, before she realized what she was doing (or she would not have possessed the courage), "You, sir, are in love!"

Mr. Mornay stared at her as if thunderstruck. When he remained silent, she gasped with fear, certain that any moment he would lash out at her for her presumption, her rudeness, her absurd accusation. He would stalk from her house and, in days to come, sprinkle the *ton* with this account of her audacity and make both herself and Ariana a laughingstock. But in the end, of course, he neither upbraided her nor denied what she said.

He simply gazed back silently at Ariana and all the anger and indignation he had been feeling slowly drained from his features, taking a good deal of his colour with it. To his astonishment, Mrs. Bentley was precisely on the mark! He loved Ariana! He was not just fond of her as he had thought. He, Phillip Edward Mornay, was in love!

Looking at her, it was suddenly clear—ridiculously so—that of course he loved her. He had, it seemed, for some time. He had known she intrigued him, delighted him, and amused him, but he had never allowed himself to even think of the word, "love." Much as he enjoyed being with her, he had not admitted the depth of his attraction, not even to himself. Feeling it now, letting it sink in on him and watching her from a distance—it was becoming painful. He was aware of an acute longing for her rising up from deep within his being, a painful longing. But then, Ariana cared for him. He had felt it was so, hadn't he?

He did the only thing he could think of to ease his sudden acute consciousness of loving her. He turned to Mrs. Bentley.

"Yes; and so you will require your niece to grant me a dance—and arrange for the wedding!" To her rapturous look, which he met with a severe one of his own, he added, "The wedding. See to it. Make any arrangement you like. Any amount of pin money you want. Everything that is mine will be Ariana's. Just be certain to get me your niece!"

It was shortly after that remarkable conversation that Mrs. Bentley had motioned for Ariana, who by now had completed a dance and was chatting with Reverend and Mrs. Chesley. Ariana had made her way over completely unsuspicious of what she was about to discover.

It did not occur to Mrs. Bentley that Ariana would be fool-headed and refuse to set a date. She was dancing on air herself at having settled ·things with Mr. Pellham. So she set about to enjoying the remainder of the evening. Now that things were going so fabulously, she became an exceedingly gracious hostess; no request was too great, no complaint met with a cold air. Nothing could ruffle her feathers from now until she died, she felt.

But of course she was wrong.

Twenty-Seven

"What—did—you—say?"

Ariana closed her eyes briefly, then began again. "I merely told Mr. Mornay there remained a matter to settle…before we go forward with the wedding."

Her aunt's eyes were wide with stricture, wider than Ariana had ever seen them, and her complexion had turned frighteningly pale.

"Do you realize what you may have done? Do you imagine a man like Mr. Mornay will wait upon your whims, gel? Indeed, he may already be changing his mind regarding the matter!"

"But he insisted we *must* be betrothed!"

Her aunt's face changed immediately.

"He said that?" Her tone was less incensed. It was not, then, as bad as her niece had made it sound. When Mr. Mornay insisted upon something he always got his way.

"And you did not deny him?"

"How could I? When the entire city knows I have been with him in his carriage at night!"

"Precisely! Indeed! You see the thing must be settled thus. I will write the banns at once."

"Aunt," she protested. "My parents must be consulted first."

"Oh, for shame, Ariana! Your parents are not fashionable or sociable but I warrant they are possessed of sense. And any sensible person would see the great advantage to yourself of this match. They will not stand in the way, I assure you!"

How could Ariana explain that her only disquieting thought—that Mr. Mornay was not spiritually minded—was sufficient in itself to prevent the wedding? How could Aunt Bentley be expected to understand the importance of a believer marrying only another believer, when she herself stood outside the faith, apart from Christ, unredeemed? Furthermore, her parents would withhold their consent to the match on the same grounds.

The two women were still staring at one another across the table. They had both slept late this morning following the prior night's excitement.

"When your parents sent you this way, they knew I would be the judge of a good match, and they were content at that. I should think a gel of your age would do likewise."

Ariana did not wish to argue, but she knew her parents had thought no such thing. Her first impulse was to blurt the truth—that her aunt was considered completely ill-equipped to judge a proper match. But for once she stopped and weighed her words, praying silently for a solution.

An idea emerged.

"My dear Aunt, I should be very pleased to set a date for the ceremony if only you would write to my family and solicit the consent of my parents. If they agree to the match," she stated firmly, "then so will I. It is that simple." She was thinking it would be a small miracle to get a response from her family at all, given their total lack of communication since her arrival at Hanover Square.

Ariana's chaperon was not pleased, but the icy notes in her voice were less pronounced when she next spoke.

"I will write at once in that case, this very minute!" Before rising from her seat she eyed her niece doubtfully. "If Mr. Mornay calls, I insist you go forth with the plans."

Ariana said nothing. *Perhaps now, my parents must respond! They cannot ignore such a letter as my aunt will compose!*

Mrs. Bentley headed to her rooms, intent upon writing the missive to her brother at once. She intended upon scolding Ariana's behaviour in no uncertain terms, which she did, laying her out as "willful, ungrateful, and undeserving." No lady of her day would have dared put off such a one as Mornay! What was wrong with that young woman?

∽∽◦∼◦∼

Ariana hoped to spend the day contemplating her situation in quietude. In her chamber she turned to prayer, and knelt at her bedside for a considerable time. How she loved Mr. Mornay. She thought of all the smiles she had seen on his face of late, and knew in her heart she had been the reason for the smiles. She was good for him, that was certain. But was he good for her? In material things, there was no question.

He was far from the ideal man she had always dreamed of, but then, in other ways he surpassed anything she had ever imagined. Perhaps not in character; besides the lack of private devotion, he was not even a really *good* man; he admitted that himself. But he was good to her. Kind. She could not think of their kiss, in his carriage, without a foolish grin popping onto her face, and the thought that she might be causing him grief was a heavy thought, indeed.

Callers interrupted her prayerful ruminations. At first it was only Lavinia and her mama come to give their congratulations. Lavinia wanted desperately to speak with Ariana alone but there was no chance, for other callers were arriving, then more and more. Ariana could not help but enjoy the attention and visits. People were delighted by the idea of the Paragon betrothed and they had resumed calling Ariana Lady Mornay.

Haines was instructed to turn away further visitors and the card tray in the hall was soon overflowing with little, gilded cards. Ariana and her aunt would have to return all these visits. And each and every person who left a card did so with the thought that Ariana Forsythe was to marry Mr. Mornay. It wasn't long before the parlour overflowed with flowers, nosegays, and other novelties, all sent for the bride-to-be.

An especially lovely arrangement came from Carlton House, inscribed with the prince's name. "Our most extraordinary congratulations to a most deserving lady." Ariana was speechless with pleasure but could have wept as well. Mr. Mornay was right: There was no way the wedding could not go forward without scandalizing all of society.

Later, she was reading her Bible, curled upon a sofa in the parlour where she could enjoy the flowers, when Mr. Mornay appeared. He had intentionally arrived late so he might have Ariana to himself. He was fully aware of the sensation he had caused the previous evening—and of how crowded the parlour had probably been all day at Hanover Square. Not many had dared call at his own residence, and he was home, according to the butler, only for those he wished to see. When Ariana saw him in the doorway she was startled, and quickly sat up.

"Don't move," he said, entering the room. "You looked charming." He came and sat across from her. "What are you reading?"

She handed him her Bible and a raised brow, momentarily.

"I see." He opened the cover and thumbed through some pages.

"Do you ever read the Scriptures?" She purposefully kept her voice light.

"Not since my days at Eton, I'm afraid. You appear to have been enjoying them, however."

"Yes; I try to read at least a few verses daily. Papa says that to read the Holy Book from cover to cover a minimum of once a year will help one lead a pure life."

He nodded, and cleared his throat.

"May I ring for tea?" Ariana suggested.

"If you wish." He seemed restless. "How was your day?"

"Just as you imagine, I warrant." She met his eyes with a small, rueful grin.

He smiled, and looked about at all the flowers and other gifts. She pointed out the arrangement from the prince and he went and read the card, and nodded.

"Deserving, indeed; for once, I agree completely with Prinny."

He stood and came to her, then leaned down and kissed her forehead.

"I just wondered..." he rubbed his chin with one hand. "If perhaps you are willing now to set a date?"

"I realize the whole town is expecting that," she admitted. "And I am endeavouring not to fret about it."

He nodded, taking a seat across from her.

"But I believe you should have thought of the social consequences before taking us out to your carriage. Though I understand you did not expect to meet with any resistance to your offer."

"Hardly," he said, relaxing into a smile. "I should have known, however, that with you, anything is possible."

"Indeed, with God all things are possible."

"That must include our wedding, then," he answered smartly. She was startled, but only smiled demurely and rearranged a fold in her gown. He had been sitting with his legs crossed, but he now unfolded them and placed his gleaming leather boots solidly upon the carpet. He leaned forward in his seat, so that he was closer to where she sat.

"Ariana, we *must* set a date. Publish the banns, and so forth. I am in mind to meet your family." He stopped, seeing her troubled expression.

"I think not yet."

He cleared his throat, his tumultuous eyes swirling darkly. "And it is still this matter of the faith that hinders you?"

She shifted in her seat. "Yes, as I tried to explain last night."

He drew off his gloves rapidly and plopped them upon a little table. He reached across the space that separated the two sofas and gently grasped Ariana's hands. They were bare like his own, and he held her soft hands firmly.

"We have time," he said. "While all the arrangements are being made. I expect in this time, your hesitations will dissolve. You may instruct me, as you wish, on any matters of faith and I will be your student."

She smiled tenderly at him. "I understand you mean well, and I am grateful for that. I will be pleased to review Bible passages with you.

Yet, please strive to understand there are some things in the Scripture that only God can reveal."

Amazingly his temper did not surface. His eyes, in fact, sparkled with mischief. "And how would you propose God should do so?"

She waited thoughtfully. "I think He must first place in you a great desire to seek Him. To understand His Word." Here she picked up her Bible and held it out demonstratively. Putting it back down, she added, "He will teach you to recognize what is sin, and to hear His voice—and to receive His forgiveness. He promises eternal life to all those who put their trust in Him, and so you must do so. As must we all."

Mr. Mornay listened, his eyes reflecting interest, but they sparkled from the sheer enjoyment of being instructed by Ariana.

She sat back in her chair. "Well?"

He gave a little smile. "I think He can manage most of that. Except the part about hearing His voice. Do you really believe you can hear from the Almighty?"

"Yes, I do, indeed. The Lord promises to direct His children, which in many cases, amounts to His speaking to us. To our hearts, that is, to lead us. Only we must be faithful to seek Him in prayer, and by reading the Scriptures. His letters to us, you see." And then her expression became troubled. "I've been meaning to tell you. I have written countless letters to my parents but have not heard a word in return! And this is unlike them. I have a wonderful family. I cannot account for their silence, and, I must add, my aunt is writing to them to procure their permission for the wedding." She paused. He was listening intently as usual, and waited for her to continue. "I fear we may have a new problem if they fail to answer, yet again. And I worry that there is something amiss—though I cannot guess what it is!"

"If they fail to answer," he said, "does it not free you to follow your own conscience? I do have your aunt's approval..."

"But they must answer! I know my parents would never hold themselves aloof from me. There must be an explanation, but I cannot think what it is! And Alberta, too, has not written!"

To his questioning look she explained, "My older sister."

"You have an older sister?" He was rightly surprised since they had never discussed her family at length.

"Oh, I'll explain that later. But I know something is amiss. Only I cannot imagine—I have tried not to fret about them—" At this point she was holding back tears.

He looked concerned, but fell silent while he considered all she had said.

"How do you send your letters?"

"I simply leave them on the hallway tray, as my aunt instructed me. Haines is responsible for seeing they are sent."

"And, to your knowledge, they *are* sent?"

"Yes, that is, the next time I see the tray it has been emptied, so I assume they have gone with the mail coach."

He thought for a moment. "Not even one letter, you say, has reached you?"

She nodded. "Not even one. And this is completely out of character for them."

"Call for Haines."

She was surprised, but did so, going toward the bellpull to summon the servant. In a few moments the butler appeared, his face expectant.

"Yes, ma'am?" He had stopped inside the doorway.

"Come in, if you would, please, Haines," Mornay said.

There was an instant look of curiosity on the servant's round face, but he hid it at once behind a well-trained exterior and came and stood before Mr. Mornay, bowing politely.

"Sir?"

"Tell me, Haines, when Miss Forsythe leaves her letters on the hall tray, are you the one who posts them?"

The man looked perplexed for a second, but then his brows cleared. "No, sir."

"Who does, then? Who posts her letters?"

Startled, Haines balked, but then mastered his expression once more. "Who would, you mean, sir, if miss *was* to leave a letter?"

A raised brow on Mr. Mornay's face revealed that he thought the discussion might be getting somewhere.

"No. I mean *when* she does. Who has been taking her letters from the tray and seeing to them?" At this, Haines dropped all pretence of being indifferent, looked squarely at Mr. Mornay and said, "I have never seen her place a letter on the tray. To my knowledge, sir, she never has."

Ariana gasped.

"Can this be possible?" Mr. Mornay asked her.

"I have left more than a dozen letters, I am certain of it!"

Haines looked dumbfounded.

"I have never seen them…" He lapsed into a troubled silence.

"One thing is certain." Mr. Mornay faced Ariana. "Whoever takes them is not sending them on. Your parents have not written because they think you have not."

"No. They would write me in any case," Ariana insisted. "If my letters have not been reaching them, I feel sure the same fate has befallen their letters to me!"

"But who? Why?" asked the butler. He was terrified of being a suspect to their minds, although he knew himself to be innocent.

"That is the question we must all find the answer to." Mr. Mornay looked at Haines and told him to ask his mistress to join them.

When, a few minutes later, Mrs. Bentley arrived, she had already prised some of the business from her longtime servant, and demanded to know the entirety. Ariana told her all she knew. Mrs. Bentley fixed her eyes shrewdly ahead, staring at nothing, deep in thought. Suddenly she looked at them all.

"I think I know a suspect!" She sounded as surprised by the realization as the others were to hear she had got one. The lady of the house looked at Haines.

"Molly. Something about that abigail has long bohered me! What do you know of her?"

Twenty-Eight

M rs. Bentley sent her letter to Ariana's parents by way of her own personal messenger, with a smaller note from Ariana explaining, as well as it could, why they might not have received any letters from their daughter, and that Ariana had received none from them. Ariana wanted to write pages about Mr. Mornay, but her aunt was in a hurry, wanting to see the wedding move forward, and would only allow the short note.

After the discussion in the parlour, they agreed to set up a test to discover if Mrs. Bentley's theory about Molly, the newest maid in her employ, was correct. To wit, was she the interceptor of the letters? Haines had not been able to give any information about her except she seemed to be adequate for her position. But Mrs. Ruskin, when sent for, had some illuminating information. As housekeeper, Mrs. Ruskin handled the hiring of domestics, needing only a final approval from the butler before taking on a body. It was she who had interviewed and hired Molly.

The girl had come highly recommended. Mrs. Ruskin was even able to locate the letter which had accompanied the abigail when she applied for the position. Mrs. Bentley opened the paper impatiently and had barely scanned its contents when she let out a great, "Aha! I might have known!"

She passed the paper to Mr. Mornay who looked it over swiftly. He recognized the name Cecelia Worthington, but it meant little to him as her family was distinguished neither in birth or fortune. He passed the pages to Ariana.

"Gracious!" She looked in dismay at the paper and then to her aunt, who was pacing with cat-like intensity.

"Of all the nerve! That woman sent Molly here for a purpose. She usually uses her 'Sophia darling' to spy out anything she wants to know, but to infiltrate my household in this manner—it is—it is unendurable! Inexcusable! Why, it must be criminal!" she concluded, hopefully.

"Only if the crime is provable," put in Mr. Mornay, to which her face dropped. He added, "Which is precisely what we shall find out when we conduct our test."

The test was simple: Ariana would write a letter and leave it on the tray as usual. Only this time Haines would be on the watch, and a footman also—just in case. One was to follow Molly after she had confiscated the letter, which they were all certain she would do. When he discovered what she did with it, he would return and make his report. The tricky thing was to decide what to put in the letter. It had to seem authentic, but somehow contain bait for Mrs. Worthington, to make her come forward. It would be all too easy for her to place full blame on the maid and feign innocence. Unless she could somehow be coerced into revealing her hand in it.

After mulling over ideas, Mr. Mornay suggested a tactic that was daring and foolproof. Rather than write a letter at all, they would infuse the paper with a strong, permanent ink powder, so that whoever opened it would be hard pressed not to find herself instantly stained with evidence. While the ink would come out eventually from her skin, it would take time—time enough for them to confront and expose her. If it sprinkled over her clothing, well, that would furnish permanent evidence.

Everyone liked the plan. Ariana got two pieces of her aunt's crisp paper—the amount she usually used. The Paragon, meanwhile, went home and fetched a small, opaque bottle of black ink powder from his study. He checked that it was tightly closed. While one needed to add a few drops of water to use the ink for writing, it was so concentrated that just one stray sprinkle of it could ruin the nicest sleeve—or any clothing—even when dry.

They all watched as he carefully and liberally sprinkled the powder inside the papers, which he had already folded once. He folded them again, very slowly and carefully, and then again, making certain no trace of ink showed through. Mrs. Bentley applied a liberal slab of sealing wax and pressed her own stamp into it; something Ariana always did, not having a seal of her own. Then it was turned over, and Ariana wrote out her family's name and direction in the usual manner. There. Finished.

The next morning Ariana went alone into the hall and placed the letter in the polished silver tray which sat upon a japanned table. She experienced a feeling of satisfaction from having done so, knowing that the "mystery of the missing correspondence," as she called it, would soon be at an end. Now, it was Haines's turn for action. Since there was usually a footman about the hall, he posted one there today but with special instructions. Mrs. Bentley had chosen Ian, a burly Scotsman, for the job, having come to trust him quite explicitly.

Ariana could hardly concentrate on her morning occupations so excited was she. Mrs. Bentley was restless, too, and sought her niece, requesting she join her in the second parlour.

"I thought we might discuss the particulars of the wedding," she announced when Ariana had come in and seated herself. But Ariana's face fell.

"So soon? We might wait for word from my parents. They haven't even heard, yet."

"But they will, shortly." Her aunt had an open tablet, a pen in hand, and ink on the table. She looked at her niece expectantly. "Mr. Mornay gave me leave to ask your preference of where you should like to set up house following the wedding. In town, at Grosvenor Square? Or at his estate? Which will suit you?"

Ariana forced herself to attend to the question, though she had no heart for it at the moment.

"I should think that wherever Mr. Mornay desires to be, I will be happy to accompany him. As long as we are together—Oh, Aunt, must we discuss this now?" She frowned at her relation. "All I can think of is my letter, and what is going to happen. That I might soon receive word from home!"

"And I wish to discuss your next home! You should be putting yourself in mind of it, Ariana."

"But I can't bear it! Not when there is some question about the wedding!" She paced the room in agitation.

"There is no question to anyone's mind, my dear. You are going to marry Mr. Phillip Mornay. There is no turning back. You must be mad to cavil at such a match! The man loves you! He gives you all that is his! I have it right from his mouth!" She paused, a painful look of confusion and disapproval on her countenance.

"I am truly sorry, Aunt. I cannot do otherwise than I am doing."

"Why on earth, not?"

Ariana sighed. "My conscience tells me I may not marry any man unless he has...substantial leanings...toward the church. A man of faith. Of spirituality."

"Fustian! *Utter* fustian!" Mrs. Bentley could hardly believe her ears.

"Oh, Mr. Mornay is many wonderful things, truly wonderful!" Ariana paused, appreciating his wonderfulness. "But he is not a man of God, a Christian in the truest sense."

"Upon my soul, Ariana, I cannot think how you could be so... judgmental, and of one who is your senior, no less! Upon my word—of course he is a Christian, his family has always been. What, were you supposing him a heathen?"

"No. I do not mean that his family does not belong to a religion."

Her aunt stared at her uncomprehendingly.

"Then what *do* you mean?"

Ariana was silent a moment, forming her answer. "That he does not engage in a personal faith, a life of prayer, of seeking God."

Her aunt shrugged. "We cannot judge what is in a man's heart! You cannot! You are obviously too young to appreciate what has fallen into your lap. I have rarely heard of so generous an offer. And if that does not make him a Christian, I cannot know what does."

"I grant that Mr. Mornay is generous. And kind—when he has a mind to be. Indeed, I grant that willingly. But these are not things, you must know, Aunt, that make us acceptable to God! This is the teaching of Scripture."

Her aunt looked at her dubiously. "The good things we do must make us Christians," she insisted. "Why, it is those things which separate us from the animals, or from savages."

"My dear ma'am, we are separated from the animals because we alone are made in God's image—no other creature in all creation has been given that honour save humanity. Even 'savages,' as you say, are made in the divine image. But we become Christians only by following Christ. We trust in His work on the cross—not our own works, however generous they be. It is through Christ alone that man can be forgiven for his wrongs and made righteous for heaven. Only through trusting in Christ!"

Ariana was nervous about daring to contradict her relation, but these were truths her aunt sorely needed, and she could do no less than try to explain them for her soul's sake.

"But then *anyone* could be a Christian!"

"Precisely!" Ariana cried, pleased.

"It does not signify what manner of wrongdoing they are guilty of?" She spoke as though the very idea was heresy.

"Not in the least!"

Her aunt threw up her hands.

"In that case, any heathen is a Christian! Any mean-minded person who crawls the face of the earth can be a Christian? You are not making sense, Ariana."

"It makes perfect sense, ma'am, when you understand no one is innocent in God's eyes, mean-minded or not. We are all, alike, in need of forgiveness—perhaps some more than others, but no one is beyond God's love, or His reach. And no one is good enough for His love on their own, without Christ." She paused, praying the Lord would illuminate these deep truths of the Christian faith to her woefully unlearned relation.

"I have been baptized," the lady stated, stiffly. "That is the atonement, and what makes me a Christian!"

Ariana had to shake her head in disagreement. She was troubled by this chasm of misunderstanding between her and her aunt's ideas of the Christian faith. She spoke gently. "No, ma'am. Baptism is not the atonement. It is merely symbolic of Christ's atonement. The Bible says there must be blood shed to pay for sin. You see, we owe a debt: a sin debt, which can only be paid for with blood. In the Old Testament, they sacrificed animals to atone for sin. And they had to do it over and over again, for no animal's blood could permanently erase the stain of sin from a human soul. But Jesus, because He is God as well as man, could atone for our sin. Which is why He died on the cross, ma'am. He was our sacrifice for sin. *He* is the atonement. But His sacrifice only brings forgiveness when we ask for it. We must confess our sin and ask His pardon. And that is what causes the conversion to Christianity. It isn't about which church you attend, but whether or not you've been washed clean of sin—forgiven!—by Christ. A forgiveness that is received by faith."

Mrs. Bentley wiped her brow tiredly. "If I understand you correctly," she said, her voice hollow, "you are saying we cannot earn our passage to heaven?"

"That's right. We cannot. Here is a verse that tells us so, plainly. 'For by grace are ye saved through faith; and that, not of yourselves, it is the gift of God: not of works, lest any man should boast.' That is from the book of Ephesians, chapter two..."

Her aunt was staring blankly ahead. Ariana went and sat by her side.

"Aunt? Are you ill?"

She came to as if out of a reverie, and when she spoke it was completely without her usual force of manner.

"This Christianity you speak of is not what I have known. And yet, I must own that I have been long afraid of God, because my works are sadly lacking. I thought I had to do so much to earn His favour and could not that, well, I simply gave up." She was looking earnestly at her niece.

Ariana spoke gently. "All you need do, my dear Aunt, is receive a gift—the gift of salvation found in Jesus Christ. Seek Him in prayer, and by reading Scripture, and read the prayer book. Surely these things are not asking too much. Knowing God is within your grasp, Aunt Bentley! Pleasing Him, too. Trust Him, keep Him in your heart, and He will keep you for heaven!"

Mrs. Bentley looked at her niece with eyes that could be called fond. She sat up suddenly.

"Wait. You do not mean you will refuse Mr. Mornay because he may not have so great an understanding as you? Of these things?"

Ariana pursed her lips in thought. "It is not that." She spoke slowly. "But knowing our need for God changes us from what we were. In fact, the Bible says, all who are in Christ are new creations—a new order of being, ma'am! We look the same, we appear like any other person, but we are renewed in our innermost beings! It is a remarkable, miraculous thing!" Her eyes were lit with excitement and her face, always pretty, glowed warmly with a beauty that for a moment did seem unearthly, and as though a halo surrounded her head. Mrs. Bentley blinked in astonishment.

"And here is the crux of the matter, ma'am," her niece continued. "Scripture expressly forbids us to marry an un-renewed person. It would be like a union of two species—unnatural, and bound to be laden with strife. If Mr. Mornay does not come to realize his need for the Saviour," and her voice dropped here, "then I am afraid there is little hope for us."

Mrs. Bentley was staring at Ariana. The otherworldly aura about her had faded, and now she doubted she had ever seen it. All she saw, in fact, was a very young, very stubborn, very foolish young woman.

"You would be content at that? You would allow him to just walk away from you? The most sought-after gentleman in my lifetime that I know of!"

Ariana's face was creased in concern. "I would be miserable! I could never be happy apart from him, and yet I cannot reconcile myself to marriage as things now stand. If we were to wed, I could never share my joy in God with him." She looked pleadingly at her relation. "Don't you see? If I am to be made one with my husband, we must be one in heart, mind, *and* spirit."

"So you would abandon that poor man who finds himself in love with you!"

Ariana sighed deeply. "You forget that I am in love, also. I have had to put myself and my future—and Mr. Mornay—entirely into God's hands. If I am meant to marry him, then he will come to faith, I am certain."

"Your marrying him would be the thing most likely to bring him to faith!"

Ariana made no reply beneath Mrs. Bentley's accusing stare.

"What a strange, cold thing you are!"

Ariana's eyes filled with tears. The hours she had spent on her knees, crying out to God regarding Mr. Mornay! The tears she had shed! Was that being a "strange, cold thing"? She stood up in agitation, wishing to avoid shedding tears before her aunt.

"I am sorry if I appear so. I assure you—" and then she broke off, unable to speak another word. She looked pitifully at her aunt and then flew from the room.

Twenty-Nine

After Ariana left, and after Mrs. Bentley had gone to the door and listened for the sound of her niece's chamber door closing down the hall, she went to the parlour window and spoke to the floor-length drapery.

"You may come out, now."

There was a moment while the drapery puffed outward, and then Mr. Mornay appeared, looking ill at ease.

"I knew it was an inferior suggestion," he said. "And unfair to her. I regret agreeing to your scheme. I am thoroughly ashamed of myself!"

"But you have seen that she truly loves you. Is that not what you wished to know?"

He sat tiredly down upon a chintz-covered settee.

"I hoped to find out what was really between us. I did not expect to discover that it was indeed *God*." He seemed weary and yet restless, and his eyes roamed the room. Mrs. Bentley cleared her throat, taking a seat across from him in a matching sofa.

"I regret she said so much about that topic…"

"No, no, I thought it was a mere excuse on her part, but it is a very real problem for her. And for me."

Mrs. Bentley rose and reached for the bellpull, but Mr. Mornay stood up. Mrs. Bentley looked at him in surprise and then alarm. She wanted to settle matters before he could leave.

"But, Mornay, you have only to satisfy her on the points she spoke of. You have merely to profess a belief—a trust—in her Saviour. Is that not easily done?"

He looked at her with a defeated expression. "It is not as if I can go and sign on. 'Twould be easier for me, I believe, if she had required me to convert to Judaism!"

At that moment the door opened and Ariana stepped into the room. She began walking toward her aunt but stopped in shock upon seeing Mr. Mornay.

"Oh!"

That she had been crying was evident: her large eyes were rimmed with red, her face was flushed, and in her hand was a sodden handkerchief, but she gave him a watery smile of greeting. Mr. Mornay was pierced with guilt and remorse—and a wave of affection. Ariana looked back and forth at them.

"I beg your pardon. I seem to be interrupting." She turned to her aunt. "But I must tell you—"she stopped and walked right up to the older woman and bent to give her a small kiss on the cheek. Mrs. Bentley stiffened involuntarily when she realized a kiss was forthcoming, and then was struck silent with surprise—and perhaps her own measure of guilt. She laughed uncomfortably. "My dear—" she began.

But Ariana was already talking. "I want to apologize for behaving in such a way that you could accuse me of coldness."

Mrs. Bentley was embarrassed, and glanced uncomfortably at Mr. Mornay. "That's quite all right, my dear." She spoke quickly, hoping to end the scene, but Ariana hadn't done.

"I know you think me ungrateful and undeserving, but I am very conscious of the honour Mr. Mornay has given me." She glanced at him gratefully, surprised to see him looking ill at ease. "And I want you to know, I have ever prayed earnestly for both Mr. Mornay and you, my dear Aunt."

Mrs. Bentley softened. "I am obliged to you, Ariana, indeed I am. And you must forget what I said, that you were cold-hearted or some such thing, for I realized at once my mistake. You are particular, but not cold," she clarified. The two exchanged tremulous smiles. But Mrs. Bentley's overwhelming desire to see the wedding move forward returned to her mind. After all, right in front of her were the principal beings who could bring it about! "And since you are such a thoughtful creature, I do not see why we cannot now, that the three of us are present, make some plans regarding the wedding."

To her surprise, it was not her niece but the gentleman who disagreed.

"Not now. Ariana and I need to talk."

Mrs. Bentley realized she was being asked to leave the room, and did so reluctantly. *If only they would leave matters to me. It is as obvious as a horse's tail they are deeply in love!*

Mr. Mornay took hold of Ariana. Gently but firmly he drew her toward him. She thought he meant to kiss her, but he drew her up against him and just held her. After a long, touching embrace he spoke softly into her ear. After listening for some moments, Ariana pulled her head back and looked up at him in consternation.

"You heard everything I said, then!"

He nodded. "Can you forgive me?" His tone intimated he did not think she could.

"Of course. I have nothing to hide." She responded so quickly and easily that he doubled his embrace, lifting her off the floor.

Ariana laughed in surprise.

"And to think of the way I scolded you that night at the Sherwoods'," he said as he put her back so she was standing, though he kept his arms around her. "When I knew 'twas likely an accident and you hadn't the least bit of malice in your whole body."

She smiled, remembering. His face then became serious and Ariana moved to the point at hand.

"What are you going to do about what you heard me speak of to my aunt?"

"What can I do?" He blinked. "What do you want me to do?"

"Are you ready to confess your sins to God? To receive Christ into your own heart, as I have done?" Her heart was beating strongly with suspense and hope, while he continued to just look at her, making no answer.

"You can choose at any moment to put your trust in Christ," she added, softly.

He looked away. "I could easily agree to that. I am afraid, however, I would be doing nothing other than satisfying you for the sake of our marriage. You would never be certain of me. And eventually, when I continue to be myself" (he made a wry grimace) "you will come to despise me."

"I could never despise you!"

He stared at her a moment. "I think you would. The way you spoke to your aunt...I could never marry you selfishly the way I wanted to, before." Their eyes met, troubled. "I was prepared to go forward with the wedding, hoping the pressure of social expectation might be enough to persuade you." He looked quite dismal as he added, "But I will not do that." He paused a moment, considering the only thing that must be done.

"Do you want me to release you? If you wish to be released from our betrothal..." His eyes took on a veiled look as he tried to harden his heart to the inevitable. His voice had sounded hoarse, nothing like his usual commanding tone.

Tears popped, unwelcome, once again into Ariana's eyes. Mr. Mornay did not want her. He had seen her level of devotion to Christ and wanted no part of it. She felt wretched. "Are you certain that is what you want?" she asked.

"What I want? By no means!"

"Oh!" She fell back into his arms, greatly relieved. "Nor do I." She looked up at him and he gave her an earnest kiss.

"But I cannot make a profession of the faith you require."

"Perhaps not today," she admitted, soberly. "But I believe that God has a call on your life, Phillip Mornay. And you must not think you can escape Him—or me—that easily!"

He held her close and spoke quietly into her ear, "I have no wish to escape either of you."

Thirty

Mrs. Bentley, to her credit, reflected upon the conversation she had had with Ariana, and fetched her little prayer book from the drawer where it stayed all week until it was needed for church on Sundays. She liked the book. It was small, a bit fat, but still could fit in a good size reticule. And the pages had a nice feel to them. She gazed at the worn cover with a stirring of old affection: *The Book of Common Prayer*. She had often discovered her niece absorbed in its pages, and she resolved to do her best to make it a part of her daily habits as well. It could surely do her no harm.

It was a small comfort, after all, to be able to do something to further one's religion. She read a morning collect at once, in the little sitting room that adjoined her chamber. After the reading, she said a small prayer. Normally she prayed only in church or at dire moments. She couldn't remember the last time she'd actually followed the readings at home. It hadn't taken long, and praying did feel nice. She would do it more often.

Afterward, like a woman who had been dreaming, she suddenly recalled she had been given the charge of seeing to a wedding! She had abundant work to do! The fact that Ariana had still not formally consented to the match did not deter her. She knew that Mornay loved her niece, and she knew Ariana loved him. Why not just *pray* for a happy conclusion? It had been quite nice to pray and now she had a good reason to do so again. Mrs. Bentley bowed her head, and, moving her lips silently, prayed that Ariana would come to her senses; that the marriage of the year would take place as speedily as could be arranged; and that Mr. Mornay would not lose patience or change his mind.

"There, and amen." She gave a firm nod of her head and moved on to other things.

Just as she rose from the settee, an urgent knocking came at the door of the chamber, and Ariana burst inside. She was lit up with excitement, and breathing quickly from having run up the stairs to fetch her aunt.

"Molly has been caught! Indeed, she took my letter to the Worthingtons' house, no small distance from here! They must be rewarding her amply! Haines has her downstairs and is waiting for you."

Mrs. Bentley jumped up, dropping the prayer book in her haste.

"Oh, Aunt! Your prayer book! How wonderful! I am delighted for you!"

"Oh, hush, stuff, and nonsense. Nothing to get in vapours over."

Ariana smiled. "Very well, I'll say no more." She leaned over and gave her aunt a kiss on the cheek, adding, "but I *am* delighted!"

Aunt Bentley was getting easier to approach, even to kiss affectionately, though she responded in a gruff voice. "Well, you did not come up here to kiss your aunt, I daresay. Let us go down and get to the bottom of this matter."

"They 'ave 'er in the kitchen, mum," said a footman, when they reached the stairs.

"Tell Haines to bring her to the parlour," she ordered, and to Ariana, "Is Mr. Mornay still here?"

"He went to fetch an officer of the King's Bench."

"Excellent! He has the consequence for that."

The women moved hurriedly to the parlour, and Mrs. Bentley immediately resumed pacing, as she had done the day before. She stopped and looked gravely at her niece.

"I will see Cecelia brought to the King's Bench or the Court of Audience. She must live to regret this contemptuous trespassing! Why, 'tis theft. To steal your letters! She deserves gaol for this."

For the first time it occurred to Ariana that her relation would assuredly seek to prosecute the interceptors to the fullest extent of the law. While it had been Ariana's property taken, the theft had occurred in her aunt's house. She was not sure who would have the greater claim to prosecute—or, conversely, not to. She hoped fervently to have some voice in the matter.

A sound at the door signaled the arrival of Haines and the maid, Molly. The little abigail who appeared, wearing chambermaid's attire, head down, shuffling her feet, looked anything but criminal. She could not have been above thirteen, and was tiny, and peeked up only once to reveal a pair of large, frightened eyes.

Haines bowed politely, and then, in a stern tone, addressed the little maid.

"Come, come, make a clean plate of it and tell your mistress everything!"

When she only continued to hang her head in silence, Mrs. Bentley could not restrain herself, though she attempted to tone down her displeasure.

"Come, child, take a seat, here."

Molly looked up tentatively, searching the faces of her prosecutors. She saw compassion on Ariana's face and automatically stepped toward her. Ariana showed her where to sit.

Sitting across from her, she looked even more small and helpless.

Ariana hurriedly spoke first to prevent her aunt from doing so. "You were hired to take my letters, weren't you, my dear?"

The little maid would not look up, but nodded.

"Was there anything else you were to do? Eavesdrop, perhaps?"

Again the slight nod of the head. Then, Ariana saw a tear fall from the little girl's face and her heart melted. Such a little wisp of a thing! She pulled out one of her fine handkerchiefs and handed it to the servant, who took it, looked at it in wonder, and offered it back directly.

"Oh, please use it."

Her aunt looked on impatiently.

"Do you know why your mistress wanted Miss Forsythe's correspondence?"

The girl wiped her face, but shook her head in the negative.

"We are wasting our time," Mrs. Bentley concluded. "To find out anything further we must speak to Cecelia herself."

The door was heard to open downstairs, and there was a shuffle of feet in the hall. Mrs. Worthington's loud voice rang out.

"I daresay there is some misunderstanding! I demand to see Mrs. Bentley at once! And you, sir, release my child this moment!"

Ariana and Mrs. Bentley looked at each other in surprise as they rushed from the parlour. Was Sophia, then, a part of the conspiracy? Mrs. Bentley motioned for her niece not to appear hurried, and they proceeded to calmly descend the staircase. Mr. Mornay had just been on his way up, but he stopped when he saw them, standing aside so the lady of the house could pass. He took Ariana's hand and tucked it neatly upon his arm. Ariana was all eyes, and after greeting him with a smile, they turned and beheld the scene below.

Cecelia Worthington was glowering at the officer from the King's Bench.

"I beg to remind you, sir, that my daughter has not been formally charged with a crime. Release her, I say!" And there, with her head bowed lower than the little chambermaid's had been, was Sophia Worthington, her arms firmly within the grasp of a large officer. She wore a bonnet which hid her face, but it was obvious she had been the one who opened the letter, not her mama, for her gown was splattered tellingly with dark ink.

"Mrs. Bentley," the officer said, in a crisp, authoritative voice. "We found this young woman in possession of a letter that belongs, I am told, to a member of this household."

"Yes! It belongs to my niece."

He rocked on his heels, evidently in his element. "And would that niece be so kind as to positively identify the letter, so we may prosecute the offender?"

"But of course!" breathed Mrs. Bentley. She motioned imperiously for Ariana to come and do so. Ariana reacted by grasping the arm of her betrothed more tightly.

Mr. Mornay looked questioningly at his beloved, saw the look on her face, and found himself stifling a grin. What a girl he had found!

He patted her hand reassuringly, and slowly she descended the steps and went toward the unfortunate prisoner and her guard. Mrs. Worthington's face was frozen in an attitude of dread. The officer dropped his prisoner's arms, took a large rag from a pocket of his overcoat, and, unfolding it carefully, produced the ink-stained papers. Mrs. Worthington began to swoon.

There was Ariana's handwriting, splotched with ink but clearly legible. Ariana saw it and knew what she had to do. Her heart felt heavy; her limbs were stiff. Slowly, she looked up at the King's Bench officer and pronounced her verdict.

"I believe there's been a mistake, sir. I *wanted* Sophia to have this!"

Her aunt gasped. The officer looked in perplexity to Mr. Mornay, who smiled wryly and shrugged. Sophia's head shot up and she stared, open-mouthed, at Ariana, but with a glimmer of hope upon her ink-splattered features. Mrs. Worthington was being supported by two of Mrs. Bentley's footmen, but, upon hearing Ariana's words, she blinked in surprise and was suddenly much recovered.

She sprang to life, in fact, and was instantly by her daughter, standing between her and the dreaded officer.

"You see, sir! My daughter is innocent!"

"I wouldn't go that far," interjected Mrs. Bentley, dryly. She was wearing a deep frown, but she saw Mornay's reaction and thought it best to follow suit. If *he* was willing to have been sent on a fool's errand, to humour her niece, how could she object? She shook her head reproachfully at her incomprehensible charge, however, and waited to see what else might happen.

Once again the officer looked to Mornay, who had joined them in the hall.

"You must do as she says," he charged, still eyeing his future bride with appreciation.

The officer obediently looked to Ariana. "Are you certain, ma'am? I was given to believe I had a thief here."

"I am certain, sir, that if there has been any theft, it will not be repeated." She looked from him to Sophia, who vigorously nodded her assent.

"Very well. It is good day, then, to you." With a quick bow to the company, he turned and left. When the door had shut behind him, Sophia sobbed with relief, looked at Ariana, and held out her arms, moving toward her for an embrace. Ariana would have accepted it, but Mrs. Bentley, seeing the inky mess on the perpetrator and the expensive gown on her niece stepped instantly between them.

"Not another step!"

Sophia halted as if stung, and froze with apprehension.

"My niece has decided to be generous. But I was certainly no party to that." She glared equally at the daughter and the mama. "Tell us the reason you planted a spy beneath my roof, and why you wanted my gel's personal correspondence."

In answer, Sophia covered her face with her hands and sobbed. Mrs. Worthington turned on her. "Come, come, Sophia, out with it! I am as shocked and displeased as Mrs. Bentley, and we must know what was behind this monstrous behaviour!"

"You didn't know?" Mrs. Bentley asked, doubtfully.

"Of course not! Sophia Worthington! Do not keep Mrs. Bentley and Miss Forsythe waiting!" Her mother rounded on her and boxed her ear. Her protective feelings for her child had vanished with the officer. Now that the danger of prison was past, the humiliation of the episode was sinking in on her. She glanced uncomfortably at Ariana but could not even bring herself to peek at Mornay. Of all people, why, oh why, did the Paragon have to be involved? Their disgrace was utter and complete!

"Well?" She took her reticule and lashed the girl with it. Sophia sobbed louder, and then wailed, pitifully. "I just wanted to kno-o-o-o-ow…about her! I just wanted to know!"

Her mother looked dismayed. "This is nonsense! *What* did you want to know?"

Sophia peeked at her mama. "You have always said I am quite the little spy; and have I not kept you informed? Where they went together? Carlton House, and Vauxhall? And so on?"

Ariana blushed, recalling that she had indeed given a true account of her activities in her letters. To think they had all been read by Sophia!

Mrs. Worthington was beside herself. She raised her reticule again and began lashing her daughter mercilessly. Sophia raised her hands to ward off the attack and resumed wailing, more pitifully than before. Haines had the sense to open the door behind the ladies, and they left the house that way; with Mrs. Worthington scolding and pummeling her daughter, and Sophia blubbering like a baby.

The atmosphere felt instantly lighter. Ariana went to Mornay, who opened his arms to her.

"I'm sorry," she said, into his chest.

"What for?"

She lifted her head and looked up in surprise. "For all your trouble, and time, getting the officer, and the Worthingtons."

He gave a little smile and reached inside a pocket of his waistcoat, pulling out a packet of letters, carefully tied with a ribbon. "I also got these."

"My letters! Oh!" She gave him an impulsive kiss. "Look, not only mine, but those from my parents! Why on earth did she want them?"

"So you wouldn't know yours hadn't been received."

Mrs. Bentley came over and saw the letters. "But to have wasted so much of Mr. Mornay's time, and the officer's!"

"Not at all," he said. "The man from the Bench was delighted to go with me."

Mrs. Bentley shook her head knowingly. "Hm, and how much did he require from you?"

Ariana's brows furrowed in concern.

"It's of no account. He was compensated for his trouble, however, if that concerns you."

"Oh, Phillip! I am sorry. If I'd known—"

"You would have done exactly the same thing," he finished for her, grinning. She smiled weakly, realizing he was right. One sight of the defeated and humiliated Sophia had been sufficient to make Ariana feel she had been more than compensated for the harm done her. The young woman would be housebound for weeks no doubt. Surely that was punishment enough.

She suddenly remembered Molly. "Will you keep the little house-maid, Aunt? What will we do with her?"

"*Keep* her?" The words exploded from her lips. "Certainly not! Keep a traitor? Pay wages to a thief? Never."

Ariana's face fell.

"Haines, please summon Mrs. Ruskin; we must have that wicked gel removed from the household at once."

As he left, Ariana turned and rushed back up the stairs.

Molly had apparently not moved from her spot on the sofa. She had, in fact, stolen out to the stairs to listen to the proceedings below. Sight of the officer had sent her into such a fright, however, she would have fled the house, only it was impossible, for a tall gentleman was upon the stairs, and others were blocking the exit. Having no alterna-tive, she returned to her former place, and so was sitting, sniffling and trembling, when Ariana found her.

"My dear," Ariana said kindly, after sitting across from her. "Don't be afraid. Will you go back to the Worthingtons?"

She shook her head, and found her voice. "No, mum. I don' think they'd 'ave me, mum."

"Mrs. Bentley will not keep you. Do you have a place to go? A home?"

The little abigail frowned. Mournfully, she shook her head.

Mr. Mornay had entered the room and was standing back, watching with that bemused expression. Ariana looked over at him.

"Do you know what I would like to do with her?"

He grinned, but shook his head. "What would you like to do with her?"

She cocked her head to one side, studying him thoughtfully. "Do you indeed want to know?"

"I do indeed want to know."

Her eyes brightened. "Splendid! I want you to take her."

His smile vanished. If it had been anyone other than her making such a request, he would have burst forth into a few round epithets, but it wasn't anyone else; it was the woman he adored. He merely scowled, therefore, and replied, "She'll be put in the kitchen; and only until she can find another situation; only until then."

He did, at least, get a warm embrace and yet another kiss of gratitude. It almost made it worthwhile.

✺

The next day, Mr. O'Brien made a call at Hanover Square. Ariana was in the parlour alone, a refreshing change for him, and he came toward her hopefully. She smiled a greeting, to which he reached for her hand to kiss it. Embarrassed by this gesture, she quickly reclaimed her hand and motioned for him to take a seat.

"I stayed away as long as I could," he said, when they were seated across from one another with a polished mahogany table between them. His sandy hair was neatly combed back, his side-whiskers and moustache trimmed according to fashion. He wore light-coloured pantaloons and jockey boots, a high collar and voluminous cravat. Mr. O'Brien did not have the air of Mr. Mornay or the fine quality of clothing, but he dressed neatly and reasonably.

He leaned forward in his seat, his elbows on his knees.

"I decided I had to hear from your own lips, my dearest Miss Forsythe, that the reports are true. Can it really be that you, so pious as you are, will wed Mr. Mornay?"

Ariana folded her hands upon her lap, thinking how to answer.

There was some question in her mind; yet they were legitimately engaged.

"It does appear to be true."

He had to question this cryptic response, eyeing her curiously.

"Is it settled? Are you actually betrothed, or can it be I may still hope?"

"It is bound to be finalized shortly; we are betrothed, you see, only we have not yet set a date for the ceremony."

Mr. O'Brien took the news well; he nodded, and then met her eyes.

"Are you in love with him, then?"

"I am afraid that yes, I am." A smile spread across her face.

"Perhaps you should be afraid." His voice was gentle, and all the more compelling for that. If not, she might have been startled; she might have felt warned for what was coming next.

"This man is so unlike you. He has none of your gentleness, or your virtue. I could hardly conceive of your marrying him—"

"I appreciate your concern, but I assure you it is unnecessary. Mr. Mornay is kind and thoughtful to me, nothing else." She paused, and added, "As for virtue, some good deeds go before men, and are widely seen, but some follow after; his are the sort that follow after. He is a good man."

Mr. O'Brien cleared his throat. "May I be frank with you, Miss Forsythe?"

She nodded. "Of course."

He spoke next in a low voice. "'Tis said he carried you into his coach; I could not reach a window and see for myself, there was such a crowd at them. But was it against your will? I assure you, you would not be the first young lady to be coerced into a union by such methods."

The suggestion irked her.

"Neither Mr. Mornay, nor anyone else for that matter, could coerce me into marriage against my will! You underestimate me, Mr. O'Brien."

"I beg your pardon," he said, hurriedly. "Do not be out of

countenance with me. You must know I asked you only out of deep and sincere concern for your welfare."

Ariana's face softened. "I understand. But you must believe Mr. Mornay is not a beast. He is prodigiously good to me." She smiled disarmingly. "Now; may I ring for tea?"

Thirty-One

The next morning Mr. Mornay sent word he would be calling for Ariana in his carriage at eleven o'clock. The footman who came with the note brought an enormous bouquet of heavy, aromatic red roses, which Ariana insisted on placing in water herself.

Mrs. Bentley was impressed. "I don't doubt but that man had these brought to town from the forcing house at Aspindon!"

Ariana hastened to be ready, but at fifteen minutes before the hour the bell rang, and it was he. When she entered the parlour he turned and just stood, staring at her with his perceptive eyes as if seeing her for the first time. She was attired in a walking-out dress of cambric with a high, ruffled neck, her hair done atop her head prettily. He went to meet her, receiving both her hands in his, and reverently kissed each one.

"Thank you for the roses," she offered. "They're beautiful!"

"As are you."

"You look above well yourself."

He smiled and pressed her hands in his own. "We are off to see my Aunt Royleforst, if that will be agreeable to you."

"Certainly, if you like. I shall inform Aunt Bentley."

"I'll get the carriage."

Ariana found her aunt at the breakfast table sipping a cup of chocolate and wearing an old-fashioned mobcap. She came to attention when she heard Mr. Mornay had called, and Ariana spotted the prayer book on the table. She felt a rise of excitement but quelled it for her aunt's sake.

"Mr. Mornay is taking me to see Mrs. Royleforst," Ariana said.

Mrs. Bentley raised her chin interestedly. "Mrs. Royleforst?"

"Yes."

"Well. Enjoy yourself. And tell Mr. Mornay—no, I'll come and tell him myself."

"He is gone for the carriage already."

"Oh, very well, but tell him there are matters we must yet discuss. I dare not bespeak your trousseau without his approval. Though he put the matter into my hands, I know he is far too particular and he must dictate which fabrics he wants for you."

Ariana responded by quickly bending and placing another light kiss on her aunt's cheek. "I must go. I cannot keep Mr. Mornay waiting." And she rushed from the room.

Mr. Mornay had turned the carriage and it was ready in the street when Ariana came out. He was about to jump down to help her up, but without waiting for help she raised her skirts and climbed up, joining him atop the board rather clumsily. She plopped, more than sat, beside him, saw his face, and instantly realized her mistake. To her relief, he laughed out loud.

She smiled demurely. "When I was younger, my mama decried ever teaching me to be a lady."

He gave the reins a sharp crack with a shout to the horses. "I suppose I should have realized that when I first discovered you in a tree! But I must inform you I think of you as quite the lady. Young, impulsive, scandalously honest, yes, but when you've a mind for it, you can move as smoothly as a queen. I've seen you do it."

Instead of heading out of Mayfair, Mr. Mornay turned into Grosvenor Square. As he pulled to the curb he explained, "I forgot a gift for my aunt. Come, while I fetch a basket." Before jumping down from the board, he turned to her gravely.

"Do not move, until I am in position to help you." The odd set of his face told her he was endeavouring not to laugh, and so she nodded with equal gravity.

"I am *immobile*, sir, until you give the word!"

As on her last visit, she enjoyed the tasteful elegance of his house. Every room was well-appointed, not in the overwhelmingly ornate style of the Regent, but just like Mr. Mornay's manner of dress: the best quality in the right proportions, for an overall effect of beauty as well as practicality.

When she was settled in his study, which she preferred to the parlour for its more personal nature, he left to order the basket. Ariana looked around curiously. There were built-in bookshelves lining two walls, and she was tempted to peruse the titles. Papa said you could learn a lot about a person by seeing their books. But it felt disingenuous, somehow, with Mr. Mornay absent, and so she did not.

The room was comfortable, though strongly masculine with a large, dark-oak desk and ponderous leather chair, and brown wainscoting. Ariana sat in a deeply cushioned side-chair, whose twin was adjacent. A large hearth at one end no doubt ensured a warm room in winter, and above the mantelpiece was a portrait of a beautiful, dark-haired lady. She wondered if it was Mr. Mornay's mama, and got up to look closely. The moment she saw the swirling dark eyes, Ariana knew her guess had been correct. The lady had his dark good looks, his presence, but without the brooding shadow he seemed to labour under.

Before taking her seat again, she noticed a few copies of *The Sporting Magazine* upon the neat desktop, as well as a large, aged, leather-bound tome. Looking at the book from her seat, she wondered if Mr. Mornay might have been reading a Bible. Could it be?

Feeling slightly breathless, she rose and quickly rounded the desk. She had to know. Yes! *The Holy Bible.* Upon opening the worn cover she came upon a register of births and deaths. It went back only two generations. She was curious to read it all but the record of deaths stood out more. She felt her eyes drawn to it and quickly scanned its contents, passing over the oldest entries, and beginning at "Edward Henry Mornay," supposing it was Mr. Mornay's father.

Edward Henry Mornay, died, 1800. Nigel Edward Mornay, died, 1800. Miranda Elizabeth Mornay, died, 1801. Three deaths in so little time! And that was the last entry.

She went back to the record of births, perhaps it would reveal the relation of these people to Mr. Mornay, but a noise in the hall sent her scurrying back to her seat.

After a slight knock, the butler entered bearing a tray with tea and chocolate. He poured her tea, and then seemed to hesitate, waiting uncertainly. He was a small, stocky man, balding, and with a serious countenance. He bowed, leaving, but then stopped.

"May I offer," he ventured, "my deepest congratulations, and say how happy we all are at the prospect of welcoming you to this establishment."

"Thank you very much." She was touched by the fact that Mr. Mornay had notified his staff. "What shall I call you?"

"Forgive me. William Frederick, at your service, ma'am. The master calls me Freddy."

"Thank you, Freddy." She smiled, and instantly won him over. She was still smiling after he bowed again and left, for he had done so with a barely disguised grin on his well-trained face, and Ariana preferred a butler who was personable.

⚭⚭⚭

After closing the door to the study, Freddy headed back to the kitchens as full of glee as that sober-minded soul could be. The master had informed him his future mistress was in the study, and he was elated by the picture of sweetness she presented. He could hardly wait to share the news with the others.

"Glory be!" he exclaimed, upon returning to that sanctum for servants, the kitchen. The others turned to listen eagerly.

"Not only is our determined bachelor to finally feather the nest, but our future mistress is a drop of sunlight."

"What's 'at? A drop o' sun? 'At's no way t'describe a laidy," Letty, a housemaid, grimaced. She looked around, grabbed a cut-glass candlestick and said, "I'll takes a look meself!"

"Oh, no, we'll have none of that," reprimanded Freddy. But Letty's face dropped.

"Mrs. 'amilton'd let me!"

"But Mrs. Hamilton isn't here, is she?" For it was the housekeeper's day off. He spoke as if speaking to a child, and indeed, though Letty was one of the oldest servants in the household, she often behaved like a petulant youngster, getting away with it because she had worked for the Mornay family for most of her life.

"I won't do no 'arm!" She folded her arms angrily across her chest and glowered at the butler, who roundly ignored her.

"Oh, why not let 'er go?" said Cook, busy filling the basket the master had requested. "We'd all like to say, congratters, that's all. An' if she does anythin' to bodge it, you can give 'er a right drubbin'!"

"And so I shall," he stated severely, giving Letty a grim look. With a whoop she grabbed the candlestick and ran from the room.

∽⌒∽⌒∽

Minutes later there was a scratch at the study door, and in walked Letty, all wide-eyed. *Lawks, it was true! A lighter-haired laidy she had never seen, and so prim and proper and kindly lookin'!* She noted the large eyes, raised in curiosity at the moment, the light green shawl over a pretty cambric dress, and fine bonnet; and even the genteel satin slippers on her feet. Letty, too, had an immediate sense that here was a mistress she could adore. Quickly laying the candlestick on the sturdy desk, she gave Ariana a slow curtsey.

Ariana felt it necessary to say something to the enormous pair of eyes gaping at her in astonishment.

"Good day."

This appeared to satisfy the servant, for she smiled, revealing a missing tooth, and then turned and strode from the room, still smiling. She was smiling when she entered the kitchen, and when she described the vision she had seen to the others.

"Bless me!" Cook exclaimed, covering her mouth with one chubby hand. "I 'ave a hankering to see 'er meself." She was actually the under cook, beneath the real chef of the establishment, but with a good reputation among the staff as a hard worker.

"Is she pri'ee?" Bessie, a scullery maid who had just come in, wanted to know.

"Mor'n pri'ee!" offered a gruff footman, who often served as out-rider on Mr. Mornay's coach. He had seen Miss Forsythe on more than one occasion and would have sent a smart remark her way in a jif—if not for her station and the master, that is.

The parlour maid's curiosity got the best of her, and soon Miss Forsythe's musings were interrupted by another faint knock at the door. In a moment the servant swept in holding a feather duster. She took a split-second glance at Ariana and then quickly crossed before her and breezily dusted the desk top, not daring to peek again; then retraced her steps, lightly dusting all the way. She stopped abruptly in front of Ariana (who was beginning to think she might have to endure being dusted herself) and curtseyed, wide-eyed, like the first servant. She then swept out of the room, all in less than thirty seconds, so that it had been like a sort of dance.

A few moments later, a chambermaid came shyly into the room carrying a rag and pail. She hazarded a split-second glance at Ariana, headed straight to the fireplace and began polishing the grate, which was clean to begin with. When she turned to leave, she too was over-come by a compulsion to curtsey, and did so, her eyes larger than the last servant's. Ariana smiled at her.

She had not alarmed her, as had the first maid, or nearly dusted her, as had the second. When, a few seconds later, yet another scratch came at the door, Ariana steeled herself to be interviewed, so to speak, once again.

This time it was Cook, ostensibly to question the lady as to her preference of fresh fruit for the basket. She took in nearly every inch of Ariana, barely listening to her response that, "Anything, anything at all will be fine, I imagine," when Mr. Mornay knocked firmly on the door and entered.

He looked in dismay at Cook bending before Ariana with a crock of fruit in her hands.

"What's this?" His hands were on his hips, and he scowled. Cook froze with fear. For a second.

"Oh, sir! Last week a lady on Grant Street ate a orange and dropped as dead as a doornail, sir! They said she never could tol'rate oranges but she went and ate one, anyroad!" She looked meaningfully at Ariana. "I 'ad to check that your laidy 'ad no indisposition to fruit, sir."

Mr. Mornay's brows were raised, but he no longer looked angry. "The basket is for my aunt."

Cook's red, round face grew even redder.

"I am much obliged to you, nevertheless," Ariana said quickly, in a hearty tone.

This put her in Cook's good graces from that day forward. Meanwhile, below stairs, both housemaids had pronounced her to be as "pri'ee as a princess." Upon her return to the safety of the kitchens, Cook added to the consensus but also exclaimed, "Now there be a kind mistress if ever I saw one."

⋙⋘

When Ariana and Mr. Mornay were finally seated again atop the board, the basket carefully stowed in back, she turned to him.

"Is your aunt expecting us?"

"No." His eyes were upon his horses as he moved them into traffic. "She is expecting me. She asked me to bring you, but since I suspected she wished to interrogate you, I said I would not." He looked at her. "Do you mind going? I believe she will encourage you, and right now I welcome encouragement from any corner."

Ariana felt a small alarm. Mrs. Royleforst was apparently a *force* to be reckoned with, but as she was thinking thus, he added, "And she will be delighted to see you." Ariana hoped he was right.

Thirty-Two

The visit began smoothly in Mrs. Royleforst's opulent parlour where they drank lemonade, and ate biscuits and afternoon cake. They sat chatting about light subjects for a proper amount of time, after which Mrs. Royleforst bid her nephew go and bring her a newspaper.

He looked pointedly at Miss Bluford, who had joined the company: Why did not she do it, since it was her occupation to satisfy the whims of her mistress? But Miss Bluford refused to peek at him, though Ariana was certain she felt the dark eyes upon her.

Mrs. Royleforst shrewdly interfered.

"No, no, it must be you, Phillip! I am intent on speaking with Miss Forsythe."

"In that case," he said gallantly, rising from his seat, "I am at your service." But he gave his aunt a strong look before he bowed and left. "Go easy on her." The door clicked shut quietly behind him. Ariana and Mrs. Royleforst faced each other.

"Miss Bluford," she said. "I am in mind to have some negus. Do see if you can make some up for us." Without a word, the woman rose and left the room. Now it was only the two of them.

Coming straight to the point, Mrs. Royleforst was astonished, she said, that any girl would refuse her nephew, and she wanted to know why Ariana had done so. When Ariana explained her hesitation as stemming from her spiritual life, the woman became annoyed.

"You should then consider it your Christian duty to improve Phillip, and you can best do that by marrying him." Without raising her voice, she managed to pack a good scold in her words.

"Only God can improve a person, ma'am," Ariana countered. "And I consider it my chief duty to please the Lord by marrying a man who shares my faith."

The lady's eyebrows went up above her small eyes.

"You are dead set against him, then!"

"No, I am hoping...the situation will change." Her words sounded lame to her own ears.

"But you are unwilling to change it yourself! Humph! I see little hope there." She gazed at Ariana with a severe expression on her face.

Ariana tried to soften that expression. "We are indeed betrothed."

"Nonsense! When you refuse to set a wedding date? I am greatly moved by Phillip's astonishing concern for you, Miss Forsythe. And I daresay you have no idea of the great honour he is offering you." She paused, looking searchingly at the girl, then continued. "If you want a man who will say whatever you want and deceive you, I warrant there are many for the taking. But if you want one who is true to his word, to his heart, and will be true to you—Phillip is your man. Despite my disappointment in your stubbornness, your *foolishness,* I advise you as a friend: Be done with your qualms, and thank God for what He has given you. My nephew may not be the man to please a crowd, but he is true to the bone, I assure you."

Ariana had no more replies. And worse, she felt a nagging conviction that what Mrs. Royleforst was saying was true: Mr. Mornay was good for his word. He wouldn't intentionally deceive her. He could have professed a false faith, but hadn't. He was a good man.

When he returned to the room the unmistakable tension in the air was palpable. He thought it best to take Ariana home. She was quiet on the return drive, and he was too familiar with his aunt not to know why.

"Would you like to talk about it?"

"No. Thank you." Then, "She despises me."

"She gave you a set-down?"

"Quite."

"For putting off my suit?"

"Yes."

"Then she does not, believe me, despise you. If she did, she would have given you numerous reasons why you are right to do as you are doing."

She looked at him, surprised. "Are you certain?"

"Completely."

When they arrived at Hanover Square, Mr. Mornay did not move to help her down.

"I am not accustomed to being patient." He turned and was facing her. "I am endeavouring to be so for your sake."

She gave him a tender smile. "You have been patient. It is a struggle for me, as well."

He looked perplexed.

She remembered the leather-bound Bible on his desk. "My best advice is to read the Scriptures for yourself. The Lord speaks to us through His Word. He will speak to your heart, I promise you, if you only open your heart to Him."

His gray-black eyes studied her intently. "You are certain of that?"

"I am. *'They that seek me will find me, when they look for me with all their heart.'*"

"I spoke to the vicar and told him, I believe, the extent of our difficulty."

"Yes?"

"His reply was that I should convince you at all costs that I am a Christian, having been raised in the church. I must say he nearly convinced me, but having heard your definition, I retain my doubts." He paused. "I do not come from a religious family as you do, but I have never, in my darkest hours, renounced the faith I was born into, and I have indeed had my share of dark hours."

She looked at him compassionately, thinking of the register of deaths recorded in the family Bible—had they caused his darkest hours? She raised a gloved hand to softly touch his face.

"Mr. Mornay—I must remind you. You cannot be born into the faith. It is not a religion so much as a friendship with God, more than that, a relation to Him. You must deliberately choose to be His relation. To open your heart to Him. That is all."

"I have never closed myself to Him!" He sounded irritated as he reached for her hands. "If you would like me to say I choose to be a Christian, as you have, then very well, I choose it."

When her countenance did not lighten, he said again, "I choose to be a Christian!"

Ariana was filled with love and sadness. Hopelessness washed over her. He squeezed her hands.

"I am willing to change for you, Ariana, as much as I can...but you must believe in me, just a little. I want to love you, and take care of you, and raise a family with you. I have never wanted such a thing before, not for a single second. You are the beginning of a new life for me, don't you see? And I want more than anything to provide a wonderful life for you, too."

He went on talking soothingly, laying out for her a picture of his assets, holdings, and properties. He described how they could come to London every season if she wished; that he would escort her to whatever entertainments she fancied. She would own equally all that was his. He was being earnest and gentle and her head was beginning to swim with the ache of knowing and loving him and yet having to keep him at a safe distance. It sounded wonderful—but it was not truly within her reach, for he was not fully hers, nor could he be, unless he was God's first.

"Do you wish to persuade me by what you own?" She cried out suddenly, unable to bear listening a moment longer.

He was taken aback. "Ariana, you amaze me. I did not hope to *win* you with this information, only to enlighten you on what sort of life you can expect to have with me. I supposed these things would please you."

"Forgive me! You're perfectly right. It sounds wonderful." She studied his impossibly handsome face. "*You're* perfectly wonderful, in fact! It would be easier if you weren't! I wish I had never met you if I can't have you!"

He reached for her, but she turned away.

"Please help me down, now," she asked.

He resignedly got down to do so. After handing her down, he kept his hands about her waist for a moment, making her meet his eyes.

"I believe Mrs. Bentley will have a dinner guest tonight." When she looked questioningly at him, he added, with a little smile: "Me."

She was pleased, and had to smile a little despite her teary countenance.

"You may give me as much instruction as you like, as much as you can pack into the next hour or two. Will that suit you?"

"Yes! I shall be happy to!" Mrs. Bentley's groom, who had been standing against the house waiting to see if his services were required, now took the reins of the team. Ariana's mind went to work planning Scripture passages she wished to share with Mr. Mornay. His willingness to explore the meaning of a true faith was encouraging to her.

Unfortunately, her aunt was entertaining a few society notables and was only too delighted to include the Paragon. Ariana did not have him to herself, therefore.

Then, shortly after dinner, Mrs. Bentley reminded her charge of an engagement they had accepted, to which Ariana would have to accompany her aunt. She sensed a relief in Mr. Mornay, which bothered her. In fact, he seemed almost eager to be off. She had no way of knowing that his eagerness was based in frustration. He was finding it difficult to balance his feelings for Ariana with the forced stagnancy of their relationship. The frustration was growing each time he saw her. Watching her interacting, graceful, sweet, and beautiful, had been about all he could bear for one night.

Ariana, too, was filled with an aching regret. During the meal it had occurred to her that she had never once prayed with Mr. Mornay. For him, yes, but not *with* him. Some awful weakness of character prevented her. And yet, perhaps this was the very thing they needed. Simply to begin praying together.

Their eyes met; his swirling and dark, and hers, without their usual sparkle. Mrs. Bentley thought she had never seen such a forlorn pair. She sent Ariana to change into evening dress, and, after the girl had shared a brief embrace with her betrothed, she turned and ascended the stairs, the picture of beautiful sadness. They watched her leave, Mr. Mornay with an unreadable expression on his face.

The chaperon turned on him.

"Why do you not come up with some plan? You are the Paragon! Surely a young girl cannot be more than you can manage."

He did not think Mrs. Bentley was intending to insult him, but insulted was how he felt. He had been fighting a growing feeling of defeat all week, and now, her words crowned it. His temper, his quick tongue—gone, at the moment. And he left the house in that sorry state. Outside, he reprimanded himself. Surely he could cope with disappointment! Why did it feel as if nothing in the whole world mattered, except getting hold of that soul-stirring blonde minx making him so miserable? He thought of going home and sitting in his study and thinking it all over. The image of the family Bible, sitting this moment upon his desk, entered his mind, and he decided he would have a look at it. That's why he had taken it off the shelf to begin with.

When he climbed into his curricle, he was intent on doing just that; going home and reading the Bible, mulling things over. He had no sooner turned onto Grosvenor Square, however, than he ran into a roadblock. Someone's gleaming black coach was standing fully across the road, obviously intending to bar traffic. A face appeared at the window, saw him, and smiled. The door opened and Lord Alvanley, one of the Carlton House set, came forth.

"Ho, Mornay! You black dog, keeping us waiting like this! Where the devil have you been?"

Phillip jumped off the board, holding to the ribbons, and went to meet his friend, who was approaching with a definite swagger to his walk. A footman followed behind him.

"Don't give me that grimace!" They were face to face in the street.

"Move your coach, then, you idiotic rascal! Don't you know better than to block the road?"

"We were waiting for *you!*" Clearly he thought that information must clear him from any wrongdoing.

Mr. Mornay turned to go. "That's what parlours are for." He prepared to climb atop the board.

"Not so fast, you dunce! Prinny is inside!" Alvanley pointed back at his carriage, and gave a snort of laughter. "We smuggled him out of Carlton House without any of his servants realizing it! When they discover his absence, there'll be an uproar! Can you see *The Times,* tomorrow? 'The Missing Regent!'" He collapsed into laughter.

Mr. Mornay was not in the mood for pranks, though the prince, when in league with others, could be alarmingly friendly to them. But he resignedly handed the ribbons to Alvanley, and headed to pay his respects.

"I can spare a minute."

Not likely! Thought Alvanley. *Now we've got you!* He nodded at his footman, who promptly took the ribbons, waited until Mr. Mornay had gone into the coach, and then began walking the horses carefully around his master's coach—there was enough room by a hair—toward the Mornay house, just as he had been instructed earlier to do.

Alvanley laughed and went toward his equipage, stopping to holler at his coachman, "Turn 'er around, Fritz!" He then climbed inside.

A few other mischievous aristocrats were inside the crowded coach with the prince, including Brummell, but they pulled Mornay into their midst. The mood was high and spirits were flowing freely. A bottle was slapped into his hand, but he put it down.

"Drink up, Phillip, you look to be in the blue devils, at any rate." The Regent welcomed him thus. Someone else piped in: "Having trouble with Lady Mornay?" And another: "Has she taken a disgust of you already? Excellent! We'll have you back to ourselves."

"Perhaps it is only his style she liked; in that case, we can send

Beau, here, to Hanover Square—a pretty pair they would make, eh, Mornay?"

Mr. Mornay allowed the comments to run their course before he turned to the Regent. "What's the plan? You look to be on an all-nighter."

"*You* are the plan!" interjected Alvanley, to laughter. "We are determined to have you join us in the most foul dissipation evil imaginations can devise. The prospect of your saintly future bride reforming you was our excuse, if we must furnish one. So we smuggled Prinny, and now we have you!" The coach was indeed leaving Grosvenor Square.

"Not tonight, gentlemen. I have things to attend to—" He moved to exit the vehicle before it picked up speed, but his way was instantly blocked, and others held onto his arms.

"I hate to inform you, old chap, but we have indeed reached the unanimous conclusion you must join us tonight," said Brummell. "And ignore Alvanley! We're merely intent on some harmless fun," and he raised a bottle to his mouth and then offered it to Mornay, who again declined.

"Prinny insisted on your company in any case, isn't that right, Your Royal Highness?" The equipage, meanwhile, had picked up speed. The coach was bulleting through narrow London streets. Even if Phillip managed to get past the men, it would be taking his life in his hands to try and jump for it. With dismay, he realized his friends meant business. He sat back with a sigh. He could see it was going to be a long evening.

Thirty-Three

*A*riana fetched a fresh handkerchief from the wardrobe. She was going through her entire stock in one night, for she had been crying pitifully. She looked down at the new one only to realize it had the letters "P" and "M" in ornate embroidery on it. How ironic that she should be using Phillip's handkerchief when he was the reason for her tears!

She wanted to confess her failure to pray with the man she loved. If only they could pray together, it might reveal to him how easy it was to talk with God.

Tonight, one prayer had led to another, and soon she was reciting her woes to the Lord afresh, though she had done so, it seemed, a hundred times. Were her prayers in vain? Why had she became inadvertently entangled with Phillip Mornay from her first day in society? Why was she betrothed to a man if he was not the one meant for her? And if he was, was she wrong to be harping on that one Scripture about being unequally yoked? But wasn't this what she had been taught? What she always had believed was immutable?

She resorted to begging God on her knees, to please, *please* bring Mr. Mornay to a saving faith. Then, she switched tactics and prayed not to love him at all if he was not to share her faith and life. Finally, she begged God to show her what to do. She could bear the disquiet no longer. She hated the perplexity and hurt she saw in Mr. Mornay's eyes! Feelings, she knew, that were mirrored in her own. Oh, why, why was God treating her thus?

She lay down, exhausted from her emotional turmoil, and still dressed in her gown, fell asleep. A few hours later, the silver moon was already dipping in the sky when she awoke with a start and a gasp. Her troubles still lay heavy upon her. Too heavy. She recognized it, she thought, as a call to pray, again. But no sooner did she fall to her knees than a ferocious restlessness came upon her. *She should go see Mr. Mornay. Now.*

What was she thinking? Go see him in the middle of the night? When ladies did not usually call upon men at any hour? She must continue to pray, that was all. But the longer she tried to pray, the stronger she felt that urgent need to go and see Mr. Mornay. It was positively unshakeable.

How absurd to think of doing such a thing! She started to argue with God and then caught herself. Argue with God? Why remonstrate if it was God calling her to do this? She was receiving divine guidance! And so she must, of course, obey! Yes, strange as it was, she must obey.

"This is Your bidding, isn't it, Lord?" She had to ask once more. She forced her mind to be still. She must cease the roiling thoughts of her heart and mind, and listen. And then, she knew. It was not an audible voice but nevertheless she heard it: *Go!* Perhaps she only heard it in her heart. She wasn't sure how it happened, but she was certain of what she must do.

Many of the beau monde regularly spent entire nights about town; Young ladies were sometimes among them. She herself had experienced coming home as the light of dawn was rising. She assured herself that her call would not seem too outlandish to Mr. Mornay, who surely was accustomed to keeping late hours.

I could see him in the morning. But no, it was no use. She had to go now. Somehow this was a part of God's plan. If she failed to obey, she would miss something important, that was certain. She straightened her gown and left her bedchamber to find Mrs. Bentley.

When she approached her aunt's door she was relieved to see light coming from beneath it. Her aunt was awake! So far, so good.

Mrs. Bentley was indeed awake. She was at her escritoire writing the banns for the wedding, after tossing and turning for hours to no avail. It was rare for her to have difficulty sleeping, and she finally thought she may as well do something useful with the time. When she heard the knock, she knew at once it was different from the usual scratchy sound the servants made, and she quickly opened a small drawer of the desk and shoved the half-written notice inside. She closed the ink bottle and hid her pen.

"Come in."

Ariana entered the room, obviously in some perturbation.

"What is it? Why are you not sleeping?"

"Aunt Bentley, is it possible—would it be too improper—for us to make a call on Mr. Mornay?"

Her aunt smiled. "Not at all! You are betrothed. I'll tell Haines in the morning to have the carriage ready, say, around noon." She stood up and adjusted her mob-cap.

"No, no, Aunt, I mean to call upon him now, this very minute."

Mrs. Bentley froze. "*Now?*"

Ariana nodded mutely.

Slowly the chaperon returned to her seat.

"Absolutely not." Her face was raised in a posture that said she was prepared for a fight. "Whatever for?"

" 'Tis imperative that I see him this very night! I need to speak with him. To pray with him. I believe our wedding may go forth. Oh, I hardly know, myself, what has happened," she cried, wringing her hands, "but I feel urgently I must see him!" In response to her aunt's unpromising demeanour, she prayed, *Lord, Mrs. Bentley must give her leave, or it is off!*

The lady rose from her seat and started pacing. She studied her niece. "You think the wedding may go forward?"

"I do…although I cannot say why or how." She recognized the inanity of her words, but was helpless to change them, for that was just how she felt. Something momentous was afoot! The sense of urgency was still heavy upon her.

Her aunt began thinking aloud.

"His house is not far from here… Perhaps I will send a messenger to announce our intentions. He can give his leave, then, and there will be no question of impropriety." She began to walk toward the bellpull, but Ariana made a worried sound in her throat.

"Now what is it?" Aunt Bentley groaned.

"My dear Aunt, can we not just go? Nothing shall be lost, I warrant you; he will not be angry to see me." Her aunt seemed to be swayed by that, thinking the same thing herself, that Mornay could only be glad if Ariana wanted to see him so desperately. It must have been due to her own desire to see her niece's wedding go forward, for in the next second she agreed to go.

Rejoicing, Ariana quickly helped the older woman out of her chemise nightdress and into a suitable gown. When they were downstairs, Mrs. Bentley put on her bonnet, tying the strings slowly, with a look almost of wonder upon her features.

"This is highly irregular; I can't imagine why I have agreed to this!" Ariana said nothing, but slipped into a light redingote of shot silk and raised the hood over her head. Haines quickly had the horses harnessed, attached the smallest vehicle that his mistress owned, a light, open gig, and came round the front for them. When Mrs. Bentley saw the equipage she gave a gasp.

"Haines! What on earth! Do you think we will go calling at this hour in an open carriage? Are you quite out of your mind?"

Haines stiffened noticeably, but his feeling of pride at being the butler of the establishment—even if he was called upon now and then in an emergency to serve as coachman, required him to make no argument. This was vexing, however, for he had felt justified in the use of the small gig since their drive was for so short a distance, only a few streets.

"I beg your pardon, ma'am." He returned the gig and got the coach. The ladies had to wait extra minutes while the horses were harnessed and the equipage could be brought round from the mews. Ariana was breathless by the time they were situated comfortably and on their way.

Haines pulled sharply to the curb in front of the Mornay house. A footman, looking prodigiously surprised, came out the front door as the ladies were leaving the carriage. He had recognized Ariana from his sleepy perch at a window and hurried out at once. Mrs. Bentley was giving orders before her foot reached the front door.

"Tell your master Miss Forsythe and her aunt are arrived. Be certain to say we do not wish to intrude upon his privacy and that we may return at another time if he prefers."

"I'm sorry, mum. The master's not returned yet."

Ariana's face dropped.

Her aunt said heavily, "Oh." Aunt Bentley then looked at her niece and said, "We have come in vain, it seems."

The footman quickly produced the butler, who greeted Ariana and her aunt with a bow. He did not look to have been asleep, Ariana thought.

"Hello Freddy," she breathed. "I have to see him! May we wait?"

Freddy immediately led the ladies upstairs to the parlour where, he said, they could wait comfortably. Mrs. Bentley did not want to wait, and her face was the picture of ill-usage.

"We shall stay for no longer than a quarter hour!" she insisted. "You may leave a card after that; but we shall positively not wait a second longer than a quarter hour! Do you understand, Ariana?"

"Yes, ma'am." She had felt convinced this was a divine mission of sorts, and now was it to be fruitless? *Send him home, dear Lord!*

Downstairs Freddy kept a sharp eye out for the return of his master, watching from a window facing the street. In the parlour, there was silence except for the steady tick, tick, tick, of a porcelain clock on the mantel. Mrs. Bentley, regardless of the clock, dragged out a heavy gold watch of her own from time to time. She had to tilt her head back exceedingly to make out the face, but each time, she succeeded.

"Two minutes more," she pronounced at last. And it was just at that second that Ariana became awash in the astonishing feeling of assurance that she was going to see Mr. Mornay. Just when she might have worried most, she chose to believe her inner feeling. The sense of urgency had vanished, replaced now with a calmness that could only be from providence, she felt.

Mrs. Bentley stood up. "It is time, Ariana. Let us go."

Ariana stood up reluctantly. She knew she had not invented the errand, or the assurance she had just felt. How could they be leaving? They were on the stairs coming down when Freddy appeared at the bottom.

"Mr. Mornay is home!"

Mrs. Bentley halted in surprise, but Ariana glowed with satisfaction.

"Quickly, let us back to the parlour!"

∽o∽

In a few moments they could hear the front door being opened and the proper, "Good evening, sir," given by Freddy. There was some unintelligible talk from below, a sound of stumbling, and then the hushed tones of the servants.

"Let—me—go!" came wafting up through the air. The voice was that of Mr. Mornay, but it sounded unusual: thick, and slow. Ariana and her aunt looked at each other in dismay. Whatever could be the matter? To add to the puzzle, a footman came bounding up the stairs and closed the doors on them.

"Upon my word!" Mrs. Bentley gave Ariana a guarded look. "Mr. Mornay must have taken ill." She had been at a complete loss as to what was happening, but this explanation seemed to answer. Another muffled sound came from the staircase. Mrs. Bentley was suddenly nervous, and stood up as well. She went toward the door.

"Allow me to take a look at him; I am older, you know, and more accustomed to these things. I will return and let you know if you may see him," Aunt Bentley suggested.

Ariana had no choice but to wait, anxiously, hoping he was not *very* ill. To her great consternation she heard a sudden loud sound, as if someone had fallen.

"I am all—right!" Again it was Mr. Mornay's voice, except he sounded closer. With a leap in her breast she rushed to leave the room. Her aunt had halted just outside the door and she instantly tried getting Ariana to go back into the chamber.

"No, you must wait, my dear. I haven't seen him yet!"

But another sound of stumbling on the stairs reached her ears and she pushed away her aunt's arms, rushing to the top of the steps. There, more than halfway up, she saw him. He was holding on to the rail and the wall, facing the wrong way, and swaying slightly, with Freddy and a footman below him. After their eyes moved to rest on something above him, he turned, swaying, and saw Ariana.

"You!" He resumed climbing and the servants hurried to help, but he pushed them away. They reluctantly fell back, but stayed close behind. When their master climbed the remaining steps with no further mishaps, they were visibly relieved.

Ariana, accosted by the distinct odour of liquor, backed away as he approached. She hurried to stand behind a chair in the parlour, as if for protection. Mr. Mornay was rubbing his eyes and looking at her as though he could not credit what he saw.

Aunt Bentley quickly intervened. "He is not well, my dear, and we should leave at once. You can return tomorrow, for I am certain that a good night's sleep will greatly benefit Mr. Mornay. We are keeping him from his rest." The man in question was swaying again, and he sat down as if aware of it.

"What brings you here?" Mornay asked, clearly trying to reconcile her appearance at this hour. He then reached down and started pulling off his boots, then allowed his valet, who had joined the other bewildered servants, to finish the job. He was utterly too fogged up with drink to comprehend the inappropriateness of this action but it made Mrs. Bentley's toes begin to curl. *The Paragon, behaving like a boor!* She hurried to her niece, taking her by the arm.

"We shall call again tomorrow. Come, my dear, we must let the man rest."

But Ariana shook herself free and walked toward Mr. Mornay.

"I am afraid, sir, that you are intoxicated," she said.

Mrs. Bentley's hand went to her heart. Mr. Mornay returned Ariana's gaze stupidly, unable to either confirm or deny her accusation. He was trying to say, "Yes, unfortunately you have found me so," but instead, without the least effort to suppress it, let out a loud, ungentlemanly burp.

"Oh, I think I must start carrying smelling salts!" Mrs. Bentley felt positively weak.

"Ariana, come here," he ordered, almost in his usual voice. But Ariana had seen enough.

"You poor dear," she murmured, stopping to pat his hand which was resting upon the arm of the chair. She then regally strode past him just as he reached to grasp her. She continued toward the stairs and nodded at an ashen-faced butler.

"Take care of him."

"If I may be so bold—" Freddy interjected, quickly. She stopped and looked at him expectantly. "The master, as a rule, does not allow himself to drink to excess."

Ariana looked away. "Then he has broken his rule, I daresay."

"Ma'am, there is an explanation. He was brought home by Lord Alvanley and Brummell. Are you acquainted with their set?"

She nodded. "I am." The so-called Carlton House set was composed mostly of aristocratic men, friends of the Prince Regent, who were witty, urbane—and noted rapscallions. "I am obliged, Freddy."

"Your servant, ma'am." He bowed and followed her down the stairs and opened the door for her. She hurried to the waiting coach where the horses were stamping their feet impatiently. She was up the steps and inside the coach before Haines could even help her.

Meanwhile, watching her go seemed to have a sobering effect on Mr. Mornay. He turned accusingly to Mrs. Bentley.

"Do not blame me!" she said to his severe countenance. "Ariana would not rest until we came to call upon you. She quite insisted upon it." She went toward the door and stood still, her hand upon the knob. "I am exceedingly sorry, Mornay." She shook her head. "Exceedingly sorry."

As she descended the steps, she reflected that, to most women in society, Mornay's state might have seemed humorous and was even expected on occasion. Only Ariana, of course, would never view it in such a light. Of all the bad luck! She shook her head, recalling she had even prayed for the success of the match.

Is this the way You answer prayer, dear Lord?

Thirty-Four

$\mathcal{J}$ ust before noon the next day, Mr. Mornay called at Hanover Square. He appeared, at first glance, none the worse for the prior evening's misadventures, but in fact was suffering from a headache which had accosted him the moment he awoke. Nevertheless, he was determined to face Ariana. He straightened his cravat imperceptibly before raising the knocker at the door.

Mrs. Bentley nervously received him in the first floor parlour.

"Well?" he asked, presently, after politely declining to sit. "Has she sworn me to the devil?"

Mrs. Bentley gave an involuntary gurgle of laughter, caused by the strain upon her sensibilities all of this commotion was wreaking.

"Worse, perhaps; she has said nothing. Not a thing!"

His look of apprehension deepened. "I may as well learn the worst. Call for her."

Ariana's aunt nodded and went for the bellpull.

"You will, of course, allow me to see her privately."

She acceded to this request, recognizing it instantly for what it was: an order. She told the footman who appeared shortly, to fetch Haines. She told Haines to inform Ariana she had a morning caller, but to insist he did not know who it was. When he had gone she nodded with satisfaction.

"Haines is trustworthy. She may not be prepared to see you, of course—"

He held up his hand. "Not to fear. I think I can handle a girl of nineteen."

Haines, meanwhile, could not. When he said he had no knowledge of who was calling, Ariana cocked an eyebrow at him and folded her arms across her chest.

"Come, Haines, you can tell me. I shan't breathe a word. Especially when I already *know* it is Mr. Mornay." Poor Haines was so taken by surprise that his brows shot up, and his secret was quite undone. Ariana smiled gratefully.

"Thank you, Haines. 'Tis just as I suspected."

∞‿∞

When the door to the parlour opened, Mr. Mornay shifted uncomfortably on his feet. Ariana walked in, closed the door behind her, and stood with her back against it, looking at Mr. Mornay with a positively angelic expression on her face. She was looking radiant this morning, the epitome of a peaceful, rested soul. Mr. Mornay's expression froze. He would not have been surprised to find her cross, morose, affronted, or insulted. But to find her gazing at him fondly, almost foolishly, was not something he was prepared for.

Seeing the look on his face made Ariana smile all the more, and then she walked over to him, stretching out both her hands to him. "My dearest!"

He took her hands firmly within his own. He lifted them, kissed them one by one, and then, overcome by this warm reception, pulled her impulsively up against him and kissed her, and Ariana sweetly kissed him back.

Afterward she removed herself from his embrace and took his hand. "Let us sit down and talk."

He followed her and sat across from her, but on the edge of his seat, so they were not far apart. Ariana looked at him a moment, and said, "My dear sir, I have finally understood what must be done. So we can be married."

"Indeed? I am eager to hear it!" He smiled. Ariana was so calm, so in charge of herself, and of him. She was beautiful and sweetly affectionate and she had said they would be married. This was quite a bit more than he had dared hope for this morning.

"Indeed." She looked at him questioningly. "It remains only to be seen if you will comply with the necessity of what must be done."

He seized her hands once more. "I am at your service, my young love. Or should I say, at your mercy?"

"I recall saying those very words to you, once. When you came and rescued me from the countess!" Her eyes shone with the memory.

"But now you are rescuing me."

"I am so glad!" she breathed. "And it is so simple! Why I did not think of it sooner, I cannot know, but here it is. You will take yourself to my father's house in Chesterton and remain there to learn and study our faith, until he sends you back for the wedding."

Mr. Mornay's expression sobered at once. "But what is the point, Ariana? Why should I leave you now, if we are to wed? I have no objection to meeting your family, indeed, I look forward to it. But I cannot fathom this request."

She was directing a patient look at him. "Because, my dear, Papa will instruct you on precisely what is between us. He is a much better tutor than I, and he will introduce you to the writings of George Whitefield, Martin Luther, John Wesley, and Mr. Wilberforce—"

"Wilberforce? You mean the abolitionist? I've read his writings."

"Others, then. Calvin, Matthew Henry, even Augustine."

"Ariana, I am not illiterate!"

"No, but the point is to read under the tutelage of my papa, and when you are ready he will send you back to me for the wedding. I have absolutely no doubt of this."

He leaned back in his seat, and looked at her quizzically. "So this is what's afoot."

She nodded.

"And this, you are certain, will settle the matter for you?"

She nodded emphatically.

He lapsed into thought for a minute. "Is this arrangement the only way I can satisfy you?"

"I'm afraid so."

These words were grave ones to him, for he felt in his heart it would be far too beneath him to agree to her scheme. He proposed another possibility. "I suspect you are equally capable as your father in these matters."

But Ariana was prepared for qualms. "My dear sir, when I saw you last night I realized the importance of your having excellent instruction. I assure you, my father is a learned man and will not fail you for good conversation. In addition, I am certain he will endeavour to enlarge your acquaintance among other Christians, many of whom you will find utterly worthwhile. I have no opportunity of doing that here in London, where I have only recent and shallow acquaintances."

He sat forward and rubbed his hands together. "Ariana, I came to apologize for last night." He paused, choosing his words. "What you saw was not a pretty sight, I grant. But I am not accustomed to behaving in that manner. It is not something I make a practice of."

"Please understand I am not condemning you for what I saw. I certainly do not approve, but that is something else. I am concerned with your welfare, believe me, but I also know that if you'll do this… well, I won't have to…lose you." Her last words were wistful, as was the expression on her lovely face.

Moreover, the second they left her lips Mornay knew he would go. Her eyes, large and brilliant at all times, were especially so now with her future in the balance. "Will you allow the banns to be published in my absence?"

"If you have not returned in a fortnight, then yes, I shall. You may hear them yourself in Chesterton since they needs must be read in my home parish."

"Do you really anticipate I shall need so long a stay?"

"I cannot say."

His gaze fell to the window for a moment while he considered what to do. Ariana had thought he might request banns and had decided to allow them. She was certain his heart was not shut to God, so that having the banns published would cause no dilemma. Was this not the reason the Lord had placed upon her that sense of urgency? So she would witness Phillip at his worst and finally come upon the solution for their problem?

"I see you have given the matter a deal of thought," he ventured.

"Yes. But I must confess the idea did not originate with me."

He looked at her questioningly. "Who—"

She leaned forward, and he was leaning forward, so their faces were close. Smiling, she whispered, "God! It was His idea, I promise you!"

He stared at her for a moment, dumbfounded.

"Is this why you called upon me at my house?"

Silence for a moment.

"Not exactly; though again, upon my word, it was a divine inspiration!"

"I could probably describe it quite differently," he murmured dryly. "But why did you come? May I ask?"

She looked down, feeling suddenly shy.

"To pray with you and—to affirm my love for you."

"You sweet angel!" he uttered, sitting up. He grasped both her arms with his much stronger ones, pulling her completely out of her seat and onto his lap. "Though you insist upon running my life, you are still my angel!" They were both smiling from ear to ear in this manner and looking at each other idiotically when Mrs. Bentley knocked and let herself in. She couldn't bear, any longer, not knowing what was happening.

Ariana slipped back into her own seat, but Mrs. Bentley recognized what she had seen. She stopped, overjoyed at the unmistakable evidence of a happy conclusion and then rushed forward.

"Oh, my dearest Ariana! My dear, dear, Mr. Mornay! I am overcome! Upon my word, I am overcome with delight for both of you!"

$\mathcal{T}$he first letter to arrive without hindrance from Chesterton expressed everything Ariana expected. Outrage over the thefts and the invasion of privacy, and concern regarding her general safety in London altogether. If letters were not safe, could people be so? There was of course curiosity regarding Mr. Mornay, coupled with a firm refusal to sanction the wedding without hearing from Ariana, first. The notes from Mama and Alberta were almost entirely pleas for more information about the mysterious Mr. Mornay. When she had folded the papers again, she looked down at the letters in her hands with a little smile.

"Soon, my dear family. Very soon you shall know all about him."

<hr>

Mrs. Bentley was furious about her brother's refusal to endorse the wedding, but her disposition improved greatly when she learned Mr. Mornay was already en route to Chesterton. (She interpreted it to mean the Paragon was intent on confronting Ariana's father, and felt certain he could only succeed.)

To distract her niece while she waited for Mornay's return, Mr. Pellham took Ariana to the long-anticipated British Museum. Mrs. Bentley cried off, but Ariana eagerly went, prepared to take notes to send to her family. From the moment they entered the building, she was accosted by acquaintances. Mr. Pellham was gracious and amusing, even when Ariana began to despair of ever truly seeing the exhibits, but she had to marvel at his social transformation. True to his word, he no longer scorned fashionable society.

In fact, as she told her aunt later, he was an immediate hit, and had even received invitations of his own. Mrs. Bentley was so delighted she could only coo, "Oh, Randolph!" and wipe a nonexistent tear from her eyes with her handkerchief.

When another letter came for Ariana from Chesterton, she was trembling with anticipation as she opened it. After initial greetings, her father finally got to the point that interested her most: Mr. Mornay. He wrote:

> *My commendation for sending us your suitor. We have received Mr. Mornay gladly and your mother already quite dotes on him. We all do, in fact. The girls were wary of him at first, but now are smitten. He does not address Alberta often, but if he does, your older sister blushes. I am myself not immune to his charm and we can easily understand how you came to favour him.*
>
> *The rector has met your betrothed (a new man, you know, for Mr. Hathaway exchanged his living for another—to the general satisfaction of all, I believe), and we have had him to dinner three nights out of four, for he and Mr. Mornay enjoy each other's company. You can be sure Mr. Timmons will expound upon the necessity of a personal faith to anyone's satisfaction. I have enjoyed sharing many of the volumes on my shelves that are dearest to my heart with Mr. Mornay, and he displays a pleasing interest in these tomes. They are all, as you know, concerned with matters of the faith. Continue to pray for him, my dear. He is a worthy man.*
>
> *Do write him; he asks for it. And your mother, as well. Give our regards to my sister. I am,*
>
> *Yr loving Papa*

Ariana was glowing with satisfaction after reading the note, and her aunt noticed.

"Why do you not take the carriage and call upon your friend, Miss Herley?" she suggested.

"Miss Herley, yes," Ariana said. "I should like that very much. Thank you, Aunt."

Ariana realized she was now in high favour with her relation. When Mrs. Bentley heard the banns could be published shortly, every last bit of hardness about her had vanished. She had become as compliant as lamb's wool in any matter regarding her niece. And Ariana's privileges had been steadily increasing. She knew as soon as her aunt suggested she use the carriage, that it would be hers for the taking from then on, as long as her aunt wasn't using it. She experienced a thrill of freedom, even though it was not quite the independence of, say, Lady Longbottom, who always drove her own little gig, led by two delicate ponies. Or that of the young bucks who sported the latest four-in-hand. No, she did not do her own driving, and still used a coachman. But she could go unaccompanied if she chose, and that alone was something.

Ariana was warmly received at the Herleys' and Lavinia insisted she send the carriage home and stay with the family for the day. It was not difficult to persuade her, for the Herleys were a boisterous family and she enjoyed the change from the staid walls at Hanover Square. It reminded her of home.

Thirty-Six

When two weeks had passed and Mr. Mornay did not return, Mrs. Bentley had the banns published—to her great satisfaction. She also put a notice in the papers.

Once again the parlour was busy with callers—also to Aunt Bentley's great satisfaction. Between entertaining the cream of society, she was occupied with the delightful business of gathering Ariana's trousseau. Mr. Mornay had sent instructions, so she had begun to make the rounds of the necessary shops, warehouses, and modistes with Ariana in tow. She bespoke everything from bonnets to stockings, which was even more fun than usual since Mornay was underwriting the expense. Not so for Ariana, however.

It took three shopping expeditions for her to decide upon a wedding dress. Not because she was suddenly concerned about fashion, but because her latent worries about her future were brought once again to the fore when they shopped. Here she was, spending Mr. Mornay's money, accepting their marriage, when in her heart there was yet an unsettled feeling. Mrs. Bentley found Ariana's indecision unfathomable.

"We are still to bespeak traveling dresses, riding habits, morning, afternoon, and evening gowns, lingerie," she finally said. "If you cannot choose for yourself, I will do so for you."

"But my wardrobe is barely worn," Ariana countered. "It is all new and according to fashion. There is no need to bespeak anything."

"Mr. Mornay is an outstanding member of society, and you are to be his wife. You must dress as his wife. You must appear in a manner fitting your station. And, it goes without saying that as the wife of the Paragon you also must be completely 'the thing' yourself."

"If we are indeed outstanding members of society, then we should set the example for others in generosity; in remembering the poor; in all manner of helping the less fortunate."

"Well, my dear, you are already known for stopping the carriage and handing out fruit and rolls to little vagabonds of the street, and I tell you, they will turn on you for it. 'Tisn't safe! Send a donation to your Societies, if you like, but I pray you do not use my coach for your charity! I shall be accosted in it one day when they see it and think you are inside."

Mrs. Bentley had gone so far as to forbid her coachman or Haines, when he drove, to make these little stops for Ariana. In response, she merely tossed the food from her window, which was perhaps worse, for a report had circulated of a stray apple hitting an earl (a pedestrian at the time) on the behind. Her aunt shuddered to think of it.

She knew Ariana was merely enduring the new round of shopping, but it nevertheless came as a surprise the morning when she was met at the breakfast table with an announcement.

"Aunt Bentley, I have determined that I shan't go to one more warehouse or shop! The extravagance is grating on me. I should rather donate the money for these things to the London Orphan Society. I leave these shops of luxuries to see hungry children on the streets! I cannot bear it another day!"

"For shame, Ariana! When a thousand other gels would give their right foot to be in your shoes!"

Mr. Pellham was visiting, and he jocularly piped in.

"If they gave their right foot, my dear Mrs. B., they would only need one of her shoes." Ariana grinned and he winked, while Mrs. Bentley behaved as though she hadn't heard him.

Ariana remembered the pages of instructions her future husband had sent her aunt. He told her where to buy what, from whom, and which fabrics were best for certain categories of clothing his wife would wear. Ariana did not mind a husband who cared more about her apparel than she did, but she was done with fittings for now. Enough was enough!

With every shilling spent, a terrible thought would assail her: *What if the wedding is not sanctioned by Papa? What if she had mistaken her own wishful thinking for the will of God?* What if? What if?...

Had it been presumption to believe that Mr. Mornay would come to his senses regarding his need for Christ? Was he too proud? What if, even now, he and Papa had had a prodigious falling out? She was eagerly awaiting a letter from Chesterton from either of the gentlemen, but none had arrived of late. Without words of reassurance, her mind entertained negative suppositions. The silence was rife with rejection to her mind, and the days became very dreary, indeed.

Her presence was requested at many an entertainment, but to avoid the incessant talk of her coming nuptials, Ariana chose to spend more time at home. She worked on her needlepoint, drew pictures in the courtyard behind the house, or stayed in when Mr. Pellham visited, which was daily.

Her aunt had postponed her own wedding until the Paragon's would be accomplished, but the two discussed plans, which Ariana found wonderfully refreshing. Instead of focusing on her future, she delighted on hearing the couple speak of theirs. Despite Mrs. Bentley's recent social success, she had decided upon a small wedding. Perhaps because she was involved in planning Ariana's, all she wanted for herself was a few friends, a small supper afterward, and then she and Randolph would be off for the Lakes. They intended on settling in that region during the winters when most of her circle abandoned town anyway. During the season they would return to Hanover Square. Mr. Pellham was thus prepared to sell his house.

Ariana sighed with contentment during the times the three of them shared. It was lovely that they would be tying the knot! If only she could hear from Phillip and rejoice in her own affairs. It helped to write to him, so she spent much time at it. When she was writing she felt amazingly restored; it seemed so simple to believe for the best. But at other times her fears and doubts would resurface, and at night, especially. She spent much time on her knees to combat them. Prayer would remind her of God's part in giving her that intense urgency to see Phillip on that fateful evening. After that, she'd been certain he only needed a proper opportunity of learning the truth from an excellent instructor. And that, shut up with Papa in his study, he could read, question, consider, and be ultimately satisfied with the miraculous simplicity of being saved for heaven by faith in Christ. Through the ages, the wisest of thinkers had been so; but what if Phillip refused the hand of grace? What if her hopes were to be dashed?

⤙∽๑∽⤚

When an invitation for an outdoor picnic with the Herleys arrived, Ariana jumped at the chance for the diversion. Lavinia's family was not so fashionable that the brightest stars of society would be there, which meant Ariana could enjoy herself without being assailed at every turn for details about Phillip or the wedding.

The day was sunny and warm. Lavinia was in such high spirits that Ariana found it infectious. She was soon enjoying a lighthearted game of bowling on greens with her friend's family. Afterward she sat resting on a blanket on the grass. She noticed a nearby grove of trees and thought with a laugh that she would not soon take to climbing a tree again! But if she had not, would she and Mr. Mornay ever have spoken? More likely he would have taken one look at her, sizing her up as another insipid female, and never given her a moment's notice. It was amazing, when one thought on it, how the most unlikely events could turn out to be the most significant of one's life.

She was enjoying a light breeze ruffling across the grass and her face when suddenly Mr. O'Brien, who had arrived late, stood before her, bowing politely. Without asking permission he took the liberty of sitting down to face Ariana.

"How good to see you, my dear Miss Forsythe!"

Ariana smiled. "Thank you, Mr. O'Brien. How are you?"

He gave her a grave look. "Not so well, I'm afraid. I heard the banns on Sunday and—I must confess, I felt a renewed conviction to persuade you not to go through with the nuptials. Is there any chance that you might yet gain your freedom?"

"Mr. O'Brien!"

"Miss Forsythe, you must give me your utter assurance that you wholly believe it is the Lord's will for you to marry this man!" When she hesitated, he added, "I could not sleep at night if I thought for a moment you had any doubts and I failed to encourage you to speak of them."

"You are very bold, sir."

"My convictions make me so. I know too much of your pious nature to remain quiet."

She met his eyes, and her doubts must have registered on her face. He sensed an opportunity, and leaned toward her and spoke in a low voice.

"You must be full of doubts, my dear; you must see the unsuitability of the match! It is plain, indeed."

"I do fret at times," she admitted. "But not on account of Mr. Mornay's character or because of anything you would think. I only fret that I may have mistaken my feelings for the will of God. I love him so dearly, you see."

"Our feelings can be our worst enemies!" his voice rose with conviction. "Of course you must doubt them!"

Her eyes filled with tears. "I do wish to know that I am following the right course!" She sobbed and he quickly thrust a handkerchief at her. "Do not try and persuade me, in this matter, Mr. O'Brien. I want only God's will. And I know that He has allowed me to—to—fall in love with Mr. Mornay!" She was crying in earnest and Mr. O'Brien became utterly solicitous. He moved nearer, and assured her of his constant prayers. How he wished he could comfort her with more than just words! Instead, he spoke soothingly, counseling her on God's faithfulness and sovereignty.

"If He has brought you to this place, then He has a purpose. He will see you through. He will make a way where there seems to be no way, my dearest Miss Forsythe. Remember the promise, 'All things work together for good, to them that love God.' Do not forget the truth of that verse, my dear."

"Thank you, Mr. O'Brien. It is a truth dear to my heart!"

"And mine." Gently, he added, "I suggest you give yourself—and your betrothed—to God, just as I have had to give you to Him. We shall all of us have to accept what He brings to pass."

"I have endeavoured to do just that," she said, with a sniff. She blew her nose and composed herself. Mr. O'Brien sat in silent admiration, watching her.

"I have wished that your betrothal to Mr. Mornay would come to an end; that he, perhaps, would cry off if you do not. Only he'd be mad to, of course! And my wishes are selfish, and for my own happiness." She was keeping her eyes averted, hoping he would cease such talk.

"But I tell you this, Miss Forsythe—I will earnestly pray for you. I will pray that God grants you the desire of your heart, and that Mr. Mornay, if he must be your husband, will be the best of husbands."

This brought a smile. "Thank you, Mr. O'Brien. You are very kind. I know 'tis at a cost. I am obliged."

"Allow me the honour of praying for you this very moment," he said, and reached for her hand. They bowed their heads, sitting there on the blanket on the grass, and prayed. Mr. O'Brien spoke first, asking God to bless Ariana and to protect her from taking a wrong path. It was a sweet, earnest prayer and Ariana was touched. She prayed for the same things, but also for him, that his living would soon be granted, and thanked God for his friendship. Afterward, smiling, they rose, with him helping her up by the hand.

He stopped, though, still holding to her hand and gazed at her soberly.

"Only promise me, Miss Forsythe, that if you have a change of heart, or are convinced the Lord would have you free of Mr. Mornay—promise me—"

She hastily pulled her hand free. "Pray, don't!"

"Please, I must! I only ask you for some little encouragement, in case—"

"I will not, I cannot give any, Mr. O'Brien!"

He looked sorrowful, but said, "Perhaps in future, then, my dearest girl!"

Without curtseying she turned and moved on, suddenly aware the other guests were no longer in their vicinity. He joined her, but their conversation remained on safe, general topics. Little did Ariana realize that her trials for the day were not yet over.

Thirty-Seven

"*A*riana Forsythe! Come, join the game!" Lavinia tugged at her arm playfully. "Come on then, we're playing hide-and-seek, and I am laughing 'til it hurts! You are missing the fun."

"Not today, Lavinia," Ariana said. It would be unwise for her, since she could possibly be discovered alone by Mr. O'Brien, and *that* she wanted to avoid.

Later, however, when they were all seated upon blankets and eating, Mr. Chesley came abreast of Ariana and Miss Herley and bowed deeply, waiting to be noticed.

"Why, Mr. Chesley," said Lavinia, in a droll voice. "What gives us the pleasure of your company? I understood you were unable to attend our picnic."

He cleared his throat. "I had another engagement, yes, but as it has been met, and I am now free, I thought I would join you after all."

"Well, how perfectly agreeable." Lavinia smiled pleasantly.

"I must pay my respects to your friend," he said, looking at Ariana, who had said nothing as yet. "Or is she too good for the likes of me, now that she is engaged to the Paragon?" This was a parry meant to require her attention, and it worked, for she looked up at him.

"Don't be absurd, Mr. Chesley. Good day."

He looked back at Miss Herley. "May I join you?" Lavinia made room for him, so that he sat between the girls. He turned to Ariana, who concentrated intently on the cluster of grapes in her hand, refusing to look at him.

"I heard the banns for your wedding; I suppose I should congratulate you."

Lavinia laughed out loud. "Of course you should, you horrible boy!"

"But how can I?" he said as if carrying a secret. "When this innocent creature is to marry such a man?"

"I beg your pardon!" Ariana was instantly offended.

"Indeed, Mr. Chesley," cried Lavinia. She hit his knee with her fan for emphasis. "How provoking you are! I insist you apologize this instant."

"Dear me," he said, affectedly. "Have I offended you? If you only understood. That is, if you knew the vile deeds of your intended—"

"Mr. Chesley! You are indeed provoking!" Ariana rose to her feet. "You have no right to speak against a man who is not present to defend himself!"

"Indeed, Harold! And you must endeavour to be polite to Miss Forsythe in any case, no matter what you think of her betrothed."

"But I am being better than polite. I have the noblest of intentions, desiring to rescue this wandering lamb from future distress." He gave Ariana a shrewd look to see what effect his comments were having.

"I am in distress," she concurred, "only on account of your ill-chosen remarks."

He got to his feet, and Lavinia hurried to do likewise. They joined Ariana, forming a small circle.

"What I know of Phillip Mornay compels me to distress you, and must be my excuse; if you only understood—and when I think I may yet spare you from a disastrous mistake—"

Ariana turned to go.

"Ariana, stay, I beg you!" Lavinia begged her with her eyes. "Mr. Chesley can be provoking, I grant you, but he is not a fabricator. Perhaps he does know of something significant. Perhaps you will thank him in the end."

"Perhaps you have allowed your curiosity to overcome your better judgment, Lavinia." She straightened her gown. "If there is anything significant I must know regarding Mr. Mornay, he will tell me himself."

"Mornay has a dark past!" Mr. Chesley instantly asserted. "Most of it has somehow been buried; but I have managed to get my hands on something that you, Miss Forsythe, could surely not allow in a man you would marry! I say that with conviction, knowing your piety."

Ariana blanched, but then gathered her strength. "I do not listen to hearsay."

Mr. Chesley called loudly. "It concerns your Mr. Mornay and a young woman near your own age." Ariana stopped. Mr. O'Brien, standing nearby and surveying the situation, heard the last statement and came to hear the matter. Lavinia grasped Ariana's arm, turning her around to hear it as well. Ariana dreaded hearing anything from Mr. Chesley regarding Phillip, for she knew he was bound to be unfair, but she was torn. Taking her hesitation as tacit permission to continue— or perhaps not—Mr. Chesley spoke softly but effectively to the little group, sharing his revelation. When it was done, Ariana was blinking back tears, but her face held a determined look to it. Lavinia went to her and gave her an embrace.

∽◦∽

Mr. O'Brien called the following day and remained in the parlour for a full twenty-five minutes.

Mrs. Bentley did not like it. "What are you thinking? To see a gentleman while your betrothed is out of town—it isn't done, my dear. The last thing you want is a breath of scandal."

"Scandalous things are not uncommon in this society." Her words were edged with bitterness. "I think I must welcome a scandal, ma'am, if that is what it takes to end my betrothal."

Mrs. Bentley stared at her, aghast, her hand going over her heart. "What is the meaning of this?" It came out as a gasp.

Ariana's face softened. "I am sorry to lay it upon you so rudely, dear

Aunt, but I could not think how to tell you." She rose from her seat and paced the room; her two slim hands came together and she raised them to her lips and nodded to herself, as if deciding upon a thing. She lowered them again and turned to face her aunt.

"I have learned something. Something about Mr. Mornay. And I—I cannot abide it!"

"What have you heard? And from whom?"

Ariana told her the source of her information.

"And you believe him?" Aunt Bentley's face contorted into a great scowl.

"I do." Her tone was subdued; resigned. "Everything I know about Phillip tells me it is true."

"What has Chesley told you?"

The lady came and stood eye to eye with her niece. Ariana could tell her aunt was agitated and upset, but there was something else she saw in the watery blue eyes of her relation which Ariana was sure Mrs. Bentley did not wish to reveal: *fear.* Her aunt was afraid of what she might have learned! Was this not more evidence of the truth of the matter? Her heart sank even further.

"Well?"

"It happened when Mr. Mornay was young." Ariana decided to sit down, and her aunt did likewise. "I think during his years at Eton, though I am not certain. He befriended a young girl whose family had suffered financial ruin some time earlier." Ariana's eyes were far away; her voice was wooden. "His father demanded an end to the relationship, and in response—" she lowered her head, but could not hide the tears in her voice. "He—he—fathered a child with her. And then, when his father would still not allow a marriage, he—heartlessly— abandoned her! And his own child!"

She looked up to see a frank look of doubt on her aunt's face.

"I cannot believe it. Another man, Ariana, but not Phillip Mornay. He has ever—until you—avoided women, particularly young ones. I have never known him to be affiliated with a single dishonourable scandal involving a female."

Ariana crossed her arms. "Well, you know of one, now. And I daresay it was this that caused him to avoid others, later on."

Mrs. Bentley pressed her lips together. "Even *if* that tale is true, which I doubt, it was long ago. What Mornay did when he was hardly out of shortcoats has nothing to do with the man he is today! I should think that you, of all people, would be most acutely conscious of that, for I daresay he has found himself another young woman, who, in contrast to his own wealth is poor, has he not? And I think I may say he has not behaved improperly to you."

Ariana was silent as she thought on this.

"Perhaps not; but his will has not been crossed in our case. If his father were alive and wished to block the wedding, I wonder how he should have behaved to me, then!"

"Now you're talking fustian! He is a different man today. And his will has most certainly been blocked," she said, with large eyes, "by you!" She nervously played at the beads around her throat. "He is offering you all that is his, Ariana! Can you truly hold against him what he did as a young buck, with barely enough brains, I daresay, to get himself dressed each day?"

"He abandoned a woman with child! It is too heartless! It—it frightens me!" She laid her head upon her hands. Her aunt gave a little frown. If only there was some way of disproving the tale—she felt certain it could not be true or she would have known about the incident. It wasn't easy to keep such things suppressed.

"It is no doubt a mere Banbury tale," she said aloud. "Mr. Chesley has seen his hopes dashed by Mornay and he seeks to put himself in your favour. Is not anything more clear than that?"

Ariana thought for a moment. If only Mr. Mornay would return! She could speak to him about it, as difficult as that would be. She supposed it was only fair to give him that chance. Suddenly an idea struck her and she looked up.

"Perhaps there is more to the story than I have heard. If you will call the carriage for my use, I believe I must go see Mrs. Royleforst!" She was herself surprised to have reached that conclusion, but she felt instinctively she must speak to someone she could trust was not hoping to sway her emotions negatively toward Mr. Mornay.

"Yes, do!" cried her aunt. "But upon my honour, Ariana, this is no great transgression that you cannot overlook!" She stopped in surprise. "Upon my honour, Ariana! 'Tis a rhyme! *Upon my honour, Ariana.*"

Ariana raised her eyes to the ceiling and went for her bonnet, while her aunt, still repeating the phrase, went for the bellpull to order the carriage.

Thirty-Eight

Mrs. Royleforst's neighbourhood lacked the aura of wealth that Mayfair possessed, but it was yet highly respectable. Ariana's arrival, therefore, when she came forth from the expensive carriage, drew only a few curious glances.

She was wearing a pale blue walking gown with long sleeves and a deep muslin ruff. There were rows of embroidery across the bodice and down the sleeves, ending with a slightly ruffled wrist and hem at the ankles. A matching bonnet with yellow silk ribbons and a little feathery puff, and a light, woven shawl completed her appearance. Her long hair was curled in ringlets and pinned up within her hat, except for a few tendrils that peeked out prettily.

A servant admitted Ariana to a comfortable parlour. When Mrs. Royleforst came into the room using a walking stick, Ariana realized she had some lameness in one leg. She slowly made her way to the sofa where Ariana sat, and then came and heavily seated herself upon the far cushion.

"Well!" she exclaimed, after settling herself. "So you've come to be friends, have you?" Before Ariana could answer, she added, "Sensible thing to do, very sensible, since we are now relations. Well, very soon to be."

"I do indeed wish to be friends."

Mrs. Royleforst feasted her eyes on Ariana, who had acquired the difficult art of looking completely comfortable in the latest fashions.

She was overjoyed that her fastidious nephew had found a wife, and she, too, wanted above all things to be on good terms with Phillip's choice. She hoped to be included in their family, for nothing would please her better than to have youngsters about her skirts.

In the past, even *she* dared not urge her nephew to find a wife. He would allow no discussion of the matter, and one might as well say, 'Do let us be as uncivil as possible to one another, eh?' For that is how he reacted. Her aging nerves and sensibilities were simply not able to withstand such treatment any more. It was a great relief to have the matter nearly settled.

And so she nodded approvingly at Ariana. "And so do I, dearie. And so do I."

She then asked Miss Bluford, who had sat down as one of the company, to fetch the tea tray. When the door shut behind the skinny companion, Ariana turned to her hostess.

"I was hoping to speak with you privately, Mrs. Royleforst."

"Oh, no, I am no longer 'Mrs. Royleforst' to you, my dear. You must call me Aunt, now."

"Thank you, Aunt Royleforst. But I have an urgent matter, about Mr. Mornay, which I need you to advise me on."

"Oh?" Mrs. Royleforst's red eyes grew round, and could almost be called large.

"Do not say," she replied after a moment's contemplation, "that it is a matter of costume. You must know that I have no talent in that regard. Phillip himself is the one to—"

"No, Mrs.—I mean, Aunt. No, 'tis nothing like that. Something of greater significance, I assure you."

"Oh." This time there was disappointment in the word. Mrs. Royleforst was afraid that her nephew's vitriolic temper was causing problems, and she was not by any means certain she could be of the least help in that regard.

Miss Bluford came back into the room carrying a gleaming silver tea service. She carefully set the tray upon a little sofa table in front of them. It was laid out with service for three, and Ariana resigned herself to a long visit. Miss Bluford was not accepted or welcomed at most social occasions and she meant to participate in this one. Her manner of participating extended to merely sitting and nodding, smiling if it seemed appropriate, and otherwise making herself as little noticed as possible. Now and then Mrs. Royleforst would say, "Why, Miss Bluford says," or, with an emphatic wave of her arm, "Miss Bluford never…!" The lady in question would exclaim, "Indeed! Indeed!" but that was all.

Two cups of tea and three little biscuits later, Miss Bluford rose to clear the dishes. Ariana was mildly surprised that it fell to the companion to do so, but recalled that Mrs. Royleforst was considered an eccentric because she employed as few servants as possible. She maintained it was to keep her house her sanctuary. Ariana was brimming with uncustomary impatience, and felt relieved to see the skinny figure retreat behind the closed door.

"I am sorry, my dear." Mrs. Royleforst also had watched her go. "We entertain so little that I did not have the heart to send her from the room. The poor dear has nothing, you know, only me, and so I try to do well by her."

"I think you succeed in that, ma'am." Much gratified, the hostess smiled widely, revealing two large dimples which popped out on the chubby red cheeks. When Miss Bluford returned, her mistress told her she needed to speak privately with their guest. The lady was not offended and offered a wobbly curtsey to Ariana and left the room once more.

Ariana, meanwhile, had been worrying throughout the visit what she would say to her hostess regarding her difficulty. How much did she already know? Ariana did not want to reveal anything about her nephew that she was not already aware of. She owed Phillip that. But on the other hand, Mrs. Royleforst could be of no help to her if she did not know about the incident.

She rearranged herself primly upon the sofa, cleared her throat, and began.

"My dear ma'am." She raised large, earnest eyes to Mrs. Royleforst's little ones. "I hardly know how to begin. You see, it regards a matter in your nephew's past, something which, I must tell you, he did not inform me of himself."

"How do you know about it, then?" Her tone was mild.

"Oh—an acquaintance told me." She paused, folding and unfolding her hands "'Tisn't a pleasant story. And the thing is, I was so shocked upon learning of it, I can hardly imagine being married—to Mr. Mornay."

Mrs. Royleforst hid her surprise and alarm. This was far worse than she expected, but she knew exactly what Ariana had heard. Or supposed she did.

"My dear," she said soothingly. "All young men are frightfully disposed to foolish behaviour in their youth. You must realize that Mr. Mornay was no exception."

Ariana looked doubtful. "Foolish behaviour, ma'am? I can hardly excuse his abominable conduct on childish foolishness!"

"Oh, my dear! I grant that perhaps he should have known better, but when young men cavort together these things happen, you know. There was no lasting harm done, I recall. It was really more an inconvenience."

Ariana blinked in disbelief. *No lasting harm? An inconvenience?*

"I daresay that one ruined life—no, two, including that poor child's—would be considered lasting harm!" Again she could not keep the tears from her voice.

Mrs Royleforst stared at her uncomprehendingly.

"Child? That man was alone in his carriage, asleep, when they removed the wheels and frightened off his horses!" Then, "Oh, dear!"

"Oh, dear!" echoed Ariana. She stood up. "Forgive me! I thought you knew! I pray you, forgive me! I had no intention—I thought from the way you responded that you knew—!"

Mrs. Royleforst motioned for her to sit down.

"I do know! I had forgotten. But I do know, yes, indeed." She drew a handkerchief from a pocket of her gown and wiped at her eyes. Ariana waited, letting her settle her thoughts, watching while the woman obviously decided what to say to her.

"You see, my dear—oh, Phillip should have told you about this himself." She paused, staring blankly ahead, remembering. When she spoke again, it was in a low, sad tone.

"There is no one, no one upon the face of this earth who could feel worse about that tragical situation than he does, my dear. You must know, his character, his disposition—were not always so dark and forbidding. No, as he got older they darkened, and this incident was the initial cause."

"If you mean to say, ma'am, that he was not always the kind of man who could do such a thing, I assure you, that will not suffice!"

"No, my gel, hear me out." She paused again. "He was only sixteen when it happened. And by the by, many said the young lady in question had arranged for the very thing, thinking it would assure her an entry into a grand family, so there's always two ways to butter the bread, you see!"

Ariana thought about that for a moment.

"Either way," continued the lady, "I do not think Phillip ever really got over it."

"What do you mean?"

"His heartache! He wanted to marry her—Miss Larkin, that was her name."

"Until his father forbade it!" (Why couldn't she speak without wanting to cry?)

"Oh, no, my dear! His father did indeed forbid a wedding; he wanted no acquaintance at all between the two. Wouldn't hear of a marriage. Wouldn't even allow Phillip to speak about it in his presence. It caused a terrible rift between them. But in the end, it was not his father who prevented it. You see, Edward, Phillip's father, implored him to visit the continent for six months and think on the matter. He was certain Phillip was ruining his life, and wanted to prevent any contact between the young people. But he promised his son that, if he would take this trip and spend some time considering his future—apart from her—upon his return, he could choose his own course, marry whom he would. Well, with that promise, Phillip agreed. But there was one condition, only one, but absolutely necessary, his father said."

"What was that?" Ariana's large eyes glimmered wetly, but she was beginning to feel a slight hope, and she listened with her whole being.

Mrs. Royleforst shook her head regretfully. "That Phillip not tell Miss Larkin anything about the agreement. He was only to let her know of the trip, allowing that it was to appease his father. He declared his love and implored her to wait for his return, only with no promise of what would happen." She paused, and sighed. "Phillip was gone only three months—he refused to stay longer and journeyed back alone. His plan was to marry her before she grew large with child, despite anything his father might say. But when he returned, after only *three months,* mind you, the young woman had vanished. For a time, he suspected his father had done something to her, and the two of them barely spoke to each other. Phillip blamed himself mightily for what he imagined might have befallen Miss Larkin. Then, we all discovered she had actually run off with another young gentleman of means. Phillip was furious! He went all the way to Yorkshire to see for himself and found that she had indeed abandoned him for another prospect. And, to his utter chagrin, he discovered she had not been with child after all. He began to see that his father had been right. She hadn't ever truly loved him; it had been a trap. Of course he was guilty of walking into the trap rather than away from it. And he has since despised the weakness in himself which made him do it, as well as any female who dares set her cap at him!" She nodded. "Yes, I have long thought his aversion to females was due to this single episode." She paused again, giving forth a great sigh. "Oh, it was a painful time for the family. Right after all this had been going on, Phillip's father died. It was sudden, and the two had still not reconciled. He took his father's passing very ill on that account. And then! He had a younger brother, you know, Nigel."

"Nigel?" Ariana instantly remembered seeing the name inscribed in the family Bible on Mr. Mornay's desk. It had been beneath the heading of "Deaths." She shuddered at what was coming.

Mrs. Royleforst nodded sadly.

"Only months after my brother passed away—Phillip's father, you see—Nigel fell from his horse and broke his neck. He died instantly." Now Mrs. Royleforst seemed ready to burst into tears. She dabbed at her eyes with a handkerchief. "It was a terrible time for Phillip. I daresay he wished it had been he who had broken his neck, not his brother." She paused and gave Ariana a tentative look. More memories seemed to float across her mind.

"I grant that Phillip was rougish and—wrong—to do what he did with that young woman, but as soon as he understood there was to be a child, I know for a fact, my dear, that he championed a marriage. If not for Edward, his father, that young lady's scheme might have succeeded."

Ariana was nodding her head in an understanding way, her huge eyes revealing the depth of emotion in her heart.

"Could he not have supplied her with a sum of money? Before his father sent him away, that is. I understand she was destitute. Perhaps this drove her to the other young man."

"Phillip had none of his own, my dear," Mrs. Royleforst said. "I do not doubt he gave her what little he could, but at sixteen he did not yet hold the purse strings!"

"And you are certain—of Mr. Mornay's feelings in the matter?"

"Oh, my dear gel! It ruined the man! He thought himself in love, and he thought she loved him! He was bitter after that. He's been bitter ever since."

"What of his mother, ma'am?"

"Ah, Miranda. Another sad story, my dear. She doted on Phillip, you know." Mrs. Royleforst took a deep breath, and was absently playing with the handle of her cane.

"Miranda was never strong; she was beautiful, and full of life and strong-willed. After Edward died so suddenly she rallied her strength for the boys. But Nigel's death was too much for her. Coming so fast on the heels of losing her husband, really, looking back, I must think it was his loss that truly started her demise. The doctor said it was consumption, but I say she died of sorrow. Phillip was like sunlight to her, but losing her husband and son within a year was too much. She died only eighteen months after Nigel. So you see…many tragedies, in such a short time."

"My poor Phillip!"

"Yes, if you had known him when he was young. Nigel and he both, they were so full of life and energy, and Phillip had not a mean-spirited bone in his body. I grant he was mischievous upon occasion—are not all young men? But I would never have guessed that he would mature into such a difficult sort of man. I believe you know what I mean."

"Yes. I wondered if some great sorrow might not be behind his temper. When we first met, I thought him such a fright!"

"Frightful, indeed! When he barks, people scatter!" She raised her tiny eyes and dared to inquire, "How did you meet, by the by? I have always wondered, particularly because you went to so much effort not to tell me!"

Ariana laughed. "Goodness! If you must know, I had climbed up into that monstrous tree on his estate, and he spied me in it, only he was good enough not to reveal his discovery to anyone."

"Oh, dear!" Mrs. Royleforst was delighted. "That was a favorite climbing tree of Phillip's when he was young."

Ariana gasped, amused. "He never told me."

"What happened next?"

"When I tried to get down, I found I was stuck, and Mr. Mornay was standing beneath me, looking up at me with such an expression that I quaked with fear! I wonder now that I didn't fall at the sight of him! I would have hung there, stuck by a thread, and looked even more ridiculous, so it's well that I didn't!"

"Oh, dear! Of all things I could have imagined…I never dreamed of such a thing!" She wiped her eyes. "What happened next?"

"Well, he climbed right up to where I was stuck and saved my gown—and scolded me—and then he helped me down." She thought of the day for a moment. "After enduring a set-down from him, he actually became quite the gentleman. I didn't know what to make of him."

"He obviously took to you immediately. As I then thought."

"Come to think on it, Aunt Royleforst, Mr. Mornay scolded me above all things for putting myself in what he called a 'vulnerable position.' He said I could have been ill-used, and he seemed prodigiously out of temper about it."

"Precisely! 'Tis never far from his thoughts. That he himself was ill-used and he, a man."

"I felt that he despised me as though I were the stupidest creature alive!"

"Yes! He has ever struggled with self-respect since that episode, and naturally, he can have none for anyone else. He feels we all invite our troubles."

Ariana's face crinkled in thought. "So, he did not force himself on this girl, or abandon her."

"No, indeed no. His father was perfectly right in suspecting that he was not the initiator. She hoped for a marriage, not blackmail, having no basis for an accusation."

They sat quietly for a few moments, Mrs. Royleforst aware that Ariana's concern was dissipating. She gave a contented sigh.

"I am so very glad I came to see you," Ariana said.

"And I too, dearie. You must promise to come often."

"I shall."

"And you feel better now, do you not, regarding this affair?"

"Oh, indeed! I am greatly obliged to you. My poor, dear Phillip. And I thought so badly of him."

"Do not be hard on yourself; no harm has come of it. And perhaps it was a good thing, for now you understand him better."

They said their goodbyes. Ariana gave her new aunt an impulsive kiss on the cheek, crowning the visit for Mrs. Royleforst. Mrs. Bentley's coachman had been forced to walk the horses, but soon Ariana was on her way home, and thinking if she could only see Mr. Mornay right now, what a warm greeting she would give him. She did not, in fact, have long to wait.

Thirty-Nine

The next morning Ariana wrote to Mr. Mornay, telling him of her visit with his aunt, and how they now were friends. She said nothing about her need to ask advice. And she added how eager she was to hear of his thoughts on Christianity as well as his impressions of her family.

She wrote:

> I am praying for you, and for us. I am quite impatient to see you again; but do not, on any account, hurry your visit. You must allow my papa to decide when it may end. A dear friend of mine, Miss Herley (you may remember) has asked a favour of me. She has her heart set on Lord Antoine Holliwell, who is Lord Wingate's younger brother, and she wishes to have you put in a good word for her with his family. Would you mind, dearest? Please let me know. Do give all my family my love—but not all my love to my family, for it most assuredly belongs to you!
>
> I will write again soon, though I dare to hope that our next meeting will not be very far in the future. I am,
>
> Yr loving Ariana

After sealing the missive with her aunt's wax and leaving it on the hallway tray for Haines, who now controlled the mail exclusively, Ariana took a brief walk outdoors. A footman followed at a discreet distance.

She returned to find Mr. O'Brien waiting for her in the parlour. He was standing, having been pacing the room, but he turned with a bright smile when she entered.

"Miss Forsythe!" He bowed.

"Good day, Mr. O'Brien." Her tone was calm. She draped off the shawl and placed it gingerly upon the brow of a wing chair. He held out his hands to her, hoping to receive hers, but when no such favour was forthcoming, he took a seat across from her and tried, in vain, to read her countenance.

She did not apologize for keeping him waiting nor inquire how long he might have done so. Instead, she waited for him to speak.

He cleared his throat. "I hope you are not displeased that I have called upon you again."

"No, not precisely. But I confess I do think 'tis best for you not to come again while Mr. Mornay is away."

His face froze in surprise.

"You see," she continued, "I discovered more regarding the story Mr. Chesley claimed to have knowledge of, and, to my great shame, I found I was too willing a listener to him. I was too easily betrayed into believing the worst about a man I admire—and love."

He cleared his throat again, sat up a little straighter, and twisted uncomfortably.

"I see," he said, unhappily.

"I heard only one part of the story from Mr. Chesley, and now I know a great deal more of it." An uncomfortable silence followed her words. "In life, as in doctrine, partial truth is a terrible deceiver."

His eyes were fastened to her face, and he slowly nodded agreement.

"I suppose you will no longer receive my calls—"

"I am sorry, Mr. O'Brien. But you may feel free to call upon me and Mr. Mornay after the wedding."

He was grateful for that little kindness, though it did nothing to ease his disappointment. "My dear girl, are you completely certain?" His heart was on his sleeve.

"I am." Their eyes met. He saw that she was adamant. He grasped for a straw and found one.

"What of the business of being bound to an unbeliever?" His question was borne of desperation and they both knew it, and yet it was a valid question.

"That," she said slowly, "is a mystery you must place at God's feet. As I have. I am bound, by duty, honour, and love, to marry Mr. Mornay."

Mr. O'Brien slumped back in his seat, and then slowly gathered himself and stood up.

"I wish you every happiness, Miss Forsythe. I pray that you may never come to regret your decision."

"Thank you." She saw how defeated his expression was, and her heart felt a stirring of pity. "But do let us be friends, Mr. O'Brien. Do not be angry, I pray you."

Suddenly he felt just that: angry. But he looked into Ariana's sweet, earnest eyes and could not remain so. She also had come to her feet and they stood only a foot or so apart.

"I can't remain angry with you," he conceded with a sigh. "I don't think it's possible."

She grasped his hand impulsively. "You are a true friend."

"Am I?" The touch of her soft hand had instantly strengthened his earlier resolve to rescue her from the Paragon. Putting both his hands around her one, he spoke pleadingly. "I must renew my warnings to you, hoping to change your mind. How can I do otherwise if I am to be a true friend? If Mr. Mornay was not…Mr. Mornay, perhaps I would not be so persistent. But my feelings for you are such that I cannot sit idly by and witness this event."

Ariana pulled her hand free, turning toward the door. She would not listen to a moment more of this.

"Is it because he is handsome? Rich? Is that why you are marrying him?"

This caused her to stop and whirl back around to face him.

"Sir, how can you insult me in this manner? If you are concerned for my happiness, then you will remove yourself from this house. And, as a man of God, pray for me and my betrothed."

"I shall! I have, and I will." He quickly joined her near the door. Her hand was on the doorknob.

"*'For what fellowship hath righteousness with unrighteousness? And what communion hath light with darkness?'* You are the light, my dear, and are you not determined to be joined with darkness?"

When she made no reply, he reached again for her hand and held it firmly.

"Consider, my dear! You are not from the same world as Mr. Mornay! I understand that, for I understand you. I share the same faith as you." Her continuing silence gave him courage and he continued, speaking right next to her head. "Can you not see how very different your concerns are from Mr. Mornay's? You care about your God and your fellow human beings. He cares about his waistcoats! You are a child of the Light; he is a son of darkness. Dear, dear, Ariana, pray do not make this mistake. It shall end in unhappiness, I warrant you."

Ariana remained speechless. Mr. O'Brien had struck forcefully the one remaining doubt in her heart. What if all her hopes, all her love, even, did not suffice to make a happy union? If they were not on the same spiritual plane, could they be one in the sense Heaven intended? What if Mr. Mornay returned and announced he had no interest in knowing God? That it was all right for Ariana to pray, attend prayer meetings and church, read her Bible and the prayer book, but that he, Phillip Mornay, would have none of it? In that case, would she not indeed be acting in a way contrary to her faith?

Mr. O'Brien knew instinctively he had hit upon something, and drew closer to her.

"I am not a perfect man; indeed, far from it. But I am certainly more able to make you the husband you deserve. And we will raise our children to know and serve God."

Ariana stared at him, her mind racing 'til she wearied of thinking.

"We may never have the wealth of a Mr. Mornay, but we will have enough. God rewards those who seek Him, and I am certain that we shall be content. And happy."

Mr. O'Brien studied her with deep blue, earnest eyes. He saw the fear and doubts on her face. Slowly, almost imperceptibly, he lowered his tall head to her height. Ariana was no longer looking at him, but just staring ahead in disheartening thoughts. Just at the moment when Mr. O'Brien thought he would surely be able to steal a small kiss, there was a sound at the door and he straightened up guiltily. Ariana came to with a start.

For some reason Mrs. Bentley had not appeared in all this time, but suddenly one of the double doors swung wide, and Ariana gasped. There stood—not her aunt, but her father.

He walked calmly into the room, and took an appraising look at Mr. O'Brien before turning to face his daughter.

"I apologize. I could not help but to overhear some of the, ah, conversation." Here he turned back to Mr. O'Brien. "And I must say, young man, you might have been quite right a short while ago. You *might* have been, but as it stands, you are now quite mistaken."

"Am I, sir?" And, to Ariana, "Who is this man? Do you know him?"

Ariana was biting back a smile, listening to him with an expression of joy and fondness.

"Oh, Papa!" She rushed into his arms. They gave each other a tender kiss on the cheek.

Mr. O'Brien stood up taller and straightened his cravat. "How am I mistaken, sir, if you would be so kind as to explain?"

"I will, indeed, my good fellow. Your mistake is that you have assumed, on past evidence, that Mr. Mornay cannot be what in fact he is: a true Christian, with the truest of conviction!"

Ariana gasped and clasped her hands together. "Oh, I knew it would be so! I knew it had to be so! Oh, thank God!"

At that moment, Mr. Mornay, who had been seeing to a difficulty with one of his horses, came to the door of the room. He saw Ariana just as she opened her eyes and met his. Hers were again filled with joyful tears, and she smiled. He noticed Mr. O'Brien at that moment, and his own smile faltered, but Ariana rushed to him and threw her arms about his neck.

"Phillip! Oh, my dearest! I have you back!" They clung together in a tight embrace for a few seconds. "I am so happy! I am so very happy!"

He smiled fully then, that handsome, rare smile.

"This is precisely why I cannot resist you. Who could resist such an impulsive, generous girl?" He was prodigiously pleased with her effusive greeting and kissed her.

Meanwhile, the rector, Mr. Timmons, who had come along in Mr. Mornay's coach, entered the room, as well as Ariana's sister Beatrice, who had not only asked to come on the trip, but also to stay until the wedding.

At that moment, Mrs. Bentley, who had been in her study attending to her accounts, entered and saw the happy couple. She began to babble and nod and grasp everyone's hand and shake it emphatically. She grasped Mr. O'Brien's hand before she realized whose it was, then said, "Oh," in a disappointed tone. He gave her a polite shake of the hand, however.

"All has ended as you wish, you can see, ma'am," he said in resignation.

"Yes!" She was startled to find him admitting the fact placidly. "And here, Charles! When did you arrive? Why wasn't I notified at once?"

"A servant said you did not wish to be disturbed."

"A servant? What servant would dare not tell me of my brother's arrival? I ought to have him horsewhipped!"

Ariana turned around, smiling. "No horsewhipping today, Aunt! It is too, too happy a day for any such thing!" She turned to face her love, still smiling, her arms still about him. Mrs. Bentley and her brother eyed the couple with satisfaction. Mr. O'Brien was moving toward the door, but he stopped by Mr. Forsythe.

"Did you witness the conversion, sir?"

Mr. Forsythe, a tall, lean man with soft eyes, looked at the young man shrewdly.

"No, sir, I did not. But I have no doubts about it taking place. Speak to the man yourself, if you like. You'll agree that he is a child of God, I warrant you." He eyed the gentleman with compassion. "And you can rest your mind regarding Ariana's betrothal. The Lord was merciful to her, and to her betrothed."

The young man looked toward the couple. "So it appears." He took a breath and turned back to Ariana's father. "Please give my earnest wishes to your daughter for her everlasting happiness." He bowed, prepared to leave.

Mr. Forsythe slapped him on the back and cried, "Do not leave in despair, m'boy! The Lord will provide the right mate for you too, all in good time."

Mr. O'Brien smiled sheepishly. "Thank you, sir. I trust that He will."

"By the by, you must meet another of my daughters." He motioned to Beatrice, now nearly twelve, who came forward with friendly but serious eyes.

"I'll marry you," she offered to Mr. O'Brien, having heard the conversation between him and her papa, and being a most discerning child.

The gentlemen laughed, which puzzled her.

"But I shall, Papa! As soon as you give your leave."

Mr. O'Brien was touched by her youthful sincerity. He bent his tall frame to meet her at eye level. "If indeed you will marry me, little miss, then we must become friends first." And he offered her his hand for a good handshake.

"Quite so!" she said, speaking just as she heard her mama do on many an occasion, as she accepted the friendship greeting. Already an exceedingly pretty child, Beatrice had a strong resemblance to Ariana, only with hair darker by shades, and eyes which were hazel.

While Mrs. Bentley listened to Mr. Timmons's affectionate account of the Paragon's stay at her brother's house, Ariana and her betrothed took seats upon the sofa and were gladly recounting their recent experiences to each other. Mr. Pellham was announced, and he, too, was soon shaking hands and nodding approvingly at the young couple.

Mrs. Bentley wished to give the pair some time to themselves. Perhaps her brother and Mr. Timmons were hungry? Why did they not sit at table in the dining room for some refreshment? She was feeling so benevolent, seeing how happy Mornay and her niece looked together, she even invited Mr. O'Brien. Beatrice, stopping only to receive an effusive hug and kiss from her sister, accepted Mr. O'Brien's arm like a miniature adult. Ariana and Mr. Mornay barely noticed them all leave, too busy basking in the light of each other's eyes.

"You must tell me everything about your experience with Christ! I am waiting to hear this. How did He reach your heart? I must know." Her eagerness made him smile.

"I'm not certain I know the full explanation," he began. "I may not answer to your satisfaction, but I can tell you the day I knew within myself that something had changed in me. Something that made me far more aware of God. I began to understand what I never had understood before, that one can speak to Him, and be in His very presence." He looked sharply at her. "Have you felt that way?"

"Oh, yes. Many times!"

He gave her a kiss on the forehead. "I never did, before. I thought I understood from childhood, about Christ dying for me, but you knew, my little love, didn't you, that I was deceived?"

She gave a weak smile, and he continued. "I spent some late nights with Mr. Timmons in his study and began to discover there was much I had never understood at all."

"You stayed at Mr. Timmons's house, then? Not just with my family?"

He smiled at the memory. "He greatly desired me to. And, when I found he was not averse to an occasional glass of claret, only one in an evening, mind you, I decided he had something to recommend him and I went."

"Do not say you stayed at his house because he offered you claret!"

He laughed. "No. I like the man. He is an excellent fencer, by the way. The claret was merely an unexpected treat."

"You *fenced* with him? Goodness! But tell me what I asked. How did God make Himself known to you?"

Mr. Mornay's head went back to rest upon the cushion, but he took one of her hands in his own, and held it while he spoke. He did, in fact, recall well the very day that his beliefs had broadened...

〰〜◦〜〰

"Mr. Mornay, I heard you mention once that you enjoy fencing, did I not?"

Mr. Mornay was in the cleric's library reading a recommended volume of sermons by the Methodist Mr. Wesley, but he set down the book and looked up.

"You did."

Mr. Timmons, the youthful new rector of the Church of the Village Square, was scrutinizing him in his typically thoughtful manner. In his late twenties, he was surprisingly intent in his conversation, quick-witted, and not above playful bantering. He was also impressively knowledgeable in history, music, art, and a host of other subjects so that Mr. Mornay regarded him with respect—not the easiest of feelings to procure from the Paragon.

"I have épées; will you do me the honour of sparring?"

"With pleasure; I need the exercise, I daresay."

"Excellent! This way, sir."

Mr. Mornay hoped Mr. Timmons was able to hold his own. It was a dead bore to spar with a partner not up to snuff.

When, a few minutes later, they were facing each other on the lawn, they raised their weapons and saluted. Each was clad only in pantaloons, boots, and a shirt, for they had removed their waistcoats and cravats. At first Mr. Timmons eyed the other man like a cat sizing up a lion. Mornay was taller and stockier than he, but neither characteristic was necessarily an asset at the sport. They agreed on points and boundaries.

As they got closer, Timmons spoke.

"For God."

"For God?" Hadn't he meant to say, "En Garde?"

"All is for God, Mr. Mornay."

Then, in a blink, Mr. Timmons lunged at him and caught him instantly on the cuff of a sleeve.

Forty

*M*r. Mornay was delighted. Here was a worthy foe; a man quick on his feet.

"That wasn't a point, you know."

"Of course I know." They exchanged smiles.

This time Mornay lunged first and was able to keep Mr. Timmons on the defense for a few good parries, scoring a cool point on the man's shoulder. The next action began with a bold thrust by Mr. Timmons, but the other man managed to quickly defer it and their blades met at the hilts. They came apart.

"No touch."

The next three actions ended similarly. Neither man seemed able to get in a good riposte.

Then, after forcing his opponent back a foot, Mr. Timmons, with a lightning-quick move of the arm, opened a path to find Mornay's chest: "a palpable touch." The score was even.

The next few actions proved that both men were capable on their feet, though Mr. Mornay more often had close calls in which he had to move speedily to deflect a point. Two actions more resulted in no gain for either gentleman. The men moved in one direction, one lunging, the other defending, then, the other direction, the defender now on the offense, and so it went for a time. If one retreated, he then gained back his ground; it appeared to be an even match.

"This is more than a form of exercise to you!" Timmons pronounced, taking a lunge at his opponent.

"I might say the same for you," replied Mornay, who deftly blocked the thrust. As their swords locked yet again and they came apart, they nevertheless maintained eye contact, making it a match of wits as well as agility.

"I confess; I was a fencing master." Had Mr. Timmons admitted this to intimidate his foe?

"How on earth did you end up in the pulpit?" was the Paragon's response.

The conversation ceased as Mr. Timmons leapt forward and gave a quick thrust to what he hoped was Mornay's neck, but the man was too quick and their blades met again.

"I felt God's call on my life." Then, looking shrewdly into his opponent's eyes, added, "We've been discussing God quite often of late, wouldn't you say?"

"Yes." Mornay waited. Where was he leading?

"So, what about you? Have you felt His call?"

Mr. Mornay's face went bland. "To enter the church?"

Timmons laughed. "God help us, no! I meant, have you felt His call on your heart? Have you decided to pray as I suggested? The sinner's prayer?"

Again they fell silent as Mr. Mornay saw an opportunity and made a firm thrust at his foe, in a region which would have put an abrupt end to his life if they hadn't been playing points. But now Mr. Timmons was too fast. He swept his arm up in a sudden riposte that ended with a veritable point, landing firmly on Mr. Mornay's well-shaven jaw.

"I'll make you a wager!" the churchman said. "The next point wins it."

"You're a gamester? A churchman by God's call, and yet you will lay a wager?"

"I am all things to all men," he said, with a dashing smile. "Are you afraid of my terms?" That was a jibe meant to hit its target and it did.

"Don't be absurd. Name them."

"If I gain the next touch, you agree to pray the sinner's prayer with me."

"Is that all?" He was scowling. "You call that a wager?"

"That's all. Are we agreed?"

Mr. Mornay was silent a moment. "There is no prize in it."

"You should be happy, then, for there is none to lose."

"I expect you should be happier over that than I. However; if I win?"

Mr. Timmons lowered his blade, pulled out his shirt, and began wiping his weapon with an intent expression.

"If you win—then I will agree to pray with *you*."

"Big of you," came the dry response. "*For* me would suit me, perhaps."

"It's with you, or nothing."

"You are determined upon it, eh? Do you imagine it will accomplish some great thing?"

At this, Mr. Timmons's face grew sober. His eyes were compassionate as he looked earnestly at Mr. Mornay.

"I don't imagine it. I know it." His hair blew lightly across his face with a breeze, and he shook it away. "When we pray, we are talking to God. Going before God, I warrant you, is a great thing in itself. Going before Him for forgiveness and redemption—well, there is nothing greater. It was for just such a prayer that Christ suffered the cross." He took his épée and pointed it gently, first at Mornay's hands, then his feet. "It was a torturous, horrifying death." He met his eyes again. "We haven't discussed crucifixion yet, have we?"

Mr. Mornay took a step back. "Oh, I can hardly wait."

Mr. Timmons lifted his sword in front of his face, and Mornay did likewise. They saluted. They started out similarly, eyeing each other. Mr. Timmons went forward first. He was quick on his feet, even faster with his arm, and determined to remain on the offensive. Their hilts soon clashed and they came apart.

"Either way, you know, it will be God's victory," the cleric said.

"I have no objection to that. But I would be pleased if it wasn't also your victory."

With a smile that belied his determination to have it otherwise, Mr. Timmons began a series of quick parries, bullying his foe, keeping him on the defense. Mornay dug in his heels and would retreat no further, and for a minute there was no sound but of wiry steel against wiry steel, weapon hitting weapon, and then they were at crossed blades yet again.

"Are you not weary, yet?" Mr. Timmons chided.

"No more than you," Mornay replied, but his breath was coming a little faster than the other man's. He was a few years older than Timmons, for one thing, and, even when younger had never possessed such energy as this fellow.

They were at it again, Mornay at first moving his foe backward, but soon Mr. Timmons rallied and suddenly made rapid thrusts in a fury of quick movements—right, left, right again—and Mr. Mornay had to back away. From a distance, an onlooker would have been impressed with the elegance of their movements, the dexterity of their wrists and arms and feet.

"I hate to do this, old fellow," said Mr. Timmons, "but I am growing weary, even if you are not."

"Do your worst." Mornay wasn't cowed. In fact, he gave a magnificent lunge and thrust, and by rights should have caught Timmons's bicep, but the younger man was too skilled. With surprising quickness, he gave a sudden upward thrust, flinging Mornay's arm, still holding the weapon, up and away with such force that the épée went flying from his hand. Mr. Timmons instantly brought his blade to bear around the area of his opponent's heart. *Touch.* He held it for a good second, then pulled away, and fell away himself, bending over to take in a few good breaths. Mornay caught his own breath. He was tired, and had lost the contest, but he had enjoyed himself immensely. He had to eye his new friend with admiration, even while he went and retrieved his sword.

He joined Timmons again to walk back to the house but the man was eyeing him expectantly.

"Well?" Mornay asked.

"Do you not pay your debts? We pray now." Mr. Timmons gave a wry smile. "I daresay you've had to pay worse in the past."

"No doubt." Mornay crossed his arms.

"No, that won't do, sir!" His friend was smiling, but in earnest. "We do not approach God our Maker with crossed arms. That is no more efficient than being at crossed swords with one another. Little can be accomplished."

"You are the rector." He dropped his arms.

Watching his companion, Timmons fell to his knees on the grass, and waited there, expectantly.

Mr. Mornay looked around. "What, here?"

"Here, come on, man! A little grass won't hurt you, you know."

Mornay reluctantly fell to his knees, keeping his eyes keenly on the other man. He didn't want to admit it, but he sensed something very strange afoot. It felt suddenly as if an unseen hand, or pairs of hands, were upon him, a weight on his entire being, compelling him down, saying, yes, do this. Pray. You must. You must!

Mr. Timmons drew himself closer to where Mornay had dropped. They were still looking into each other's eyes, Mr. Timmons with an otherworldly sort of compassion, and Mr. Mornay with caution. Mr. Timmons was the most surprising person he had encountered since meeting the little blonde minx.

"Close your eyes," the rector said.

"Is that entirely necessary?"

"It is, sir." A wan smile.

"After you, then."

This brought a laugh.

"So be it!" Mr. Timmons closed his eyes, and then peeked. "You're still looking!"

"And you're not?"

"It is a debt of honour, recall." This was no less than brilliant. Debts of honour, as all gaming debts were considered, had to be paid as soon as possible and in full. A man could owe his tailor money for a year, his shoemaker and silversmith, even longer; but a debt of honour required immediate payment.

Mr. Mornay made a dismissive gesture with his eyebrows, and then closed his eyes.

Mr. Timmons started to pray, "Heavenly Father." He stopped. He peeked. "Mornay, you must repeat after me."

"What, like a child?"

"No. To *become* a child. A child of God." He motioned with his head for him to get ready and once again Mr. Mornay closed his eyes.

"Heavenly Father."

"Heavenly Father."

"I come before You knowing I have no right to do so."

Mr. Mornay repeated the words, and then each of the following lines afterward.

"I come as a sinner."

"Asking for Your mercy."

"I come confessing that I have sinned against You."

"Asking Your forgiveness."

"Not because I deserve it."

"But because Christ, in dying, forgave me my sins."

"Because Christ, in dying, paid the debt of my sins."

"I ask You to take me as Your child." This line was repeated with difficulty, and only after a long pause. Mr. Mornay was astonished. He felt something happening within himself. He was suddenly conscious of feeling as though he were in God's presence. Not out on the grass on a man's lawn, but at the feet of God. At the very feet of God! How could it be? How could a simple act of prayer result in such an impression on his senses? Why had he never felt such an impression in all his life before? He had prayed before—hadn't he?

"To come and live inside me, in my heart." Again the words were difficult to pray. He was aware, keenly, that *God* was his audience. *God* was listening. If he said these words to God Himself, he had to mean them. He had to want what he was asking for. Was it a miracle of some sort? That he did? He prayed the words, choking them out, as it were, with shocking force of feelings.

"To take my life and make it Yours." Mr. Timmons added, waiting for Mornay to repeat them. But he balked at this.

"I'm not signing my life away, to join the church as you have, am I?"

Mr. Timmons laughed gently. "No, my man. We are merely inviting God to begin an awakening within you. So that you are aware that you do not live just to yourself, but to Him. Not just for yourself, nor for Miss Forsythe, but for God."

The line was repeated. Mr. Timmons added thanks, and then prayed heartily for Mr. Mornay's newfound faith, after which they finally rose from the grass.

The cleric extended his hand. "Congratulations, sir. If you meant that prayer, and my feeling is that you did, you are now a child of the King."

Mr. Mornay shook his hand, but was silent. He *had* meant it, surprising even himself. Indeed, he had meant every word.

"Aren't you more a Methodist than an Anglican in your manner of prayer?" Mornay asked, while they returned to the house. "I once read the minutes of a meeting of Calvinistic Methodists, and you pray and speak of God as one of them."

Timmons only smiled. "I am called to the Anglican church." After a pause, he said, "I am a Christian, leave it at that. And so, as of today, are you."

∽∾〇∾∼

Mr. Mornay came out of his memories, looking down at Ariana. "I wasn't entirely sure he was right at the time, though I agree, now."

"I'm so glad!"

"I did mean what I prayed. I have felt a change within myself, too. I have a greater awareness, first of all, of God. I find myself talking to Him! Do you do that?"

She nodded, turning her face up to his.

"I am confounded that God has saved me for heaven when I have done nothing for Him."

"He loves you. He loves us all. We can never deserve it. But I am certain you will do things for Him." In a droll tone, she added, "Actually, I have suggestions for you regarding that. In case you need ideas."

"Still running my life for me, eh?" He kissed her affectionately, "Little did I know that I would thank you for insisting upon my packing off for Chesterton, but I must."

"I know how you may!" Her eyes came alight, and she quickly filled him in on Lavinia's request regarding her hopes of marriage to Lord Antoine Holliwell. While she was speaking his features grew dark, and then forbidding, and she felt the excitement dying rapidly from her breast.

"I cannot consent to this, Ariana. In fact, if you care for your Miss Herley you will tell her to drop all contact with Holliwell instantly."

She studied him silently for a moment. "Do you disapprove of Miss Herley to such a degree, then?"

"I have no objection to Miss Herley. It's Holliwell who is unsuitable. I would not encourage the most desperate young woman in England to seek a match with him, or any of his family."

"Holliwell is unsuitable?" She was dazed by the thought.

"Worse. He is a scoundrel, a rake, and a thief. I should think your Miss Herley must run in the opposite direction or her good name will be ruined. You must tell her so."

"I must!" Ariana gasped. "As soon as possible!"

"We can call upon her directly following supper, if you like."

She smiled, pleased at this offer. He was not usually sociable with her circle of friends. She smiled even wider at his next words.

"I will speak to her father myself, if you wish, because I want to please you, my angel."

Ariana was so touched by this she was momentarily bereft of words.

"I love you!" was all she could say.

"I love you more," he replied.

It occurred to her just then that she had a wedding to plan. Not a maybe wedding, or a perhaps-there-shall-be-a wedding, but an honest-to-goodness one, and suddenly it seemed of the utmost importance to finalize the plans.

"We must discuss our wedding! Who shall perform the ceremony? Where shall we go, afterward? When shall my wardrobe be moved to your house?"

He laughed aloud. "Your parents and I discussed it at length and your papa is no doubt informing your aunt of the plans as we speak. Speaking of which, you must show me your trousseau so that I may approve it."

"Approve it! Did you not dictate what was bespoken? How can you fail to approve it?"

"I must see the cut of the fabric...The shade and style exactly. Grow accustomed to it, Ariana, for I will always oversee your wardrobe."

The swirling black eyes were looking deeply into her own, and Ariana decided at that moment there was no one else on earth whom she would rather have overseeing her wardrobe—or, for that matter, anything else of hers.

Discussion Questions for *Before the Season Ends*

1. *Before the Season Ends* is set in Regency England. What are some new things you enjoyed learning about the period?

2. Ariana believed strongly in honouring her faith and her Lord. How do you think a woman who lacks strong convictions can strengthen her faith? Do you know a Christian without strong convictions? How could you use the Bible to try to help her?

3. Ariana spends a lot of time praying and seeking God. Hebrews 11:6 states that "without faith it is impossible to please God, because anyone who comes to him must believe that he exists and that he rewards those who earnestly seek him" (NIV). Is Ariana rewarded? How? Are there troublesome things you have brought to God and been rewarded for by His answer?

4. There's an old poem that says, "God works in mysterious ways, His wonders to perform." At one point, Ariana is mystified by how her necessary affiliation with Mr. Mornay can be of God. Later on, she realizes that it is. What are some of the mysterious ways the Lord has worked in your life that seemed negative at the time, only to bring great blessing in the end? Share and discuss an instance.

5. When Ariana doesn't hear from her parents, she just "knows" something is wrong. Is your family so close that you would have this reaction? What would be a good way for someone to strengthen their family's ties if they aren't close? What is one thing that you do to help strengthen your own family?

6. Ariana makes a great effort to distinguish between "mere religion," and "soul-saving faith." Can you describe the difference in your own words? Why is this difference so important?

7. In the end, Mr. Mornay says he was amazed to discover that he could actually sense the presence of God. Have you ever experienced that? "Knowing" that God is there, with you? If so, think

about it. What were you doing at the time? Were you praying? What difference has it made in your life?

8. Tell about your experience of sensing God's presence. Do you think it could happen again? Why or why not?

9. Based on 2 Corinthians 6:14, Ariana insists she cannot marry "an unbeliever." Notice, however, that there is no restriction regarding the class, rank, or ethnicity ("race") of a potential mate. What does this tell you about God? Does He see people as we do, or view them as equals?

10. Share how this book has been edifying or refreshing with someone else.

If you enjoyed *Before the Season Ends,*
you'll also love the sequel,
The House in Grosvenor Square.

❦

As Ariana Forsythe plans her wedding to Philip Mornay, she must adjust to the realization that she is soon to become the wife of an extremely wealthy man. She wonders if it's wrong to rejoice that her future husband is rich. But she promises herself to use her new position to do what she can to aid the numerous street waifs she sees all too often in London.

During a tour of her future home—the house in Grosvenor Square—Ariana makes plans to redecorate according to her tastes. But when Philip arrives home later, he is informed that an expensive silver candlestick and a miniature portrait of George III have gone missing. Moreover, each time Ariana visits the house, accompanied by a friend or relation, another item disappears.

Shortly thereafter Ariana is abducted as she leaves a performance at Covent Garden Theatre, leaving Philip to unravel the pieces of the mystery. Where has his future bride been taken, and by whom? For what reason? How does Ariana's faith play a role?

Finally, after the safe return of his intended, how does Philip—a man of intense discrimination in his tastes—find the many alterations in his house? And what on earth is behind the sudden influx of bills from every charity in London, all thanking him profusely for his uncommon generosity? Will he have second thoughts about his future bride?

Readers will find romance, intrigue, humor, and inspiration in this new book of spirited romance for the Jane Austen soul.

Coming April 1, 2009

*L*inore Rose Burkard lives with her husband and five children in a town full of antique stores and gift shops in southwestern Ohio. She homeschooled her children for ten years. Raised in New York, she graduated magna cum laude from the City University of New York with a Bachelor of Arts in English literature.

Linore wrote *Before the Season Ends* because she could not find an Inspirational Regency Romance on the bookshelves of any store. "There are Christian books that approached the genre," she says, "but they fell short of being a genuine Regency. I finally gave up looking and wrote what I was looking for myself." She has begun four other works of fiction in the same category, and also enjoys writing articles, reading, parenting, family movie nights, swimming, and gardening.

Linore can be reached at: *admin@LinoreRoseBurkard.com*

or

Linore Rose Burkard
c/o Harvest House Publishers
990 Owen Loop North
Eugene, OR 97402

Be sure and visit her on the web at: *http://www.LinoreRoseBurkard.com*. Sign up for her free mailing list, and get news and announcements of her latest writing projects or books.

A Short Glossary for *Before the Season Ends*

abigail: (n.) A lady's maid; any female maid (servant)

Example: "I see you've hired a new abigail."

ague: (Rhymes with "achoo!" Pronounced "ah-gyoo") Originally, malaria and the chills that went with it. Later, any respiratory infection such as a cold, fever, or chills.

Assembly, Assemblies: Large gatherings held in the evening for the gentry or the aristocracy, usually including a ball and a supper. Almack's in London was the ultimate Assembly in the early part of the nineteenth century. A number of high society hostesses had autocratic power of attendance as they alone could issue the highly prized vouchers (tickets)—or not—as they chose. Competition to get in was fierce. The Duke of Wellington was once famously turned away for being late.

B

ball: A large dance requiring full dress. Refreshments were available, and sometimes a supper. Public balls required tickets; private ones, an invitation.

Banbury tale: A story with no basis in fact; a rumour; nonsense.

banns: The banns of marriage were a public announcement in a parish church that two people intended to get married. They had to be read three consecutive weeks in a row, and in the home church of both parties. After each reading (and this was their purpose), the audience was asked to give knowledge of any legal impediments to the marriage. If there were none, after three weeks, the couple was legally able to marry within the next three months, in a church. To bypass the banns, a couple could try to get a marriage license instead. Without banns or a license, the marriage would be illegal (null).

beau monde, the: The aristocracy and the rich upper class. The "fashionable" elite. In practice, anyone accepted into their circle, for example, a celebrity, became part of it.

blunt: (slang) Cash; ready money

C

Carlton House: Given to the Prince of Wales by George III upon reaching his majority, Carlton House was in a state of disrepair (for a royal, at any rate). The house consequently underwent enormous alterations and changes, and was the London palace for the Regent. He spent a great deal of time there but eventually came to favour the palace at Brighton—an even larger extravagance. The Brighton "Pavilion" is today a museum, but Carlton House, unfortunately, no longer exists.

chamber: A private room in a house, such as a bedroom, as opposed to the parlour or dining room.

chaperon: The servant, mother, or married

female relative or family friend who supervised eligible young girls in public.

chemise: A woman's long undergarment which served as a slip beneath her gown. Also, a nightdress. (Previously, the chemise was called a shift.)

chintz: A patterned cloth, usually floral, with a pleasant satiny "shine" for texture.

chit: A young girl

clubs: The great refuge of the middle- and upper-class man in eighteenth and nineteenth century London. Originating as coffeehouses in the seventeenth century, clubs became more exclusive, acquiring prime real estate on Pall Mall and St. James' Street. Membership was often by invitation only. Among the more prominent were Boodle's, White's, and Brooke's. Crockford's began to dominate in the very late Regency.

consumption: pulmonary tuberculosis (TB)

corset: A precursor of the modern bra, usually meant to constrict the waist to a fashionable measurement as well as support the high bust required for a Regency gown. It consisted of two parts, reinforced with whalebone, that hooked together in front and laced in the back. The garment could also be referred to as "the stays."

countess: The wife of an earl in England. When shires were changed to counties, an earl retained the Norman title of earl; his wife, however, became a countess.

cravat: (pronounced as "kruh-vaht," with the accent on the second syllable) A loose cloth that is tied around the neck in a bow. Throughout the Regency, a fashionable

gentleman might labour much over this one detail of his appearance, hoping to achieve a number of different, much-coveted effects.

curricle: A two-wheeled carriage that was popular in the early 1800s. It was pulled by two horses, and deemed rather sporty by the younger set.

curtsey: The acceptable mode of greeting or showing respect by a female. By mid-century the curtsey was less in evidence except for social inferiors such as maids to their betters, or by any woman presented at court.

cut: An effective means of social discouragement that involved pretending not to know or see a person who was trying to be acknowledged. A woman might use this technique to discourage unwelcome attentions from a gentleman; but many others cut people, too. Getting the "cut direct" from a social superior was vastly humiliating.

Ð

Debrett's: An annually published guide to the peerage, often called simply, "the Society Book."

dowager: The name given to a widow of rank. For example, if you were a duchess, and your husband died and your oldest son was married, his wife would become the duchess, and you would become the dowager duchess.

draper (linen draper): Merchant who sold cloth

drawing room: A formal parlour used in polite society to receive visitors who came to pay calls during the afternoon.

first floor: The second floor in the United States. The English called the street-level floor the "ground floor." Entertaining was never done on the ground floor.

foolscap: A paper of certain dimensions, some varieties of which originally bore a watermark of a fool's cap and bells.

footman: A liveried male servant beneath the butler but above the boy or page. He had many duties ranging from errands to lamp-trimming to waiting table, or accompanying the lady of the house to carry packages when she shopped, or to deliver calling cards when making calls.

fortnight: Two weeks.

fustian!: "Nonsense!" "Don't be absurd!"

G

gaming: Gambling. Nothing to do with "game" in the sense of hunting, or innocent playing of games.

gig: A one-horse carriage. Light, two-wheeled, and popular in the early century.

groom: The servant who looked after the horses

Grosvenor Square: (pronounced "Grove-nuh") A part of Mayfair, considered the most fashionable square in London. Mr. Mornay's town house is in the Square.

hack: A general-purpose riding horse, but the term might also refer to a "hackney coach," which was a coach-for-hire much like a taxicab today.

L

Ladies' Mile: A (horseback) riding road in Hyde Park for women

lady's maid: The servant who cared for her mistress's wardrobe and grooming. A French lady's maid was preferred, and she was particularly valued if she could do hair in all the fashionable styles. A lady's maid was an "upper servant," and could not be fired by the housekeeper; she might also be better educated than the lower servants.

lorgnette: Used by ladies, the lorgnette was a pair of eyeglasses (or a monocle), held to the eyes with a long handle, or it could be worn on a chain around the neck. The monocle used by a man was called a "quizzing glass."

laudanum: A mixture of opium in a solution of alcohol, it was used for pain relief and as an anesthetic.

livery: A distinctive uniform worn by the male servants in a household. No two liveries, ideally, were exactly alike. Knowing the colour of the livery of someone could enable you to spot their carriage in a crowd. The uniform itself was an old-fashioned style, including such things as a frock coat, knee breeches, powdered wigs, and a waistcoat.

Mayfair: The ritziest residential area of London, in the West End, and only about a half mile square in size.

mews, the: Any lane or open area where a group of stables was situated. The town houses of the rich often had a mews behind them, or nearby, where they kept their horses and equipages when not in use.

muslin: One of the finest cottons, muslin was semitransparent and very popular for gowns (beneath which a chemise would be worn).

O

on-dit: (French; literally, "It is said.") In the Regency it was slang for a bit of gossip.

P

Pall Mall: A fancy street in the West End of London, notable for housing some of the most fashionable men's clubs. Carlton House faced Pall Mall.

pantaloons: Tight-fitting pants that became fashionable beginning in the early 1800s, and which pushed breeches out of fashion except for formal occasions. Pantaloons had a "stirrup" at the bottom to keep them in place.

parlour: The formal or best room in a modest home. Grand houses often had more than one; a "first" or "best," and a "second parlour."

peer: A nobleman, that is, a titled gentleman with the rank of either duke, marquis (pronounced "mar-kwiss"), viscount (pronounced "vy-count"), or baron. The titles were hereditary, and the owners were entitled to a seat in the House of Lords.

pelisse: An outdoor garment for women, reaching to the ankle or mid-calf, and often hooded.

pianoforte: A piano. Genteel young women were practically required to learn the instrument.

pin money: A colloquialism for a woman's spending money. The allowance agreed upon in her marriage settlement, to be used on small household or personal (vanity) items.

R

regent: A person who reigns on behalf of a monarch who is incapable of filling the requirements of the crown. When George III's relapse of porphyria rendered him incapable of meeting his duties, his son, the Prince of Wales, became the Prince Regent. The actual regency lasted from 1811-1820.

reticule: A fabric bag, gathered at the top and held by a ribbon or strap; a lady's purse. Reticules became necessary when the thin muslin dresses of the day made it impossible to carry any personal effects in a pocket without it seeming bulky or unsightly. The earliest reticules (apparently called 'ridicules,' as it seemed ridiculous to carry one's valuables outside of one's clothing) were, in effect, outside pockets.

rubber: In games like whist, a rubber was a set of three or more games. To win the rubber, one had to win two out of three or three out of five.

S

season: The London social season, in which the fashionable elite descended upon the city in droves. It coincided, not unnaturally, with the sitting of Parliament, though the height of the season was only March through June.

smelling salts (smelling bottle): A small vial filled with a compound that usually contained ammonia, to be used in case of fainting.

spencer: For women, a short jacket that reached only to the high empire waist. For men, an overcoat without tails, also on the short side.

squire: Nineteenth-century term of courtesy (like "esquire") for a member of the landed gentry.

𝒯

tendre: (French adjective, meaning *soft, tender*) Regency slang for "a soft spot"; an attraction to.

ton, the: (pronounced "tone") High society; the elite; the "in" crowd; those of rank, with royalty at the top. To be "good ton" meant acceptance with the upper crust, and opened many doors in fashionable society. Occasionally, those without fortune or pedigree could enter the ton—if they were an Original, for instance, having something either sensational or highly attractive about their person or reputation; or could amuse or entertain the rich to a high degree.

𝒱

valet: The "gentleman's gentleman." The male equivalent of a lady's maid, his job was to keep his master's wardrobe in good repair and order, help dress his master, stand behind him at dinner if required, and accompany him on his travels.

Vauxhall: A famous pleasure garden, across the Thames from London.

𝒲

wainscoting: Wainscot was a fancy, imported oak. The term "wainscoting" came to mean any wooden panels that lined generally the top or bottom half of the walls in a room.

waistcoat: Vest

For more information about the Regency period, see the author's website at:

http://www.LinoreRoseBurkard.com